# JUSTICE

## THE VENDETTA TRIFECTA - BOOK 3

## A.J. SCUDIERE

GRIFFYN INK

Justice

FIRST EDITION

ISBN: 978-1-937996-39-0

ISBN: 978-1-937996-33-8

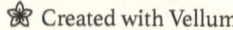 Created with Vellum

*This one is for my family--Guy, Jarett, January, Eli . . .*

*There are more of you in my family, but these guys are the ones who put up with the deadlines, the editing (not pretty!), and the general "no, I can't, because I'm killing someone. One of you needs to make dinner!"*

# ACKNOWLEDGMENTS

As always the book you hold in your hand is my baby, but it takes a village. This village is made up of many people:

Dana--who beta read, gave notes, and occasionally cried and got mad at me.

Eli--who makes me make deadlines.

Guy--who made dinner more times than I can count.

Daddy--who has always believed in me.

The entire Smyrna, GA, police department--who opened their doors to me and let me interview, take notes, and follow them like a puppy.

Gene "Zhenya" Suhir--who made Annika's Russian conversations fluid, convincing, and, well, *Russian*!

Dan Ruke--as always for the brilliant cover work!

# CHAPTER 1

I t was the shock wave from the bullet and not the sound itself that woke her.

She was already in motion, already on her hands and knees, having been shoved or kicked from her bed. Rocketing away from the danger before she even registered it, she was hidden before she became fully alert to the fact that a gun had been fired in her bedroom. She couldn't sort out who had fired it or what damage they had caused, only that she was trained to get away.

Rolling under the bed quickly, her mind and her heart warred with each other as she pushed at the panel that was her only escape. The bed had been built without box springs. Rough wood slats held it at a normal height off the ground, leaving enough space below to hide. A metal sheet lay on top of the slats, lining the bottom of the mattress and thus shielding the space—the extra paneling intended for an event just like this one. Hopefully it would protect her from bullets above her.

Alert now, Sin shoved at the trap door built low into the wall. The space was just big enough for both of them, but she saw she was here alone. Working from habits developed from hours of practice, she popped the locks free and silently swung the door out. Grabbing the weapons beside her, she rolled into the brush they had let grow up near the house. She crouched silently, listening for the noises that would kill her.

This was not the plan.

Lee was not with her.

He was behind her, somewhere in the small cabin, and she wasn't even sure if he was still alive. Sin had followed the number one rule: get out. Number two: come back alive to save the other one. But all her instincts had pushed her to stand and fight with him, not leave him to defend himself alone. Whatever they faced, they were always deadlier together.

So why wasn't he here?

As she huddled, listening to the sounds from inside, she registered several things. She was wearing only flannel pajamas and fuzzy socks. While they would keep her warm in the cool Appalachian night, the bright colors and the dancing apples design would make her an easy target. She had her sais, held together in one hand, probably automatically pulled from under the pillow when she had rolled from the bed. Or gotten kicked out, she couldn't say for sure which. In her other hand, she held a set of kamas. These she vaguely remembered grabbing. Stashed in the space under the bed, she picked them up as she pushed out the trap door. Lastly, she registered that there were no more sounds of a fight coming from inside.

There were low voices. Thumps. Dragging sounds.

Sin tried not to imagine that it was a body they were dragging. She couldn't distinguish Lee's voice, but it didn't matter. Two voices meant he was definitely not talking. There was no one here he would converse with but her.

Concocting a hopeful scenario, she imagined Lee had killed one of the intruders and managed to escape. Thus the remaining two would be discussing and removing their dead partner.

Hope was a tenuous thing. In the split second her eyes had opened as she rolled from the bed, Sin had seen two people standing in her room. Her escape achieved by rote muscle memory, she hadn't been awake enough to check faces or take note. But her memory was sharp that there were two.

Her memory also said one of them was Yulia Churkin, but that was impossible since Sin had killed Yulia herself months earlier. Clearly, her mind was not functioning well and had inserted a known face on an unknown intruder.

With her legs tucked up and her arms wrapped around her knees, weapons gripped properly now, she would have looked more scared than dangerous to anyone who approached her, but she was definitely the latter.

She also had a decision to make: stay here and cover up with the camo blanket or run for it?

If she ran, they might see her. If she stayed, they might find her or blow up the cabin or burn it or . . . Sin didn't put anything past the people that raided her world tonight. She didn't know them personally, but she knew exactly what they were about and exactly what they were capable of.

The weight of memory came over her, heavy and cloying. She fought mental pictures of another night when her home had been invaded, her safety pierced. That time her reactions had been startled, disbelieving. This time she understood exactly what the invaders had in mind.

Her heart crushed at the thought that Lee might still be in there and he might not be okay. But she had other worries, too. If she was going to get him out alive, she had to be ready.

So she held her weapons in her left hand and grabbed the go-bag waiting for her to her right. Bugs crawled on it, forest dust had settled into the folds of the bag, but she didn't notice. With a quick scan of the area revealing nothing she could see or hear, Sin made a run for it.

The noises behind her changed, became higher pitched with faster movement. She'd been seen.

Her pajamas were almost as bad as neon; she couldn't hide,

couldn't evade. The pink pajamas with yellow, green, and red apples had made her smile, but now might get her killed.

*No.*

The singular sound burst through her brain.

*No.*

She knew more than they did. Her brain worked as she ran. She may be in bright clothing and she may not have a gun, but she had weapons in her hands and she would not go down without a fight.

*She would not go down.*

Slowing, Sin avoided the fallen branches in her way, cracking them would give away that she was leading them on a chase. She couldn't afford a rolled ankle.

Ducking behind trees and darting one way then another, she let her pursuer catch up to her as she fought to catalogue what she could. Male. Shorter than Lee. Heavy. Hitting the ground hard. Thus, not trained in stealth. Men who used knives tended to be lighter on their feet, thus, this one was likely carrying a gun.

She grabbed dead branches as she ran, conserved her energy, and tucked right, not letting him get a bead on her even as he got closer. Chucking the branches ever farther in front of her, Sin continued to make a low level of noise.

He came right beside her.

The bait had been easy, the fight would not be.

So she came out swinging.

She went for his jaw, the only thing showing above the edge of the jacket. The bulky clothing showed he was not ready for a hand-to-hand fight and Sin assessed him quickly even as she hit him three times in rapid succession.

He didn't move well, but the padding of the jacket kept him from feeling the full wrath of her hits. Her fingers already stung a little, indications that she'd nailed bone, and hard.

His gun was at his side, ready but not held out, and only as she hit at him did he bring it up.

That was what she wanted. She'd been delivering hits, but not ones that would lay him out, in hopes of getting his weapon.

Stepping swiftly to the side, she didn't let him get her in his sights, but grabbed for his wrist even as he raised the gun. The silencer on the end of it turned her stomach—that was why she hadn't heard anything.

But there was no time to think about it.

His wrist wasn't much exposed and she used the v between her thumb and first finger to slide down to the skin beneath the edge of his sleeve. It was enough to get a good grip.

She twisted for all she was worth.

He didn't hide the sound that came from his mouth as she tried to snap his bones.

Still, she couldn't see his face. The dark seemed to eat every bit of light except that which mocked her as it glowed from the smiling apples on her.

Finally, he let go, giving Sin the weapon.

Quick steps and a bone-deep knowledge of her surroundings allowed her to step back and fire three times at him.

He bolted, far and fast. This time it was him ducking between trees and using them for cover. But why hadn't she hit him?

---

The night was slightly warm in her leathers but Sin didn't notice. She had filled the loops and special pockets in her pants with the weapons she had clutched on the way out of the cabin. The jacket was already fully loaded when she pulled it from the bag. Long ago, she had designed it to hold whatever she needed and what she needed were rows of slim pockets to keep simple throwing knives inside the front plackets. She needed reinforced, squarish pockets near the elbows to both protect her when delivering a hit or a block and to hold throwing stars. She had added a hunting knife to a pocket she had stitched at the small of her back. Guns aimed backward, resting in pockets specifically designed for them, at easy reach and out of the way of the kamas and sais she would likely reach for first.

She never intended to become proficient with firearms, knowing from an early age that bullets were sometimes traceable, guns registered with serial numbers and the like. Knives were not.

She had not intended to get involved with anyone. She'd been only eleven the first time her home had been invaded, her parents executed. Twelve when she discovered it was the Kurev Mafia behind the hit. She'd been fighting ever since. Even as a kid, she'd never thought she would have any kind of life with anyone else. Never thought her current suspicions would be borne out.

But Lee had changed all of that.

He'd lost his first wife and child to the Kurevs. He'd come home one afternoon to find their bodies riddled with bullets. Even worse than Sin's situation, Samantha and Bethany's deaths had been intended as a warning to him.

The two of them lived with the Kurevs as a shared enemy for years. He understood her angers and her fears. He was a shelter to a girl who didn't think she needed any. And he let her be the heat to a man who had gone cold in his soul.

Despite all that, she waited out here alone.

Despite the fact that she had gotten away, the stillness of the woods around her spoke of violation and solitude.

She and Lee had a plan in place for a day like this. There was a plan for every possible day they might face. Plans kept them alive and whole. Or at least she hoped they did.

Plan one was to get far away, together if possible. But that was no longer an option. She had no clue where Lee was right now and she tamped down the fear that he wasn't anywhere anymore. They had several spots in the woods and signals they could—should—mark into the trees.

*Meet me here tomorrow.*

*I passed by here but couldn't stay. Meet me at the next point.*

And of course the most disturbing option: no markings at all. The messages were all in codes—broken branches, patterns in the sticks, leaves and dirt, scratches on the trunks. Things anyone else wouldn't be able to read even if they could figure out that it was a complex system of communication.

The two of them practiced reading the signals, trailing each other through the surrounding mountains, tracking only by footprints and messages. They had even been forced to use it once when a bear and her cubs had come too close to the cabin and stayed too long the previous winter.

Sin knew the system worked. But now she feared there would be no marks left for her to read.

Noises to her right changed her alert to action and she sprinted several yards to a tree she knew well. Her motions and even her shoes had been altered to be as hard to track as possible. She was out of the way before anyone would have noticed.

The colors of her leather clothing weren't pitch black, but shades of darker grays. The night was rarely jet and the singularity of too much of the same darkness would make her easier to spot. While her skills and her toys had gone lax for a handful of years in the middle, she was now even better than she'd been before. Lee made her better; she made him better. She was quiet not only to her own ears, but to his. They moved as a unit, improved as a unit, and while she was out here alone, the skills she'd added to her extensive list were invaluable.

She also knew the area here, loved it like a mother loved every smile on her baby's face. Sin knew how the weather changed the trees, how the trees bent and broke, how the branches cracked against the ground hardened by winter. She read it and reacted to it.

So she knew which tree to climb up, which branch to step out on, where to hold, to reach across to the neighboring tree that could not be climbed. Given its tall, bare trunk, it was unlikely anyone would even look up into it, if they were looking for her.

Tonight she had left wearing only bright flannel pajamas. Unfortunately, anyone who came here—out into the wilderness of the Appalachians, to a lonely cabin that had no natural visitors save the occasional bear—would be expecting her. They would know better than to think she was traipsing the woods leaving signs of where she'd been, where she was headed, and maybe doing so in bright pink pajamas. Sin would do no such thing.

She had no watch to check, but she knew it had been two hours. It didn't take long out here to learn to read the clock of the trees, the animals, the lacking light. It was six a.m. and at this time of year that meant another half an hour before the sun would begin to faintly open the sky.

Crouching in the upper branches, all but obscured from view, Sin watched as two figures approached from the other side of the cabin. Her vantage point gave her a wide range and the two were far away, but she could see enough that she had to steel her heart against the knowledge that neither of them was Lee.

One was a brute of a man—broad-shouldered, burly, more muscle barely edging out finesse. The weight of him alone made Sin think she should be able to hear him from up here, distinguish the sounds of his heavy boots from the scampers of the animals nearby. The other interloper was thinner, maybe just a little taller. They both wore jackets against the chill of the Appalachian night, the clothing obscuring the form so Sin couldn't tell if it was a man or a woman. This was the one she would focus on if the fight came to her.

This person walked like a fighter with the grace borne of years of practice. The heavy man would go down with one or two hits, but this one would take work. This one moved like a martial artist . . . or maybe a gymnast? But Sin shook that thought off. It was just bad memories coming back to push at her because she was feeling vulnerable now.

Peeling her eyes from the two who had not even once looked up, she scanned the area for Lee. She had changed her clothing at one of their designated points and left him a marker. Told him she was fine and she would be back.

Though she could see plenty far and her eyes had adjusted reasonably to the dark, nothing else popped out at her. She knew where to look, knew where Lee would go, but couldn't spot him at any of those locations.

She consoled herself, thinking that he was far too skilled to let her see him. If anyone else were up high, looking around, he wouldn't want to be found.

Next she scanned the skyline. There were several such points they'd found where trees could be climbed and perched in, vantage points taken. They only considered spots with several options for access and egress, like the one she was in, but she saw nothing and considered that Lee was staying close to the ground.

Sin thought it was reasonably likely that Lee had been shot in the encounter. Still, she knew from past experience that bullets hadn't stopped him before, and she hoped that was still the case.

The two figures were clearly communicating though neither spoke loud enough for her to hear. For a moment she wished for one of Lee's listening dishes; it would be seen up here, but she desperately wanted to know what these two knew.

As they approached, she could make out a little more. The short man was bald, his eyes deeply set, mean-looking even from this distance. This was the man she'd fought.

The other retained the tall, willowy attributes she'd noted in the first place. Dark hair was either cut short or slicked back; the deep of night obscuring any further details. In her mind, the figure became Yulia Churkin, but Sin knew Yulia was gone—just one of many Sin herself had been responsible for dispatching, but one of the few whose deaths were unclear. Most of those she had killed had been easy to watch go. Skill might have been required to win the fight, but none was necessary to deal with the death. For a long time, she had regretted nothing, but in the past few years a handful of deaths weighed heavy on her shoulders, Yulia's among them.

So she wasn't surprised that she saw the woman in the shadows. After all, she'd been seeing Yulia in the shadows for a while, and she didn't doubt that it was simply another trick of the night.

Lee was what she worried about. Her scans still didn't find him. That didn't trouble her. Sin knew he was hard to find, even for her, even for the one who best knew where to look. What troubled her was that there was no sign of him. He would have left her a message, pointed her in the right direction, at least let her know that he was okay, if he could.

The fact that he hadn't done so carved a slow hollow in her chest, piece by piece chunking out a larger section of her. Sin held steady to the belief that he was bulletproof and she stayed in her tree.

She had three other locations to check around the perimeter of the cabin. It was entirely possible that he'd gotten out and gone the opposite direction. It was plausible that he'd done it on purpose—to draw these two away from her.

Until the sun came up bright and shiny over the deep green of the mountains all around her, she didn't move except to turn her head. By then, the two were long since gone, having wandered full circles around the cabin, looking, but missing all the signs she'd left behind in her haste to get out. They had wandered far into the woods about an hour ago, disappearing into the thick trees, their exit punctuated by the distant sound of a vehicle engine. They had walked within yards of her training room and by all appearances hadn't realized they passed the camouflaged structure. Sin stared at it, identifying not the lines of the tent topping, nor the drape of the camo netting and the branches that obscured it from view, but knowing exactly where it was. Perhaps Lee was inside, despite the fact there was no sign of life there. She would check.

She stayed in her perch for another hour, when her black form in the tree would read as incongruous should anyone spot her. The foliage was likely enough to keep her hidden, but she still made her movements slow and precise as she crept her way down the series of branches that led her safely to the ground.

After checking the tree she had marked in case Lee had managed to sneak past her, she headed to the second way station, telling herself that the lack of response meant nothing. Two hours later she had completed the full perimeter, checking all the stations they had set up. Though her hands were free, she was now laden with go-bags they had stashed at each place. Each station had supplies for both of them, enough to keep the two of them alive and hidden in the mountains for an extended period of time. She'd eaten one of the granola bars but hadn't been able to stomach anything else as her worry had grown with each unmarked meeting point.

No Lee. No sign of Lee.

But Sin kept going. He was out there and she would find him.

Instead she found tracks of thick-tread tires, some huge SUV they must have driven in here. Drops of blood dotted the area around tracks and led here from the general direction of the cabin. Sin concluded that it couldn't be Lee's because why would they bring him out here? Dead, he was of no use to them. Alive, he was lethal.

One of the shots she had heard must have been fired by Lee. This blood would have to belong to a third one. Surely they would have come here with three or more to try for her and Lee. One-to-one would not be sufficient. It would be stupid. Sin knew these people, and they were not stupid.

Making her way to the Kitty2—Lee's clunker-on-the-outside/dream-in-the-engine car—she walked the edges first and determined that the branches hadn't been touched before she started pulling them aside. Even then, she worked carefully. She knew all too well someone could have slid an explosive into place or attached something to the car to track her.

After finding the car clean, she started the engine, backing out of the small "garage" they had built. Almost out of habit, she stopped a car length back and stepped out to rebuild the space she had left. By the time she left, the day had passed well into afternoon and the area showed no traces of her car having been there unless someone knew exactly where to look.

Only she and Lee knew exactly where to look. At least, she hoped that was still the case.

She pulled over and changed clothes in the car before driving to the low-end motel they had chosen in advance. She rented a room under an ID she'd had tailored the year before but hadn't yet used. With a sly smile she spoke to the desk clerk, her voice rusty from disuse, from being so harshly ejected from her bed and her home.

"Hey, I'm waiting for a guy . . . about this tall—" she held her hand up over her head, then gestured to her arms. "Muscled, he'll ask for Leah. Send him to my room?"

All of it—the clothes she wore, the words she said—had been planned in advance. She simply hoped the rest of what they had planned held as well. Lee would show up. That was the plan.

The next day, she left the spare room key in the designated spot —under a rock at the far end of the parking lot, in the grass beneath the big tree. Lee could get into the room if he showed up and she wasn't here.

Sin began the long trek back to the cabin. She started out in street clothes, but after she left the highway for the old back road, she passed only a few more miles before pulling over and quickly changing. A few miles beyond that, she rolled carefully off the road and into the brush, the dirt and rock path allowing only the hearty and the already-knowledgeable to pass.

It took the whole day to re-check every station, but she found each exactly as she had left it. Lee's go-bag remained with a small pack of medical supplies and clothing. The leaves remained exactly as she had placed them. The branches unaltered. The trunks bore no scratches, not even from real animals, as though they too knew not to come back here.

With each mile she walked, each position she checked, her heart grew heavier. She still didn't know how to handle it. Despite the handful of years with Lee, she had lived longer on her own. Still spent her formative years molding herself without real guidance or even input from anyone. So the sensation of caring remained as uncomfortable as it was painful.

Sin could no longer deny that there should have been something.

Lee would not have left her with no information of his whereabouts, his safety, unless he simply wasn't able. So she held out hope for the last station and when it didn't come, she checked the balance poles, the fight room, every last place he might have gone. Then, finally, she stood still and watched the cabin.

The front door remained slightly ajar from two nights ago. In the bedroom window she could see the cracks radiating from the shot, even if she couldn't distinguish the hole. The small structure screamed of abandonment.

Though she wanted to rush inside, tear the place up, Sin held herself in check. She was nothing if not methodical and now, when her world was teetering once again on the brink of collapse, she reverted to her old ways and fought to hold onto only what she knew for a fact.

Scoping the place out took time. Time she wanted to burn. Time she allowed herself to cling to possibilities. But eventually, just in case someone was watching the front of the cabin, she entered through the trap door she had pushed herself out of over a day ago.

Reversing her earlier actions, she slid into the space under the bed and fought her knowledge of the smell. Forcing herself to roll out from her position of sustained ignorance was difficult. Still she managed to make herself stand and survey the damage.

The bed was a mess. Though simple, the sheets and covers had once been comfortable. Now they were tangled, shredded, pockmarked. Their dark color was tinted with darker stains. Too many, too big to be minor.

The pillowcases and covers bore their original designs of dark swirls so an intruder would have a harder time distinguishing where the people lay in the bed, wouldn't be able to tell the face from the pillow. But now the pillow she had slept on lay on the floor and the dark designs of the sheet failed to conceal a bloody smear on her side of the bed. She was unable to ignore that the smear looked like it had been made by a hand the size and shape of Lee's.

The mattress on his side of the bed was blown open in one spot and her analytical mind could not stop the processing that was occurring. She guessed the energy to split the mattress had come from a close-range shot, maybe forty caliber. Blood stained the area. The blown apart material revealed the red had sunk in, seeping through several layers, indicating a large quantity of blood.

Sin had seen this much blood before. On more occasions than one person should. Every time, the person bleeding had been someone she had cut, shot, stabbed.

Cutting off that line of thought, she stepped carefully around the bed, following the smears and drips that told her the victim—not Lee, she couldn't think that way, didn't want to—had been pulled from the bed.

There was a story in the markings, one she didn't want to

read. But she prided herself on the truth. On not letting emotions get in her way. So she looked. Calculated. And understood.

The victim—the body—had been dragged away, bleeding profusely the whole time. He might have been alive at the time he was slid across the sheets, but he hadn't been conscious.

Lee was not a small man, and it looked like it had taken two to transport him. It was clear the body being dragged offered no help and no hindrance. No foot print was clear, but she could see where he had been tugged, hoisted, hauled. The smears along the outside of the doorway, bloody handprints that weren't Lee's, the pooling of even more blood that then soaked into the rough wood flooring, told her they had stopped for a moment and rested their heavy burden.

Sin wanted to believe that his extraction meant his vitality, but she was well aware that the Kurevs would not believe a death without solid proof. And she had no doubt that the two remaining Kurev brothers were pulling strings on the other side of this.

So she stood in the doorway looking at the marks leading away from the cabin, the ones she told herself had been the two intruders hauling away their third, and she understood the reality of things.

There was no sign of Lee. The last thing she could point to when he was alive was him shoving her off the bed, waking her, saving her. She had checked her clothing for her own purposes when she removed it as sometimes you found the damage to the fibers before you felt it in your own skin. There had been no bloody handprint on the back of her pajamas. So Lee must have been fast, pushing her out of the bed before he had bled enough, touched something, whatever he had done to leave that handprint on her side of the bed.

Then, after he had bled enough to smear everything, he had reached out for her.

Sin hadn't been there.

She stood now, staring out the open cabin door, evidence spreading out beside her and in front of her. She fought against the sensation that she was cracking apart.

In that moment, hope bent and broke under the weight of the truth.

# CHAPTER 2

Nick woke slowly from a hard sleep. He was pulled through the sludge that layered his dreams as though by a large hand saving him from drowning. Like a drowning victim, he fought it all the way.

When he finally opened his eyes, it was to grit and darkness. Nothing spoke to him, told him why he was awake when he had finally achieved a much needed deep sleep. The place lay quiet under a blanket of Georgia humidity. An unassuming house in an unassuming neighborhood, it spoke of single man, cop salary, simple dreams met.

None of it was true.

In his dreams—when he slept hard enough to have them—Reese was back with him. His whole life, family members had died on him. An uncle would be there one day, gone the next. As a kid, he'd had a funeral suit for every stage of his growth, and only later had he realized that was not the norm—not the sheer size of his "family" and not the fact that they seemed to drop like flies. But Reese had been the first death he'd felt in his core. He didn't just miss her, he simply couldn't breathe sometimes.

Worse, he didn't know if what he truly missed was her or the ideal he had of what she could be. The knowledge of the second possibility didn't lessen the dull thud of loss that accompanied him everywhere. It didn't change the sharp piercing of his heart that happened at random times, always hitting him when he wasn't prepared. As though he could ever be prepared.

Sometimes, when he dreamed, he lived another life.

Asleep, he married Reese. Silly, since it had never been a waking goal of his. It had all been too new when she was ripped away. He believed he saw children they had together. Sometimes they looked like him, sometimes like her. And sometimes he woke with cold sweat plastering his hair to his head, sticking the sheets to him.

Tonight had been hard. Tonight the children looked like Kolya Kurev. Nick dreamed his half-brother Kaspar held a gun to Reese's head and Nick feared losing her. In the odd state of dreams, he hadn't yet lost her, but simultaneously knew she was already gone. The combination made him cling harder to the phantom of his own imagination, made it harder for the unseen hand to lift him through the layers and wake him to whatever was happening in the Georgia air around him . . .

Nick lay still, allowing the world to slowly right itself around him. Birds called outside his window, the southern heat making sure they were never truly quiet. Cars passed, not on his street, but on the main road a block away, and in the distance a siren wailed.

His phone lay dark on the nightstand beside him. The gun he kept loaded still created the requisite lump under his pillow and he could discern nothing wrong with the night.

In spite of having no idea why, he couldn't shake the feeling that he'd woken for a reason. His life was upside down, but he'd made friends of his enemies, and they had no reason to wake him at this hour.

Shvernik had taken out Reese with a single shot, and Nick's brother-in-law Lee had retaliated with a handful of well-aimed bullets that hollowed out Shvernik's skull. Despite the gunfire and the deaths, Nick had come to understand that none of it had happened at Kaspar Kurev's behest. In fact, his growing association with his brother should be keeping him safe—safer than he would be on his own.

Nick still controlled Atlanta and the surrounding areas. He still butted heads with Kaspar occasionally. But things had settled, the rest was details. At least from that direction, nothing should be waking him now.

Finally fully alert, he sighed silently into the dark and slid his hand under the pillow. His fingers wrapped around the gun and he heard the zip of the hard plastic and metal as it slipped along the cheap fabric of his pillow case. Throwing back the covers, he stood on silent feet, his t-shirt and flannel pajama pants a concession to the thought that people might visit him unexpectedly in the middle of the night. It seemed more dignified than trying to face down an interloper in the nude.

He was more irritated than anything. It had likely been a wily raccoon that woke him or maybe a coyote, hungry, coming down from the hills, setting the neighbor's dog to barking. Something like that. The armed sweep of his house was cursory, performed so he could get back to sleep, maybe change the direction of his dream should he be able to get back deep enough to believe.

With the gun loaded but loose at his side, Nick paced his home, restless in what he knew was a useless exercise. But he was awake and he wouldn't sleep again if he didn't know for certain.

Probably because he was so sure that no one was there, he didn't see her, sitting in his recliner until after he'd walked past her. At first just reacting, Nick swung his gun until he pointed it center mass.

Unlike the rest of his family, most of his training had come while on duty. He didn't have the lax grip or the callous disregard for life of the Vasilescus that had come before him. He also didn't have the street swagger that the current generation of Kurevs seemed to think was cool. He aimed not as a threat, but in preparation.

She didn't flinch.

That, as much as his recognition of her as a person, led him to lower the gun and plop down onto the couch.

Though he had heard from her here and there—they exchanged ridiculously off-date birthday cards and the occasional one-way text—he hadn't seen her since she hauled her husband out of sight while he stalled the officers coming around the corner to a murder scene. At least, that was how it was later classified.

"Sin." He wanted to be enthusiastic, engulf her in a hug, do the things a brother would normally do given a surprise visit from his sister. He did none of them, unsure how she would react.

Aside from a curt nod, Sin made no move to jump up and embrace him. She didn't even answer him, simply sat there as though she were contemplating the world. So Nick sat nearby, contemplating her.

His half-sister looked enough like him to fit the bill, but mostly they both looked enough like Kolya Kurev to clearly be his children. Sin had gone after Kolya for the deaths of her parents—the people who had raised her—not knowing the man was her biological father. Lee had eventually put the man down. For which Nick didn't have the slightest concern.

Kolya donating sperm to Nick's mother had destroyed her life and directed Nick's, but he was here now and he didn't begrudge the fitting death for the man he'd always known was his father but had never actually known. Nick had never been certain how Sin had dealt with finding out she was the mafia kingpin's daughter. Her emotions over that alone had to be as tangled as the rest of it, except she didn't seem to have many emotions. Nick wondered if that made it harder for her or easier.

He had hoped to find siblings, maybe a family, in his searches. Sin was the closest he had come. Though he now worked lock-step with Kaspar Kurev—their half-brother—Nick couldn't think of him as family.

Looking around the darkened house, he didn't see what he expected. "Where's Lee?"

She didn't answer for a moment, and Nick wondered if she still didn't trust him. She and her husband were likely passing through on some op. He would have been grateful for the visit, but after a heartbeat Nick felt the apprehension press in on him. Sin had never been one for social visits, and there was something here that told him this wasn't her idea of a drop-in.

"Dead."

He cocked his head, the word taking a moment to register. When it did, the thought blew him backward into the couch, the harsh weave of the cheap cushions scratching him through the thin shirt, the foam padding rejecting him rather than accepting him. For a moment the word reverberated through him and he thought of Reese. It had been her death in his house that had compelled him to move. He'd sold or thrown out all his furniture, hence the scratchy couch, the low end sheets. The lack of comfort from any quarter as Sin's single word swirled the air around him, changed and toyed with him until he was certain he hadn't heard it.

"What did you say?"

"Lee's dead." This time two words. Again delivered without inflection. Another person would have thought she was without feeling. Nick had worked with her long enough to see that she was on the verge of shattering. She was disturbingly strong; a lesser person would have broken long ago.

He didn't ask again. He couldn't offer a hug because she was isolated in the recliner, but he put his hand out and covered hers, shocked when she allowed it.

They sat that way for several minutes before he followed up. "Do you know what happened?"

"Kaspar sent two people to the cabin. Assassins. They got in before we woke up. I have no idea how they did it. I didn't wake up until the first shot was fired. I think that shot killed Lee."

Nick waited her out while she paused. He sat on the edge of the sofa now. His bare feet feeling the cheap wood veneer flooring beneath his soles. His pajama pants and thin t-shirt hardly worthy of the news of his brother-in-law's passing. Though he hadn't known Lee as well as he had Sin, the man had proved himself worthy and even avenged Reese for Nick, blowing Shvernik's face off to the point where the hitman had to be IDd by fingerprints. It seemed almost impossible that Lee was gone.

Furthermore, Sin had most of her facts all wrong.

---

Owen Dunham was sitting at the table, Annika helping their three-year-old, Virginia, relay the latest story from "school" when he heard a faint chime coming from the bedroom.

He had no idea how he heard it. This particular sound was coming from a carefully hidden spot, buried under two t-shirts and a drawerful of socks.

His wife looked up at him; he wasn't the only one who had heard it. The non-expression on her face, the slight nod, told him he should go ahead and answer it. Annika was as curious as he was. The phone had remained dead silent for nearly six months.

His heart was beating hard by the time he carefully set down his fork and made a cheap excuse to their girls for just a minute. For Charlotte, the gesture probably harkened back to another time when she was younger. But if she was bothered by him jumping up from the dinner table and dropping everything the way he used to, she didn't show it. Owen left them all behind as he headed toward the source. The hallway seemed longer now, the bedroom door heavier, the air thick with anticipation, even though the messages often were as simple as a belated "Happy Anniversary." There was no reason to be anxious, but he was.

The small black plastic burner phone lay silent under the clothing, having beeped once and done its job. Owen took a breath before popping it open and pressing the button. He told himself the message would be innocuous, but he wasn't prepared at all for what he saw.

L is dead

His heart, beating too fast already, went suddenly to a cold stop. He thumped himself on the chest several times, as though he could literally restart it.

Finding himself sitting on the edge of the bed in shock, Owen took stock. Forced himself to breathe. Normally he didn't respond to the messages right away. Normally he just smiled to himself, contemplated the well wishes or the favor she might have asked of him, and returned to his regularly scheduled life. He usually returned messages several days later, on a separate phone, to a different number, from a different location. Virtually untraceable.

Normally, he would have grinned at all the cloak and dagger moves, admired the clever plan. But now he was choking on the regularity around him. The message had to be wrong.

He stood, reached into his closet and into the backpack behind the shoes to pluck out the second phone. Different make, different model than the first. It would dial to the alternate number where she would be awaiting a message.

It was an imperfect system. If someone raided his house they would find both phones. If they hacked the backlogs they would find messages, find the pre-paid cards he used to pay for the upkeep of both burners. Though he didn't use the same card to buy them, he did use the same kind of card. Still there was no reason for anyone to suspect a retired FBI agent/college professor of staying in this kind of contact with anyone, let alone the woman on the other end of this phone.

Opening the second phone, he powered it on, impatiently waiting for it to run through the entire booting scenario.

Annika came in, worried. "What is it?"

When he didn't answer, she looked into his face and understood. "It's bad."

He only nodded, his life for the moment punctuated by the soft beeps and blurps of the phone loading all its systems when it was only needed for texts.

Owen didn't hand his wife the first phone. He'd told her once he never wanted her to touch it. She wouldn't have to testify against herself or him if it came to that, but he needed to know that there would be no physical evidence of her association with the phone or the messages. He could only sleep if he knew he would be the only one implicated. So he held the phone up for her to see, the horrible message still shining its pixilated awfulness on the screen.

Annika gasped. It was worse than she'd imagined even after seeing the look on his face. "It can't be right."

Owen, thinking exactly the same thing, was finally able to access the second phone and typed in his response.

Are you sure?

Sin had to know that was coming. Had to know he would clarify.

It was hard to even conceive that Lee might be gone. The man had been sharp, fast, and ruthless. Who could possibly have gotten ahead of him? And how had they gotten Lee but not Sin? She was clearly out and about, having gotten to her phones and was at least upright enough to text him. Though Owen had to wonder how upright she could be without Lee.

He hadn't seen Lee the last time he'd seen Sin, but he'd heard him. One short sentence in the deep voice he'd heard only once before. Owen had recognized a wealth of information in the sound. He heard respect for Owen, for all he had done and not done for them. And he heard love—deep, abiding love—for Sin.

Or maybe he just imagined it all.

He didn't imagine the way Sin leaned back toward the woods when she stood in front of him, the way she seemed to always pull like a compass needle to the point she knew where Lee stood sentry behind her. The man had trusted her faith in Owen, yet he protected her anyway. The loss of Lee made Sin a bit of a wild card. Owen knew their story, knew well what she had been before her husband came along. And he knew she could be flying off the handle now, though that wasn't coming through in the texts.

The chime of a returning message broke his thoughts, pulled him into the room, back into the loose hold Annika had on him, her chin on his shoulder reading the new message as he did. It was longer this time. Not broken into shorter texts as it was harder to trace one message than two.

Certain.

I'm confident it was K. N says no.

Heading South.

*Shit.*

"What?" in that singular word, Annika's still faintly lingering Russian accent hit the opening sound harder than necessary. Probably only Owen would hear it. But he heard it.

Looking her in the eyes and feeling the old pain of being ripped away, he translated. "She thinks it was the Kurevs."

Annika nodded. "I got that. And that Nick says it wasn't. Do you know about that?"

Owen shook his head. "I only know what you know these days. I know she maintained a relationship with her brother, but that it's loose. I heard rumblings in the bureau that made me think maybe Nick had hooked up business-wise with the Kurev family, but I don't know why he would after they killed that woman in his house."

He rubbed his temples. His brain still worked like a hamster running the old FBI investigation wheel, but did so without the constant input. These days Owen's mental backstories were more fiction than fact and he had to wonder what he didn't know about Nick Stelian and his current operations.

Owen considered Charlotte, left sitting at the table in charge of her baby sister. He considered the last line of the text and the code they had agreed upon once before she sent him these phones through two different shipping methods, two different carriers, to two different addresses for him. Sin was nothing if not careful.

"I don't know if I'm pregnant or not." The words seemed out of nowhere, but Owen followed. There had been a handful of miscarriages between Charlotte and Virginia. There had also been the travesty of his job and how he had always feared it would rip them apart. Annika apparently feared no such thing. But the stress of it had been too much. Then he left the Bureau for teaching and, suddenly, Virginia had come along. They were trying for a third, but without much success.

Him picking up and going on a wild goose chase was not in their plans. But it looked like it might be in the cards.

*Shit.*

None of the hundreds of cases he handled in his time with the Bureau had affected him the way Sin's case had. No one had gotten to him, both figuratively and literally, as she and Lee had. She was one of the reasons he had quit. And probably one of the only reasons he would go back.

He pointed to the last message Sin had sent.

67.5 degree shift. Clockwise.

Annika calculated, "So that means . . ."

Owen nodded. "She's coming here."

---

Sin sat in the driver's seat of the Kitty2, knowing she shouldn't be there. This was Lee's baby; Lee liked to drive it. While he let her behind the wheel plenty, he cringed when she drove, as though she were a lunatic out to hurt his car.

No one cringed now and her skin went cold with the thought. By sheer force of will, she pushed the feeling aside.

The car stayed parked in the still night air. The air at Nick's house had been thick, carrying the scent of heat and vegetation mixed with city. Here, the first cold snap had come through, and the already drier Chicago air started to slice into her senses. The cold kept her alert when the ice inside her didn't.

Parked on the side of the street, Sin sat casually still. The front street and the alley were both lined with tiny houses, spaced neatly, each alike enough to be a neighborhood and different enough to not be cookie cutter. The area was not new enough or rich enough.

This whole neighborhood needed help and four doors down it was getting the wrong kind.

All the traffic through here stopped for the same small house. Though this was clearly a neighborhood where families tried in vain to raise their kids well, and people scraped for every dollar they had, one house had no such problems. Sin wondered if Lee had maybe come through here when he came to Chicago on his own just over a year ago.

He might have sat on this block and watched this very house.

He could have known what she knew: that Roman Kurev monitored this area with all the care of a dog shitting on a clean lawn.

Lee had reported much of that back to her in messages of few, carefully chosen words. Just like that, the idea bored into her that there would be no more messages. Suddenly, a deluge of memories swamped her, threatening to take her down with it, and making her useless for the job at hand.

Fighting her way back to reality wasn't an easy task for a woman who didn't cry and wasn't used to feeling much of anything. For a harsh moment she hated Lee for bringing this to her. Hated that he once said they had a short shelf life. Hated that he had been proven right.

What saved her was her anger. More than she hated him, she hated *them*. The Kurevs had brought this to her doorstep on a night long ago. *They* had laid it at her feet and expected her to ignore all the injustices and simply walk away. To maybe just fade away, like her sister. To maybe live with it and carry it herself.

At one point, she had placed it all on the Kurevs' doorstep again. Only then had she walked away. She had been done. Finished. The scales had been righted to her satisfaction and she asked only to be left alone. It wasn't her fault they refused to do that.

Now, they had once again taken everything she had. Once again, they'd come right in through the door—though she still had no idea how. They added swift fuel to a fire that had begun to go to coal. So here she sat. Waiting for Roman. Fighting her way out of the memories and wishes that swamped her with never-to-be, she watched the people passing in and out of the back door.

At last, Roman emerged. Alone, like the idiot he was.

Nick swore the Kurevs had not burst into her home, had not killed the one person she truly loved. Had not driven a wedge between her and the brother she was coming to care for by putting them on opposite sides of the issue.

For a moment she contemplated the possibility that the Kurevs hadn't been responsible, but she quickly wiped the thought clean. The Kurevs were responsible for far too much for her to feel any guilt, even if this were an honest mistake. And there was no one else who even could have come after her.

The only other people who would be looking for her would be the FBI—if they had put their old notes together, followed her through the Diana-and-Will years and found her in a cabin in Appalachia. Or the White Oak Police Department. She knew they were searching for their missing officer and her equally missing husband. They had no evidence that led them to suspect foul play. But Sin had high ranking-friends in each of these places—so she knew damn well no one would come in, guns blazing, and take out Lee while trying to take out her.

This had to be the Kurevs.

She turned the key, starting the nearly silent engine and followed the loud purr of Roman's bright orange Corvette. The idiot didn't even understand that he should drive a low-profile car.

She didn't let him get far.

Just two blocks over, the neighborhood somehow became more rundown than the one she had just left. Perhaps they were too poor to afford even the meth the Kurevs pedaled.

Without thinking, she sacrificed Lee's car, ramming the back bumper of the tiny, showy Corvette and crumpling it.

She could see the man—her half-brother, really—looking into the rear view mirror and seeming to realize for the first time that she was back there. So she she hit the car again. And again. And again.

Until he jerked the car over to what passed for a curb and got out. So did she.

All bluster, he stood, pulling his gun as he rolled to his feet from his little coupe. He looked slick and he held his gun like a fool. Though his hand didn't waver and he didn't hold it sideways, Sin could see that his aim was off. Even if she stood stock still, he wouldn't hit her.

Who had trained Roman to shoot? Had he learned on the street with his father's hitmen? Had Kaspar given his baby brother instructions? Regardless, the youngest Kurev brother didn't hold a candle to her. Lee had trained her. And she would use that training to get Lee back. She needed his body, needed something to bury, needed her own closure. The poetry of retrieving him with the guns he taught her to use wasn't lost in the moment.

Time hung around her, cloaking its passage in her thoughts, her own gun appearing in her hand as though by fate. She had grasped a single sai in the other, and without thinking twirled it as though she were sitting at a desk, bored.

She lived a life that should have been fueled by adrenaline and heat. Instead she was cool, calm, unconcerned.

"Roman." She said only his name, both wanting to say it correctly—Ro-*mahn*, and let him know she actually knew who he was—and not wanting to speak any more as she heard someone else coming up behind her.

She'd chosen this neighborhood for the high probability that she could shoot this man in the street and the residents would all close their curtains, trying desperately to not be witnesses. Some fool was joining in. A mistake.

"Dian—" he stopped himself as the half-name and the voice penetrated her brain. He tried again, this time getting it right. "Sin."

But she didn't turn.

One brother in front of her, the other behind. She almost smiled.

Instead she walked up to Roman, closing the ten feet separating them. The look on his face turned from angry to confused at her willingness to move toward a loaded gun. Her own firearm was held in her hand, not loosely, but benign-looking at her side. Though she hadn't initially thought of it that way, the twirling sai in her other hand was an excellent distraction, and now she used it.

He shoved the gun at her as though physics didn't exist or maybe he thought he could use the tip to push her away. Taking advantage of that motion, she flipped the sai up and quickly tapped his gun hand to her left, pushing his aim out of her general direction.

Sin stepped back, a precise motion, a dance, placing her where she wanted to be. She knew guns and she knew anatomy —all gifts from Lee. Gifts that she would give back to Roman. She didn't want the muzzle blast to tear him open; she wanted clean shots, through-and-through. And she delivered.

Two rapid trigger pulls left him staring at her before the pain of what she'd done set in. Crimson patches bloomed on his shirt and she could see the war inside him: shoot her or worry about his wounds.

She saved him the trouble. "It won't kill you."

Lifting her leg carefully, Sin planted her boot against his chest. Strong beyond what she appeared, she pushed him. The motion she supplied would not only drop him but trigger his pain reaction.

He nearly screamed as he fell backward.

Now he looked at her like she was a demon risen from hell and Sin reveled in the idea. Standing with her legs straddling him for a moment before he tried to get away, she quelled his urge with a foot planted on his knee and an aimed gun. "I want my husband back. I get to bury his body. Tell your shithole of a brother."

Roman shook his head. "I don't even know who you are." He was scared though he tried not to show it.

"You should."

Just then the brother under her boot spotted Nick over her shoulder. "Nicolae! Stop this crazy bitch." His words, his attitude, commanded it.

Nick did no such thing. "That crazy bitch is your sister."

Only then did she feel. The sharp piercing in her chest that reminded her the world was all wrong. The burn of lightning cracked her heart in two, and she fought with everything she had to contain it. Damn, Nick.

She almost spat at the man on the ground slowly bleeding blood of the same type as hers. "I am no sister of yours."

For a moment, they stared at each other, Roman assessing her features and seeing the reality in Nick's words. Sin understood that the truth of genetics did not make the truth of the world. When Roman started to sit up, Sin decided she'd had enough of this little family reunion in this shitty little neighborhood. "I killed Ivan."

That got a reaction.

She leaned in closer. "Tell Kaspar. Deliver Lee to me. Or I'll pick you off, one by one. Do you understand me?"

He only nodded in response. His gut had to be hurting, his hand snaked in to cover the wounds as though he could hold the blood inside. Though the reaction was normal, it was useless. As long as he got to a hospital within the hour, he'd most likely live. The cell phone in his pocket made that extremely likely, which was a good thing. Sin didn't want to have to deliver her message again.

For a moment, standing there in the street, the dark Chicago night resembled the darkness in Appalachia. She could feel the foam of noise guards in her ears, see old soda bottles and other trash dancing on strings in the wind, strange targets for her to practice on. She could hear Lee's voice correcting her, telling her to do more exercises, to strengthen her fingers for her grip on the butt of the gun. Gently telling her not to let the gun recoil on her so much, even though she insisted it didn't.

Pain and anger flared like solar heat, burning away the sensations.

When she looked down, Roman was the only thing in her vision. So she shot him once more, in the shoulder, before she walked away.

# CHAPTER 3

Nick watched Sin walk into the deep recesses of the neighborhood. He counted the fifteen steps she took before he could no longer distinguish her form from the darkness. She was simply too good at fading into the shadows.

He always thought of her as his sister, though she was only aware of their relationship for a while and most of that time had been spent at a significant distance. He didn't know where she stood. Figuratively or literally now.

Nick was certain he would never have found her if the Kurevs hadn't initially come after her family. She still seemed to think of that night as a singular event: the hitmen had come in, bound the parents, and raped both the girls—which they weren't supposed to do. After that initial assault, the hitmen executed both the parents and left the girls alive—which they were supposed to do.

That was the first clue.

Kolya's men didn't leave survivors, so why these two? Past history showed it wasn't because they were kids. That oddity led Nick right to her. Right to his sister.

Her reaction to that first assault put her squarely into Lee's crosshairs. If Nick had the right of it, her skill at revenge started an FBI chase that left her free to live under a forged identity and to somehow do it with the respect of former FBI agent Owen Dunham.

The problem was Sin was wrong. The fire that forged the steel that she was made of was not a singular event. It was a bullet hole, leaving a spider web of cracks and ramifications that spread across the entire surface. It cut lines into lives well beyond what Sin could see. Even now, with Lee's execution, the cracks were still growing, still reaching out further in bursts and pops, radiating from that first night.

His sister had not shed the effects of what had happened to her. She probably never would. She was likely incapable. But Nick didn't judge that as he was just as incapable.

His path hadn't been split by one explosive event the way hers was. His happened as a slow, incessant chipping away for all the years of his life. Only recently did he gain the understanding of what a single moment could do, how a shock could shatter everything. He paid a very high price to understand his sister better.

Roman moaned at his feet and, feeling childish and spiteful, Nick kicked him before stalking off into the dark.

The man on the ground was genetically as related to him as Sin, but Nick had never felt anything from his brother. He had no issues walking away from the man bleeding on the side of the road, a lone streetlight flickering overhead. The others had all gone out and in this neighborhood no one came to replace them.

Leaving Sin's car behind—it was Lee's car, Nick was pretty sure—felt odd to him and he glanced into the windows as he passed. What he was checking for, he didn't know, but he didn't see anything. No bags, no trash, nothing that would identify her.

Sin wasn't one for errors. If she was leaving the car then she had cleaned every trace of herself out of it. Aside from wiping her prints or possibly wearing gloves, she would have worn only leather clothing, nothing that would leave fibers behind. She would have vacuumed the car, scrubbed the outside and left no identifying pieces inside. Her braid would be hair-sprayed within an inch of its life; she would have worn mascara and some kind of eyebrow makeup to make sure no stray hairs gave her away. Nothing would link her to this scene or this scene to the Christmas Killers of old.

The street became darker as Nick walked, but his eyes adjusted. Behind him he could hear faint beeping and murmurs as Roman dialed and arranged for his own ambulance. For a moment he considered fetching his own car, then decided against it. It was only a rental and the police wouldn't impound it, as he had parked in a spot a few houses down. He wasn't part of the accident and even if something were learned, it would be nothing new. The second Kaspar showed up, Roman would let his brother know that Sin had shot him, demanded Lee's body back, and Nick had watched. He'd probably also tell that Nick had kicked him. Not that hard, but it probably hadn't been the best decision.

Once again, Nick had chosen sides.

Only the side he had chosen had disappeared down the street.

Picking up his pace, he checked alleyways and yards. But if Sin didn't want to be found, she wouldn't be. He could only wander through the open space and hope she wanted to see him. For a man used to running things, it was an awkward place to be.

He turned left at the end of the block on a gut decision and another block later spotted her casually passing under the cone of light sputtered out by another lone lamp. Had he not seen her at exactly that moment, she would have been lost in the dark again. She wore a hoodie now, but he recognized her gait even if he couldn't fathom where that jacket had come from. Sprinting, he caught up with her, only to have her turn at the last moment.

"Don't. Just let me do this."

"No." He called it back as softly as he could, but with as much as he could put behind it. All of it was made harder by the fact that she enforced the space between them, motioning for him to come no closer.

"We're on opposite sides of this one."

"No we're not." He sighed. He had no more sides, only this web he had woven and he found himself getting stuck in it more often than not.

"I'm going after your business associates. I will take them down. It will have effects that you won't like." She shrugged beneath the jacket; she had to be frying in there but looked cool and calm.

"They aren't my business associates anymore. If you're convinced they came after you and took Lee—" it was the only wording he could use. Nick had no idea how she'd schooled herself to say her husband was dead with such a casual tone "—then they aren't any associates of mine. If there's one thing I learned from my grandfather, it's that family comes first."

"They're your family, too. And your grandfather was mostly full of shit."

He laughed, the tension of the moment slipping into the darkness around him. Walking forward, finally bridging the gap, he said, "Yes, he was, but he was right about that. He just had no idea who my family really was. It was Reese, it's you, it's Lee. There's not much left of it. But it's not that man on the street back there, and it sure isn't Kaspar."

Her shoulders—held so straight and proud—sagged. Without Lee, Nick was all that was left for her. She didn't resist when he hugged her.

The whole thing was beyond fucked up. But he was determined to untangle it and leave Sin standing upright. She deserved that.

Owen had expected to see Sin. He didn't harbor expectations of how it would happen, but he hadn't expected her to turn up at the threshold to his office. He sure as hell hadn't expected the man behind her.

Owen was still floundering for what to say—should he greet her or act like he didn't recognize either of them?—when she held out a piece of paper and spoke. "I just wanted to hand in the topics you wanted for my recommendation letter. Thank you for writing it. It's due soon."

He only nodded in response, dumbstruck by the way she morphed back into the student she'd once been.

The two then disappeared down the hallway, Nick Stelian less malleable in form than Sin. He still moved like a cop, and Owen wondered if it was a kindred recognition . . . Though he never would have thought of Stelian's type as his kindred.

When he flipped open the paper it was typed up with the usual information. Her name, her class record, inserted from when she'd actually been a student, and various other things that fit in a rec letter. In the middle, however, for anyone looking for it, were the time and date and location for a meeting.

She'd chosen the hiking path where they'd met up before and he wondered at the decision. He later debated it with Annika. It was Annika who argued that the pros outweighed the cons. The cons were that they'd been there before, the pros that there was no evidence that anyone knew they had met. Sin had done her job keeping Owen's help out of the light. Also, the place was busy enough to not attract attention when two cars headed that way at roughly the same time. And there were no security cameras in the woods. No one would know they had literally crossed paths.

So now he walked the trail beside her, one hand holding hers while the other fidgeted restlessly in the large jacket pocket. He tried not to let his digits slide into place around the trigger and the butt of the Beretta there. It was stupid really.

Of course Annika was smarter than all of them put together.

"You know she's faster than you." His wife smiled. "And Nick probably is, too."

"Thank you." The sarcasm reminded him the gun was just for comfort, though it wasn't doing its job.

Her grin cracked a little wider. "I'm pregnant."

He stopped, the world slipping as though it had been held by a string suddenly cut. Owen felt his heart get bigger, then contract back just a little, protecting itself against the possibilities.

"I know." Her smile turned thoughtful. "I got curious and checked this morning. Obviously, it's way too early to do anything or make any decisions, but I wanted you to know."

The world slowly popped back into place, the slicing calls of birds in the trees above them, the grind of cars in the distant lot. The sight and smell of the woods and the background noise that was never distinct yet never just white permeated back through his senses. He thought of other celebrations that had ended in tears. Times he wondered if it was his fault and doctors saying that it often went this way, just because. Still, his feelings didn't go away just because medicine said so.

It was another factor in the path ahead. Probably why Annika told him now.

But her mind was already on another track, and though their hands were clasped tight in solidarity, she was well ahead of him in some ways. "It's not a bad idea—the gun. Though you aren't as fast as her or her brother, you're better than some of the others."

That made Owen suck in a breath as they turned off the short walking trails and up into the hiking area. Suddenly he turned to her, wondering if she should come along, and knowing he couldn't leave her. "Anni? Should we cancel—"

He didn't get to finish.

"Of course not. Her husband died. And I'm not an invalid. Right now, it goes the way it goes. Honestly, it's a gamble and my money's not on the best outcome. I don't want to miss anything for something that's probably not going to pan out."

Her frankness startled him. Owen had not seen it coming and for a moment he wished the hits would quit. Both good and bad, the world was swinging for him today.

Annika tugged him up the trail, urging him not to linger. From past experience he knew comments about slowing down or "her condition" would not be welcomed.

Always a trained agent, though he was eight years out of the Bureau now, his eyes swept the surrounding area of their own accord. The back part of his brain logged everything—other hikers, animals, anything out of the ordinary. But the front part contemplated all the new developments, so the time slipped away from him and Annika was sucking in her breath at the view they had reached long before he expected it.

There was a moment of pure tranquility as he gazed out over the landscape, the earth falling away in front of him, a sheer face of rock that was as deadly as it was beautiful. Certainly the park had warnings, gates, devices to stop stupid or suicidal people, but they managed to leave the view intact. So Owen stood and stared out over land seemingly untouched by man, while he held the hand of his pregnant wife and contemplated the joy of creating another person.

Then it fled as though pushed by a force field.

He could almost feel her approaching. Owen understood his wife's awe at the view. He'd only seen it twice before; the first time quite a while ago. Then, like many wonderful things too easy to access, he hadn't come again until he needed to meet with Sin. She'd been going by Diana then. It had been a while, and he hadn't been here since. So he let his wife have the moment to watch out over open land while he waited.

Annika's voice broke through the sounds of the forest. "They're almost here."

She never stopped amazing him. He'd always known she was

smart—smart enough that it was worth bending a few laws and telling her about some of his stranger cases from his FBI days. When he'd first started tracking Sin, they thought they were tracking a small, Asian man with a grudge against the Kurevs. It was Annika who first suggested that the Grudge Ninja was a female. It was Annika who soaked up everything like a sponge and turned it into something useful. She was the one who suggested that the grudge Sin held against the Kurevs before would be no match to the one she harbored now. Something Owen had not yet factored in.

So he shouldn't be surprised that his wife simply picked up all his best surveillance techniques.

"Dr. Dunham." The voice came from off to the left. It clearly belonged to Sin. Diana. Cynthia Beller. She had been each of them. Maybe she was none of them.

Turning his head to answer the sound, he nearly laughed as Annika did, too. In fact, in another two years they would be Dr. and Dr. Dunham. The small amusement took the edge off his worry that Nick Stelian was waiting in the brush, the way Lee had been the last time he and Sin had met up here. Nick was not the expert Lee was and Owen was nervous until the man made an appearance right behind Sin.

For a moment, the four of them sized each other up. Clearly, Sin and Nick had not been expecting Annika, and Owen sure hadn't expected to see Nick face-to-face. It wasn't a good match. At least no one knew who Sin really was. But Nick, . . . Nick had two faces, two lives. The surface knew him as the very competent and community-oriented police detective in White Oak, just outside Atlanta. But below the surface, Nick was the head of the Vasilescu crime family. He'd perpetrated a hostile takeover on his own grandfather and hadn't shed a tear when the old man died less than a year later. He was also in bed with the Kurevs—his and Sin's half-brothers. While Nick ran a relatively benign organization that did as much outreach as gun running, the

Kurevs had no such proclivities. They died, killed, and razed the world around them in pursuit of their own name, money and power.

Owen didn't like the idea of Nick anywhere near Annika, but it was a little late for that thought to pop up now.

Still, as all those thoughts raced through his head, his mental track hit a brick wall when he really looked at Sin. They had been intertwined for so long—even before they knew each other. He'd first nurtured a grudging respect, followed by a deep understanding, then finally a kinship.

He wanted to reach out and hug her, to offer fatherly compassion for the loss written on her face. But she wouldn't appreciate a hug. She didn't touch, didn't connect in the normal way.

Annika, seeing what he saw and possibly more, didn't know that Sin didn't hug and reached out to the girl. Owen was already wincing as the air electrified. The two women, also twined by fate, touched for the first time.

Sin, accepting the wild embrace Annika offered, clutched at his wife and sucked in air as though she had been unable to do so until this moment. She buried her face in Annika's shoulder, turning away from her watch, leaving her vigilance in the dust as she let Annika hold her in place, palm to the back of her head as a mother would do.

The grief that hit him was unparalleled by any he had known himself. Owen looked at Nick, who seemed just as thunderstruck as he was that Sin allowed this, that she dropped her guard. As he met Nick's gaze for the first time, the two men realized simultaneously what it meant for them. Sin trusted each of them with her life. They were her guard, allowing her the support Annika offered, and Owen felt a surge. Sin did not trust easy.

Quietly, he and Nick stood watch for however long it took for Sin and Annika to hug it out. Without words, they divided the territory, Owen sliding his fingers along the Beretta in his pocket,

Nick's stance changing as they watched the forest depths for stray bears or Kurevs.

She didn't cry like other girls. There was nothing in Sin like other girls, so the grief poured out, a silent river rent apart and lessened by the bond she and Annika instantly formed. Somehow, Sin understood that Anni understood. She didn't know that Anni had been born in Belarus under the USSR and immigrated to the US after her father was murdered, probably by the government. She didn't know Annika's grandmother had been detained as a spy, forcing Anni's mother to pack her child and flee in the dead of night. His wife had been nine. Though no one had Sin's background, Annika could relate.

Owen didn't count the time, he simply waited until, by some mutual agreement the two women broke apart, still no words exchanged between them.

With a sigh that seemed to release just a little more of her sadness to drift upward and away, Sin finally added her voice to the sounds around them. "Dr. Dunham, Nick . . . Nick, Dr. Dunham and his wife."

With that stilted introduction, Owen found himself accepting a friendly handshake from a man he never wanted to be friendly with. Inwardly he cringed at his own voice. "Call me Owen. It's about time."

His half-smile was for her, but it too neatly overlaid the churning in his gut at what he was getting himself into. "This is my wife, Annika."

There was a surreal moment, as though it was a garden party or a school function, and not a meeting between an ex-agent and two known killers. Owen didn't know what to do next, but Sin and Annika did.

Sin looked to him, her eyes imploring him, even though he had no idea what she might want. "I need your help."

"With what?" He couldn't say yes, didn't know what she needed.

"Nick didn't believe the Kurevs were involved with Lee's murder. He's been working with Kaspar for over a year now." So unlike Sin, she sighed again, full of exasperation. "I want to believe it wasn't them, but I can't think of anyone else. Can you find out if I'm missing someone?"

The voice that responded wasn't his. His mouth opened, but it was Annika who answered. "Of course we can."

Of course Annika said yes. Owen wanted to believe that she was just being nice, that she didn't know what she promised. But he was pretty certain she knew exactly what she said, and he was just as confident that she wanted in.

She knew Owen had friends still in the Bureau. They both knew Nguyen—his favorite lab geek—was now head of lab services and out for Kurev blood. The man was also a secret fan of the Grudge Ninja and kept an eye out for any of her work. Sorely hurting for some action for a few years, Nguyen soothed himself with bad things that happened to the Kurevs and he haunted Owen with the occasional update.

"What about Roman? You already burned that bridge." Just before he left, Nguyen had pinged him with pictures of a 9mm bullet pulled from Roman Kurev. Geek to the core, Nguyen had made friends with police officers and agents in Chicago and was often notified and even occasionally sent actual evidence in things Kurev-related.

Shrugging, Sin almost smiled. "I had no bridges to burn."

Annika joined it. "Roman is your brother, is he not?"

A shake of the head. "No. DNA means nothing to me. My father was my father. Kolya had nothing to do with me except to trigger all of this. Roman, Kaspar, even Ivan . . . I have no brothers there."

As Owen watched, Nick flinched at her casual dismissal of DNA. But as soon as the expression passed, a simple bump of her elbow signaled between Sin and Nick that it wasn't DNA that tied her to him.

Sin watched Owen carefully.

He said he was willing to use FBI connections to help her find the information she needed. It wasn't revenge this time, it was about finding Lee. It was about not letting her husband's final place be among the Kurevs. The very thought tore her to pieces. So she tried not to think it.

The Kurevs had done enough to him. They wouldn't be in charge of his death any more than they already had been.

"Can you tell us what happened?" Annika's gaze was soft but intense. There was a tone that told her saying no was an acceptable answer, but Sin knew from past experience that trustworthy people could help.

Was Annika trustworthy?

It must have shown on her face, because behind his wife, Owen gave a small nod. They had never spoken of his wife; this would only entangle them more. But the tangle was necessary. She had to get Lee back.

So on a leap of faith akin to going over the cliff at her side, Sin took a breath and started. Without giving anything exact, she told about the cabin, how far out it was, the lack of visitors. Other than one older man who lived alone in the mountains wandering by and sharing a sandwich with them, no one had been there before the assassins came.

"Except the assassins." Annika inserted when Sin came to a stop. "They had to be there before."

Sin shook her head. "We were careful."

But Owen countered, "They got in. I don't know that you can be careful enough. Satellite images can be hacked—"

"We covered everything from the top, too. Diverted the smoke from the chimney. Ran a gas powered generator." Sin shook her head. It didn't matter what they'd done. "Regardless, they found us."

It was Annika who offered consolation again. "But maybe you stayed alive years longer because of those precautions."

Sin was wondering whether the simple postponing of the inevitable was worth all the work, but Annika's voice stopped that.

"Would you trade a single day you had for an easier life?"

Sin shook her head again. Still, the way Annika and Owen were looking at each other made her think maybe the question wasn't solely aimed at her.

Owen's response helped seal it. "The more I know the more I can help. So, you don't have any evidence that they had been out there before?"

"Other than the fact that they came in so cleanly and easily that night? No." At Annika's next question she had to admit that she hadn't seen or heard anything until they were standing over her. That she wasn't even sure she'd woken at the gunshot but maybe had only woken because Lee shoved her out of bed.

Annika prodded again. "Before that, did you ever feel like your home had been violated?"

"No. Even that evening was normal. We ate dinner, read for a while, paced out a fight, ran a drill, then got ready and went to bed. We were tired and fell asleep. That's it. Lee was beyond saving before I even woke up." She shrugged, the rise of her shoulders helping to push down any feelings. Her success would be linked to her ability to stick to facts.

"Were you drugged?"

Everyone turned to look at Annika, even Nick who had remained silently watchful. His words were soft. "Shit, Sin."

Thoughts reeled in her head. Could it be possible? She didn't want to latch onto easy absolution, but the idea teased her, offered her sanctuary, explained the missed shots. "So how would they have done that?"

It was Owen this time, picking up his wife's thread. "Through your water supply? Your food? Maybe in the air. They drug you, then walk right in, no stealth required."

While she couldn't see the whole plan, she acknowledged the possibility. Sin didn't want to believe she and Lee had become so lax that two assassins had made it through the front door and to the end of the bed without alerting either of them.

Looking to Dr. Dunham—*Owen*—she considered his strong convictions. Now she needed to gauge what would mean the most, how much his morals would have to bend to help her. She needed him, and soon. She was running on a limited clock.

# CHAPTER 4

O wen watched his email ping again. But it didn't contain the information he needed.

*Call me. I have things you want.*

While Owen wanted the things, he didn't want the vocal contact. During his years with the Bureau, Nguyen had been his go-to guy, so much so that Owen had told the Bureau to simply fly the scientist out for certain cases that came with big red bows. Nguyen had broken open so many clues in that investigation, given Owen the leads he needed.

To this day, Nguyen had no idea that Owen had eventually found the ninja. Spoken to her face to face. Befriended her as best she would allow.

It was Nguyen who kept Owen abreast of developments after he left the Bureau. When Owen stopped tracking the Ninja, the lab tech had picked up the discarded mantle and run. With his Agent friend no longer supplying his fix, Nguyen was searching her out himself. He was tracking the gunner, too, maintaining files on each of them, cataloging possible cases.

Even Owen didn't know if the two had been out and about, if they had done anything to merit getting another case file. He didn't ask, didn't want to know. He was a lawman to his core ... or so he'd thought until she'd come along.

Nguyen was a scientist to his core. He loved a puzzle and he like to grab clues out of the air. The man had been in the business longer than Owen, long enough to know what was important now, what to ignore, and what to file away for later. He could incriminate a suspect from a misplaced eyelash or the position of a footprint. He could string together partial fingerprints. Owen didn't doubt the investigator could pick up stray thoughts that hapless criminals had left lying around at their crime scenes.

So Owen was very afraid to speak directly to Nguyen without the filter and time lapse of email. But he was going to have to give to get. And he was going to have to guard his words carefully, or Nguyen would tease out the details without Owen's consent.

Since it wouldn't serve to wait too long, Owen picked up the phone and waited out the ringing. He had not been this nervous in a long time.

"Dunham!" Owen could imagine him standing in the morgue, in front of a filleted body, more involved in the death of the person than the life. "So you're back on the trail of our girl?"

Owen cringed at the terminology of Sin as 'our girl.' Though he hoped otherwise, it was crystal clear that Nguyen's enthusiasm for Sin's style and skill had not dimmed.

*Shit.*

He had to say something. The two had kept in touch a bit, so there was no room for a "how's it going?" or "what have you been up to?" Owen dove in. "Yes and no."

"Go on."

Yes, Owen thought, somehow tell him only what he needs without outing Sin and without tipping him to what's really happening. *Easy.* "I've heard some rumblings, that's all. There was nothing, then you said Roman Kurev was brought into a Chicago hospital, gut shot. Spent hours in surgery."

"Please." Nguyen's disdain shone across the distance. "Kurev's suffering a gut shot and a shoulder wound. Probably a street kid. Did you get more than what I sent you?"

"On the internet. Just a little side blip on a page, but it popped." Owen rubbed his temples. He wasn't a good liar, and was glad he'd actually found something on the internet regarding the shooting before he contacted Nguyen via email. "So what did you find?"

"Death of a high-ranking Kurev associate, Bear Kimmel."

"Kimmel?" Owen had never heard of the guy. It was both gratifying and disturbing to know that his work had moved on without him. The Kurevs had changed in new ways that he was not informed of.

"Bear Kimmel is—was—an enforcer for Kaspar Kurev. Not the smooth operator kind that we can't get a hand on, but a big, meaty, greasy beast that no one wanted to tangle with. We know exactly where he's been and what he's been doing, but he's Teflon in the courts." Nguyen's sigh gave Owen the much needed reminder of why he left the problems of the Bureau behind.

"So why did that pop on the Ninja radar?"

"Because when we found Bear he was tied up with a big red bow."

*What?*

*Had she worked a hit? With all the trouble with Lee?* "When did he die?"

"A week ago."

It wasn't Sin. The time frames simply didn't work, but he couldn't tell Nguyen that.

Nguyen went on, running roughshod over Owen's thoughts. "The bow was all wrong. Different kind of ribbon, let alone different dye lot. And the methods weren't as precise, but there was something there."

"So why does it pop? Just as a copycat?" He was confused now but working to not give anything away.

"The method, maybe the killer talked to our girl."

"Suspects?"

A laugh came across the phone. "Yeah, that's part of the pop." He couldn't see Owen's frown. "The only suspect is the wife, Ann Evalyn. But she's as Teflon as he is."

"What's the tie?"

Nguyen's laugh was both hearty and heartened. "She's a ninja-wannabe. She started taking mixed martial arts as an adult —so she doesn't seem to have the stealth or poise our girl does."

Owen noted the lab guy still spoke of Sin in the present. Though, to the best he could figure, there'd been no new breaks or any real news on the case for years.

"She's a regular at the shooting range, too."

Owen made a noise of understanding. The info was nice, but not enough. He'd never lost his old agent sense of need for more —more clues, more evidence, more hunches, more to hold onto.

"Thing is, Mrs. Kimmel is known to be batshit crazy." He paused a moment. "The agents pulled interviews from the shooting range. She draws faces on the targets. Writes her husband's name across the chest. Her fellow black belts don't like to be paired with her in class."

"What?" This sounded like an active case.

"Yeah, apparently one of the agents went in to 'try out' the class, and she kicked the shit out of him. Dirty style too." Nguyen chuckled a bit. Maybe he just had a thing for women who could kick his ass. "Anyway, the manner of Bear's death roused concern our girl was teaching her. It's also possible Kimmel just heard the stories from the inside track, but it's being investigated."

Owen had no doubt that Sin did not have any part in that one. She'd been a cop for too long, the blue lights suiting her sense of justice and need to balance the scales when she was living in the open as Diana Kincaid.

"Thanks man." The words didn't stop his brain from wondering what would have been different had Ivan Kurev not found her just outside Atlanta. Lee would be alive, that cop the assassin Shvernik had killed would be alive. And Lee and Sin would still be living quaint lives in a quaint house; something Owen had always wanted for her. He wanted her to taste the normality that had fled her life years before, become the most she could be.

But maybe she had. Maybe it would have happened anyway. It seemed Ivan was trying to impress his brother by finding the ninja. Well, he'd found her. The sad fact was that Sin and Lee had left a very wide swath of destruction behind them and there was no way someone wouldn't turn around and find them. Maybe it had always been a matter of time.

Owen hung up as Annika came into the office.

But she spoke before he could. "It's summer. Cancel your classes. Help her."

His head was shaking before his wife finished her words. "I don't know that I'm the right kind of help. Let's just say that her style doesn't fit my morals."

Annika sank into the comfy chair in the corner. It was there for when the kids needed help with their homework, for reading and looking at blue sky out the window. And now Anni used it, rubbed her palms out over her knees, took a deep breath, and stared him down. "Why not?"

"I don't kill. I don't get revenge. I don't stalk, invade, . . ." He shrugged, not knowing what else he could say. Sin was an assassin; he wasn't.

"Your morals are not offended. You understand that you might have made the same ones had you walked in her shoes." For a moment Annika paused, waiting for him to tell her she was wrong. He wouldn't. She wasn't. "You only know that you aren't built to enact her methods. But you can help her. You can find the information she needs. Go to Chicago, check in with the Bureau there and help her find her husband's remains. Should she cripple the local crime lords while she's at it, more power to her."

"Anni—"

She didn't let him finish. "Your morals would be more offended if you don't help."

It was his turn to breathe deeply, and he spoke his concerns though his wife seemed to believe the decision was already made. He was starting to think it was, too, but he tested it for firmness anyway. "I have classes to teach."

"There are other professors to teach them. They need a professor. She needs *you.*"

"What about the girls? It's summer."

Annika laughed at him. She did that often when he was being stupid. "You were going to spend the summer teaching. Now, you'll go help a friend, be a good person, come back happier and spend the rest of the summer with them."

"The money? There's a baby on the way." Another child, another mouth. It could be easier or harder depending on the money situation. He worried about those things.

"We have savings. And it is still very early. We don't really know that there will be a baby. It's gone south on us before." She shrugged, seemingly at ease with the fact that fate could and just might deal her another bad blow.

"What if something happens and I'm not here?"

"What if?" She threw her hands up. "I'm a big girl, Owen. You cannot hover over me. I'll survive and if I really need you, I will call you on this handy device called a 'phone' and you can come home on this thing called an 'airplane.' I hear there are flights nearly every day now."

Her sarcasm wasn't lost and he had to grin.

Yes, they had both known how this would go. Yes, she was right. She usually was. Still he threw out his concerns just in case she hadn't thought of them. And mostly because once Annika was done slicing and dicing his logic, he felt better about the decision. He wanted to help Sin. Anni made it okay to go.

He plucked the burner phone from his pocket.

Owen knew he shouldn't have it on him. Just having it was

suspicious enough. Should anyone track the number it would triangulate to Sin eventually. She was smart enough to not read messages—and thus ping the cell towers—in areas she frequented. But how long could that go on? How could she stay in serious communication if she didn't have the phone readily available and check it often?

Things were getting tangled.

He punched in the text message anyway.

---

"I walked away from a bleeding brother!" Nick was frustrated as hell. "Dia—"

He didn't know how to do what she wanted, didn't think he could pull it off, and couldn't even seem to call her by the right name.

In the beginning, when he'd first located her, he'd known she was Cynthia Beller. But his research showed she was living as Diana Kincaid. Now, since she'd left that behind, she was probably the most herself. She seemed more comfortable in her own skin, even if her husband had been killed. "Sin."

"Tell them you were tracking me." She didn't throw her hands in the air, didn't waste gestures or even breath—as though she didn't have any of it to spare these days. "The Kurevs will let you back in. Tell them you knew Roman would get help, and you had to follow me."

"I kicked him." Nick hadn't believed that the Kurevs had come after Sin. He and his brothers had a standing agreement. Invading his sister's home, killing her husband, and attempting to kill her was a grievous betrayal of their collaboration.

Unfortunately, Sin had a point. Who else could it have been?

Unfortunately, if he had to choose, he'd choose her over the brothers. And she was going to make him choose. It didn't matter if the Kurevs hadn't been involved. Sin would hunt them, and force someone to tell her where her husband's body was. Even if she was proved wrong, all of Nick's carefully constructed holdings, webs of networks, plans . . . would all go down the toilet with her search.

"So you were trying to look like you were on my side." To her it seemed obvious.

To Nick it seemed like a terrible gamble to walk back into the Kurev den and explain that everything was okay. That he'd kicked the younger brother of the bloodiest crime family in the ribs and left him in the street to die of a gunshot Nick had done nothing to stop. Beautiful plan.

Sin, however, found no matching sarcasm to go with the track playing in his head.

She stared at him. Waited for him to agree with her. Waited for him to be the brother she needed, though she had never needed one before.

This was his fork in the road.

Help her now or she would disappear on him.

Of all the half siblings he'd found, she was the only one who'd wanted anything to do with him . . . which was maybe because he didn't tell her of their relationship until nearly too late to do anything. Of all the half siblings he'd found, she was the only one he actually liked. "I don't know that you're right about the brothers."

"I do." It wasn't arrogant. It was simply sad and certain.

"But count me in." Screw the empire that he had built. Stolen. Resurrected. There were a thousand ways to look at it. Now he only looked at it as a loss. Well, he'd been growing tired of that side of the business anyway.

"No." Her refusal surprised him. "Just talk to the brothers, like you usually do."

This time it was his turn to refuse. "No. I'm all in or I'm not. Lee was your husband; we find him. You bury him. You—"

Nick found he had no words because he had no idea what she

would do after that. Her raised eyebrows and the sardonic twist of her lips suggested neither did she. He didn't let that stop him from what he was saying, so he started over. "I'm in or I'm not at all. That's it."

"You'll lose your badge." Her voice was flat. Her expression was, too. She'd never been overly demonstrative, never the bright bubble that Reese had been. But when they lost Reese, some of the spark she'd found fled with the loss of her friend. And now, what little had been left after that seemed completely snuffed out.

"My badge is just a front, we both know it."

"It's not. You love it." The small movement of her ribs as she breathed, the lack of movement of anything else, the simple statement told him she paid far more attention than he generally gave her credit for.

"I can afford to lose the badge. I can't lose my sister."

Behind the hard shell, she cracked.

His little sister. Too similar looking to dispel the rumors of her mother and Kolya Kurev. Too long on her solely focused path. Too damaged to even need a hug. Her surface didn't change, nothing he could put his finger on anyway. But he knew her. He *knew* her, and Nick could see the changes, see the hit his reminder had dealt. He couldn't grab her, shake her, yell that he loved her, that she was the only family he had left.

For a moment, Sin didn't move.

Then, after a long, shallow breath, she looked up at him, eyes clear if a little over-bright. "Once I hear from Dr. Dunham, we can head to Chicago. But you should try to keep your badge."

"I'll try to keep my head is what I'll try to do. It's far more important than my badge." He sat next to her in the shabby motel room, bouncing on the edge of the oversprung bed, and they began to plan.

# CHAPTER 5

S in sat in the crook of a tree, pondering her situation.

Having decided that he liked his head attached to his body, Nick had contacted Kaspar by phone, rather than in person. No matter that Sin kept offering for him to denounce her and hold onto his Kurev ties, Nick refused. He was staying with her, and he wasn't going to visit anyone with the last name Kurev in person until he had a better handle on things.

The upside of the phone call had been that Nick told Sin to listen in. Because he gestured her over, holding the phone where they could be ear-to-ear, there was no ambient noise, no *click*, of a second handset involved.

Though she listened carefully, she was unable to stop analyzing the fact that the man on the other end of the line shared the same amount of DNA with her that Nick did. The same amount that her sister Wendy had. This whole farce left her father's percentage of genetic relationship to his younger daughter at zero. Then again, it had always been zero. They just hadn't known it. Hearing Kaspar's voice on the other end of the line, reminding her of such things, turned her stomach.

"So what if I did?" His tone through the phone had been flat, much the way she thought a shark would sound if it spoke. Nick asked if Kaspar ordered a hit on Sin and Lee. "What are they to us other than a prick in our side?"

She didn't know if the slip in phrasing was accidental or intentional, couldn't tell if he thought he was funny. Unable to react, she held tightly to her anger because the man on the other end of the phone likely knew where the remaining parts of her husband were. And the very idea that Lee had been killed by the Kurevs, then remained with them, was more than she could bear. It disturbed her that she was praying they had dumped his body somewhere. Clenching her teeth and hoping the grinding of her jaw didn't make any sound, she waited as Nick responded.

"Because she's our sister."

"Her blood means nothing. Does yours?"

Sin startled as Nick threw his head back laughing, the movement jerking the placement of the phone. "More than yours."

Though she had strained to listen to the response, there wasn't one. Or if there was, they didn't hear it. Nick had clicked out of the call. Rummaging through his pockets, he brought out another burner phone. Like her, he had different ones for different purposes. Unlike her, he didn't memorize the phones and numbers. He used a coding system that he scratched into the casing, and he checked several different phones before finding the one he wanted.

Sin thought those etched numbers were going to get used against him one of these days. But before she could even grab the passing idea and anchor it, he was chatting into the next phone. He'd hung up, called a second number, spoke. Hung up. Called a third.

As she watched, she'd been reminded that Nick had a vast network.

Maybe that was why he coded the phones. Lee always accused her of never learning to see beyond her own sphere. He was right, she knew. Even when she met Lee, they started as a very uneasy alliance—two solo artists knowing they were better with some kind of agreement. Eventually they had become so much more. Still, two had been her limit. She couldn't fathom the small empire Nick ran. Her work with Lee was the only reason she even had the skills to work with Nick now. To tell Owen Dunham what was happening.

It had all led her up this damn tree, where she now wedged herself between some too-small branches on a too-crisp fall night, watching into the windows of the Kimmels' home. Dr. Dunham had tipped her off to the murder of Bear Kimmel. So now she and Nick watched to see if Ann Evalyn Kimmel might be a fan, might wish to be of some help.

Nick was pressed into the perfectly manicured foliage against a short brick wall dividing the sections of the newly built neighborhood. Small parabolic listening dish in one hand, headset in one ear, the other open to listen for noises, he fidgeted a little.

Sin might have been able to imagine it was Lee over there, quietly eavesdropping into the house. But there was no way that was him. Though their sizes were similar, Nick was blunt force trauma where Lee had been grace and agility. While Lee would have folded himself into the shadows, Nick looked as though someone had jammed him back there and he couldn't get comfortable. He didn't even seem to understand that you didn't get comfortable, you just sat still.

Turning her attention back to the window, Sin waited through the complex evening routine of a lone woman. Owen had pulled a full report on her. Ann Evalyn Kimmel was a trained martial artist, though apparently 'artist' was a strong term. She was a poor quality mother—between the daycare and the nanny, Mrs. Kimmel often went long periods without seeing her two boys. The older one seemed to have other places to go, which Sin thought was probably good given the parents he inherited. Now it seemed Ms. Ann Evalyn had sent the boys to live with a cousin . . . Indefinitely.

Clearly her grief ran deep. Deep like the plunge down the front of her dress. Deep like the red on her nails she'd gotten done earlier that day despite the perfect purple manicure she already sported. Deep like the color of her lips and brows as she painted them on to go out and paint the town.

Sin had lost her patience with the woman a full twenty four hours earlier.

While she was on a clock, she had to exercise patience here. Sin wasn't sure she'd have time to try a second tactic should this one fail. This woman was a valuable card if a bit of a bitch.

If Ann Evalyn Kimmel was a fan, she might be willing to let Sin in. Might be able to get her to someone who knew where Lee was, someone who would tell her. Hell, the woman might have even heard something useful. So Sin watched. And tried to ignore Nick.

It was an hour before the widow was done primping and preening. An hour before the slick and shiny chauffeured car pulled up and the self-important man got out and met her at the door. Both of them wore smiles that suggested they were on the wrong side of her husband's death.

Nick slid out from his space, listening equipment left behind for her to wrap up and hide, so that he could follow the two wherever it was they went. He'd supplied Sin with earpieces and communications devices so the two of them could stay in touch while he trailed the couple. So he could warn her if they turned back toward the Kimmel home. Sin and Lee had never really used this kind of tech much, their silence so valued. Nick was not a stealth predator.

So she was on her own almost thirty minutes later when she checked out the house. The equipment was put up, carried back to her car. She had wandered the neighborhood, wearing a yoga suit with sleek purple-on-blue coloring. The fabric might ID her should she leave some of it behind—and chances were good that she would leave some trace fibers—but hopefully she could keep from leaving any personal evidence behind.

Sin walked briskly like she was exercising as she scoped the place. She'd worn a blond wig, more gold and highlighted than platinum. She needed something that blended in around here, but didn't catch the streetlights and shine like day. Most of the women here had either sleek, dark coloring or else they were bright, glowing blond. Some were oddly both.

The people here were vulnerable, too many of them waving at her as though she were a neighbor, as though her appearance alone made her a friend. Smiling blandly, she would wave back while she cataloged what she saw—where the patches of trees were, how dark the neighborhood got at night, how many cars passed, how many lights stayed on—she wondered if they knew about the snake in their grass. Had they talked to the Kimmels? Had Bear watered the lawn and waved as these nice people wandered by?

Sin had pressed on. Parked her things out of the way and stood in the bushes behind the Kimmel home, the stucco wall at her back already cracking despite the still-fresh newness of the fabricated neighborhood. Sin turned the jacket inside out, and the deft removal of three pins let the wig slide off, leaving her colors nearly full black.

Usually she staked out a house more than this. Usually she had time to. At least she had Nick, following Ann Evalyn Kimmel, the only resident of the house. Kids were gone; there were no servants; Bear was no longer.

Previously, Sin had depended on standing trees, a long favorite decor of mafia homes as they disrupted police listening devices posted at the requisite legal distance and made it difficult for telephoto lenses to shoot through obscured windows. Old growth near the house was easy to climb. But here the height of the house—taller than the spindly trees—was a disadvantage.

Then again, the height—taller than the street lamps out front—was a point in the favor of anyone on the roof. The incredibly close neighbors were a distinct problem no matter how she cut it.

Calling to her, the arches of the patio offered the best path up. She had never quite mastered her fear of a backup home alarm system, she more preferred never to bother them. Standing on the low wall that ringed the patio, she reached up. Only by bracing her feet against the pillar and holding on with her hands could she shimmy higher. Soon the top of the pillar was too wide into the arch and she had to improvise. A decorative bit of brick stuck out, a fashionable corbel on the top, and it was sheer strength that pulled her up this time.

Finally she was standing on the roof of the patio. The multi-gabled construction now worked in her favor, as she stood in the shadows created by the varied levels of rooftop on the single home. Sadly, there were no vents on this level.

This time there were no arches. Instead, the brick face on this level resembled shale slices. As she searched for a way up, she realized the design could be her friend. Luckily, the unevenness gave her hand-holds and foot-holds.

Sin had to grip tightly, as she was climbing at a strict vertical, her body hanging out, only the grasp of rough shale in her hands keeping her from plunging backward. But she didn't have far to go, and she was lying on the roof in a matter of minutes.

She wasn't worn out. She knew to climb quickly and surely. Her muscles would tire not from distance but from time, so she was up and flat against the shingles before anyone would hopefully see her. There was little light up here, the moon in near newness and the sky in cold Chicago mode. Though she was north of the city, this was more like where she'd grown up. She remembered the sweet heat of a Chicago summer as only a child could, and the abrupt snap of cold that signaled the coming winter, and of course the snow.

Tonight was like that. Though her neighborhood wasn't like

this one—hers had been older though still plenty upscale—it brought back memories and swamped her with awareness she'd never considered before.

On the roof of the Kimmel home, where she was supposed to be breaking in, Sin stopped and wondered if her old neighborhood had gone completely crazy over her parents' murders. If maybe the neighbors never really felt safe again. Bear Kimmel had not been killed here, which was why she could walk into the neighborhood even when she shouldn't. The people who saw her smiled as though of course she would want to walk around and admire their beautiful houses.

Her brain clicked over and images of Wendy came clear. Wendy looked like Dad. Wendy, with her lighter colored hair and bigger eyes, had more of Dad's shape of face, more of his look, certainly she had his expressions.

The shadows lulled her deeper into her thoughts. They should have been sad, but over the years, Sin had found some forgiveness in her after all and the thoughts were more contemplative than anything. They were also something she didn't have time for up here.

She'd waited long enough. Anyone who thought they'd seen something would have long since figured they imagined it and go back to not looking at the neighbor's roofline.

For a moment, the clouds moved, revealing what little light the moon offered up, and through the light cut an eagle. Sin could tell from the outline. Crisp as fall apples and the spines of the books her father had showed her, the shape of the bird was clear. A bald eagle. They were coming back to Chicago. The creature that had been near mythical in her childhood was becoming commonplace. She watched him circle, once, twice, but she couldn't stare for long. She had work to get to.

So she slunk along the steep shingles and pulled a screwdriver from a pocket. Too dark to see, she felt her way around the base of the attic vent and used the tool as a pry. In a moment she had it set aside where it wouldn't tumble away, and she slid down the hole it left. It was a tight fit, and she got stuck but managed to push through, thinking only of the evidence she was leaving and grateful that no one would look here.

No word from Nick, which meant that she was good to go . . . or else that Nick had gotten killed or caught or simply couldn't talk. Though Nick didn't do furtive surveillance on foot all that well, he rocked it in the car. He could follow anyone anywhere, take out their tires, and make them glad to see him when he showed up to "help."

Inside the attic, Sin pulled up the door and let down the stairs and snuck into the house to see if Ann Evalyn Kimmel was too batshit crazy to be of use, or just crazy enough to help her.

---

Nick had stayed behind the other car, watching but keeping out of sight. If they had any idea they were being followed, it didn't show. Usually first thing someone did when they thought they had a tail was take odd turns and see if the car followed. It was absolutely the wrong thing to do. Anyone with no reason to fear the police should head straight to the nearest station, but no one did that.

What Ann Evalyn Kimmel and her date did was take a poorly chosen route to a bad neighborhood where they pulled up for some kind of roadside drug delivery. Ann Evalyn was stupid enough to stick a recognizable hand out the window with cash, then pull it back in with something else clutched in it.

It didn't matter what Nick really did. The blue polyester bits of his uniform that seemed to have worked their way into his bloodstream wanted him to open the car door, flash his badge, and arrest both of them on an array of charges. One of which should be 'stupidity.'

After that, the two hit a club. There Nick had flashed the

badge and been let in without much more than the barest glance at his credentials. It could have been a child's shiny bit of plastic for all the perusal his badge brought, which was exactly what Nick had hoped for. The bouncer let him in because Nick knew the way of it. His arresting people on drug charges actually made the place more famous. The bouncer might alert some of the staff, but never let it be generally known that a cop was slipping inside.

The club had been dull, Ann Evalyn Kimmel shining a bit too bright in her drug-fueled burn, her already overinflated sense of self-esteem only heightened by whatever she had taken. The man with her was also clearly high, but not anywhere near as buoyant.

Hours later, Nick was only running on the fumes of knowing he was doing this for his sister. Ann Evalyn was starting to come down and actively scouting new hits from the other patrons when she got a call that stopped her forward momentum and had her grabbing the arm of her date. She didn't seem mad that she had to pull him from the club and rip him like Velcro from the front of a younger woman. Ann Evalyn was on a mission.

So was Nick.

He followed her out the front door, trying not to make eye contact with the bouncer who seemed disappointed that the club hadn't been shaken down and patrons hauled out with cuffs, flashing lights, and blue officers drawing attention. Ann Evalyn huffed impatiently waiting the few minutes it took for the driver to bring the car around.

Though Nick had grown up with the kind of money and power that could lead to her attitude, he'd never had it. Maybe because no one had ever instilled in him an inflated—or any— sense of self-worth. Anything he believed about himself, he'd proven repeatedly. So he didn't think twice about grabbing his own car, and waiting for the black sedan to pull up and swallow a slightly worse-for-the-evening looking Ann Evalyn and her date.

Finally, she was doing something of value to him. As they

traversed city streets that were only slightly clogged with traffic on a week night, the neighborhoods got more interesting.

Yes, he thought as they turned along the water's edge, the road tracing the shoreline on one side and the mansions of the rich and famous on the other. The people in the black car probably didn't care. Ann Evalyn seemed to have known where they were coming all along, her half-smile at the initial call and the impatient foot tapping made up for the fact that she couldn't see out the tinted-to-near-midnight windows of the sedan.

The massive, metal gates of the private property opened. While Nick could easily have followed them in, he drove right by.

Tapping the button at his waist, he spoke into the air in front of him, knowing the mic hidden in his collar would pick it up. He didn't say his sister's name, only what she needed to know. "She's here. They just pulled up. Exactly like you thought."

# CHAPTER 6

Owen sat at a massive wood table trying not to get pulled under by unexpected memories. The table itself felt wrong—not the right size, it didn't sport the thick, single-cut plank of surface he had sat at for so many meetings before. The chairs were different, the furniture having entered another era of décor and investigation while he'd been out of the Bureau.

Still just sitting down brought back the wave of feelings. The concerns that the world would go to hell if he didn't do his job well enough. The knowledge that it wouldn't—he'd had to remind himself daily—but that it really might for a few people if he didn't get enough evidence to fully prosecute, if he didn't run down the perp and take him off the streets, shut down the money laundering that fed the drug trade that supported the ring stealing kids in Guatemala and bringing them here as prostitutes.

He had to consciously take a breath and remind himself that it wasn't his circus anymore. It was all still happening, but he was no longer in the fight.

Nguyen had taken him on the tour of the new lab. The new domain was inhabited by a variety of techs, MEs who worked solely for the lab, as well as evidence collection and prosecution specialists. Owen had marveled at how well his friend tolerated them all in his space. Later it had become clear that he didn't really, he liked to remind everyone that it was all his lab and they were just his guests.

In Nguyen's office, Owen saw some things never changed. There was still a drawer stacked with photos of dead and decaying bodies. And under the photos was a fresh bag of Reese's sticks.

Owen had raised his eyebrows. "What? No mini-snickers?" Those had been his go-to candy when Owen was in the Bureau, but it seemed things stayed the same and they changed without him.

Nguyen offered one to Owen, who was still trying to hold his stomach together given the image of the severed and shredded arm that the candy had been tucked under. He politely refused. Maybe things were more the same than he gave them credit for.

So he sat at the table and pored over the extensive files in front of him. Despite the time it had taken to convince Annika not to come and for her to line up a sitter and convince him he was wrong, the filing had still mostly not been ready when he arrived yesterday.

A young agent had been assigned to help him and Owen experienced a surprising shock that he wished Blankenship were here to dig the files. But Blankenship had moved on to DC, heading a research division. Last Owen heard, the man was training researchers, many of his early awards and promotions due to his work on the Christmas Killers case. In the meantime, he'd apparently cracked a few other big investigations, making Owen shake his head.

Instead of Blankenship, Owen was now being helped by the unfailingly polite Agent Pillow. At first the kid—seemingly straight out of high school—brought him coffee, asked if he was comfortable and basically acted as a gopher . . . until Owen asked about several missing or blacked-out sections in the files.

"Yes, sir, those are redacted."

Tex. The kid's name was Tex. Owen wondered where his cowboy hat was and what a kid named Tex was doing in the Chicago branch.

"I have clearance." Owen tried to push gently. The kid had already made him wait before giving him redacted files.

"Actually, sir, the redactions are correct." Tex smiled politely and Owen reminded himself he'd wanted to punch Blankenship in the face a lot of times too.

Was he stuck with the clearance level of the first year agent who'd brought him the files? After thinking of a relatively polite way to frame the question, Owen was shocked by Agent Pillow's answer.

"I have clearance, but can't share that with you." He nodded and smiled as though that made the error okay.

Clearly a better agent than Owen had given him credit for, the kid read his expression and answered before he could ask.

"It's not a mistake, sir."

"But all agents—" Owen had started before he was gently interrupted.

"There's only one agent in the room, sir. Let me know if I can help in any other way." With yet another polite nod and half-smile, FBI Special Agent Tex Pillow left Owen sitting there staring at his hands and his redacted documents.

After he got over the initial shock of the put-down, Owen let the unexpected feeling of freedom wash over him.

He wasn't an Agent any more. Though he consciously knew that, the feeling meant more to him. He wasn't allowed the redacted materials, but they couldn't take the skills, the techniques from him. Nguyen would tell him almost anything. He was no longer bound by the oath or the codes he'd lived his life by. He could really help Sin.

And he'd learned enough.

So he drank the coffee and read all the un-blacked out sections before thanking the young agent and heading off. He called Annika and met up with her at a small chain diner, where he had yet another cup of coffee and tried to have a conversation in the middle of downtown Chicago about the history of their largest crime family.

"I need lunch." Annika announced a while later. A raised eyebrow that Owen shot her revealed that she had more to tell, but wasn't going to share unless he fed her.

Two hours later they had eaten burgers smothered in barbeque sauce and covered the small table in their suite with dirty paper napkins and plastic silverware. By the time they finished the cake, Owen fully agreed with his beautiful, smart, utterly amazing wife.

"We have to tell her."

---

Sin sat at picnic bench freezing her ass off. Though she didn't show it, it was definitely harder to remain still than it had been in the past.

From age eleven until she really got to know Lee, she was fueled by one thing: fix what had been wrong. This meant taking out the people who killed her family. There had also been peripheral people, those who ordered the hits, who worked high within the network. There had been what she called "side kills," people who were hurting other innocents, people she could take out and help others not go through what she had. And there had been the kingpin, Kolya Kurev.

Her mouth quirked at the thought. She still wasn't ready to deal with the fact that she carried the man's genetics in her system.

She'd run on different fuel when she'd been Diana. Though she never really accomplished it, the drive had simply been to act and maybe even achieve some level of normal. For the first time, she welcomed opportunities outside her usual sphere.

She'd attended the theater with her husband. Graduated college. Held a job. Made work friends. Though it looked normal, none of it really had been. Her best friend was killed. Her boss turned into her family. And the single line of hate she'd left in her earlier trail had turned out to be a maze full of monsters fighting their way out—fighting to find her and put her down.

Now that she'd lost Lee, her fuel became different yet again. She needed him back, needed the closure that his return would give her. She was wise enough now to truly understand what she fought for. To know who exactly it was that she fought. And to understand that her fight would tangle more threads than it cut.

She was going to do it anyway.

So she waited at this picnic table at a state park, thinking for the first time that there had to be a better way. A better—warmer—place for them to meet up. Somewhere that wouldn't capture them all on some surveillance camera going to the same place at the same time.

Nick arrived next, shivering in the snap of Illinois air and unafraid to show his discomfort in front of her.

"So, how's tricks?" He blew into his cupped hands and almost smiled.

"I slept." An understatement if there ever was one. Safe in her hotel room, screamers on the windows and doors—tiny devices that would shriek if glass broke or the door or window opened—she'd sunk down into the big fluffy bed. Having rented the room under a false name, and having worn the blond wig and some strategic makeup, she went bold-as-you-please up to the room. Head high, she still managed to keep the security cameras from getting a good straight-on shot of her face. Makeup didn't change the biometrics that facial recognition software relied on. Though she didn't think any program would bleep out "It's her!" it would certainly add the blond woman in the nice hotel in to the pile of faces to check. So she simply avoided angles that would capture her.

Nick smiled and nodded, "I tried. Ann Evalyn is a hot mess and she's making me re-think a bunch of stuff. My brain was going too fast."

*Interesting.* "Like what?"

"Maybe I need ninjas on my team." He shrugged. He ran a lower key operation. No meth, no heroin. It was getting hard to get any of the harder stuff on the streets of Atlanta. "Kaspar's been pushing me to expand business. And I'm pretty sure the last dealer I took out was one of his. He thinks if I won't do it, he should. Doesn't understand that it's not that I don't want to *sell* it, it's that I don't want it there. Period."

She smiled.

It was bizarre talking to Nick about his drug trade. With her, he could start with something about the Vasilescu network and by the end of the sentence be talking about his work as a detective in White Oak.

For a while, Sin had struggled with his absolute power over certain things in his city. She and Lee had long, deep discussions about what Nick was doing. Though she'd never judged her brother—simply had refused to let her mind make a call on it— she hadn't condoned his work either. Not until Lee had asked what was so different about Nick's current work and her old work?

Sin had stopped stark still at that. *But I vetted them all!* The words rang through her head. *I knew exactly who I was taking out and what each of them had done.* Lee must have heard her thoughts, because he simply said, "And so does Nick."

That had been several years ago now, that Lee had turned her thoughts on their heads. She had not once had cause to question Nick's judgment since then. So she listened now as he mused, but they were interrupted by Owen and Annika Dunham coming up the trail.

Handshakes passed all the way around, except for a hug Annika offered to Sin in the way of women. Sin gratefully accepted, but as they all sat, Owen complained. "Anni shouldn't be out here."

"I'm fine!" she punched him in the arm, maybe a little too hard.

"She is fine." Owen looked to her and Nick, "But she's also pregnant. So I'm going to keep this fast—" his words tripped a bit as his wife punched him again, harder this time.

Then she interrupted. "I have a tendency to miscarry." She rolled her eyes. "It's not anything I do, but Owen seems to think he can change the way of things with hotel rooms and vegetables."

"And heat." He looked again at Nick and Sin as though they were the reason he was getting chastised.

Sin didn't respond. She was too busy shuddering at Annika's comment about "tending to miscarry" and wondered how the woman could be so blasé about the statement.

It was Annika again, who turned the topic and put the show back on the road. "I'm from Belarus. A cold park bench doesn't scare me. So let's get down to business." She smacked her mittened hand on the table, the sound muffled by layers of knit and maybe the fuzzy faux-fur that lined the cuff.

Her own ass freezing, Sin turned to her brother. "Nick, you want to tell what you know?"

With a nod, he offered what he learned following Ann Evalyn to the club. "I watched that woman for four straight hours and I honestly would not be surprised by a mental disorder diagnosis. But Diana—*Sin*—didn't find anything in her home indicating she was on any actual medication, but she is exactly as batshit crazy as the rumors say."

He folded his hands and when no one else spoke, he continued. Sin already knew this part. "She was out on the town, but while she was partying, she got a call and headed north, waterside to the Kurev mansion." He paused to breathe in. "Though I never saw her there on any of my previous visits, she was welcomed into the home. All of them recognized her on sight. So she's definitely in the fold now."

Owen looked back and forth between Sin and Nick, probably wondering how they were going to use this information. Maybe wondering if he even wanted to know how they were going to do it.

Sin took over before Owen could become concerned. "Her home is very interesting. I used Luminol and found several old bloodstains. All seemingly cleaned up, none large enough to indicate a death."

For a flash of a moment, she saw the stain on the bed in the cabin. She hadn't cleaned it up. Forcing her attention back to the present, she continued. "There was a variety of medication available—mostly prescription pain meds that didn't appear to be her own." When they looked to her, she explained. "Not street offerings either. No bottles with her name, but definitely high end, unmarked containers . . . Almost like the pills were a gift. But more interestingly, she has a safe in her closet which opens with her oldest child's birthdate—" she paused while they all suppressed a chuckle or a head shake "—and in it are two guns."

Sin continued. "She also has a cool trap door to a panic room built into the back of her closet. It looks like she goes in and out a lot."

"Panic room? Those aren't common in her neighborhood. Do they build those in McMansions?" Annika looked confused.

"Actually, I over named it. It's just a hidden room. I don't think the walls were anything other than normal drywall and there was no communications system." Sin shrugged. "What was in it, though, was really interesting. A bo staff, kamas, and sais."

"All the things used on her husband." Owen murmured to the trees around them. "Things she claimed she didn't train with."

Sin smiled. "These were a bit . . . flashy. I really don't think they belonged to Bear."

From everything they had gathered, Sin got the distinct

impression that Bear Kimmel didn't do anything that had a close relationship with finesse.

It was Annika who strung all the pieces together. "So she's in with the Kurevs, from probably before her husband got killed. So she likely knows at least some inside info about the Christmas Killers?"

The other three shrugged, but it was Nick who picked up the tail. "So either Ann Evalyn Kimmel acted alone and tried to frame the CKs or the Kurevs helped her do it."

"Why would they help?" Annika was leaning over the table, interested in the conversation. Owen pulled her back and put his arm around her, though whether he was just keeping her warm or concerned about her involvement was unclear.

Nick didn't seem to see the byplay, or if he did, he simply was a master at ignoring it. "Maybe they wanted him gone. They initiate Ann Evalyn and get rid of Bear in one move."

"Initiate?" Annika moved further into the comfort her husband offered. "Is that like some gang thing? Does the mafia do that?"

The questions were rolling out of her and all were pointed at Nick. No softening of anything there. Sin liked Annika from the start, but her straightforward approach made her even more endearing. Sin thought she was the only one who called Nick a mafia don to his face. But here was Annika Dunham, asking her questions about the "way it was done" and waiting for her answer.

Nick laughed a little.

They were out in the middle of almost nowhere, allowing Nick the chance to actually answer. "No, not like that. But they'll keep some kind of evidence of her killing Bear. They help her cover it up, but maintain whatever they have so that they can threaten her with it. They can easily leak to the cops later simply by handing over the evidence they have."

Annika was nodding. "It has to be murder or something very high up the legal food chain, or else there is a statute of limitations and the person's indentured servitude would eventually run out."

No, Annika was no slouch. And the way she was looking at Nick now it was clear she wondered if the Vasilescu family ran that way. A few blinks later, she decided that it clearly did not and she stuck to the conversation at hand. "So we are pretty sure it was Ann Evalyn."

Sin nodded, thinking only to answer, but unable to miss the communication between Owen and his wife. Clearly it was Owen's turn to speak and so Sin was looking at him before he opened his mouth.

"I wanted to know if I had your permission to send a team in to the cabin. To do evidence collection."

The blow felt physical, as if he had punched her in the stomach. And though he hadn't moved at all, she reached around to protect her middle, her brain and guts churning. It took a moment for the roar in her head to die down enough to untangle the web of her thoughts. She knew they were all watching her, even though no one spoke. No one wanted to disturb the widow. Not beyond how she had already been disturbed.

Finally she managed a word. "Why?"

"Evidence? See if we can find out what happened? If they did poison you?" He leaned forward, seeming sympathetic, but there was more to his expression. Dunham wanted something specific from this investigation.

Shrugging, she told him what she had to. "I trashed the place." There was a beat where they all looked at her. Annika the most confused. "We can't leave evidence behind. So I ran at first, just like we planned. But when Lee didn't come, I trashed it. If someone goes in, we can't have them find anything that might link the cabin to the Christmas Killers."

Annika had started nodding a few words in. Sin had broken chairs, shoveled out the fireplace and threw the ashes into the woods. She removed perishable foods, but left evidence of the creatures who had gotten bold in the few days she'd been gone. She left the door open, knowing nature would handle some of the destruction herself.

However, Sin had not been able to trash the sheets. Having decided that they were too dangerous to leave behind—they were covered in Lee's blood after all—she had started to peel them from the mattress. But she simply hadn't been able to. As soon as the first corner had lifted, the bloody section had moved all as one piece. So much blood that it had dried and wouldn't fold.

Sin filleted grown men alive. She'd seen Lee's bullets take the back of a skull with them and spray brain matter everywhere. She'd seen intestines and muscles and none of it had made her lose it the way the sight of those bloody sheets had. So she'd left them. She'd need to trash the mattress, too, destroy the evidence there. But she didn't have the time to light a bonfire nor to hide the billow of smoke she would create in doing so.

Telling Owen all of this turned her stomach again. And she thought his solemn nod conceded the problem. His words shocked her to the core.

"I'm only going to do this outside the official jurisdiction of the Bureau. I've been reminded that I'm not an agent anymore. Which means that I can hire my own investigator who can find what he needs for us and keep it all quiet."

Sin shook her head.

"There may be prints. Evidence of drugs. Even footprints can reveal a lot."

"Who would you hire do this?" Sin asked, her hands now solidly wrapped around her middle as though she could hug herself out of missing Lee.

"Let's just say he's a fan."

That at least made her smile. "You have fans?"

"No. *You* do."

Only Nick and Sin were startled by this. Annika outright

laughed, but Owen continued over his wife's giggles. He offered a guarantee that the information found would come only to them. None of it would be used against her. "Look. You have evidence of me meeting with you now. Someone turns you in, you turn me in."

"I don't have anything." She wasn't saving evidence, holding it over his head. Sin didn't operate the way the Kurevs did.

He grinned. "It doesn't matter. Any investigator who does any reasonable digging into you these days, will be led right back to me. Besides, the first question they would have to ask is 'where did the information come from?'"

So it was coming down to an issue of trust.

For a moment she looked at him—her mentor, college professor, the one who led her into law enforcement. And the same man who had hunted her for several years before that. She didn't think he could set her up for a fall.

Sin offered only a nod. Her consent made Annika quiet, the giggles stopping in a concerning way. It signaled a change in the conversation. The news he had promised them.

Annika was going to deliver it.

Calmly, she pulled a packet of papers from the huge bag she'd brought with her. Sin had assumed it was just her usual purse, but that had been a mistake.

Nick frowned at her. An expert at knowing when to talk and when to listen, it made him a brilliant detective and a fearsome mafia don.

There was something in Mrs. Dunham's expression. The dulcet tones didn't mitigate the sharpness that Sin could feel coming.

"I checked medical records—"

"Why?" Nick interrupted. Annika was gearing up for something, but he asked what Sin needed to know.

"Because *both* you and your sister were left alive. Why? Unless there was a possibility that *she* was Kolya's child." Annika shrugged as though her curiosity made it okay to dig through other people's records.

Sin wasn't upset by it, she always wanted to know more, but she wanted to know why. "But we know I'm Kolya's child now. Not Wendy. How would he not know?"

Annika shrugged as she pushed the papers forward. Sin put her hand on the top of the folder, claiming the evidence, but not opening. She wanted to hear this woman's conclusions first.

"Maybe he knew his hitmen were hired thugs and it was easier to say 'leave both girls' than try to explain. Maybe he thought Wendy was possibly his, too."

That gave Sin pause. She knew her mother had an affair with the man. She'd seen pictures, evidence that the two had been in contact before her mother became pregnant. The evidence of their affair was carried in every cell of her own body. The dark chocolate color of her hair, the shape of her eyes. "Could she have been?"

It seemed unlikely. Wendy even looked like their dad. Flipping quickly through the paperwork in front of her, Sin didn't let the woman answer. "How did you get these files?"

"I called, said I was an executor of the estate. Since your parents were killed before HIPAA privacy laws went into effect, most offices don't know how to deal with it. I faxed a 'document'—" She made air quotes "—and got the records in return."

There was a pause, then Annika filled it. "If you follow the sequence of events, you'll see we didn't go far enough last time." Last time she found out she was Kolya Kurev's daughter; Sin thought they'd gone plenty far enough.

Annika didn't.

"You had surgery, and your father found out your blood type and thus found out you couldn't be his. He must have found out more, because eventually he triggered . . ." She didn't finish.

But Sin made a motion to keep going. They all knew that her

father had gone after the man screwing his wife, and brought a mafia hit down on all their heads.

"Well, apparently he was tested, and he had Wendy tested, too." Her eyes looked sympathetic.

*That* made Sin afraid.

"You're father tested twice at the clinic. It became pretty clear that he was sterile."

*Well, Shit.*

# CHAPTER 7

Nick watched Sin, saw her grief showing through as she sat on the end of the bed and stared straight ahead. The emotion wasn't naked, but it was far more than she usually let seep through.

He'd done it the first time—hit her with a slap of information that left her cold and on uncertain ground. Told her she wasn't her father's daughter. He wouldn't have thought this news would be quite so devastating after all she'd learned in the past, but apparently it was.

Nick had never told Sin but he'd invested research time on her father. The more Nick learned, the more clear it became that the man was fully aware of what he was doing. In the right circles he had the reputation of being one of the best in the business.

Sin sat quietly, bleeding the whole story out of clearly open wounds.

Unlike Owen Dunham, Nick had no qualms about being seen with his sister around town. Even though he'd stood by, watching as she shot Roman and then he'd stepped over the man, Nick wasn't sure he was completely on the Kurev shit list yet. They would question his alliance, certainly, but he was confident the Vasilescu business was too big for them to simply take him out of the equation. He'd spent time making sure his people wouldn't work with the Kurevs, and also that the two remaining Kurev sons knew it.

It had been dark when Sin fired bullets into Roman, and Nick wasn't convinced their brother would recognize her if he put her in a wig and let her do her thing. He wanted to broach the subject with her, but she was sitting there, staring blindly, as though waiting for the world to end around her.

Maybe he needed to have a better plan in hand before he talked to her. Either be able to talk around it or convince her that his way was best. She liked to work her own way.

Given the deadly move against Sin and Lee, Nick was done with the Kurevs. He no longer wanted a partnership. He wanted the whole thing. And Sin could help him, whether she intended to or not.

Instead of telling her this, instead of asking for her to join him, he simply offered her food. She wasn't eating often and when she did, she seemed to pick at it. He'd known her for years and his sister had always had a healthy appetite, but since they came to Chicago, not much.

"Sin, you have to eat." He made a point not to call her "Diana." She needed to know he was there and to lean on him. Sin didn't lean on anyone. Anyone but Lee. And it had taken Lee years and several near-death experiences at his future wife's hands before she'd even come close to leaning on him. Nick didn't have that kind of fortitude or time. So he forced the issue.

She didn't disagree about the food, but when they got it, she didn't really eat it either.

"I had enough." She'd pushed the half-full plate away, mumbling about not being hungry and Nick wondered where his forward-pushing, in-your-face sister had gone. And if she was ever coming back.

When he finally gave up and took her back to her hotel, she swore she was heading directly to bed. His own night was not finished, he had ties to sever. It was time to start sawing at his bindings.

Though he ran his own family, the Kurev boys considered him beneath them—seemed to think it was okay to threaten his empire, to scoff at his methods. Nick knew better; they didn't have the local police happily in pocket like he did. In Atlanta, he laundered money in plain sight. Everyone wanted to be in with Nick.

Nick was known as a good guy. He worked with the PD both from inside and outside the organization. He funded college for a number of officers' kids. He did good deeds, cleaned his streets, created communities and networks in the rougher neighborhoods and ran cocaine and sometimes guns. He offered clean houses of prostitution with willing participants in a city far from Nevada, and he made a ton of money at it—money that he couldn't show to anyone. Money that meant nothing sitting idle in Caribbean accounts.

Owning Chicago would be big for him.

He could do it, too. He'd taken the Vasilescu family one step at a time. He'd turned his grandfather's best men, ran a game of human chess, and said "checkmate" before his grandfather realized he was being played.

There were people here in Chicago ready and willing to work with him. Nick had a handful of back alley interests—people he'd made alliances with and promises to in the event of a future change of hands. Nick almost smiled to himself. The future was here.

Though he had a gun in the room with him, he only had the one. It wasn't huge—just a 9mil—and he spent a moment checking it, chambering a round before he slipped it into his holster and covered the whole thing with a dark fleece jacket. He needed to be armed, but he needed to look like he belonged.

He then pulled a longer coat. Though he would leave it open to have access to his gun, he would blend in more with the coat on. The hat covered his ears and was chosen for its dark gray color, though the coat was brown, none of it would identify him from anyone else on the street. His boots and the frayed cuffs of his oldest jeans wouldn't give him away as a visitor.

About to break a sweat under all the layers as he stood in the hotel room where he'd turned the thermostat to an Atlanta clime, he headed for the door. It was time to start the opening moves with his inside guy.

Nick hit the street and the bracing cold hit him back as day dropped off into night. Reaching his hand inside his coat, he let his fingers brush the butt of the gun, reassuring himself it was ready. Then he moved past that and pulled out his cell phone. Texting, he alerted one of his inside guys that he wanted to meet.

He was only a block down the road, not yet to the L and the swarms of people who would be waiting there for the crowded journey home, when his phone buzzed. Caleb Riker had texted back.

Tell me you're moving pawns.

---

"She's crazy." Owen didn't like the words coming out of his mouth, but he didn't think they were wrong.

"I don't think so." Annika's reply was delivered as so many of Annika's comments were: casually. She spoke as though her thoughts were clear and clearly reasonable. As though she wasn't saying that Sin's plans were okay.

"Lee is dead. She's walking into a hornet's nest and she's doing it alone." He believed more in the need for a funeral—a rite for the people remaining—than in a burial for the dead. And he had a hard time believing that Sin felt there was something for the soul in the ritual preparation of a body. Maybe that was because he believed that if there was an entry to Heaven, there had to be a better method than "Did you bury him properly?" Because Owen wanted no part of that Heaven. Good men like his grandfather turned away because he had the misfortune to drown in a lake and not have his body found. Bad men allowed because their families followed code. And men like Lee—whom Owen really didn't know where he belonged—left to the devices of the Kurevs and Sin, his immortal resting place decided by the winner of a terrible game. No, Owen couldn't fathom that.

It was Annika again, still casual, still clearly somewhere else, who gave him something to latch onto. "I imagine it's simply the last thing she can do for him. If she doesn't, then she admits he's gone and walks away from everything they had." She shrugged. "We have a strong marriage, but we aren't bound up the way they were."

"It wasn't healthy." He frowned at her.

"I didn't say that it was." She didn't react, just sat there, secure enough in her correctness and in her ability to sway him. "It's what they were, though. And it wasn't a choice. It was their only option. I can't imagine losing that. So I understand her need for closure." She paused just for a moment. "I suppose it's possible she's doing this on the off chance that there is something out there. That his soul may need a proper burial to tilt things in his favor. I see why she's so hell bent on finishing."

It almost bothered him the way she could so effortlessly speak what rambled in his head. She plucked it from his thoughts with ease and sent it back to him, neatly packaged. But it didn't bother him that she understood him so well. She still loved him.

He shifted the topic before she could. "I don't want you to do anything like this for me. I'm happy rotting in a field somewhere."

Annika only smiled at him as he switched topic again. "So when do we tell my mom that we're pregnant?"

That stopped her. She stared. "When we can hand her a baby?"

"She'll be mad if we wait that long."

"Of course she will." Anni shrugged, no love lost over the thought of his mother's anger. "And we will apologize with a baby. If you tell her before and something happens there will never be an end of it."

He couldn't argue with that. His mother still considered it a sin that Owen hadn't disclosed his future bride's immigrant status upon the first date. Everything she learned was a secret he kept from her. Only in this case it really was. The woman had called Anni and expected to be consoled over the loss of her future grandchild the first time they'd had a miscarriage. Annika had finally had to tell his mother to stuff it, that her own grief trumped her mother-in-law's.

"So when do we tell her?"

"When the baby is born, or when she shows up unannounced and I am visibly pregnant. Though I am not above lying to her and saying I simply gained a lot of localized weight." Her arms were crossed. Owen was pretty sure she was serious. "Stop trying to argue me out of this, and just place your call."

Not to his mother. He knew that. He wanted to wrap Annika in something puffy and park her somewhere safe. Instead she was here in Kurev territory, following a woman hell bent on poking the hornets' nest. Owen picked up the phone. He knew the number by heart, though it had changed several times over the years he kept up with it. The familiar voice answered, must have been sitting at his desk.

It took a second to identify himself and why he was calling from a hotel outside Chicago. As he spoke Owen looked out at the steel gray sky, the clouds rolling closer. This high in the building, it felt like they were coming right at him. "Get to a new number. Act like your favorite bad guy and call me back at . . ." He gave only the area code and hung up.

Then he grabbed one burner phone and texted Nguyen's cell with the three-digit prefix. Then he emailed the last four digits. The scientist would put it together.

---

Sin had a plan. After crashing for the night, she started thinking about how she was going to make it all work. This was a decent hotel. She needed to gather her disguise, check out of here, and check in somewhere else as someone new. Then she needed to make contact with Ann Evalyn Kimmel.

Sin worried about her disguise, wondered what would be good enough to get past Kaspar Kurev. Or better yet, past Roman. Though she understood he wasn't in the house much these days, which worked in her favor, he still might see her. And it wouldn't do her any favors to be outed as herself.

She was contemplating how dark it had been when she'd shot the man and how likely it was that her voice would give her away, when she heard a knock at the door.

Nick was probably the only one who would knock here, and it wasn't his knock. It was rather late for the maids. If it turned out to be room service, she was going to assume the Kurevs had found her and bolt through the connecting door, through the room she'd rented next to this one and off the balcony into the pool before they got through the locks.

She plucked a Springfield from the small desk and headed around to the side of the door. Most hotels had small hallways ending in the doorway, this one had a wall next to the entry, a huge selling point for someone concerned about bullets preceding any guests. Flattening herself beside the entry, she was thinking about how to figure out who was on the other side when the voice came through.

"It's Annika."

Sin paused and asked, "Is everything okay?"

She was contemplating how she would know—what she could ask Annika that anyone forcing her here wouldn't know—when it occurred to her that it didn't matter. Annika might not tip her off if there was trouble. She might not even think to do it. But as Sin rapidly thought this through, more words pierced the cheap panel door.

"C. Macey Cooper."

An old alias. Owen had shared a lot with his wife if she was pulling that one out. It was one of the names she'd used when Owen was still FBI, still trying to stop them from stopping Kolya Kurev.

Annika was good, too. The name made a point to Sin, let her know that Annika was the real deal. She opened the door.

"Hello." Annika smiled as though this were a social visit. Then hiked her huge purse up onto her shoulder, and Sin eyed it warily wondering what awful secrets might be hiding in it tonight.

Sin was just waving the other woman into the room, analyzing what weapons she might have on her or what the purpose was for this visit when the other woman smiled. "I don't bite."

"I do." It was a fast response and Sin almost regretted it the moment it came out of her mouth.

It was rare for her to have no idea what a person wanted from her. Or rather in this case, there were simply too many options. Given Annika's seemingly sunny personality, she could be asking Sin to brunch the next day. Or she could be here to tell her to stay away, to not drag Annika's husband down this dark rabbit hole when there was a baby on the way. Sin looked at the woman's eyes as she came into the room and chose a chair situated at the small table near the window.

For a moment, Sin wanted to say, "Don't sit there. Don't be visible where bullets can find you." But none of that made sense. Who would snipe Annika? This high up in the building?

Exhaustion swamped her as it did sometimes these days. It

was so much work, maintaining two connecting rooms herself. She registered a false male ID into the other room and messed up the bed so the maids wouldn't think anything odd. In addition to the adjoining rooms, she needed a floor that was low enough to run the stairs should trouble come from above, but high enough to be above sniper range. She liked to be over the pool so she could jump if she needed to. So much to manage on her own. How had she done it for so many years?

Then she reminded herself that her clock hadn't been ticking then. While certain hits needed to occur in certain windows, she'd picked her own targets, made her own plans, and took the time she needed to do it right. Now, this time crunch was uncomfortable, and not something she needed to handle with everything else on her plate. Nor was the woman who sat and smiled at her as though they should become best friends.

So Sin played the game. She sat on the edge of the bed and asked politely, "What brings you by tonight?"

"I want to help." The other woman shrugged, her brown curls bouncing with the motion, her general demeanor almost too bright for Sin's eyes. But it was easy to see that a keen brain lay under all that hair. And somewhere, buried under the mother and the simple sweater set, was a woman who wanted adventure.

"I'm not offering tours." Sin had been the child of a woman like this: a wife who needed adventure. Sin had thought it the most wonderful thing in the world while she lived it and the most awful thing was having it ripped away. She would never be party to that for another child. The Dunhams had two daughters and a third on the way. "You can help research, though."

Briefly she wondered what Owen would think of her tossing research in his wife's direction, but she was too busy scoping out the woman in the chair across from her that the words didn't register at first.

"I already did." Annika waited a beat before spilling her beans. "You know they were hunting for a small Asian man up until you took out the campus rapist. Even then, they still couldn't figure it out."

"But you did?" Fascinated, Sin leaned forward.

"A female attacker was the only thing that fit. The lack of a fourth set of footprints at the scene meant the victim and the ninja were the same person." Annika shrugged.

Sin almost scoffed at the term "ninja." She'd never considered herself such, but it was a cool title. "So you're the reason they closed in on us. We could have had another good year or two."

Probably a good ten years older than Sin, Annika didn't look it. Her smile was secretive and she wasn't intimidated by the younger woman who could kill her fifteen ways without a weapon. Sin liked that.

Annika spoke in a clear, calm manner. "I have been helping you for years. I convinced Owen to give you that recording. I offered similar hair for a switch. There is not any evidence of you at the FBI. Not from while my husband was there."

Sin fought to keep her surprise hidden, but according to Annika's grin, she didn't do a sufficient job.

"I know you worked alone for a long time. Then you worked with your husband and I understand you were a very good team. And now you are alone again, but you know how to work with a partner and you know that many things work better, *safer*, in pairs."

Sin listened, wondering where it was going. Why the stress on certain words? But Annika wasn't done.

"I won't kill someone unless they directly threaten me or a child of mine. And right now those are the same thing." She grinned and pointed at her belly. "But I can help you with Ann Evalyn Kimmel and with the Kurevs."

Though Sin had no idea how this housewife proposed to do that, she was more curious why. "What would make you risk that?"

"Because, my husband has always gone out and made the

world a better place. Because these men need to be stopped and I'm in a singular position to do it."

Sin quirked her head. She could think of a thousand other people who could step up . . .

But Annika saw through her. "No. *Only me.* I know your background. I figured you out when no one else did." Annika looked proud of herself on that one. Sin didn't really know what to make of it. "I know what's going on with the Kurevs. I know their faces but they don't know mine. I know their history, but they don't know me. I've seen your work and I'm not always confident of your methods but I have no qualms with your results."

Sin was shaking her head.

Annika railroaded her. The sweet sweater-set and bouncy hair was a lie. This woman was a shrewd player who wanted in and Sin was going to have to work harder to keep her out.

"I can shoot a gun with incredible accuracy and I have no issues pulling the trigger. My husband has taught me all kinds of self-defense—" she held up a hand, seeming to know Sin's protest. "I understand that's mostly useless here, but I'm not a puppy that you will have to protect."

"I—"

That was it. Sin only managed to get the one word out.

Annika looked at her, nothing sweet remaining. "The Kurevs are expecting you. You propose to get entre via Ann Evalyn Kimmel, but you are still *you.* They won't expect *two* of us."

Sin blinked.

It was crazy.

But valid.

She was shaking her head as Annika's next words hit.

"Ya tvoya loochshaya nadezhda."

"What?"

"Exactly." The other woman smiled. "I am your best hope. I'm Russian. I immigrated to the US when I was nine. I'm fluent. I remember the homeland. I fit better than you do." She paused. "I can get information you can't."

Standing before she knew how she got there, Sin didn't like the fact that she was considering this. "Why would you do this?"

Annika's eyes teared up. "Because I can't imagine losing my husband. I can't imagine not knowing where he is. Because I'm not really going to *do* anything. I'll go out in public and speak to some people. That is all."

"You're getting tangled up with men who don't play nice. You have a home, kids." Sin protested.

"And these men will not be around long." Annika almost smiled. "Sure, I might make the Kurevs a little irritated at me, but I am not shooting anyone. Once you have Lee back, you and Nick will remove the Kurevs. I know this. I won't even be a memory. I will speak to Ann Evalyn Kimmel. She can introduce us to other key players and I will learn useful information through conversation out in public. That is all I am offering."

Sin only stared.

"Because these men are evil. I understand my husband's need to remove them." She sighed. "Life is a risk. My mother and I snuck out of our country, crossing borders under tarps and tools, hidden in truck beds. We went into Poland into a village and paid for help there. We found passage to Mexico but once there, were robbed. My mother spoke no Spanish. We cobbled together money for a coyote to take us across the border. We walked forty miles in the desert with heavy packs of water and little food. On my tenth birthday we hid from the guards who patrolled the border and at the time thought nothing of shooting the people who came through. We didn't understand what they yelled about."

"Holy shit." Sin had not seen that coming.

Annika shrugged. "When I turned eleven, my mother and I got an apartment of our own. I then spoke fluent English. She managed to get Visas for us. Probably because my father and grandmother were killed by the KGB back home. At age twelve, I became a citizen. I later graduated high school, clothed and fed. I went to college, met Owen. My life is better every year since we came here." She sighed. "I am unbalanced. I have so many things and I have not paid for them."

Sin shook her head, what did she mean?

"I do not contribute, though I am working on another degree. I will go to work in a few years and help others. But I have so much. And I can help you. It is simple, I am good at it, and you need me." Before she finished, Annika had reached into that big bag and pulled out a box.

Hair dye.

Sin shook her head. Maybe the woman was delusional? Instead she protested the only way she knew how. "You can't use that. You're pregnant."

Annika laughed. "I spoke with a doctor and I checked for certain chemicals. I'm safe."

What was Sin going to do with her? She couldn't deny that the crazy offer sounded useful. But before the thought could form, Annika had her again.

"So, I suspected, but now I am more certain."

"What?" Sin still didn't see it coming.

"You wouldn't know that a pregnant woman shouldn't use hair dye." Just a moment of pause. Then the shock. "Unless you were pregnant, too."

# CHAPTER 8

S in stumbled back, Annika's words tumbling through her brain. Part of her wanted to tell the woman to get out. The other said she simply needed to nod and let Owen's wife hug her until she felt better. But there was no "feeling better."

"Okay, that's a yes. Or you would have already said no." Annika looked at her as though Sin's face would reveal more.

Surely it didn't. Her face never really revealed much. She could make it cold as deep winter, as untelling as midnight.

Sin tried waiting her out, but apparently the other woman was better at it than she, or maybe there really was something to that crap about pregnant women. She'd inadvertently joined a club she had no intention of ever belonging to.

Annika made the first real move, which was good because Sin had no idea what to say about the situation. Until now, mostly she ignored it. Without Lee there, it had been the easiest method.

"You have not told anyone, have you?" Annika was standing in front of her now, though Sin didn't remember her moving. The other woman was taller, which normally wasn't a threat. Sin enjoyed that people underestimated her, took her stature as a weakness, but it seemed none of this worked against the kind of soft assault Mrs. Dunham brought.

She shook her head, no.

"Did Lee know?"

Again, a head shake no.

"Have you seen a doctor?"

Sin wondered if the woman was trying to get her to open up by asking simple questions first then going for the kill once Sin started sharing. "I went to a walk-in clinic after Atlanta." She was eight weeks along and trying not to imagine how Lee would have reacted as there were so many options.

He might have been angry that their precautions had failed. It wouldn't have been a good time even without all this. He might have been excited about a child, thinking about one last big play, then finding a better life, another chance to live above the surface under another name. Even though Sin was confident based on evidence from last time that it wouldn't work. He might have been scared, and that was probably the most likely scenario. The last child he had—the only child he'd ever had—was gunned down by Kurev associates. His only consolation had been that the girl had been having a good day by all accounts and that she was with her mother at the time. Though the fact that her mother died with her wasn't any points in anyone's favor.

Sin appreciated that Annika didn't try to hug her again. She was too smart for that. "From one mother to another—"

Sin held up a hand, moved sharply to cut the words off, but the movement was so much more. The strength, the snap behind it made it all clear that she could cut off far more than words. Do much more damage than simply making sharp suggestions that someone shut up. "I know what I am, and I am not anyone's mother."

Annika smiled. "I didn't think I was ready either. But you get ready. You'll be better at it than you think."

Laughing out a harsh bark, Sin sat back on the bed, the movement bouncing a little. Her stomach turned slightly, though whether that was an effect of the pregnancy or a natural reaction to her thoughts, she didn't know. "It's not that. Even if I wanted this—which I don't, I really don't—I'm in no position to raise a child."

"You'll find a way." There was a simple knowledge behind the words. But Sin's knowledge was much more complex, much more tangible.

"You must know about Bethany." Lee's daughter.

Annika nodded.

"You know about Reese?"

Another nod.

"Look at what happened to Lee. We were in a cabin in the mountains. Entirely off the grid . . . Not bothering anyone. Well, not at that time. And look what happened." She leaned back, wondering what the hell she might have done to the child already, just by being herself, and said, "I can't provide the number one thing a child needs. I can't offer safety from mortal danger."

For the first time Annika seemed to acknowledge the truth. There would be no golden "Mommy moments" for Sin and her child. The child's father was already gone before he even knew and that might be the only blessing.

Annika sat herself back down, the box of hair color forgotten amid the newer, richer information in front of her. "What will you do?"

"I have no idea. Lately, I've been ignoring it."

"If you don't make a decision soon, you'll have to carry the child. The options will close in on you sooner than you think." Annika shrugged. "You can't ignore it more than another day or two."

Sin was ignoring that, too. There were ways to get out of it. But she couldn't stomach the thought of most of them. "Probably, I'll have him and leave him on a doorstep somewhere. Someplace I know they'll be good to him."

"Will you follow him?" She seemed casual, Sin thought,

asking kindly about Sin's plans to give away her child, and for a moment Sin saw beyond her own sphere.

In her mind, she spoke, *I'm learning, Lee. I promise.*

She saw that this woman was carrying a child she was convinced she might lose. Annika was prepared to deal with the loss and the grief that would come with it. She spoke calmly to another woman, nearing the end of her own first trimester. Sin had read enough in the past several weeks to know that her chances of losing the child naturally were decreasing by the hour.

She still believed that Annika's nightmare was her own best recourse. Better if the child never saw the light of day. It had no father. Its mother had no maternal instincts. Sin had spent enough days in foster care to know those didn't just appear because a woman gave birth. Unfortunately, it also taught her what happened in a child that was given away by the parents who created it.

There were no good outcomes here.

Sighing, she stood up, hoping that would indicate that Annika should leave. "I don't know what to say. After we finish in Chicago—after I get Lee back—then I think I'll have the child and spend my time researching families." She'd have to find a new ID, one the Kurevs couldn't track. Leave the child with someone who could raise it as their own.

But Annika didn't leave. "I need to color my hair. Can I do it here?"

"Something wrong with your own room?" She shouldn't have been rude, but Sin didn't want Annika along. Unfortunately, she was right about two women coming along with Ann Evalyn Kimmel. No one would suspect it. Add in that Annika spoke fluent Russian and honestly it was brilliant.

Sin loved it. And she hated it.

"Owen is going to hate me. I can't afford to lose any friends." She shrugged. "Even if it is a really stellar idea."

*Shit shit shit.* She had to make a call here. Was Dr. Dunham's friendship more important than finding Lee?

Lee was gone. Dr. Dunham was still around. Aside from Nick, he was the only one who knew her story and still seemed to like her anyway.

She had too many big calls to make here. Keep the baby? Or save it from the pain of the future? Could she find it a good life without her? Give Lee a proper, final goodbye? She didn't seem to be able to let go of the idea of finding him. Every time she decided it wasn't worth it, it came back in a rush of necessity. Tugging at her, pushing her. But at what cost?

Annika sat still. "Owen is out of town right now. He's with the investigator that he hired, on his way to your cabin. So I was hoping for some company to color my hair. Maybe some tips on how to do it right. I know you know."

Sin nodded. That she did. She had way too much practice.

Annika sighed. "I know my husband. He may be angry with you for about two minutes for 'letting' me come along. But he will know you did nothing of the sort. In the end, it will probably make you better friends—as he'll commiserate with you about how obnoxious I am when I'm right. So help me dye my hair so I don't give us away."

She stood, took the box with her and headed into the bathroom.

"Bulldozer" was definitely the right term, so Sin followed the other woman into the bathroom and found herself dispensing hair and make-up tips like an evil Cosmo article. She had Annika portion out sections of her hair to leave as highlights in the near-black dye. Sin showed the woman how to not look like a fresh dye job. She talked makeup to change the appearance of the shape of the other woman's face.

And all the while she planned how to make Ann Evalyn Kimmel want to take the two of them in.

Owen sat in the car beside Nguyen for the first time in a long time. Though they had spent much of the ride into the Appalachians catching up in general and discussing the Ninja in particular, they had lapsed into a peaceful silence. A third man sat in the back seat. Riker—recommended by one Nick Stelian.

Owen wasn't sure how he felt about this man he didn't know, or about any of it. But Nick assured them that Riker was not only a trained investigator, invaluable at a crime scene, but that he was firmly in Nick's pocket. Though the Kurevs thought Riker was their man, Nick had actually turned him some time ago, with relative ease. Also, Riker had been collecting evidence against the family for years.

So Owen had to trust that Nick was right, that this Riker guy wanted the Kurevs brought down as badly as the rest of them did. And that he knew how to keep his mouth shut when it counted.

Though they had flown down together, meeting Nguyen at the airport, Owen hadn't had time to really talk to the investigator. There wasn't much they could discuss on a crowded plane. Despite the fact that no one was listening to a word anyone else had to say, it wasn't a risk Owen was willing to take. So now he grasped the opportunity of the silence, looked into the rear view mirror, and started speaking.

"The cabin is deep in the mountains. We have a hike to get there." It wasn't Riker, but Nguyen that Owen worried about on the march. Still, the lab geek's desire for all things Ninja would keep him going. "These two lived off the grid there on more than one occasion, but I'm not sure how long. I don't know who—if anyone—occupied the cabin in between their stays, so I don't know if you'll find evidence of anyone else.

"These two were known as 'The Christmas Killers'—"

"Holy shit!" Riker interrupted him, for the first time excited. Well, for the first time making a facial expression of any kind. "I heard about this, some kind of Kurev story." He paused, soaking in the information. "It's a couple?"

So it began, with Owen filling in the legend of Sin and Lee, making decisions about telling it as it actually was or keeping the awe alive and maybe retaining further respect and diligence from these two. Did the legend make Riker more or less likely to keep the secret?

Owen just didn't know.

Then he was at the spot where Sin had told him to turn off. It wasn't a road, just a flatter section at the side of an uninhabited stretch of highway. But the mile markers matched, or he would never have pulled off the road here. He'd bought a beater four-wheel just to get to the cabin and was now grateful that she'd recommended it. It wasn't easy pushing through the brush, trying to stay in the shallow path that told him he was headed the right way. She wasn't kidding when she said it was hard to find and harder to get to.

It took an hour of the three of them navigating carefully— Nguyen and Riker seeing only branches and scrub, Owen focused on avoiding rocks, ruts, and ridges that would damage the car. They not only had to get in, they had to get back out.

Sin made him swear not to program them into any GPS unit or any other tracking system. Though she'd given him every advantage—directions, coordinates, and the turnoff, none of it was easy. She'd recommended an early start and several days' worth of food. Told him how to start the generator if they wanted.

Yet the day had passed the highpoint a while ago. He was crawling so slowly that he figured someone who knew the trail better could go twice his speed. Even so, he still nearly hit the tree in the middle of the tracks.

This was where she'd told him to stop. Not like he had an option.

Now the hard work began. Turning to the other two, he told

them what he knew. "It's just over a mile, and it's a hike. So anything we need, we have to carry."

While Nguyen had heard this before, it was Riker who took the news better. He happily piled on bag after bag, crossing the straps until he was burdened with more than his fair share. The lab guy, easily out of place, already looked worse for the wear. Grabbing his evidence collection kit, and overnight bag, he showed no shame allowing Riker to carry another of his bags for him.

Owen pulled out the hand-drawn map Sin had made and pointed them downhill. "This way."

It was all he could do not to say "Sin says" or "Sin and Lee" ... So far he hadn't once uttered a name. While he was pretty sure that Nguyen had the names or at least access to the files, Riker didn't. Owen wasn't going to be the one who gave it away.

It was an hour later that they crossed the one mile mark and Owen saw the first signs that indicated they were close. She said they would see the bottom of the valley and the cabin was just up the other side. Low enough into the hollow to be nearly invisible, for the smoke to dissipate before it cleared the surrounding peaks, high enough to stay out of the spring floodwaters. Here, nature ruled on daily details.

"Holy shit!" Riker dropped the bags in his hands and stepped forward. He'd run into something of interest and veered a little off to their left. While Nguyen stepped almost directly into Owen's footsteps, Riker explored a bit and apparently was rewarded for it.

Looking like a mime as he touched the trees, he marveled over something only he could see. Then Owen suddenly saw a wall of leaves undulate under the detective's hands. The workout room Sin told him about. "Find the front. It should be built up on a platform, there may be things inside."

Riker disappeared inside and a minute later Owen and Nguyen heard a second "Holy shit!"

They turned, heading toward where Riker had disappeared, Nguyen calling out, "Don't touch anything. Don't destroy evidence!"

"What's the verdict? Check out the room or the cabin first? We're here." Owen spotted the tiny building through the trees. Where most homes were built in a clearing, this one was one with the woods, though Owen couldn't tell what was older: the wooden structure or the trees.

At a first glimpse it looked too primitive to live in. Sin had warned him, it wasn't easy in the cabin.

Nguyen must have been thinking much the same things. He looked skyward at the dark that was fading faster than in the cities, probably a bit concerned about the strange noises of the surrounding woods. "We may have a lot to set up tonight before we check everything. We need heat. I think we should start with the cabin."

Owen agreed but held his tongue, waited for Riker's vote.

"Either way."

So far, the detective had turned out to be as easy to work with as Nick had suggested. Which bothered Owen a bit when he admitted it to himself. He didn't want to like Nick Stelian. He didn't want the man to be right . . . about anything. It had been hard enough on Owen, realizing that he sympathized with Sin, that her values overlapped with his more than they clashed. Her brother was even further out of the fold than she, and Owen found himself waiting for Nick to screw up and suggest something too illegal, too dangerous, too stupid.

But he didn't.

Apparently he even chose co-workers with sound work ethics and reasonable demeanors. Riker—whom Nick spoke highly of —had been set up by the Kurevs, then forced into their pocket to stay out of prison for the crime they'd framed him for. An otherwise straight cop, Riker seemed to think highly of Nick. And it all pissed Owen off.

He pushed it aside as Nguyen scanned the area before gingerly setting down the few bags he carried. Without saying anything, the lab geek held his hand out to the side, stopping Owen's forward momentum and starting an investigator's slow track around the building.

Riker stood sentinel at the entry to the workout room, watching Nguyen walk the perimeter of the small building. Still Nguyen didn't let them in. Pulling a flashlight from his bag before he entered, he pushed at the door in a high spot using his elbow. From where he stood, Owen could see him sweeping the light back and forth, then crouching low and aiming it nearly parallel to the floor. Owen knew what Nguyen was doing: looking for any footprints. Evidence that disappeared in direct light often popped at an oblique angle.

Owen had passed the information that there were only 2 rooms and yet it was a full half hour before the investigator came back out and told them they could enter.

"Here. Riker, you can put your bag down exactly here." Using his finger to gesture, he delineated an imaginary box where Riker could lay things and where he couldn't. "Owen, you over here. Then put my stuff here. No!"

He put his hand out to Riker. "Not the table."

"I wasn't going to." The cop looked a little offended and Owen wondered if this was going to be a problem. Cops so often ruined good FBI crime scenes, simply because they didn't encounter them every day. No matter how good Riker was at collecting evidence, chances were that Nguyen wouldn't trust him and would probably offend him. Often.

The lab manager offered only a nod of acknowledgment and turned to the fireplace. "I'm going to check this out before we get it going."

"What about the generator?" Riker asked what Owen was thinking.

But Nguyen shook his head. "Tomorrow maybe. We need

daylight to see if it was tampered with." He knelt carefully in front of the bricked-in hearth before reaching out, eyes on the job in front of him, mouth still explaining why they couldn't just fire up the heat. "It would be really easy for them to make the generator the problem. Build up some toxic gases, then—when our Christmas Killers are passed out—come in and do their damage. We sure as hell aren't sleeping with it on until we know it's safe."

Owen was already setting out the doctor's sleeping bag and thinking how that made perfect sense, but they needed that fire going soon, because the night was getting cold. Fast.

Watching out of the corner of his eye while he worked, Owen put together sandwiches while Nguyen inspected the fireplace. He pulled red marked evidence bags out of his travel kit and scooped and saved ash from several different spots. Using a marker he labeled each one, then folded the bag, stickered it and signed across the seal.

Owen wondered why use standard procedures for everything, when it was all going to a private lab anyway. Nothing here was going to a court of law. Protecting the chain of evidence was completely unnecessary. He opened his mouth to say something then thought better of it.

Let Nguyen do what he wanted. It didn't hurt anything. If he hadn't yet figured out that Riker was a decent cop in the back pocket of the Kurevs but betraying them to Nick Stelian, then maybe Owen didn't need to tell him.

"Ah!" One set of fingers blackened at the ends, the others grasping a dinner utensil that he was never going to be used for food again, Nguyen shined the light down and grinned at something he'd sifted up. "Paper."

Owen smiled back but thought a lot of people probably burned some paper in their fireplace. He was torn between the need for the truth and the need for heat.

They hadn't brought a heater with them. They'd debated it, but there were too many other cool toys that Nguyen wanted.

And they had to hump all their stuff and all the evidence they collected back out to the car. Yeah, Owen was looking forward to carrying those evidence bags. Nguyen certainly wasn't the one to bear all the additional weight.

Owen and Riker had both finished their sandwiches and Owen stood up to face what he knew he needed to. So he was standing in the bedroom doorway, looking at the rumpled bed and the sea of blood that had congealed on it.

He was mid-thought, *Lee died here*, when Nguyen cheerfully spoke out. "You can light the fire now!"

Owen was glad that Riker moved to do it. He couldn't pull his eyes from the bed and the devastation it represented. Also, his fire building skills were probably lacking. Likely Riker was the faster, better candidate for the job.

He noticed that Nguyen hadn't put any of them into the bedroom to sleep. He didn't want to sleep there anyway.

While Owen had seen numerous crime scenes, dead bodies, and blood left behind, it didn't affect him the way this did. He rarely knew the victim. And while he couldn't say anyone but Sin actually knew Lee, he had struck a simple accord with the man. Moreso, looking back now, Owen had almost believed him immortal.

Just look at what he'd accomplished. How could someone come in and simply shoot Lee, kill him, in his own bed?

It seemed impossible. But Owen knew that was Lee's blood in that bed. And like Sin before him, he knew it was enough. The scene belonged to a murder.

The fire roared an uneasy sound, the logs starting to pop under Riker's care, the heat beginning to permeate the room. As Owen lay down in his clothes, he pulled the sleeping bag up around him, wishing it would make the floor less hard or the scene around him less disturbing.

He didn't believe in ghosts.

But tonight he almost did.

Tonight he almost wished Lee would show up and give him something he could use.

---

The house was old hat now. Sin was used to scaling the wall of Ann Evalyn Kimmel's McMansion, and that was what worried her. It was when you became solid at something that you screwed it up. Usually Lee was here to keep her alert. They reminded each other how to work carefully; they had each other's backs.

Sin pushed that thought aside now and checked over her own shoulder.

She'd recognized a couple of the neighbors, waved as she walked in and worked her way through the routine she'd set. Each time she came into the neighborhood in the track suit jacket and yoga pants, the blond wig and the whole get up.

She changed the jacket, reversing it to black, once she was in the Kimmels' back yard and out of sight. Pulled the hood up to conceal the blond of the wig—as she would need it once she was inside. Tonight the wig was firmly anchored. Tonight the green contacts were in place. It was so hard to find dull colored contacts. Everyone wanted bright, unearthly colors. Sin just wanted to blend in.

She was on the roof and in the attic faster than before. No pausing for the neighbors, no watching for eagles. In and clean.

She didn't flip on lights, just turned her jacket back to the colored side, left the hood down, and looked like yoga-girl except for the thin leather gloves she wore.

If Ann Evalyn Kimmel were smart, she would realize what the gloves meant: that Sin wasn't leaving any evidence behind. Therefore, the hair wasn't her regular color and wasn't even her hair.

That would all become important evidence if Ann Evalyn didn't take the bargain.

Then again, if Ann Evalyn didn't like what Sin was offering, Ann Evalyn might never tell anyone anything again. Sin really had no problem with that.

So she left the lights off and wound her way into the master bedroom. Though her husband hadn't been in the grave long, Ann Evalyn already clearly dominated the room.

A comfy looking chair—that appeared to have never been used—sat by the window and Sin curled herself into it. Tucking her feet up, she grabbed a nearby magazine and by the light filtering around the trees and the blinds, she read up on how to curl her eyelashes.

She waited.

# CHAPTER 9

O wen awoke to a crick in his neck. And one in his back. And a cramp in his leg. For the briefest of moments, he thought about bitching about it, then he remembered the blood in the room next door. He decided to be grateful for the aches and pains.

Nguyen had no such compunction. "Goddamn, if I didn't really want to be here, I'd be dammed pissed about sleeping on this floor."

He sat up and rolled his shoulder, giving a few audible pops that made Owen draw back in concern. Clearly the noise didn't bother Nguyen, so Owen held his commentary.

It was Riker who jumped right up, his expression bordering on cheery. If he had any pains, he hid them well. Too well.

They were all still in their clothing from the night before, but only Riker pulled off the look with anything but shame. He had his sleeping bag rolled and a granola bar eaten before Owen was fully upright or Nguyen quit bitching. "I'll head outside and look around."

Without many other options, Owen had to trust the man's version of "look around."

There was no evidence he had an agenda other than the one

Owen gave him, and it was a little late to be worried about it now. The three of them were in the back of beyond, with no real contact to the outside world. They would be missed in a few days, sure, but that could easily be a few days too late.

Owen had stashed a satellite phone that he simply hadn't mentioned to the others. If anything dirty went down, things would depend on his being able to get to it.

Using the diagram Sin had drawn for him, he looked for the location of the well and the piping that brought water into the cabin. He checked the placement of the generator in the back and the wiring they'd buried . . .

Owen kept the map to himself, too, letting Riker look around on his own. He might just find something because he wasn't given a direction to look.

Owen followed the younger man out when he finally cricked himself upright. But even then he didn't join in as Riker filled paper evidence bags tucked into a belt he seemed to wear for expressly that purpose. A carabineer clamped a kit bag for something else, and a holster held a gun out of the way but easily in reach. Owen didn't doubt Riker's abilities, he was just wary of any man who popped up so easily in the morning. It didn't seem human.

Grabbing a bottle of the water he had schlepped in yesterday, Owen pulled the tiny travel toothbrush from his bag and headed out away from any evidence to brush and spit. He was not built for this. Had he ever stayed awake for forty-plus-hours straight? Survived by sleeping in a utility van and drinking only bad coffee? He remembered that he had done those things, he simply didn't remember *how*.

Riker was around the back, carefully tracing the perimeter of the house and Owen let him go. Turning the other way, Owen headed out for the workout room, once again, nearly walking into it before his eyes and brain adjusted to what he was seeing. Then, of course, the room became obvious, but he had to give them credit for disguising it so well.

Pulling back the curtain made of army-grade camo netting, he stepped inside and felt he'd entered another world.

She'd told him about this room, about where it was, what he would find. He was prepared for the step up onto the rough wood plank floor. Her description made it sound crude. So while it wasn't finish carpentry, it was much nicer than he'd expected. He scanned the place, then turned for the light she had hung and hit the switch, illuminating the hidden space. He spotted the car battery she'd mentioned, sitting and corroding, still jumper cabled to the practice dummy.

He recognized the electronic opponent from late night infomercials and he fought the urge to punch the thing, see if he could make the lights blink. He remembered the ad and wondered if Sin had set it to the lauded "taunting" mode. Probably.

Beside him a wooden post, most resembling a too-sturdy coat rack, stood sentinel. It waited for its master to come back, the stubby arms holding still at heights to mark kicks, punches, maybe even a head butt. A heavy-bag, silent and unmoving, hung next to a speedbag—both probably Lee's—bolted to a cross beam set into sturdy branches of a tree that made up one corner of the room.

He'd stepped into another world. A world not his own, and one that did not welcome him. All the pieces stood still, as though if they didn't say anything, he wouldn't see them.

For a moment, the patterns of her life reverberated around him in the cold quiet. She'd lived here for more than two years total of her life. She'd taken what was clearly a run-down cabin and filled the gaps, both literally and figuratively, and made it work. She'd built a practice room so she didn't lose skill just because she'd lost contact with the outside world.

Lee had made her a home here.

Owen stepped back outside, shaking off the feeling of violating a privacy and enjoying the small heat offered by the sun filtering through the too tall trees above.

He looked up. His eyes now attuned to the camo netting, he could see that they had used it everywhere. Branches and netting crossed over the roof of the house; they snaked up into the trees, tenting and splitting. This, too, she'd told him about, to break up the smoke coming from the chimney, to keep them from sending up a signal of their whereabouts every time they lit a fire.

It was ingenious. More than she'd given it credit.

It was almost a physical sensation—the punch of what she'd accomplished, what she shrugged off, and what she might have become if she'd grown up even semi-normally.

They would never know.

He walked around to the back of the house where he ran into Riker once again. This time the man was checking the well system, pushing aside some of the vines that had covered over it. Spotting Owen, he began a report.

"The vines look like they grew here, but they aren't attached to the well the way they should be. That means they were placed here. See?"

He pointed to small black dots on the crude brick work around the low rim. "These are where the vines attach. The black pads left behind mean the vine was ripped away at this level. This looks to me like someone consistently pulled away the vines and then moved them over the well to disguise it. I'm guessing that was our girl."

Owen noted right away that the cop had adopted Nguyen's terminology for Sin. He didn't like it, but held his tongue. "Why not someone else? Trying to get to the well, but disturbing the vines repeatedly so that when they actually do something, it's not noticeable."

"Too much work. Wouldn't these two have noticed something messed with repeatedly? Even if it was just a little?"

It was a valid commentary. But Owen didn't put that kind of effort beyond Sin, so he didn't put it beyond the people hunting her. He only nodded to Riker. "Is it tampered with?"

"Looks like." He didn't look up, just reached back into a pocket and pulled out a small, powerful flashlight and shined it where he pulled back the vines.

He didn't want to ask. Owen knew that on top of this, Nguyen was in the house, probably testing the blood on the bed, dusting the place for finger prints. But this was in his face. "What is it?"

"Drill mark."

"What?" He was already on the move. It couldn't be that easy, could it? He asked the cop.

"Sure it could. Drill when they aren't here. Then sneak back and load whatever you want into the water system. It's not hard." He still hadn't looked up. Tipping his head, he checked another angle.

"Maybe they did it?" Owen was reaching and he knew it.

"Did they tell you they did?" This time Riker looked up, but did it without changing his grasp on the vines, still working hard not to disturb evidence. "You have the inside scoop about this place. Not just where it is, but what's theirs, so we can sort out what's not." He waited a beat before he continued. "Since you didn't say they did it, I'm guessing they either didn't or they didn't tell you about it. Also, if they'd drilled the hole, wouldn't they keep a better eye on it? Plug it? This has been left open a while, but. . ."

Riker gestured Owen over to take his own look.

In the dark of the trees, the light shined a precise circle around the metal sheet that someone very long ago had fashioned into a well topper. It was mortared into place poorly, but the mortar hadn't been disturbed. It was old enough that a good shift in the lid would have left behind fresh crumbles. None were there.

Owen noted all of this. But it wasn't what Riker's light shown on. The metal inside the bore hole was still a bit too shiny.

Just then, a noise inside the small building had them popping to attention. Another followed, and just as Owen was turning to run, to see if his friend had managed to hurt himself in the middle of his evidence, he heard the words.

"Holy shit!"

---

Nick wouldn't wear a tie tonight. Though he preferred to look professional, he didn't think having a silk strap around his neck was very intelligent.

The suit was a slick gray, professional but maybe just a little south of upright. He'd fit right in with Kaspar and his crowd. His brother dressed just a little over the top. The large diamond on the pinky ring, the pinstripe in a deep blue that bordered on purple, the things that said they had money to burn and the brass balls to flaunt it.

Nick had this one suit that he wore for such occasions. The legs were just a touch wide—which was fine because he wasn't a thick man. It allowed him to load his ankles. It should have been a weird feeling: a gun on one side, a knife strapped to the other. But it wasn't. He had a leather scabbard on a belt under the waistband of his pants. With the jacket on, it was unnoticeable. Sin had taught him to practice, hours of pulling out the knife in a smooth movement, how to reach for it without being noticed, how to put it back and make it almost just disappear from his grip.

He was ready.

Of course the slick suit was covered by the same long thick coat he'd worn out before. But tonight he looked like a Chicago businessman and he was about to become one.

Sin had convinced him that Kaspar and Roman had come

after her. They'd commented about taking his business. Tonight was step one to stopping their momentum.

He arrived at the club, his driver dropping him curbside slightly early. Nick wasn't much for drivers, but he wanted the simplicity and safety of a pick-up tonight. He didn't have Sin at his back, and while he believed he knew what the brothers' reaction to his bomb tonight would be, he couldn't be certain. There was always the possibility that the driver would be taking him to a certain dermatologist just outside of town.

Nick had made sure a table waited for him early. Kaspar would be fashionably late, believing as children often did that making people wait made him more important. Roman might not appear at all. Nick fought down the urge that these two did not deserve to be running an empire, but that was how it worked. The sons inherited . . . whether or not they deserved it, were suited to the work, or even wanted it. Once again, Nick was left considering that he shared the same amount of DNA with Koyla as both Kaspar and Roman did. As Sin did. Yet there were clear delineations of insiders and outsiders.

He was erasing those lines.

The table was at the back of the room. Typical mafia stuff. Nick liked the rounded booths in this place and the fact that while it was popular and packed, he could still buy the seat he wanted when he wanted it. He liked that he didn't have to get into a pissing match over the lone seat with its back to the wall.

No one here looked at him twice as he ordered a sparkling water with a lime and lemon curl. It was a simple but calculated move to appear as though he was drinking. Let Kaspar make the errors tonight.

The drink came and he nursed it for about ten minutes. In case anyone was watching, he sipped carefully, consistently, and bit by bit relaxed back. With a smile, he signaled to his server to get him another one and while he waited, he ordered an appetizer and ate it before he checked his phone.

Covert glances at an old family watch allowed him to easily stay on top of the time without looking like he was doing it. Kaspar was now over fifteen minutes late. Nick had been here by himself for over thirty. Though he didn't care about the mind games and the tardiness—the steamed clam appetizer had been fantastic and he didn't have to offer to share it with that little shit —if Kaspar didn't show, Nick would be pissed.

He shifted position, checking first one pocket, then the other as the server took away them empty plate. There were no messages from anyone. He didn't expect any from Dunham; the FBI agent was in the hills and out of contact. His wife was likely shopping. Sin was tracking down Ann Evalyn Kimmel and hadn't wanted him along tonight. No, the only person calling him would be Kaspar and it hadn't happened.

Nick was debating just how much longer he would stay. If his brother was too late, he should arrive to an empty table. Five more minutes? Ten?

He was thinking about whether to order another appetizer when he spotted Kaspar in one of the many mirrors around the place. As his brother appreciated the show of his own entry, Nick paid no attention and signaled the server to order his dinner. Nick didn't stand.

"Vasilescu." Kaspar said the name as though Nick needed reminding that he wasn't a real Kurev. With one practiced hand he unbuttoned his jacket as he slid into the booth. Behind him Roman stepped up and moved to the other side as Nick fought a sigh. So easy to predict.

Hopefully just as easy to take down.

They had him pinned in the middle. He just didn't care.

"Did you order without us?" The reproach in his brother's voice wouldn't last long. The kid thought he was the top of the food chain. Nick was going to eat him whole.

"You were late." He shrugged, drank from his sparkling water and stayed laid back. He refused to hand over the respect Kaspar demanded.

There were niceties, the brothers ordered food and did not hold back on the alcohol. So it was another thirty-ish minutes before Roman even brought up that Nick had stepped over him and left him in the street.

"Of course I did. I was following her. You had a phone."

"You left me bleeding. Shot." Roman stared.

"It was a flesh wound." Nick stared back, silently accusing the younger man of being a pansy-ass. "You had a good five hours for an ambulance to get to you and save you. She wasn't trying to kill you. And clearly you've healed up just fine."

To prove his point, he tapped his younger brother on the chest. Nick fought a grin as Roman fought to hold back his grimace.

Kaspar had remained silent while his brother tried desperately to start a bickering match. Nick shut it down with simple answers and the insinuation that Roman wasn't man enough to deal with a gut shot. He wouldn't last long in this business if that were truly the case. But now the older of the two joined in. "Why did you follow her instead of helping Roman?"

"Wanted to know what she was up to." He shrugged and welcomed the dessert he'd ordered to be rude. The others had barely gotten their meals and Nick was digging into some tiramisu that was far better than the conversation.

"Were you trying to capture her? Shoot her? Were you interested in her?"

The word "interested" came out with a twist of speculation, which made Nick's stomach roll a little bit. They didn't know that Sin was their sister. Not that she would ever do anything with either of these asshole idiots, but that Kaspar had clearly thought it bothered Nick in his core. He debated telling them, but that would be Sin's decision, not his. So he simply repeated, "Wanted to know what she was up to."

Kaspar didn't respond.

God the tiramisu was good. Nick wished he didn't have to eat it with a side of Kaspar's arrogance. "She said you have her husband."

"We do." Kaspar spoke around the bite he was taking. Uncouth.

Nick looked at this man, the image flashing in his head that he could have been raised this way. For a moment, he was grateful to his asshole of a grandfather. Surely Koyla was an ass, too. But Bun—longtime head of the Vasilescu organization—had made sure that Nick was raised with standards. Not love. Not understanding. Not a real home. But at least he had standards.

He carefully ate another bite of his dessert, taking his time. Thinking what cards to play. "Are you going to contact her?"

"How?"

Nick laughed. "I get the feeling all you have to do is say so. She's the kind to have eyes and ears everywhere." *Like right here at your dinner table.*

"I don't like that." It clearly twisted Kaspar up to think Sin was watching him. His next words proved it. "I deliver the message to her. Not her coming to us."

The next words out of his mouth nearly choked Nick. As much as Kaspar was an idiot, he did manage to lob out the occasional curveball. Nick tried to catch this one.

"Can you get the message to her?"

Why would they think Nick could do it? Did they know . . . Suspect Nick was playing the other side? Was this a test? And if he played it too cool would that possibly cost Sin the chance to get Lee's body back?

On the one hand, the drive to get her husband's body back was pointless. Nick remembered standing graveside at Reese's funeral. How he hadn't truly believed she was gone until the funeral.

Maybe Sin was smarter than him. She seemed to know she needed that punctuation.

"I think I can find her. You want me to run her down?"

"That's your only job right now."

As though he was their errand boy. Little shits.

But he held his tongue on that thought. "What do I tell her?"

With that they stood up and left, their dinners only half eaten and the bill unpaid. Not that Nick cared. What Nick cared about was that they left him holding a whole hand of cards he had not gotten to play.

But as he waited while the Kurev boys walked out the front door, a manila envelope dropped onto the table beside him. It simply said, "Lee."

---

Sin was almost impressed.

Ann Evalyn Kimmel did not freak out that a blond girl in yoga pants was curled into her reading nook.

Nope, Kimmel entered the room with a gun out, loaded and aimed. Which meant she'd retrieved the gun before entering the room. It was possible, maybe even probable, that she kept it in her purse. If Sin was doing what Ann Evalyn was doing, she'd keep a loaded gun in a big bag at her side all the time. But she didn't judge Ann Evalyn by her own standards.

The fact that Kimmel didn't stumble onto her, meant she figured out someone was in her house before she got to the bedroom door. That's what impressed Sin. There were two options. Either Ann Evalyn knew Sin had been here recently and was keeping an eye out or else she always swept her home when she entered.

"Who the fuck are you and why are you in my house?"

Sin smiled. "I really wanted to read about . . . The best workout gear for my body type." She held up the magazine, but

didn't untuck her feet. She didn't want to antagonize the woman.
Then again, she was implying that she didn't even need to have
her feet on the ground. Smiling, she set the magazine down
slowly enough to show her hands were empty and spoke.
"Seriously, I wanted to meet you."

"Why?" The gun didn't waver, though Ann Evalyn's grip left
something to be desired.

"I understand that you removed your husband."

No response.

Sin let her voice harden just a little bit. "Then blamed it
on me."

Ann Evalyn visibly jerked at that. "What are you talking
about?" But her voice wasn't steady and neither was her hand any
more. If she was half as smart as she thought she was, she would
be very afraid right now. The fact that she'd blamed her
husband's death on Sin meant she knew what Sin could do.
Probably, she didn't know the half of it.

Now she stood and walked toward the woman. "Oh come
on, Ann Evalyn. The big red bow, the throwing stars." Sin
winked and enjoyed the involuntary intake of air she saw from
the other woman. "Did you print articles about what he'd done
and tack them to him? I heard they found him lying on the
floor. I admit I'm very disappointed anyone thought that
was me."

"You don't know what you're talking about."

That made Sin genuinely laugh. "Oh honey, I know more
about it than you might ever think."

Ann Evalyn didn't give, which had Sin walking right into
the gun.

Sin got close enough to push the gun aside. While it meant
the bullet was no longer aimed at her, she didn't think the danger
was past. This woman had taken down her hitman of a husband.
She might have had the element of surprise on him, but she'd
done it hand to hand. So Sin held her ground. She kept her hand

on the gun, covering Ann Evalyn's fingers, keeping it aimed away from both of them.

"What's your name?"

"I'm not giving you that." She offered a small, knowing smile. "You either already know it or you're trying to get it."

"How do I know you're her?"

*How long was this going to go on?* Sin needed to get to the point. "The very fact that I'm here, that I know what you did and how you did it, means that I am exactly the one you think you can blame your husband's murder on. Whether you get away with it is up to you."

The fist nicked her in the chin.

The punch was short and fast. While she'd seen it coming, she hadn't seen it with enough time to get entirely out of the way.

Using her momentum from dodging Ann Evalyn's rings, Sin took advantage of the placement she still had on the woman's gun hand. Though she had only pushed the weapon out of the way, afraid that setting her fingers on the right pressure points would cue the woman to react, now she had no concerns about what the other woman might do. So Sin pushed against Kimmel's knuckles and forced her to drop the gun.

It hit the carpet with a thud worthy of its weight, but Sin was already ducking another punch.

She'd taken plenty of hits before, though her goal was always to avoid them. In one way she was on new ground here; in general she didn't fight women and Ann Evalyn's rings were something new. If they caught her face, it would be hard to cover.

As the next swing came nearer to her eye than the one before, Sin suppressed a sigh and stopped fighting 'light.' Pulling the woman off balance with her grip still on the hand that had held the gun, her other hand shot out and up, into a solar plexus that wasn't as soft as it looked.

Ann Evalyn had been working out.

But the hit still registered. Knocking the society doll back meant the punch coming at her swung wide and fell short and Sin used the opportunity to push back and try to end the fight.

Through heavy breaths, Ann Evalyn stood at the ready. Her hands were out at her side, but she shook them periodically as though she had excess energy to throw off. The thought flashed through Sin's head that the woman might be on something, but she didn't have time for the answer.

Holding her own hands steady and palm out in front of her, Sin tried to start a conversation. "Let's not fight."

"Yeah. You don't want me to kill you." Ann Evalyn narrowed her eyes.

Well. That was not a friendly overture. "You need something from me, and I need something from you. Let's not kill each other and try to make it work out for both of us."

"I don't even know who you are." Ann Evalyn barked out the words, the stress of the situation showing on her.

Sin fought back the laugh that wanted to come out and tried to remain calm. She repeated. "You framed me for your husband's murder, but I haven't decided whether to be angry or flattered. I'm leaving that decision up to you."

When Ann Evalyn didn't respond, Sin went back to the chair she'd been sitting in, wanting to pull out the proof that she was who she said. Giving the woman her back was a sign of bravado or trust.

Ann Evalyn took it entirely the wrong way.

Sin heard only two steps, then other woman was on Sin's back, her hand snaking around Sin's neck.

# CHAPTER 10

"**B**itch." Sin whispered the word just as her air was cut off.

Ann Evalyn's full weight hit her spine and Sin used the opportunity to step forward. She didn't stagger as most people would. It was an odd moment to think fondly of her deceased husband, but in his own way, he'd helped her out today. If she could throw Lee—a six-foot, two-hundred-pound, trained fighter—Sin could throw Ann Evalyn.

*What a stupid name*, she thought not for the first time, and used a lurching step to bend her knees without the other woman necessarily catching on.

She needed to end this quickly, but leave Ann Evalyn alive and friendly. Unfortunately, Sin didn't have a lot of time to execute her plan as there were sparkles beginning to dance at the edge of her vision. *Dammit.*

Grasping the arms around her neck, Sin pushed. One shot, then her vision would go. Ann had the hold mostly right. Then again, Sin had always believed it didn't really matter just how "right" you had done something if it worked.

So she grabbed Ann Evalyn's shoulders and bumped her hips out, sending the other woman flying.

*Whoops.*

But Sin was too busy taking in her own restoring gulp of air to care too much that she'd overshot her throw.

Ann Evalyn rolled. Right into the corner of her room. Almost behind the big overstuffed chair that Sin was pretty sure had never been sat in before her. More importantly, it was a good weapon.

It was lightweight, hard, and oddly shaped. Sin's foot snaked out and caught the front scrolled leg, flipping the chair towards herself as Ann Evalyn resumed her stance.

The other woman reached for the chair but the top side was padded, and though she caught it, Sin pulled it easily from Ann Evalyn's grasp.

She tried a move, but Sin held her off, chair between them. Though, honestly, it turned out to be a nice looking piece of shit. There was every possibility that slamming Ann Evalyn with it as hard as she could would hardly leave a mark.

Ann Evalyn feinted one way, ducked the other, but Sin moved the chair with her, keeping the woman in the corner, her back literally to the wall.

"What am I?" Ann Evalyn was furious now. "A lion?"

"You're snarling like one."

Blue eyes narrowed at her but nothing else happened.

A moment later, the two of them were still in a standoff, when Ann Evalyn visibly startled and her eyes darted off to just behind Sin's shoulder.

"I'm not falling for that. No one is here." But Sin did put down the chair and even faced it toward Ann Evalyn. Carefully, she sat down, but shot her hand out rapidly, stopping the woman from coming at her. Chair or no, Sin was in charge here.

"Don't. We're here to have a discussion."

"What? I don't want to fight?" Sarcasm firmly in place, Ann Evalyn leaned back against the wall, seemingly conceding that she was trapped.

Sin didn't trust her any further than she could throw the

woman, and as of two minutes ago, she'd learned that exact measurement. "We need to talk."

Ann Evalyn rolled her eyes.

"We have two options. One—I dispose of you. Making certain that everyone in all organizations knows that I did not kill your husband. Or Two—you decide to work with me."

For a moment, silence reigned.

"Someone's coming to meet me. He'll be here any minute."

"You're lying. No one comes to meet you. Not on Monday nights, or any evening. It's two a.m. Try again." Sin appeared patient. But she wasn't patient. She had shit to do.

Sadly, the current incarnation of her plan involved a willing Ann Evalyn Kimmel. If this didn't wind up as intended, Sin would need another plan and fast.

"How do I know you're her?" Another snarl.

"I don't know that you ever will. But I've given you a small demonstration. You can get more, but you may not survive it." She bounced her leg as though she had nothing better to do.

The mafia wife seemed wholly unable to make the decision. She looked borderline ridiculous in her disheveled party clothes. Part of her mascara had migrated beneath her eyes; her eyeshadow and lipstick had smeared. While she sat there keeping an eye on her quarry, Sin cataloged this and wondered how much of what had been on the woman's face was smeared across the back of her own jacket.

She wanted to reach up and touch her fake hair, be sure her wig was still in place. But it either was or it wasn't, and touching it would only draw attention. Keeping her hands at her lap, Sin waited.

After about two full minutes, the words came. "What do you want?"

This was the hard part, telling Ann Evalyn what she needed. She did not like depending on the other woman. So she took a deep breath in and reminded herself it was about Lee. "I need you to get me and my friend in to see the Kurevs."

Ann Evalyn threw her head back and cackled.

Sin thought about how to kill her. A triangle choke hold seemed the most fitting. No slicing and dicing. Ann Evalyn's crimes had not been horrid enough to warrant that, but the choke hold would also shut her up. "And this is funny because?"

"You," She waved her hand up and down. "I don't think they work with yoga moms." She laughed again, "Do you have an info graphic to present? Market share analysis?"

Sin smiled. Not a pretty smile either. "Nope. I do think I've proved that I'm hardly a yoga mom. I'm whatever I need to be."

Sin enlightened her. "I'm friends with your neighbors, the gate guard, too. They already like me better than they like you." The right side of her mouth pulled up in a small mock of a grin. It was an expression she'd gotten from Lee.

Sin fought the urge to explain about her husband. She didn't think it would garner any sympathy. After all, like a mantis or some other insect, Ann Evalyn destroyed her own husband.

Small shifts in the other woman's stance told Sin that her information about the neighbors didn't sit well. Still pinned into the corner of her own bedroom, her body stayed rigid, defiant. "So?"

"You know who else I'm friends with? An FBI Agent!" She grinned and almost clapped her hands with joy. Never mind that it wasn't technically true. Sin wasn't sure she'd call them 'friends' and Dunham wasn't even an agent anymore.

Ann Evalyn's eyes narrowed. That was a neat trick, Sin thought, they were already so narrow, yet she somehow managed to look even more put out.

"How do you think I'm sitting here? How do you think I stayed out of jail for so long?" She leaned back as though she were bored. "And that's not even the issue. I know you did it and I can prove it wasn't me. I have the evidence, the resources and the channels. The Kurevs already know it was you—it's how you got in the door with them."

There was no hiding the slight jerk. The information was a surprise.

*Amateur.*

"I can go right to the police. . . and not the ones in Kaspar's pocket."

All the whimsy left and Ann Evalyn's smile slid right off her face. The look replaced with a dangerous countenance, backed by steel.

"I'm in your house. Didn't trip the wires—and you know your system is good. I know what you did and can prove it. I know where Kaspar's cronies are and who they are. Do. Not. Fuck. With. Me."

Sin sat back. "You have two choices. You help me get in or you don't. In option one, you introduce my friend and me as personal acquaintances and recommend us to the Kurevs. You get us access inside the home. Option one has the advantage of cover for me and life for you."

"Option 2?" It was asked with a sneer.

Sin did not like this woman. But she did have the possibility of making her own life easier, and Sin and Nick had not been able to locate anyone else who could do it as well or as soon. "Someone finds you dead here tomorrow or whenever they sell you."

Sin sat through another extended silence, as always, ready for anything.

In that moment she realized it wasn't true. She believed she was ready for anything, but the events of the last week showed her how wrong she was. At least, sitting here, guarding Ann, she was in her element.

"One."

That was it. Just the one word. But Sin was tired. "Excellent."

She didn't move. Just pulled out her cell phone and called

Annika. Standing up, she wanted to stretch but didn't. "Now walk me out the front door."

Again, she gave the woman her back, showing trust, or dominance. Again, Mrs. Kimmel made bad choices.

Just one step was all she needed, the heavy thud into the plush carpet revealing that Kimmel was coming at her.

Sin swung, right arm flying backward, left arm reaching around her back, just as she had made Nick practice. Her elbow connected with Ann Evalyn's jaw even as the woman's manicured hands reached out.

Unable to stop her own forward momentum, Ann Evalyn ran her very nice dress into the silencer on the end of Sin's 9mm gun.

That was going to leave a mark. Sin pressed the gun forward, letting Ann Evalyn feel the strength of the barrel and the woman behind it.

Her hands dropped.

At gunpoint, Ann Evalyn walked toward the front door and reached for the knob.

Sin rapped the back of the woman's hand as she reached to open the pretentious double lock. "Security code."

Grudgingly, Ann Evalyn moved to the box and started punching digits.

"Wrong code."

Again, the eyes narrowing.

Man, this woman was pissed off. The plan might not fly. Her voice was as surly as the rest of her. "I just changed the code."

"No you didn't." Right now, Sin loved her brother more than anything. Lee had been good at rewiring the system, but it was Nick who got close enough to Ann Evalyn at her club the other night, tampered with her phone, turned it into a broadcasting device they could listen in to whenever they wanted. Keypads with associated tones were about the dumbest thing, Sin thought. She knew what the correct code sounded like.

This time the right notes played.

As the door opened, Sin saw Annika sitting in her rented Mercedes, fitting right into the neighborhood if not for the three a.m. time. Having smoothly stashed the gun, Sin waved, grinned and turned to give Ann Evalyn a girl-hug. Then she smiled again.

To anyone on the street it would have looked like she was thanking the woman. But with her face turned so no one, and no security camera, could lip read her, she reiterated in a dulcet tone, "Don't fuck with me." Then she bounced down the steps and into Annika's waiting passenger seat.

"How did it go?" The other woman asked, the nearly black hair seemingly changing the shape of her face, just as she had said it would.

"Only as well as expected." Damn, she was tired. She used to stay up all night. Used to climb through windows and listen into conversations as alert as you please.

"It's the pregnancy." Just those three words from Annika, and Sin realized she'd slid back into the seat, her back done with staying straight, her eyelids already drooping.

"Don't worry. I don't think it's obvious." She took a turn and Sin waved and smiled at the man at the gate. He was reading a paperback and barely looked up. Annika continued. "It's normal."

"Good." She sighed and just managed to stay awake until she reached the hotel. She came and went as the blond woman. Sin —as herself—had never been here.

Annika wished her goodnight and headed back to her own hotel, never climbing out of the car or asking for more. Owen's wife had cleanly passed every test, every check point Sin had put before her. Tonight, she'd simply been a pick-up driver. At a time past two a.m.

Annika had excelled.

Ann Evalyn had been a bitch.

The elevator felt sluggish, the hallway longer. When Sin arrived in her own room, she found Nick, already sitting at the small table. She'd given him the spare key, rented the room for two, and having him come and go reinforced her story. She just hadn't expected him to be here now.

He held up one of his many phones. "Nothing yet—"

But the sound of a standard ring cut off his words. "Well, there we go," he said to Sin, then held up a finger for her to wait while he pressed a button and spoke.

The ringing went on while he talked, but that was supposed to happen. Nick's voice was solid, serious. "Kaspar doesn't like being awakened in the night by a woman who let someone break into her house. This is your last warning. Next time, Option two is enacted."

Then he waited.

Though Ann Evalyn didn't say anything, she disconnected before the ringing stopped.

Sin wondered if the socialite was shaking in her boots. Clearly, her phone had been doctored. Though Sin and Nick hadn't wanted to give that fact away, it was better to rein in the woman than have to go it alone.

"Now we wait." Sin sank onto the end of the bed, hands planted on her knees, shoulders drooping.

"You look tired." Nick said it calmly, but his expression was a bit worried. "You know what. I've got this." He held up the phone. "I'll stay up, no point in two of us doing it. And I'll come get you if she tries something else stupid. In the meantime, do you think you can get to sleep?"

Sin laughed. "I think I may already be asleep."

With a grin, Nick leaned over and kissed her on the forehead. She almost startled. Aside from fighting and Annika's almost forced hugs, she was rarely touched. But clearly she needed it.

A kiss on the forehead from her big brother.

Who would have guessed?

Nick let himself out the door and she forced herself to stand up, flip the locks behind him. She had plans. Brush her teeth, take off the wig, her shoes. But she didn't do any of them.

Crawling up onto the comforter and leaving the soles of her shoes hanging off the end of the bed, Sin fell immediately into a drugging sleep.

---

Nick hadn't given her the envelope that Kaspar had passed to him. Sin seemed off. She'd seemed tired and that was probably good.

Nick understood. She'd always been driven, much like he was. Though he hadn't suffered a single defining event, he'd suffered all along. She'd chosen Lee. Chosen that life and found something good in it.

But here she was, once again, having her life ripped out from under her in a short time. As much as it was the same, it was horribly different this time.

This time, she hadn't seen it happen, not really. She didn't have a body or closure. In the original accounts of the attack when she'd been a child, she'd tried to save her parents despite the gangland style bullets they'd each taken through their skull. But she'd tried. Sin, at eleven, could say she'd done everything in her power.

As an adult, she couldn't say that.

His sister had been running on odd cycles since she'd turned up in his easy chair a week ago and probably even before that. She'd waited, how long? Maybe four days for Lee to come, before she returned to the cabin. Before she realized she was once again on her own.

So if he could let her sleep, he would. If he could hold off some of the shit the Kurevs were dishing up for one more day, he would.

He sat in the hotel room next to hers, unwilling to leave her alone.

Nick desperately wanted to text either Riker or Dr. Owen

Dunham about what was happening at the cabin. Had Sin and Lee been drugged?

It seemed they had to be. He couldn't imagine any other way one of these pricks could get the jump on them. His heart turned over for her. She was taking it as well as she could, even though she often looked a little green around the gills.

Flipping the envelope over in his hands, he thought for a minute.

He was awake, but most of Chicago wasn't.

He couldn't really order room service, and a beer and hot dog was an L ride away. This weather wasn't something he was built for.

He wanted to have Sin running this city, but knew she wouldn't get her hands into any part of what she'd worked so hard to scrub away. Though she had no tolerance whatsoever for the Kurevs, she'd found an uneasy truce with Nick. Showing that her relationship with him changed her views, even before she had the whole picture.

He wondered if she was paying for it.

Or if Lee already had.

Shoving that train of thought aside, he picked up his phone and dialed a number he knew. Dana Block likely wasn't awake, but she answered her phone with a nearly chipper "Hello?"

She would know it was him. That burner phone rang only on his line. He didn't identify himself; they both knew the rules. But the thoughts he was thinking . . .

He had to talk to her, see if it was even plausible. Because what good was the number on his Caribbean bank account? He didn't have Reese. He didn't really have Sin. And though he had Atlanta, he didn't have Chicago.

Yet.

"I've been thinking."

He could almost hear her smirk. "Are you in town? Because I'm pretty sure I can hear the gears in your head from here."

"You probably can." Despite what she did, she was a good person. One of the best. One of the believers. He needed that. "Can we meet?"

"Now?" Her tone was incredulous.

So despite the cheer infused in her voice, she really did seem to realize it was the middle of the night.

"Tomorrow's good."

Nick needed answers.

---

Owen and Riker had run in at the sound of Nguyen's exclamation.

"Did you see this? Did you know?" The lab guy was on his hands and knees, his blue gloves marked on the back, with time on, time off, room he was in. He was saving them all in bags in case he inadvertently touched any evidence. The man was nothing if not thorough.

Owen wondered if he was going to bag his pants, since he'd been kneeling on the floor. But Nguyen was too busy gesturing. "Look, there's a space here!"

Owen knew what he'd found, but Riker dropped to his knees to investigate. "Damn. It looks like a regular bed, but it's fortified." He reached under and knocked on the metal sheeting that both supported the mattress and protected the space. "That is slick."

Nguyen grinned, his love for all things Sin clearly growing by the moment. "It gets better. Trap door."

He pushed on it and Owen watched as the two men baby-crawled under the bed and out the other side. For a moment his brain overlaid the sound of their glee with Sin's terror. When she'd last crawled out that hole, she'd woken in the night to gun shots, blood, and Lee pushing her out of bed. These two were treating it like a fun park, despite the evidence in the mattress right over their heads.

Once the two came back inside and finished admiring the panic options, they spent three more hours sweeping the place before heading out, carrying the added weight of evidence this time. Once again, Caleb Riker humped most of the burden, while Nguyen carried mostly just his thoughts.

Owen had packed his concerns as efficiently as his things. Though they hadn't been a lively group on the way in, the three men were positively somber on the way out. Owen stayed silent, holding out for cell signal, waiting to hear from Annika that she was okay.

The fact was that Annika was going to be okay regardless of him. He had learned years ago that she didn't need him. Of the two of them, she was the more capable, the more resilient. But she liked him and she kept him around, and he needed her voice in his ear, letting him know she was still here, still his, still in one piece. It kept him in one piece when things around him fell apart.

Like they had in the past forty-eight hours.

Owen had found nothing. But Riker's drill hole in the well cap was telling. When they tested the water in the house, there was a trace of GHB. That was definitive proof.

Caleb Riker had also found the generator had been tampered with. The leaves and debris on the ground had obscured the damage—as they had been meant to. The very things that Sin and Lee used to hide their own presence had hid the signs that they had been found.

Together, Owen and the detective had dug up a small pipe. Run from the output on the generator, it gathered not all but most of the gas emitted and piped it directly into the bedroom. Carbon monoxide gas could be fatal, but it appeared they couldn't get enough of it.

Also, anything strong enough to have a real effect would likely alert one or the other of them. Sin and Lee were not regular people. If one of them had started acting funny the other would have taken care of it. So that couldn't happen. Not if the assassin wanted to make it real.

So they'd been hit with GHB then with CO gas.

*Shit*, Owen thought, there had almost been no way around that. And there was every possibility there was more in the water, but they hadn't brought tests for it. To be sure, Riker was hauling a good sized sample of it back to civilization.

Nguyen had also taken a portion of the bedding with him in a paper bag. He lifted fingerprints, though Owen and Nguyen both were convinced none of those would belong to anyone other than Sin or Lee. These guys had drugged the pair in at least two different ways simultaneously. They didn't fuck around. They wouldn't leave prints behind.

What they did leave was markings in the woods.

Owen and Nguyen didn't have much trouble at all finding where they had parked, that they had driven in an SUV, four-wheeling their way in.

Part of the reason it had been easy to find had been the blood. A trail led from the small house out to where the vehicle had been parked. In places it was clear that blood had spilled in some way, or the assassins had seen it and used something to push dirt over it. It didn't make it any less obvious. And Owen wondered why they had done it.

What he did know was that they had dragged a body of the size and shape of Lee Maxwell. That body had been bleeding badly.

The real news was startling, and as the three men quietly drove down the road toward Atlanta, Owen wondered how he would tell Sin.

Nguyen had checked the bedding. The ground. The trail. And there was a problem with Sin's conclusion. A problem that would hurt her more than she was already suffering.

After Nguyen checked out the bedding, traced the blood trail into the woods and then came back, he stood before Owen and presented his findings.

"The thing is, it's a lot of blood. If this were an open case, we'd be looking at a murder." His hands had gone to his hips, fisted, as though he were still wearing gloves. The lab never left the man. Gloves or not, he was careful about what he touched and how. "But the amount . . . it's not conclusive. We'd investigate a murder, as that's what I think is here. But it's not definitive."

"What?" Owen and Riker had looked at him, speaking simultaneously.

"The blood trail—" Nguyen pointed in the general direction. "The spatter suggests a body still actively bleeding. They dragged a dying body, not a dead one. So they either shot him and dragged him all that way while he died, or they did it super-fast."

He shrugged. "Did our girl see them take the body?"

Only able to shake his head, only able to relay what he'd been told, Owen said, "No. She watched the house for a while and didn't see anything."

No. If she'd seen it, Sin would have followed them. Drugged or not, she would have hunted them down and dispatched them post haste. There was no way she would have let them take Lee.

"So, they didn't shoot and run."

"What are you saying?" Owen had asked, though he already had an idea.

Nguyen looked dubious. "If I had to commit it to a report, I'd have to say I'm not sure he's dead."

# CHAPTER 11

S in was rudely awakened by Annika Dunham, who seemed to think it was a good idea to make sure Sin was eating properly. She decided to begin with breakfast, which was another bad choice when Sin was finally really sleeping.

Sin growled. "I've been eating solid foods since I was six months old. I think I understand how to do it properly."

The evil woman only smiled and said, "I'll wait while you shower."

That meant removing the blonde wig, washing her own hair, drying it and then putting all that shit back on.

Though she fully expected to emerge from the shower and find Dunham's wife sitting in the stuffed chair and knitting booties for either her future child or Sin's, Annika was doing no such thing. She was teasing her hair into a giant mass of dark waves and sliding slick burnt orange heels onto her feet over socks that somehow looked so wrong they were right.

Sin only stared.

"Seemed like we should head out as the new us." Annika grinned. "Be seen in public together, just in case Ann Evalyn gets any silly ideas about backing out of your little plan. And you actually need food."

She didn't comment on the baby or any of the rest of it and silently turned around and headed back into the rest room. She had no qualms about making Annika wait while she got ready.

An L train ride and egg burrito later, Annika left her back at the hotel. The whole time, Nick had been checking in, reporting on Ann Evalyn. She hadn't used the house phone or cell again since late last night and there was no word on movement from her home. And when could Sin meet?

"Right now." She practically growled that, too. Why did it feel like everyone wanted a piece of her?

Pulling out the hairpins, she yanked the blond wig and massaged her scalp. Sin wanted to watch crap TV, maybe some courtroom show where the judge yelled at the people defending themselves, but she couldn't do it. She was a shark, always moving forward, unable to stop and relax until her job was done.

And it was not yet done.

So she turned on the news and checked for any updates on the Kurevs.

In the old days, it was good to be Capone. Everyone knew your name and shook in fear. These days, the Kurevs made certain that only the few that needed to know ever even heard their name. When Sin had been a kid and started researching, it had taken her more than a few years, more than a handful of tries, to find the name behind the hit on her parents. So she didn't expect to hear it from the lips of any of the talking heads.

What she did think she might stumble across would be stories pertaining to the business. Something she could tie back to the family that ran Chicago. Something that would tell her what they were up to this week and what might be distracting them, creating a soft spot in their underbelly. Because Sin would be waiting.

Waiting wasn't all it was cracked up to be. Her world felt wrong. Off in a way it hadn't in years. When she lost her parents, she was consumed at first with being afraid. Someone had simply come into her safe, normal home one night and ripped her world to shreds. Sin had been a child. Unable to defend herself, make her own decisions, or fight the powers that be. She'd eventually converted that overwhelming fear to a feeling of invincibility.

Though much the same thing had happened to her this time, it was still wholly different. She was now skilled and willing. No longer stuck trying to simply find her own way, she was working to protect someone else while feeding the deep need in her to get Lee's remains.

At least Nick was coming. At least he'd called ahead. As much as she didn't want to see him, didn't want to be bothered by someone else's agenda right now, she also wanted to see him. He anchored her.

Which meant her world was wholly fucked up.

When the head of one of the biggest mafia crime organizations in the US was your anchor, you were pissing in the wind. Sin knew it. And it didn't change anything.

She heard the mechanical click and whir of the door lock as it obeyed Nick's key. She tried to put on a pleasant face. He was her brother. She should be polite.

Or so she thought until she saw his face.

Starting with a sigh, Nick spoke. "I met with Kaspar and Roman last night. Tried to lay some foundation for you, or even get them to just give me Lee. This showed up mysteriously after they left." He held up a thin manila folder.

"What's in it?" It must be something good if he came over to deliver it rather than telling her. Maybe it was—

"I don't know. It says 'Lee'." He held it out, but she didn't want to take it. "I didn't look. It's yours and I respect your privacy."

As she reached out to take it, t her fingers hit the manila paper, and she was struck by a massive wave of fear. She wasn't ready. Her voice caught. "Do you think it's pictures of Lee?"

Though she knew he was gone, she hadn't been forced to face any actual evidence of his death. But this felt like there was something thicker than just paper inside, maybe a picture. Maybe the thing she didn't want to see. "You open it."

She jabbed it back toward him and Nick obligingly took it.

As she watched, Nick slowed. As though he were in jello, he took the pages from her, and began to pull at the clasp. She knew he was fine, it was just her perception, her fear, running the world in slow motion.

He reached in, pulling out a picture, just as she had suspected. For a moment, she took satisfaction in being correct about what had been in the envelope, but then it registered: the widening of his eyes, Nick's mouth going slack.

His words came through, deep and long, as though she were listening underwater. "Sin. Look."

He jabbed the print toward her too fast for her brain to put together what she was seeing. The colors swirled. Then Sin tried to grab something as the world around her twisted and darkened too.

Even as the lights sparkled at the edge of her vision, the last thing she saw was Nick, reaching toward her, shouting something. But burned on her brain was the picture.

A battered man was tied to a chair.

Lee.

Owen stayed in Atlanta with Nguyen, though he'd driven Caleb Riker to the airport almost as soon as they'd regained civilization. He knew the detective worked for both the Kurevs and Nick, though Owen quit trying to wrap his brain around who was screwing who on that one. It was easier to return Riker and simply keep their findings to Nguyen and himself.

But, of course, that couldn't happen. When Owen asked about a lab, Nguyen had called in a favor from a friend in town. He'd gained them both access to the facility, the sterile spaces, the machines. But anything they searched on the system would likely be recorded or at least able to be called up later if someone wanted it.

Nguyen probably would need help—lifting fingerprints, feeding them into AFIS, doing a point match—and Owen was of no use at any of it. In fact, once a long time ago, Nguyen had pointed out that Owen was a contaminator of the worst sort, leaving hair, fibers, and "greasy fingerprints" everywhere he went. So he was stuck sidelined while the other man worked his magic. He had only two consolations. First, the evidence, though incriminating, couldn't get linked back to Sin. And secondly, he wasn't busy, so he could call his wife.

After winding his way back to the lobby, he dialed and it took only two rings before she picked up. "Hey! You are back in civilization!"

"Yes." Owen could feel the smile as it spread on his face. Just hearing her voice calmed the storms that sometimes struck up inside him. "We just got back into cell range about two hours ago. I'm at the lab now."

"What are you doing?" The curiosity came through. Always.

He laughed at it. "Nothing. Talking to you. I have no lab skills. What about you?"

She laughed back at him, soothing his soul for just a moment before she spoke. "I'm trying to brush a huge mass of tangles out of my hair. I teased it up to go out to breakfast with Sin."

He was frowning, but before he could ask, she told him.

"We are out in our new gear. She's a blond, I'm a blowsy Chicago wife. We were trying it out. Teasing your hair is not a good idea!" The humor came through in her voice, but all thought of laughing had fled from his own thoughts.

"Why are you dressing up as a Chicago wife and . . . ?" And what? He didn't even know, but he knew Annika, and that scared him. He thought about reminding her she was pregnant, but only wound up reminding himself that would just piss her off. She'd cite medical statistics pointing out how full of shit he was until his head hurt. And she'd be right. He was acting on superstition. But dammit, he wanted her to act on it too! She never did.

He could hear her pause. She wasn't going to tell him the whole story.

It was a burner phone he'd called her on. He didn't want people listening in on sensitive information. He also didn't want her location pinpointed. Though she didn't violate any of their 'rules,' her next words didn't change anything for him.

"Remember where I am from?"

Of course he did. He almost rolled his eyes at the silly question. He knew almost everything about her, so he clearly knew . . . *Oh, shit.* "No! You aren't getting involved."

"No. I'm not. I'm just going to get some information. That is all."

"No!"

In the silence he could hear the long echo of his mistake. One small syllable, but a massive error. He could hear the foundations of his world crumble as his ill-chosen word bounced off them.

She broke the silence. "You might want to re-think what you just said."

He was fucked. There was no controlling Annika. She listened intently and took what he had to say to heart, and then made her own decisions. She sometimes placated him and did what he asked because he asked nicely or because it meant a lot to him. But if he said no, if he forbade her from doing anything she hadn't already agreed to, then he might as well stand in front of a moving steam roller as attempt to change things. In her own way, she was as logical and stubborn as Sin.

That scared the hell out of him.

So he swallowed his fear for her and said, "Please don't."

Her voice got softer, if not her decision. "I'm helping her. She needs it."

"But—"

"There are things you don't know."

He was opening his mouth to protest again, but the words that emerged were Anni's words, in Anni's voice.

"Owen, there are always things you don't know. The world doesn't run the way you think it should. And people live lives very different from yours." She sighed as though thinking, but she didn't say more.

"What is the more?"

He knew the words even before she said them. "It is not mine to tell."

He'd heard that before. So he reverted to the only thing he could do as things began to spiral away from him. Sin had been drugged. The girl he thought couldn't be surprised had been invaded and hadn't even woken up for it. The man he thought couldn't die was likely dead. And Annika, who mostly liked being at home and planning their daughters' birthday parties, stood solidly for her convictions and said things like "It's not enough to say so, someone has to act. Someone has to be the first to stand up."

So he reminded himself that she had escaped communist Russia as a child and lived to tell about it. She had stood stronger than him through three miscarriages and that it was him, not her, who was afraid now. Owen reminded himself that she was logical, not crazy, and that she had two daughters she worried about, too.

He reminded himself to trust her. Though it was hard, he simply said, "Please stay safe."

There was no way to keep the plea from his voice. He couldn't wrap her in bubbles and she would kill him if he tried. He admired Sin, but he didn't want his wife to be more like the girl. He was walking a sharp edge and he'd already nicked himself on it telling Annika 'no'. It was a rookie mistake—he'd been married to her long enough to know better. It seemed it was only he who was too stupid to learn. So he told her he loved her and turned back to Nguyen and the lab.

He couldn't shake the feeling that things were wrong. There was something Annika knew that was too big to tell. If it was unconcerning, she would have simply said what it was. But this meant someone had talked to her, told her something of value that changed the game for her, something Owen shouldn't know.

Annika wasn't one to keep secrets from him. She'd flat out stated that it was not hers to tell. So he knew that she knew something . . . and his head felt like it was about to explode. It felt like it would be easier to listen to Nguyen explain the intricacies of DNA testing than to figure out what Annika knew. She was a fucking steel trap.

He smacked the phone against his leg, hating himself just a little bit.

Annika's ability to keep a secret had kept their marriage together for so long.

The years he'd worked around the clock for the FBI, he'd come home and spent their precious little time telling her about his cases. She cracked some of them. Brought him home sooner, made him a small god in his division. Owen had given her classified information. And she'd given them both an anchor in the times when their marriage ran on very little interaction of substance.

That very same ability was shutting him out now.

The irony that Anni was with Sin in Chicago—the town where it had all started—while he'd been with Nguyen at the cabin—where it had all ended—wasn't lost on him.

His friend was hunched over a slick table with a magnifying screen lit from underneath, lost in his work. Owen wanted to push him to go faster. Find what they needed and get back to Anni before Sin dragged her into something terrible. But Owen was impotent here.

He could no more speed up this process than he could stop

his wife.

Seeing that there was nothing here for him until someone generated a name or something he could look up, he soothed himself by calling his daughter. "Hey Charlotte! How are you doing?"

She spoke of band practice, homework, and gymnastics. Though the last gave him pause he tried not to show it. So much like her mother. He listened without commenting as Charlotte proceeded to tell him how she'd fallen from the bars, suffered a mild sprain to her wrist and been banned from anything on her right hand. And could he tell the coach she would be fine? Of course he couldn't. Charlotte hung up angry. And Owen sighed and hoped to catch a moment to talk to Virginia.

His younger daughter complained that her host family wouldn't let her watch a crappy cartoon. Then the parents informed him Ginnie hadn't eaten vegetables in four days.

He was striking out with all the women in his sphere. He couldn't get a child to eat vegetables let alone convince a pregnant woman not to infiltrate a known mafia kingpin's inner circle.

Coffee.

The thought popped into his brain as something he could actually accomplish. So he excused himself from the lab and drove away in search of a decent brew.

Though he found a spot soon and got a latte that seemed nearly heaven-sent, he took his first sip and savored it despite the realization that it was just a drink. It was no more going to save him than a purple flamingo was going to fly by.

So he headed back to the lab, the coffee having disappeared before he parked. He threw out the cup on the way in the door, since security was tight enough here that the cup would have been questioned. When he finally made it down the hall, Nguyen looked at him, startled.

"There you are! Where have you been?"

"Coffee run." *He'd been missed?* He didn't think that would even be possible.

His internal dialog didn't matter at all. Nguyen had him by the elbow and was pulling him back to the computer. "I checked the prints—pretty cursory job, but enough to sort. Most were our girl and her guy." He still didn't have names. Owen didn't supply any despite the pause, and in a moment Nguyen continued.

"There were two additional prints besides theirs and ours—I found two sets of yours! Have you been there before? Or can you actually throw fingerprints on the wall just by showing up?"

Though his mouth quirked, Owen didn't get to respond.

"You contaminated that scene, man." Then Nguyen tugged Owen's elbow again as though that would make his eyes go some particular direction. "So there were two others. One set only produced partials and there's no way I can even try to match anything on those. But we got one whole print. Dude fucked up!"

It was like he'd won the lotto.

"Look!" Nguyen tugged the elbow again.

"I sorted the AFIS results myself. I need a second expert to confirm but . . ."

"But you can tell me who it is?"

"Of course." Nguyen batted off the question. "The second is only for legal issues."

"Then we don't get one." Owen said, but Nguyen was already onto the important things.

"It's this guy. He's considered a possible associate of the Casazza family in New York. His name is Patrick Kelly Gilligan."

"What does he do?" Owen did not like this.

"He's a reaper. Collects debts or bodies, but his fingerprints are on some very nasty scenes. FBI is all over him." Nguyen lived for this stuff. All about the science, he often didn't remember there were people on the other end of the story. Then again, while Owen burned out, Nguyen was still here with light in his eyes. "Word is he's called 'The Mechanic.'"

# CHAPTER 12

S in's brain roared and there was nothing she could do to shut it down.

Words filtered through from the outside in deep, elongated sounds that she could barely understand let alone string together. Someone was pushing her. Some of the sounds were Nick nearly yelling at her. What he'd been saying she had no idea.

Annika had come, too, and the three of them had discussed how to find out if Lee was alive, how to get him out. Annika made subtle and not-so-subtle hints to tell Nick about the pregnancy, but so far Sin had resisted. Eventually the buzzing in her skull had ratcheted up again and she sat down to do her own thinking.

So now the two of them stood in front of her, looking at her like she was crazy, while they talked on the phone to someone. Sin guessed it was Dr. Dunham, but she wasn't sure. She couldn't devote much mental space to the sounds beyond the crashing in her brain.

Lee was alive.

Barely.

Probably.

Kaspar Kurev had him.

Though she couldn't put together what was happening outside her body, inside her head thoughts, ideas, and plans were jumbling around at warp speed.

First, she reconciled herself to the fact that Lee had been alive at some point after being dragged from the cabin. Which made the whole thing make more sense. They'd taken him alive to use as their hostage to get to her. Surely they wanted Lee, but what the Kurev's really wanted was both of them.

Sin had gotten away because Lee saved her. Now she needed to save him.

If he was still alive.

Unfortunately, they couldn't be sure. They each examined the picture, an eight by ten glossy with enough detail to see that he was alive, tied to the chair he was in, and badly beaten. He wouldn't give her up, she knew that much. Sin didn't have faith in a lot of things in this world, but she believed in her husband.

While she would have gladly traded herself for him on any normal day, this was no normal day.

Did she ask for proof of life?

This was clearly not an old photo. She and Nick agreed it wasn't altered. Though she knew that back in the days just after Kolya had ordered Lee's first wife and their daughter killed, he went a bit crazy. The Kurevs delivered a strong message to him— beating him within an inch of his life. But this picture wasn't from that time. His physique was different now. Then he'd been a mild mannered accountant, earning big money and making a nice place for his family by not thinking too much about what he was doing.

That Lee had looked different, acted different, thought differently than the Lee she had always known. This was *her* Lee in the chair.

Lee wasn't so much tied as chained to the metal chair. The man in the chair was clearly someone to be reckoned with. That was her Lee.

Just three weeks ago, she would have gone in, guns blazing, sais twirling, but she wasn't in that position now. Though the picture was relatively recent, it had been over a week since Lee was captured. A week-old picture wouldn't be distinguishable from yesterday's. While yesterday's date was burned into the picture, it could easily have been altered. With only the print copy in hand, there was no metadata to check. Still, even that could be messed with.

Her head hurt. She thrived on knowing her goals. Uncertainty hadn't been an issue in her life for the longest time. When she met Lee, she stayed on track. When she decided to stay with him, she integrated him into her goals. Only when they were in White Oak, only when she had friends and concerns beyond herself and him, did the decisions become difficult.

Now she had to decide: go after Lee at possible cost to the baby? Or leave Lee alone and shelter the life inside her that may never come to be?

The problem—well, one of the many problems—was that there was no certainty in any of it. She didn't know if Lee was alive, didn't know if the baby would make it. Didn't know where Lee was, even if she did decide to go get him.

So she had to go in and find him and not hurt the baby. No small order there. Ultimately, the picture didn't change the task, only the time frame. If Lee were alive, she needed to get to him while he was still alive enough to stay that way.

Lee was a known quantity.

The baby wasn't.

Though she would do everything in her power to protect her unborn child—the child she would never raise—she would choose Lee first. Lee would want the baby safe. She did, too. But the man in the chair needed out, .. now.

She only hoped the Kurevs understood that this was the flag. Like fighters telescoped their punches, showing a trained opponent what they were winding up for, this move opened things on a grander scale.

Sin would get Lee.

Not a single Kurev would be left standing when she was done and so help anyone who stood in her way.

---

Nick watched, worried, as his sister sat in a haze. Her words were sometimes a little slurred, sometimes a bit out of order.

"Her blood sugar is low." Somehow, Annika just looked at Sin's bad posture and diagnosed the problem.

"How do you know that?" He looked to the other woman. The big teased hair and strong make-up startling him each time he saw it. This was not the same woman who sat quietly by her husband during the meetings. Even then, Nick had suspected she was doing more than just soaking up all the info like a sponge.

She looked perfect to party her way into the Kurev household, and Nick had to admire Annika's versatility and her fortitude, but he didn't understand how she claimed to understand his sister so fully when he thought they'd just met. "Is it a mom thing?"

Her dirty look set him straight. "No, I just know things you don't."

What did she know? Something was up with his sister. Something other than her husband dying and leaving her alone, getting resurrected from the dead, and needing rescue? Or maybe Sin had simply, finally, cracked.

Annika was in Sin's face, telling her, "You have to eat."

No questions, no doubt. The woman held food to his sister and Sin chewed and swallowed as though not even aware she was doing it. Annika monitored her intake until she was satisfied, though Sin still didn't come out of her head for a while.

While he watched this odd show, Nick's phone rang. Only a

low buzz, rather than a full song, the phone vibrated against his pocket, which at least helped locate it. Still, there were two phones in that particular pocket, and he took a moment to check the number etched on the back. He didn't want to admit that he was afraid it was Kaspar, calling to find out if Nick had located the girl and delivered their message.

As usual, Kaspar's requests put him into a tailspin of moral decisions. His compass never quite survived unscathed an encounter with his half-brother. He wasn't prepared to answer that call, so he was grateful the ringing phone was the line he'd given Dr. Dunham.

"We have information. Can you get everyone together?"

"We're already here."

Just as he said those words, Sin stood up, her eyes clear, her focus in front of her.

Nick put the agent on speaker. As they each chimed in, Sin's voice rang clear. "I'm here."

For the first time, Nick thought she really was.

Though there was some distortion from the speaker, Dunham came through clear. "Sin, they did drug you. And they were really underhanded about it too."

"What do you mean?" Even as she said it, she slumped back onto the bed. Guilt rolled off her in waves, replaced by relief. Clearly, without alerting any of them, she'd shouldered the thought that it was somehow her fault, and the burden had finally been lifted.

Dunham's words helped even more and Nick had to wonder if the man could somehow see across the miles and knew what he was doing for Sin just by talking. "They drilled into the well and drugged it with GHB. From the pattern of vine removal and replacement that Riker found, it looked like they did it several times, probably upping the dosage."

Nick knew GHB—a common date rape drug, it was clear,

odorless, and tasteless. In well water over time, the two would never have noticed it.

"Then," Dunham continued, "they also took a portion of the emission from the generator and siphoned the carbon monoxide back into your bedroom. You didn't stand a chance. I have no idea how Lee even woke up to push you out of bed."

"He saved me." The words were soft, reverent. And so was Dunham's response.

"Yes, he did."

For a moment, they all simply dealt with the new information. Then Nick guessed that Dunham couldn't see into the room, because he spoke before Sin could gather herself back together well enough. "We lifted some fingerprints that weren't yours."

In the background a rough voice came on. "We lifted a lot of Dunham's prints, too!"

"Shut up, Nguyen." Dunham must have been shaking his head. "There were partials and one different whole print. So at least two other people in the house."

That matched what Sin said she saw. Though given the new information about her and Lee being drugged, Nick now decided to lean more on the evidence. It was the police detective in him.

"The partials are useless," Dunham added, but Nick knew that. "The one whole print yielded some disturbing news. It's attached to one Kelly Gilligan—a hitman out of New York. He's mostly known for doing work for Vani Casazza—"

Nick's breath sucked in at the mention of that name. Vani had slid neatly into her husband's throne about fifteen years ago when the man mysteriously died. It soon became clear that anything Mario had accomplished was because of his wife. And despite her unusual rise to power, her ruthlessness made the transition smooth. Nick had spent much time praying he didn't tangle with Vani. If this guy was one the Casazzas were using, then he was bad, bad news.

"They call him 'the Mechanic.'"

"Oh God, why do they call him that?" Nick rubbed his temples and waited for an answer.

A pause. Then Dunham's voice again. "A tendency to dismember his victims . . . Then sometimes rebuild them in . . . Odd ways."

Annika looked a little green around the gills and Nick didn't blame her.

"That's who took Lee?" Sin's voice was clearer than it should be, given the circumstances. So were her eyes. She was gathering information, a hunter in her own right.

"We think so. There's more, Sin."

"Tell me." She was standing firm, though something—a look, some meaning—passed between her and Annika. Nick wasn't privileged enough to understand it, and it seemed they weren't going to fill him in.

"There wasn't enough blood to determine that Lee was actually killed." Dunham talked over himself, probably making sure Sin didn't read the information as anything certain, not realizing she already knew more than he did. "Don't get me wrong. It was a lot. But Lee *might* have survived."

"I know." Bell clear, her voice rang out, and Nick could almost see Owen Dunham rock backwards. "We just got a photo. We have to determine if it's current, but Lee was alive and upright after he was taken from the cabin."

---

Owen heard only silence from the other end of the phone, despite the number of people all talking through the speaker. This decided shift changed the game entirely. So, as he relayed information about Gilligan and his past activities, his mind was turning.

He didn't like Annika being involved in this. Not before and certainly not now. The Mechanic made Sin and Lee look more like Kevorkian—benevolent helpers moving souls where they needed to go. Owen knew Sin and Lee had tortured more than one man and not for information either. It was their own brand of revenge, of tipping the scales. It was a calling card and a message to anyone else who wanted to step out of line that someone was waiting. And even though Owen understood what they did and overall approved of their choice of targets, he didn't want Annika becoming best friends with Sin.

Unfortunately, as Owen was often reminded lately, what he wanted Annika to want or do and what Annika wanted to do and often did, were not the same. He constantly had to remind himself that his wife was smart—brilliant even—and that she'd actually been through more than he had in this regard.

"Annika?" He asked it into the ether in front of him, into the tiny mic in the phone and the open room in Chicago.

"Yes, Owen?" Her voice was sweet. The old underlying Russian accent rubbed her 's' sounds and kept her from laying into the 'w' in his name. Usually he love the sound, but right now it scared him.

"Is there some way we can speak privately?"

He heard the shuffling and wished he was there. If he could touch her, remind her what she risked . . . "A few seconds more."

He loved that she was literal with her time. She didn't use the generic, or lazy as she called it, American "one minute" which often meant "however long it takes me." So he wasn't surprised when, about four seconds later she said, "Okay. I'm alone."

*That was fast.* "Where are you?"

"Sin gets two rooms. It works as cover and escape and apparently when one needs to be on the phone alone. What did you need?"

"Given the new information are you still planning on helping Sin out with Ann Evalyn Kimmel?"

"Of course. When we merely thought we were retrieving a

body, it was less important. We know Lee is alive. We *must* help." Her conviction was wonderful.

And terrifying.

His reluctant grin must have shown through the phone line, because she asked him, "What?"

"I was just hoping that was off the table. That there would be a completely different plan now."

"Oh no. In fact, we decided it was the best plan and that we would just move a little faster."

Of course they did. And they needed his pregnant wife. Owen felt his stomach turn as he forced himself to ask questions calmly and not yell orders across the miles. "Is there any chance you might reconsider your role in this?"

"Oh, honey, no." She sounded sad that he still thought she might back out. Like she was disappointing him with her answer. Well, she was. "I couldn't back out before. I'm the only one who can do this. I speak fluent Russian. I can overhear things, I can get in the door when others can't."

"Other people speak Russian." He grasped at straws as they flew by, just out of his reach. And he continued to miss them, as Annika pointed out.

"Yes, but they can't align with Sin. They don't know about the Kurevs the way I do."

He regretted telling her what he had. "You don't know her. You don't know what she's capable of."

"But I do." Her voice was gentle. He was the child here, and she was delivering the news he didn't want to hear. "I know her as well as you do—" when he started to protest, she cut him off. "I know some of the same things you know about her. A lot of them. I think more like she does than you do."

*And didn't that just scare the shit out of him?*

"And while you know some things I don't," He didn't really. He'd brought most all of his cases home to his wonderful wife with her sharp mind and ability to keep secrets. "There are things

I know that you don't. So . . . I think I'm making a sound decision here."

"That's the point. There are no sound decisions."

"If it were you, I'd reach out to her. She would walk through fire for you."

Yes, Sin would. Just like he would walk through fire for her. Wasn't he already back in the FBI's pocket? Wasn't he away from his kids? But he wasn't sure he was willing to send his wife into the fire in his stead.

Annika's voice was soothing and he tried to feel it. "I'm counting on that. We may need her one day. She'll be here for us. I'm being a good friend, and I'm being a good person. I would want any and all help getting *you* back. So I'm going."

"That's the problem, Anni." It was maybe the one thing she didn't understand. "You remember how burnt out I was. When lives are at stake, each task becomes even more crucial than the last." He sighed, remembering those days. "The first step feels like one step, like you can turn around, but I don't think you can. You won't be able to back out." His words came faster, his tone more desperate. "You think you can see what you need to do. You do that one thing and it will all be fine, it will be over or the next person will pick up, but they won't. And you'll have to do the next step and the next, and if you don't someone will die. You can't see what will be asked of you, Anni, but I can."

"No, you can't."

"No, I can't, but I can see that it will be more than we think, harder than we expect, and more dangerous than is okay."

"I know. But I am in. If I do not do this, how can I live with myself? She needs me and Lee needs me and . . . I need you to understand." Her accent got stronger when she was angry.

*Oh, but didn't he understand?* He'd worked this way for years. Always the only one who could save the missing, the damned, the one in need. He never made it home when he said he would, and half the time he turned around and was back out the door before he slept in his own bed.

Back in the day, he'd loved chasing Sin and Lee, because as the bodies piled up, he just didn't care. He didn't feel any need at all to save who they were killing. It was stressful, sure, but about as easy on the burden as a case could be.

Maybe he deserved this. "I love you, Anni. Remember that, and keep yourself safe." How many times had she said that to him? How many times had she sent him off to do what he felt compelled to do and she waited behind, not knowing if he would come back on time or at all, but knowing full well the danger in what he did? This was the universe telling him it was his turn. This was what Karma felt like.

The Gods of the Obvious seemed to think so, for as he turned to look out the window of the laboratory lobby, the sun hit just the right point to spear him in the eyes. His mind blanked at the red-tinged whiteness as his world went bright but blind.

She said she loved him, too, but in the background he heard her speak something to the person who asked if she was finished. He couldn't make out the sounds, maybe because his brain was trying to grapple with the loss of sight. He was reaching back for the desk he remembered was behind him, turning away from the glare that sought him out, and trying to let his eyes readjust to the simple vision of linoleum flooring that he was hunched over staring at.

"It's a bitch, isn't it?" The guard's voice was rich and deep and seemed almost like the Gods were saying something more than *Bad time of day, huh?*

"Yeah." He sputtered out as Annika's voice came back on the line.

"I have to go. That was Nick. We're going in tonight."

# CHAPTER 13

Nick was nervous, the evening had shortened dramatically, and he had an errand to run before Sin and Annika headed into the lion's den. He desperately wanted to offer to go with them, but he wasn't sure if the Kurevs would recognize his sister. He wanted to believe she was good enough at her subterfuge that they wouldn't, but was he willing to bet everything on it? He didn't know yet.

He'd been set to meet with Dana Block the next day, but he was certain now he had to ask his questions before he met with the Kurevs tonight. He had to know how to cover his ass in case he changed his mind.

Sticking his hand in his pocket, he felt past two cell phones and briefly wondered how many pounds of extra weight he was carrying in burners. Only in Chicago did he keep them all on his person, and then only when he wasn't near the Kurevs. With them, anything he carried became a calculated risk.

He was trying to identify the proper phone and figure out how the evening was most likely to go down when Sin stepped up and grabbed his arm. Annika had stepped into the restroom for a moment and the two of them were nearly alone.

"There's something you need to know." She tilted her head, looking concerned and wary all at the same time.

"Can it wait?" Having at last located the correct phone, he wanted to make his call and squeeze in his meeting before things started happening tonight. His finger pushed the button on its own. Nick wasn't sure his plans would work even if he left right now, and—

"No." The added seriousness in her always-serious gaze stopped him dead.

"What is it?" The phone still hanging loosely from his grasp was now nearly forgotten as he stared at her, unable to place what she was about to say. His body tensed for a blow and for a moment he wondered if she was knocking him out of the loop. Asking him to stay away from her rescue efforts because of his association with the Kurevs. She'd never liked it, and who could blame her? His goals and her goals were sometimes at odds and usually each simply ignored it in the other.

So her words were a complete shock to a system he thought had gone numb.

"I'm pregnant."

"What?" The bolt that passed through him left empty spaces and the certainty that he hadn't heard her correctly.

Sin seemed to understand that and she gently repeated the words, just as quickly following up with, "This doesn't change anything."

She was so wrong. "It changes everything."

A niece. A nephew. His brain didn't quite fit around the new thought. He'd always assumed he'd have a family one day, the Kurevs, other half brothers and sisters that he found along the way, eventually a wife and kids of his own. Life had dealt small blow after small blow and ended with several grand ones in the form of Reese and Lee. Incident by incident, his family had shrunk to Sin and Lee. And now maybe just Sin. But maybe this new life, too.

"Was this planned?" He asked when he knew he shouldn't, and even through the swirling conjectures and doubts in his head, Nick couldn't help but think her timing couldn't have been worse.

She jerked back, giving Nick his answer before she spat out the words. "Oh, hell, no."

"Are you going to have it? Keep it?" He continued on, pushing where he had no right to push. Asking where he had no right to know. "Because, if not, I'll raise it. I'll give it a good home."

The doubting look she gave him told him what she really thought. "Yes, I'm having it. This is Lee's child. But I'm not raising it and neither are you."

He noticed she didn't say "Lee and I" just "I" . . . She wasn't counting on getting her husband back. Though he saw echoes of hope in the backs of her eyes, he knew she wasn't quite confident he was still alive.

"Neither of us can provide the safety a baby needs. We don't have any." She turned away. "And right now—any choices I have to make—I'm banking on Lee, not the baby. I'm still early, my risk of miscarriage is still high, and I don't know how to give up my child."

Her voice hitched, ever so slightly, on the last word and Nick caught the stray sound, understanding more than she'd meant to say. For her, it would be easier to lose the baby than to have to give it away.

Before he could reply, she shook her head at him. "It doesn't change anything in the end. But if I do something that you don't understand, maybe this is why."

He couldn't help frowning at her as his phone buzzed a message, letting him know the world still went on even as his collided into something massive. Frowning at Sin, he asked, "What do you mean it 'doesn't change anything in the end'?"

"I mean," She sighed. "If I have the opportunity to both protect the baby and save Lee, I'll do it. But if I have to make my own choice, I'll choose Lee. It's a decision I made nearly a decade ago and I won't undo it."

The sound of her voice seeped into him as surely as her convictions did.

This, he understood.

For a moment, fissures he thought had long since healed cracked opened again and he wished for a short, shining moment that he had the chance to make this same choice for Reese. If he could sacrifice something else and have her back, he . . .

What would he do? Give up his sister? The only sibling—out of far too many—to reach out to him and hold on when everyone else simply didn't care.

His brain faltered as his thoughts careened around corner after corner. "The GHB, Sin." He stopped. It hadn't fully come together in his mind, so they weren't cohesive yet.

Sin, however, seemed to understand and her deep breath in told him this wasn't the first time she'd considered the implications.

"I don't know what that does to a baby. I looked it up, and there's not enough data." She shrugged, though if that was because she didn't care or if she simply couldn't change what was, Nick couldn't tell. "A lot depends on how much and for long. The carbon monoxide was bad, but I don't know how long or how often I was exposed. And I can't find a damn thing about the combination of GHB and carbon monoxide on a developing fetus."

It was another reason she'd chosen Lee. Another reason she wouldn't get attached. Another reason Nick had to be behind her.

So he nodded, trying to understand her decision. Trying to convey that it didn't matter if he understood. He would be there for her.

It was yet another reason to meet with Dana Block.

Nodding to his sister he called the lawyer again.

---

The information was pouring in and Owen didn't like any of it. "The Mechanic"—one Kelly Gilligan—had a file that spanned paper and digital data. For over a decade the FBI had this man on their watch list, but had never been able to pin anything else on him. On his good days he made a very angry Sin look tame by comparison.

For a moment Owen had to stop and reconcile what he knew of Sin with what he was seeing of this man. They both killed. They both killed violently. They both killed repeatedly.

So why did Owen understand Sin—pardon her in his mind even?—when Gilligan was clearly someone he would sic Sin onto if he were aiming her where he wanted.

While he reminded himself that Sin went after the bad guys, most of Gilligan's take-outs were pretty heinous themselves. Gilligan was a remover of loose ends. The one who took out the ones the mafia was tired of. The ones who got in the way. The ones who flipped sides.

Though Vani Casazza seemed to be his main sources, the Mechanic wasn't owned by anyone. He chose his jobs himself, from what Owen could figure. There were reams of information on the guy. Dozens of agents had taken on the task of trying to find a loophole or physical evidence. They tried to take down the Mechanic without becoming one of his victims.

No one wanted to be one of his victims. He tortured them for fun. Dismembering them and putting them back together in grotesque ways. This, combined with a disturbing ability to keep them alive for as much of it as possible, had earned him his moniker. Was that the thing that allowed Owen to hold Sin's "work" separate from Gilligan's? She seemed to take satisfaction in the completion of her task. There had been times where she'd pushed suffering on her victims, but mostly she removed them. Painfully, but efficiently.

Gilligan seemed to get actual pleasure from what he did.

That, to Owen, was sick. Sin was understandable—just look at what she'd come from. But she hadn't cracked. She wasn't batshit crazy the way the Mechanic was. He seemed to kill whomever he was paid enough to take out. Sin always had hard evidence on her scores. Owen knew her, knew she didn't kill quickly or lightly, and that she was always certain she'd gotten the right guy.

While Sin found satisfaction in removing a rotten soul from the realm, the Mechanic never seemed to be satisfied, if judged from the sheer volume of his work. Much of it could be traced back to even before the FBI had matched a stray set of fingerprints and found out that the man they'd been seeking was Gilligan. But he'd gone off the grid right about then, probably having realized he'd left those stray prints behind.

As Owen searched through the files he saw that dozens of agents had their names and research catalogued here. If you were bored, or needed some practice, it appeared you were put on the Mechanic Case. Flipping through, he found himself wishing more of this file had been redacted. Instead, he faced a deluge of information, each bit more concerning than the next if only that it contributed to the sheer magnitude of the Mechanic's work.

Owen read until he had a headache; he'd reconciled his belief in Sin and his conviction that the Mechanic needed to be taken out. He seemed mentally stable if not completely sane, and that was the thing that would give him the advantage. Owen had no issues with pointing Sin in the Mechanic's direction, except that he was no longer positive she would emerge the victor. A sobering thought about the girl he once thought invincible.

Then again, he'd thought Lee was immortal, too, and look where he was: either dead or in the Mechanic's hands. Just the thought turned Owen's stomach and for a moment he prayed that Lee was well and truly dead.

Another thing plagued Owen as he worked his way through

the file. Though many agents had their hands in it, one of the most recent signatures that kept popping up was that of Agent Austin Pillow. Suppressing a sigh, Owen fought back the memory of his clipped remarks to the younger man and Pillow's reply that only one of them was an agent.

All the while, the back of his mind poked at him.

The Mechanic was after Sin. If Lee was alive he was hopefully being held by the Kurevs and Gilligan was long gone. And Sin was taking Annika into the thick of things. Tonight.

There was no stopping either of them.

He only hoped there was no stopping either of them.

Time was ticking. But Nick hoped he could make it count tonight.

Dana sat drinking a coffee she'd ordered while she waited for him. That was their usual meeting in public. Never together, not really. She sat on the opposite side of the shop, and Nick called her. They spoke on the phone, in eyesight of each other.

If he needed papers and she had something on her, or if he needed to leave something with her, one of them would head to the restroom and leave the drop in the hall. The other would pick it up, both would leave separately, but could see to confirm the drop had successfully been kept out of other hands.

Their locations were chosen because of the ability to speak within sight of each other, for having a restroom hallway that wasn't heavily traveled, for having good coffee and sometimes a croissant or two. It was Chicago, even with their limiting criteria, they had options.

Nick first met Dana at a Kurev gathering. Both had embraced the irony that the Kurevs brought them together, when both had a bone to pick with the brothers. But until now, neither Nick nor Dana had thought about going for the jugular.

"You have your accounts." Her voice was lilting. She was

smart. And in another life, one without the slice and sting of Reese, he would have gotten more involved with her. Or at least tried.

"I do. I want to protect them. Regardless of which way the market goes."

Dana was the architect of their shorthand, able to easily inform him of what he needed without dropping any security risk buzzwords into their conversation. "What would change the market?"

"I'm considering shifting the corporate direction." He fidgeted with his tie. How to convey to her what he needed?

"Go on."

"I'm considering getting into corporate takeovers. Buying up existing conglomerates and dismantling them."

She paused, considering his position for a moment. Then responded, showing that she both understood and had questions. "For re-sale?"

"No."

"Do you have a specific corporation in mind?"

"I do." Taking a sip of his coffee, he leaned back, fidgeted with his tie and looked around. He'd put on a full suit for this meeting, simply wanting to look less like himself. No one appeared to be listening in. But all the games had changed drastically in the last handful of years.

Sin and Lee had been at the top of their food system. He'd had his own ecosystem which had bordered on the Kurevs'. Now his brothers had become an invasive species, leaching their way into his territory and his business. Lee had been toppled and Sin was teetering at the precipice. The sharks circling underneath had become smarter. The new assassins who'd gotten into the cabin were just more of the same.

The situation was shifting under his feet. And if change was coming, Nick wanted to orchestrate it.

Dana was there to help him do it—if it could be done.

"Will you take over the existing market?"

His visual sweeps of the store saw her picking at a muffin, eating small bites and looking at some magazine that appeared to be a glossy women's rag. He almost laughed. Anyone following Dana should know that was out of character for her. But no one cared, though someone should; Dana was almost always negotiating slick deals for clients whose names no one really knew.

Just like everyone thought that Uncle Dom and Slidell were running the Vasilescu holdings in Atlanta. Some people knew about Nick, and those who did knew to keep their mouths shut. Most were after the other two men, pegging them as cocaine and gun dealers, in league with heavyweight attorney Phil Megan.

"No. I'll dismantle the existing market."

He could see her frowning as he heard the words come through his own earpiece. "Markets are markets. You can't dismantle them without a campaign."

"You're right. They'll reform. But I'm thinking of getting out of the business."

The frown deepened and she leaned over the magazine, her straight brown hair obscuring part of her face as her finger traced an article. She was good at this. She looked like she was chatting with a friend and at any moment would say, "Girlfriend, you need to dump his sorry ass." Instead, she was discussing crime lords, off-shore Caribbean accounts, and dirty police officers with Nick. "Entirely?"

"Yes, both ventures." He was seriously thinking about it. He couldn't enjoy his money as a detective. He couldn't stay in Atlanta if he got out. He'd know too much. Most of the people involved in his true line of work were as batshit crazy as Ann Evelyn Kimmel or as power-hungry and self-aggrandizing as Kaspar. If he was lucky, someone as clueless as Roman would take over. But even his youngest half-brother wouldn't let him simply stay out of the way.

No. Nick was either going to hold both areas entirely. Or he was getting all the way out.

But what would he do if he were well and truly out? Sit on the beach and watch the Caribbean waves break all day? That sounded wonderful for a day or two, but after that it was mind numbingly awful.

He briefly entertained joining his sister. He could train beside Sin, become a weapons expert—he was already pretty damn good on the gun range—and fight the good fight.

Nick almost laughed out loud. Sin was Sin because of her drive. Nick didn't have it. The ball of hate at his center was much different from the one that fueled her. Also, he didn't have the stomach to do what she did. He always considered himself some kind of benevolent dictator, but not a killer. He reconsidered his earlier statement about getting out of both businesses. "Maybe."

Then he took a breath in. "That's what I need you for: I'm considering my options."

"How do you propose it? You'll need to get out clean."

She meant no one coming after him. He'd thought of that.

Then he said the words that scared the shit out of him. But the idea had been dogging him for days. Enough to make him call this meeting and understand his options. While he wasn't committed to any one course of action yet, he was taking the first step. Possibly right off the edge.

"I think my business will qualify for federal grants in this takeover."

Dana sat bolt upright and sucked in an involuntary breath. Nick heard it even across the coffee shop.

# CHAPTER 14

S in was nervous. Just being nervous was enough to make her tendons shake a little. When she thought of what was at stake, she nearly shut down.

Lee.

Life or death.

The thought would slam into her, rattling her thoughts, her plans, her very being.

No matter how many times she turned it over, she couldn't shake out an answer.

Nick left. Annika went back to her own hotel room for a nap and suggested Sin do the same. As though one pregnant woman embracing her impending future was the same as another dreading it. Sin couldn't sleep, rough thoughts dodging her feeble attempts like coyotes baying in the distance.

One by one she considered and discarded ideas.

What if she just left Chicago? Lee was probably dead, she was probably on a fool's errand anyway—one that would leave her dead, too. If Lee were still alive, he would tell her to leave him behind, especially if he knew she was pregnant. So wouldn't she be fulfilling his wishes if she just picked up and left? Found a nice family that wanted a baby and left the child there for them . . .

It was an odd fantasy. But even in her best imaginings, she was plagued with thoughts of 'what if? What if she could save Lee? What if he wasn't already dead, but poised for a breakout and with a little help from Sin he'd be on with his life, none the worse for wear?

She didn't believe it. It would not go down like that, she knew it in her heart. But '*what if?*'

What if she went in, guns blazing, sais flying and anger fueling her on a deadly spree through the Kurev household?

There were parts of that scenario she found wildly satisfying. She had no love for the men who were her genetic half-brothers. She'd had no love for the third brother, the one she killed. It probably helped that he'd been aiming his gun at her when she went for him. Those scenarios helped quell the misgivings.

When the options for her future were played out and her brain still didn't shut off, she was sucked back into the past.

Alone in the hotel room, blackout curtains drawn, she found she could no longer stay one step ahead of her own worries.

She'd known she was Kolya's daughter for a while. Though she'd labeled Kaspar and Roman as her half-brothers, Nick she thought of only as "brother." For some reason the genetics in him seemed stronger than in the others. Maybe because he put stock in them, when the boys who bore the Kurev surname didn't.

She'd had these same thoughts before, and they didn't plague her the way they had once, but what she hadn't yet given voice or thought to was that she would bear Kolya's grandchild. She had not yet contemplated the true downfall of her parents. She had originally believed they were innocents in a random killing, but Lee later suggested her parents had been targeted.

Lee's much earlier words had later allowed Nick's statements to sink in. Which had in turn paved the way to understanding and belief when he told her that he was Kolya's illegitimate child . . . And so was *she*. It allowed for comprehension when Owen told her that even Sin's sister Wendy had not been their father's child.

For so long, Sin faced the world as an adult with a child's strict moral view.

Her parents, her perfect parents, ripped away cruelly. Her sister abused and eventually driven to her own death.

It was only later that Sin admitted her anger with Wendy for giving up and letting go. And only much later than that when Sin began to understand her sister's grief had been so much different than her own.

No, it was not so simple. Her parents had died from their own transgressions. A long fall from the pedestal she had placed them on. She was no longer a child wearing the blinders of grief, holding tight her belief in a black and white world, coping in the only way she knew how.

Her family had fallen away. First her parents, then her faith in her sister, then Wendy herself. Lee had opened the first crack of light to see that her parents were human, fallible, and maybe even the authors of their own demise . . . And therefore her pain.

It was too much to bear. Too hard to think about.

In some ways, Lee had it easier. She didn't say this to him, but in his beginning, he was the betrayer. In hers, she was the betrayed.

His justice was atonement for his own sins. Hers was for sins committed against her.

But what was she now?

How had she never faced choices this hard before?

In the end, there were no choices. There was only forward. The only way to quell the voices was to go into the Kurev home and find out where Lee was. Then find Lee. Alive or dead.

That was a simple mission.

Complex in its execution, surely, but at its heart it was the kind of thing Sin thrived on: a goal.

With that finally settled, her body relaxed into much needed sleep.

---

Nick didn't realize how much he hoped the evening would fall apart until it didn't.

First, he headed into the hotel to pick up Sin. Unless they had cameras in her room they would never know she wasn't a green eyed blonde who favored sharp heels, bubble gum, and sunglasses. She was ready for him even though he wasn't ready for her.

It took a moment to stop looking for the telltale bulge of her pregnancy, but he couldn't find it. If he couldn't find it, then no one would know unless they were told. A small measure of comfort.

And she wouldn't tell anyone. Look how long it had taken her just to tell him.

That secret was at least as safe as it could be.

She sat quietly in the passenger seat of the car until they arrived at Annika's hotel. Heading in, they neatly turned and spoke to each other, carefully avoiding all the cameras. For a moment Nick thought he had a future in security. Cameras were never placed well, and the few that were never seemed to be backed up by a secondary, meaning that a knowing criminal could easily avoid any head-on shots. Hats, glasses, and even Sin's disturbing bangs could all act as concealers. It was his greatest frustration as a cop and his greatest ally when he was on the other side of things.

Though Annika made them wait for just a moment, she wasn't anywhere near late enough for Nick to be able to cry uncle on the evening. After fuming the bathroom with a cloud of hairspray to maintain the look she was going for, she stepped out, the mist still hovering around her.

Nick gagged, his lungs contracting for a moment. "Damn, Annika—" He didn't get much more out, he was too busy trying to breathe. "You're pregnant. That can't be good for you. . ." He hacked again. "Sin is too."

The back of his throat rebelled, but the women seemed immune. Both stared at him as his eyes watered and he was just getting it together when Sin looked at Annika and said, "Do it again."

"What!" Instinctively, he turned away, holding his arm crooked over his face, trying to ward off the evil that was aerosolizing around him.

The hiss of the can notified him that Annika was at it again.

Calmly, not about to lose a lung at all, Sin explained. "One—her hair needs to stay in place. No self-respecting gold digger would let her hair fall. You have to know the part to play the part—"

Nick started to interrupt but stopped himself. He didn't want to know how she knew.

"And two—that's her real hair. She can't leave it at the scene." Turning to Annika, she asked, "Did you brush it, then spray it, then run your hands over it?" Pausing as her new friend—or maybe "accomplice" was a better word—nodded yes, Sin asked, "Eyebrows?"

"Leg hair, too."

Delivered deadpan, it startled Nick to the point that it made the girls laugh. He was glad they could giggle like that, given what they were headed to. For a second, it stopped him cold. Sin had only ever laughed like that with Reese.

He knew.

He'd watched Sin from the moment she hired on at his precinct. He'd drawn her there. Known she was his sister for several years before he told her. How did you tell someone that you'd tracked them across five states and two identities? And that she was the daughter of the man she'd built her life around destroying?

So he hadn't been surprised that she was far more serious than silly. But there was something about Reese that had made them all happier. The brightest, sunniest of them all. And Nick hadn't laughed like that himself since Reese had died.

Here Sin was, laughing with the FBI agent's wife.

Dunham could string him up by his toes. Make his Caribbean accounts worthless from behind prison bars. Nick was trusting that Owen would do no such thing. He hadn't turned in Sin, after all. She would have made him a household name, but Dunham hadn't done it.

Nick wasn't quite as big a fish as his sister, but the Ex-Agent owed him no allegiance either. He was left dependent on the kindness of strangers.

Annika looked at him oddly, "I didn't hairspray my leg hair."

He nodded, as though, *of course you didn't.* He really hadn't a clue.

Sin filled him in. "You hairspray everything. Any hair left at the scene can be matched."

"It's not an exact science." You could say two hairs matched, but you couldn't prove they were from the same person without DNA found in the root.

"Leave nothing behind." It was a grim smile she offered him, set to the tune of the evening.

Only then did he notice that both women wore mostly synthetic fibers. He'd be willing to bet they were purchased at big box stores —meaning thousands of women would own the same garment and they'd be virtually impossible to trace. Sin's jewelry had to be fake, there was no way the woman owned something as frivolous as a diamond that large. And the thin chain meant that it would fly away in the event of a fight. Also, it was tucked along the collar of the halter top she wore, probably a careful decision as the chain wouldn't contain any skin cells rubbed from her neck. Her jacket was leather, the only natural material on her. A unique piece, it classed up the generic outfit, and leather didn't leave fiber behind.

She must have noticed his scrutiny. She saw that he catalogued Annika's leather skirt, the leather in their shoes, the soles generic black. Her gaze was piercing and soft at the same time. "Paranoia keeps me alive."

He knew that all too well. He'd lived it himself, barely escaping a bad end at his own grandfather's command because of his own paranoia. It suddenly didn't feel like the security blanket it should be.

Quickly the moment passed and the women stood looking at him as though he was the one holding them up. He was. "Shall we?"

Holding the door open, he trailed them out into the hallway, both women in conversation, keeping their eyes toward each other and looking only across or down. Nick was impressed with Annika's skills in avoiding the security camera. In the elevator, both played with their sunglasses, blocking not only their eyes, but their cheekbones and eye orbitals—the markers facial recognition software used to distinguish one person from another.

Annika was too good at it.

He ushered them both to the car, quiet in his thoughts, worried about the evening. While he'd known Sin was the best of the best, he hadn't expected it from Mrs. Dunham. But why hadn't he?

Somehow, Nick had adopted Owen Dunham's view of Annika —as someone to be protected. He hadn't paid enough attention when Sin told him it was Annika who really cracked the Ninja case. It was Annika who fled Belarus and the KGB as a child. A history like that made for no ordinary soccer mom. The slight accent she carried, the slight likelihood to drop contractions, were the only real indicators that Mrs. Dunham was nowhere near as harmless as she seemed.

Lee was in the best hands possible.

They were pulling into the almost Stepford-like subdivision before he knew it. Once again, the gate keeper wasn't doing his job, this time asleep behind the desk, feet up, book open on his chest in a blatant display of unconcern. The gate was wide open, so Nick pulled through.

When they pulled up to Ann Evalyn Kimmel's house, it was Sin who popped out of the backseat. Annika stayed in the front passenger's seat, the arrangement all carefully planned ahead of time. Ann Evalyn would sit behind Annika, not behind Nick, the driver—where she might grab him and throw the entire car into chaos. Sin was in the back with the woman, with easy access to shut down anything that went awry.

Ann Evalyn would probably notice the set-up. No one cared. She should know she needed to watch her back. Still, Sin turned her own back to the woman as they descended the stairs. They had been inside for a few minutes, and according to the plan, Sin would search the woman, check the phone to make sure it was the right one—the one Nick got notifications from—and that she didn't have a spare.

They got into the car without fanfare and almost without any conversation at all. But then Sin tossed something out the window as they pulled out of the subdivision.

Only when the window was back in place did she inform the front seat, "She had on one of those fitness charm necklaces. If you get in trouble, it GPSs you and calls your friends. She had one on a bracelet, too!"

Nick watched the turns, though it was only the other cars he needed to worry about. He knew the way to the Kurev home probably even better than he knew the way to his house in White Oak.

In the rear view mirror, Nick could see the sullen expression on Ann Evalyn's face. Sin kept thwarting her and she clearly didn't like it. His heart beat faster thinking that their entry into the Kurev home depended on this woman.

His eyes scanned the streets and other traffic, because even if Ann Evalyn did everything she was told, they would still get in trouble if someone was following him. Given his unsteady relationship with his half-brothers, he didn't doubt the possibility.

But no one had pinged his internal radar. If he was being followed, it would have to be by a tag team, changing out cars to keep him from recognizing the tail. Nick doubted his brothers thought he was that valuable, but he kept his eyes peeled.

The sheer volume of cars on the road slowed their progress, but they finally made it into town. "Here you go, ladies."

He used the term loosely, wondering if there was a 'lady' among the three of them. Sin and Annika didn't thank him. Both played their parts, carefully watching the third woman. Ann Evalyn was necessary, but not trustworthy. Ann Evalyn didn't thank him for the ride either, but that was because she was a bitch.

They would hit the club together. Serious work for Annika and Sin, but the three needed to be seen out and about for a little bit. Especially, if Roman was at one of his favorite haunts. His friends would at least be able to see the three together and "partying."

Pulling away from the curb, he fought the traffic around him. He tried to keep his breathing even as he headed for the Kurev house.

---

The club wore on Sin. She'd never understood the fun others found in dancing in a room filled with noisy music and general desperation. Then again, she'd met Lee when she was just nineteen. Well, nineteen going on ninety. Clearly, other people loved being out, being seen. Just as clearly, Ann Evalyn was one of those people.

The woman positively preened in the presence of the fawning strangers. She had the best meth, the coolest baubles, and the most intriguing drink in her hand. What startled Sin was that it only took Annika about ten minutes to abandon her, emerging from the bar with her own brightly colored drink, and hanging on Ann Evalyn's arm, demanding that "Annie" be introduced to all the coolest people.

Sin smiled at the bartender, slickly getting the most interesting looking drink out of him without having any idea what she'd actually ordered. One taste told her she didn't really want to know.

An expert at blending in, Sin worked hard to be sure that it didn't look like the effort that it was. Annika, however, shed her old skin and waltzed in like she owned the place, leaving Sin smiling at some overly affectionate young man while she envied Annika her wedding ring. Though even that didn't stop some of them.

Owen probably had no clue his wife—his pregnant wife—was out basking in the sordid praise of strangers, throwing out smiles and sly grins like candy at a parade.

It was nearly an hour later when she managed to corner a very drunk Annika in a thankfully empty ladies room. She'd left Ann Evalyn behind, needing to corral the train wreck. It was all she could do to refrain from knocking the glass out of Annika's hand. Though maybe she wouldn't need to. Annika had been drunk enough to drop her last drink, and accept a new one from the man at her side.

"What?" The head turned, the big curls not moving and not leaving evidence behind.

Fighting hard to keep her jaw in place, Sin moved it twice

before making sounds. She wasn't often this surprised. "You're not drunk."

"Of course not." She didn't add that she was pregnant and not stupid.

Stammering, Sin stepped back. "I'm sorry."

Annika smiled at her, "Don't be. I'll take it as a compliment."

But just then the door pushed open behind them, and Annika set her drink on the counter, sloshing a little as she began to dig through her purse for something. "Go." The consonants came out mushy again, and Sin fought her own grin as she listened, "Tell Ann Evalyn that I want to go to an after party."

Triumphantly, Annika held up a lipstick, giggled, and swatted Sin out of the restroom, absently hitting another club-goer as she gestured. In turn, she offered a shocked apology, sloshing still more of her drink down the drain. She probably hadn't drunk a drop.

The weariness of the club finally having passed with her revelation, Sin developed her own slightly sloppy demeanor and beelined for Ann Evalyn. It was time for the real outing of the evening.

Sin watched closely as Ann Evalyn placed her call to her own driver and the three women exited the club. Mrs. Kimmel looked just a little bit high on something, but Annika's performance was stellar. Seemingly tipsy, she was just enough unstable to look like easy pickings, but steady enough to not get picked. For her part, Sin played bored.

The back of the car made her uneasy. Ann Evalyn was within arm's reach of Annika, which made Sin uncomfortable. On the one hand, Annika was becoming a friend, and she didn't have any of those to spare. On the other hand, Annika was almost something she'd borrowed from Owen, and it would kill him if anything—*anything*—happened to the woman he clearly loved beyond measure.

Bright heat formed prickles at the back of her nose and

random muscles in her body tensed as she fought to keep thoughts of Lee at bay. Sadly, the simple mantra was that he might already be dead. Nick had spoken the words out loud: possible fool's errand.

While Sin was perfectly willing to be the fool, it would not be at the cost of Annika. She swallowed hard, fighting the tears that threatened to surface. It had never been this hard with her parents, maybe because they had been *dead*, not maybe dead. Maybe was a hard place to live.

Just as she was getting her thoughts under control, the driver rolled down his window and spoke at the gate. With the privacy partition up and the smooth ride of the big car, she'd almost missed it.

"What?" Ann Evalyn acted like a spoiled child at Sin's hard stare. "I know what I'm supposed to do. No worries, Bitchy McBitcherson."

*Oh dear God.* She was working with a moron. A deadly, spoiled moron. She'd have to be on the lookout not just from the Kurevs, but from this petulant woman.

In a moment they were parked at the front of the house and were walking up the cobblestoned drive. Ann Evalyn was a bit unsteady on her spiked heels. While Sin also had heels, she'd worn some serious lace up boots, much sturdier than they looked with a heel that wouldn't break, but would knock someone out if applied to the side of the head with reasonable force. Let Mrs. Kimmel break an ankle, Sin couldn't think of a more deserving person.

A slight man, obviously staff of some kind, and obviously well trained to blend into the background escorted them through a series of halls.

Tapestry rugs clashed with bold colored paint. Small tables with crenelated edges stood flush against the walls as though waiting for someone to need a marble surface partway down the hall. Urns held proud flowers in colors that had no bearing on the decor and paintings hung in six-inch thick frames that were as much works of art as the paintings they held. For a moment Sin thought she saw a Vermeer and wondered if it was stolen before she reminded herself that she was not here to bring the Kurevs down.

Not yet.

Letting the plush carpeting sway her feet, she remained a little unsteady, trailing her fingers along the wall. It would smear any prints she left and give her an additional sense to help remember the way out of here if she needed it.

At last, the man pushed open a seemingly random door in the hallway. "Visitors, sir." Then he faded into the background again.

Roman Kurev was barely bothered to turn from fixing himself a drink, but Kaspar nodded a hello to Ann Evalyn then checked out his guests, his eyes landing right on Sin.

# CHAPTER 15

Owen didn't like any of it. The file on the Mechanic didn't yield anything new as he read. His stomach rolled as he tried not to imagine what might have been removed if this was what was left.

The Mechanic was apparently a solid businessman. There were instances when he turned on the very people who hired him, but where Owen could piece it together, the employer had held out on him in some way. It turned out it was a very bad idea to not pay the Mechanic. Kelly Gilligan did not give second chances.

Owen could only hope that the Kurevs would think themselves above the mechanic's laws and thus find themselves under his fist. Unfortunately, Kaspar was a good businessman himself and would probably maintain a steady relationship.

That was the crux of it. It seemed pretty clear that Kaspar had hired the hit on the cabin. Though there was no real evidence, there was plenty of circumstantial to go around. Given Kaspar's history of repeat business with the Mechanic, it seemed Kurev was satisfied with what he received.

Apparently the Kurevs had visited Vani Casazza on more than one occasion. In fact, these occasions lined up such that people the Kurevs disliked turned up dead in Mechanic-like ways in very coincidental time frames. Lastly, the Mechanic seemed to currently hold an apartment in a security building in Chicago.

Owen both wanted to laugh at that and to barf up his lunch. The laughter because the deranged assassin seemed to think he was better off with a security doorman. Barfing because it was way too close to Annika and way too far from where he was.

Nguyen was still finding details from the cabin, holed up in his borrowed lab here in Georgia. He calculated out how much carbon monoxide and GHB might have been administered. He asked for Sin's blood so he could test it, but Owen refused. Who knew how star-struck his friend would become if he met Sin in person? And it was also a felony. Bad enough that Owen had the identity and location of an unknown fugitive. He wouldn't put Nguyen or even Sin in that position. But he couldn't stay and babysit anymore.

Standing abruptly at his decision, he shoved the papers down into his briefcase. No worries about getting permission to take the file; he'd simply say he assumed the copies were his. More importantly, he had to get back to Anni as soon as possible and he headed from the lounge back into the lab, knocking on the open door to alert Nguyen as he came in.

"Are you good here? I have to get back to Chicago." He hoped his voice didn't shake like his heart did.

"I'm fine." The lab geek waved him away, barely looking up from his screen.

It was the best Owen was going to get. Still he lingered for a moment, looking over Nguyen's shoulder at the peaks marching in neat pairs on the page. As he watched, his friend tapped the screen with a blue latex covered finger and a set of peaks lit up. He scratched something in his notes. Then he did it again at another peak. A third time, a phantom peak lit on the screen, but in red.

"What's the red?" Owen almost kicked himself as soon as he asked it. He just opened the door to a three-hour lecture.

"Well, this is a DNA analysis."

Yeah, he wasn't that dumb. He couldn't read the peaks like a book, but he knew what DNA graphs looked like.

For some reason, Nguyen took his eyes off the screen and partially turned in the chair. We collected all the prints, and I matched some of the partials. The DNA looks sound."

Owen didn't even know what that meant. What was unsound DNA?

His confusion must have shown on his face. "Unsound would be that I mixed several peoples DNA instead of making a big batch of one person's. It was a crapshoot, but I got it."

"How can you be sure?"

This time he grabbed a pen and used it as a pointer to tap at the screen. Owen winced and wondered what the local guys thought of his friend coming in and taking over the lab and touching the computer screens. But they were all neck deep in something of their own.

"Here's the kicker." He pointed to two peaks that meant nothing to Owen. "This is female. Since we could rule out our girl as a match, and our guy, and we matched Gilligan, these are the only prints left. And they are all from one woman."

*Well, that was something.*

Owen was getting ready to say exactly that, but Nguyen didn't have time for observations other than his own. "Some of these sets of genes indicate things. I mean I can't identify her but I can tell you a few things. Like she doesn't have any genes for obesity."

Clearly the person who snuck into the cabin in the night was not struggling with weight issues. He sighed, but his friend didn't hear it.

"And she has brown eyes."

*Oh shit.* That was something actually useful.

Maybe.

"She's of some Slavic descent. . . Not like fifth-generation American, like first gen or both parents. Or not American."

*Holy shit.*

Pulling up a chair before he even realized he was doing it, Owen waited for more information.

"She's negative for BRCA—that breast cancer gene, the bad one. She's not a descendant of Genghis Khan."

*Not helpful, not helpful*, Owen thought. But the words kept coming. "She likely has curly hair, a high reading ability and is a sprinter."

His head swam, it was a lot of information, but how would it help? Probably the most useful was that it was another female. In that line of work, females were rare. Probably not as rare as most would guess, but it did considerably narrow down his suspect pool.

If he had a suspect pool.

The sheer volume of what Nguyen was spouting off from information obtained from poor quality fingerprints was head-spinning. The utter uselessness of most of it was disturbing.

He had to get his brain back in the game. Had to leave the building, book a flight, and get his butt to Chicago where his wife was doing insane things all in the name of helping a friend.

His friend.

And "friend" was a loose term.

"I gotta go." He clapped Nguyen on the shoulder, pushing the chair back and wondering why he'd even sat down in the first place. "Let me know what else you get."

It was a formality that he said it. But he got a hollered out, "Looks like she's cilantro averse!" as he passed through the doors and back out the lobby.

He nodded to the guard and headed into the glaring sun, hoping there was still a flight to O'Hare that he could find a seat on. As light hit him, so did a disturbing sense of foreboding.

Sin glanced around the room. More lush paintings abounded. The fireplace was marble, the tables and couches antique. A mahogany pool table stood in one corner, getting use now that a party had grown up from their initial visit. It seemed the Kurev boys knew Ann Evalyn as a good-time girl. At a soft request she had called friends, Roman had pulled out his phone, and moment by moment the party had grown.

Even Nick showed up, drank some amber colored alcohol and talked shop with Kaspar and Roman. No eye contact was made until they were introduced. Nick not recognizing any of them would help solidify the idea that Sin was "Hayley"—friend of Ann Evalyn, party girl, and basic idiot.

She shook Nick's hand without the usual firmness of her grip. A good handshake had been solidified by her time as an officer and the need to assert herself as a strong presence from hello. Now, the limp, soft, almost offering-for-a-kiss handshake of "Hayley" felt uncomfortable, but Sin didn't let it show.

"Nicolay?" She drew out the ending of his full name. Kaspar had not given him the title of family in any way. Simply, "This is Nicolae."

The resultant cringe all three men involuntarily offered up at her mangling of the olde world name was fun to watch.

"Just Nick is fine." Even his hand didn't know what to do with her dangling fingers waiting almost for a blessing to the back of her hand.

Kaspar had only nodded to her, but Roman had given her a "Ya vamee ocharovan." Which she didn't have to pretend to not understand. When she shrugged helplessly, he winked. "Enchanted."

She smiled instead of shuddering.

Annika had been introduced as "Annie" and had given solid handshakes and polite but firm looks in the eye to each of the men. She was being billed as the smart one. Thus no one would be surprised that she spoke several languages fluently, had an advanced degree, or a calculating gaze. With the newbie, it was better to stick to the truth.

Aside from seeing him across the room a few times, that was all she had interacted with Nick, or either of the Kurev boys. She'd lingered around the room, making inane comments, getting herself the most complex mixed drink she could, chugging just enough to make it look like she was partying, then warming it in her hands until she could claim the ice melted, making it undrinkable. By the time she'd claimed the vodka tonic, she was pretty sure her reputation as an idiot and a flirt was solidified.

An eclectic mix of people had shown up surprisingly quickly. Somehow she'd thought the Kurevs would draw a mostly Russian crowd, but that was likely her embedded ideas of their father's family, ruled by tradition. These boys were running things differently. While the percentage of Russians was greater than in the general population, she learned that one man was from Ukraine, another from Estonia. Two men very recently from Spain, judging by thick accents, tried to hit on her in tandem. Two Irish men and an Irish woman were at the party—though one man was standoffish and cold, the other two plied her with drinks and dancing.

The crowd was amazingly diverse in heritage, though seemingly single-minded in their ability to come at the beck and call of a known mafia associate. Probably drawn by the lure of open Kurev gates and free drugs and alcohol. Some had spilled out into the hallway, and some had spilled yet more mixed drinks onto the priceless furniture. Sin reminded herself that she didn't care.

She giggled like a schoolgirl, smiling almost shyly as Kaspar had once turned his attention on her. Roman had been a second test, since he had looked directly at her as she pulled the trigger on him just a week ago. Either she had passed with flying colors or the Kurev boys were remarkable actors. In a fair estimate, Roman looked far too stoned to be good at much of anything tonight, leaving Kaspar as her only worry.

Walking up to the bartender who materialized as the party guests had, she held out her glass of vodka tonic. With a shrug and a side glance, asked him, "Is it déclassé to get more ice in this?"

Smiling, he simply scooped nearly perfect cubes into the tall thin glass, bringing the clear liquid to the top with only a few telling bubbles.

It wasn't like she was going to drink it anyway. Like the blond hair, green contacts, and the clothing, the drink was nothing more than a prop. The thought that she might be in the same building as Lee had kept her senses sharp. Though she hadn't heard any telltale thumping coming from stray parts of the mansion, the growing population of the party was a good cover for her to sneak away if she could. She hadn't planned it, but the opportunity had sprung up.

Working her way back through the crowd, she found Annika talking to someone she didn't recognize. From a distance, Sin raised her eyebrows, silently asking if she could interrupt. A return smile, a little too broad and excellently drunk looking, returned her answer.

Sin was proud of herself. She'd learned all these signals by watching, never having had need of them before recently. She'd only worked with Lee, and his codes had been logical, logistical, and far more discrete. The standard party fare had taken some coursework on her part, not having a chance to develop it through normal means.

Reaching out, she snagged Annika's free hand. "Annie! I must find the ladies room. Come with me." Then she turned to the man, apology on her face while her brain cataloged everything she could about him. She'd flip through files and mugshots with Owen later to see who she could identify.

"Sorry, have to go with my bestie!" 'Annie' shrugged. "Hayley? We'll come right back, won't we?" Annika kept her eyes on the man she was speaking to, even as he looked her up and down, her wedding ring not a hurdle to his conscience.

"Of course." Sin dragged her away, chatting with their heads together, speaking of inane party things until they were out of earshot.

They found a nearby restroom with relative ease, though they hadn't asked directions. It provided an excuse for Sin's absence later.

She didn't put bugging the guest bathroom above the Kurev brothers. Standing in close to Annika, she washed her hands, using the water to cover any sounds, and moved her head, shifting her long hair to keep cameras from catching sight of her mouth moving. Getting her lips read could get her killed.

"I need to explore as best I can. I'm going to disappear for a little while if that's okay with you?" Her words were at odds with the slight shrugging motion and the tilt of her head. All of which was designed to suggest she was whispering party secrets to her best friend.

"Yes. What's my plan if you don't come back?" Annika offered a perfect mimic of Sin's safety strategies. Thank god. She was a disturbingly quick study and Sin loved the woman a little bit more every day.

"Go home with Ann Evalyn any time after two a.m. if I'm not back." That would give her an almost two hour window, and she'd either get back, get herself out—which she was perfectly capable of—or get Lee out. She prayed as much as she was capable of for option number three. "Don't wait around. As soon as you get the opportunity after that, just go. And if you feel threatened in any way, get out. I can take care of myself. I need you to get back to Owen."

A small nod confirmed the plan and Sin went on quickly before they ran out of handwashing time. As it was, they were already a little too clinical for a party. "Are you getting anything?"

Annika turned off the water and began to chat openly. Her speech could be interpreted any number of ways, but the message was clear to Sin. "Oh, Hayley! I met this guy, Sergei, and he's totally . . . *up* there. Like, making bank." She giggled, "Says he's doing secret work and can't tell me about it. He loved that I speak Russian!"

"That's amazing. We'd better get you back in to him then." *Holy shit.* Annika had landed a decent sized fish. They left the rest room hand-in-hand only because Sin had seen a few of the other party girls doing it. Blending in was essential.

Annika beelined back for Sergei, finding him on a couch and squeezing in next to him. It was brilliant, and could conceivably get her friend in trouble, Sin thought. But she pushed the thought aside. Trouble for the three of them here tonight was a more than fair exchange for Lee's life. Though honestly, she and Nick had Kurev troubles long before now.

It was another fifteen minutes before she managed to beg out of the conversation, claiming to see someone down the hall that she absolutely must speak to. Being a mental midget was great cover, but holding back retorts and fawning over ridiculous statements by puffed up macho men was harder than most anything else. But she'd done it and she was down the hall, past the partiers and around the corner before anyone noticed.

Quietly opening and closing doors, she checked out room after room. She passed two offices, a guest suite, and a library that surely was just for show. There was a den, a sort of private playroom, different from the obvious room for entertainment that the others occupied. The house seemed even disturbingly larger from the inside.

Though Nick had told her what he knew of the place, he hadn't been able to give her much info about the back. He'd not been further back than the party room they were crowding into and spilling out of tonight. He told her the Kurev boys were welcoming to after-parties, that they liked to have people in the house, particularly drunk women. While he'd not fully handed her the keys to the kingdom, he had given her the lock picking kit for it.

Her heart pounded slightly less after she turned the corner and found herself in another back hallway. Back here, there was less chance of being caught, greater likelihood she would find what she needed. Better odds that she could take someone out without shutting down the whole party.

When she hit a back staircase, Sin examined it for a moment, deciding to go down. The narrow staircase was tread in wood planks worn in the middles from many feet going up and down them over time. A servants' staircase, it likely led to tucked away places off the main portion of the house.

Going with the theory that Lee would make a lot of noise if he could, he was more likely down than up and she hoped she didn't run into anyone coming the other way.

# CHAPTER 16

O wen's plane touched down in seemingly slow motion.
He'd left Anni message after message, and knowing
that tonight was the night she was headed to the Kurev mansion
made the lack of return messages more difficult to brush away.

He worried about her pregnancy. He worried about her being
Sin's sidekick. He worried about her being in the presence of Ann
Evalyn Kimmel and the Kurevs. While he trusted Sin and Nick to
do their best by her, their best wasn't always enough—as
evidenced by the current predicament. So Owen worried.

He called his daughters, thinking it would calm his nerves.

It almost did. It would have if the conversation had not
consisted of a weary Charlotte saying that she missed him and
her mom with equal parts need and disdain. The call might have
soothed him had Virginia not been so excited about her school
project—a batch of cookies—that she shouted nearly every word
at him.

He wasn't sure which was better or worse, the need or the
yelling. He wasn't sure when baking cookies had become a
graded project for school. And he wasn't sure when he and his
brilliant, sweet wife had started associating with known drug
dealers and cleaners specializing in wet work.

Rubbing at his face as the plane came to a standstill on the tarmac, he wished for his old days on special flights. Instead he was now a civilian again, stuck on a waiting plane because supposedly civilians didn't deal with men like The Mechanic.

An hour later he'd claimed his bag—the last one coughed up by the carousel—and dragged it out to catch a cab. The line of waiting cars had dispersed one by one as he'd waited, leaving him standing in the taxi line by himself, no taxis in sight.

He called Annika again.

The phone picked up before she answered. A giggle, a muffled word, and then, "Oh, it's my husband. I should maybe answer this." Then a string of words in Russian that sounded rather intimate.

He should have said yes when she offered to teach him.

It hit him as he stood there in line. His wife was in reaching distance of the remains of the family he'd spent years circling. They had no idea who she was. And he couldn't afford to tip them off. "I'll call you later. I'm in town."

It was safer with less talk. Surely Kaspar and Roman would not recognize his voice. But . . . What if they knew? Or found out? These guys had paid leaks in every law office in the US.

Though it was hard, he left Annika in her own care, trusting that she was capable, knowing that she was far wiser than he in many situations. Owen hung up the phone.

---

Sin found herself knocking on Ann Evalyn's door in the broad light of the afternoon sun. The air still pricked cold fingers at her, reaching for everywhere she didn't have at least two layers of clothing on, but Sin didn't feel it. She remembered the cold season before winter well enough.

Perhaps Ann Evalyn was still asleep at just after two p.m. They hadn't delivered her home until around three. Sin's search had yielded nothing in the way of Lee. The basement in the house held servant rooms as Sin had suspected. But many of the rooms were occupied not by people but by carefully grouped supplies.

Though small, maybe six by eight feet, one room held enough meth to get Chicago high for about a month. Pinkish in tinge, the quantity and color let her know it was their own creation. They dyed it, tested strange batches for their chemical code and promptly killed anyone trying to sell a knock-off on the streets. She'd read the reports. She stalked these guys the way teenaged girls stalked rock stars, except for the crying and screaming parts. Sin knew what they were up to.

Another room held an assortment of machinery that she couldn't identify. Still another held a disturbing myriad of laptop and tablet computers. Not all the same brand or size. None in boxes. Were the Kurev boys working run-of-the-mill robberies? That didn't make sense. The only thing she was certain of was that it wasn't legal.

Several other doors had held people behind them. Using Morse code, she knocked the letter L in staccato beats, knowing Lee would be listening for it.

But she didn't find him. She only found a few concerning folks who would open their door, look around and yell out to stop fucking with them, or find an empty hallway and mutter something about "assholes" and head back in.

None of them saw her, but if they compared notes, they would learn something.

In the end, she found a pile of evidence against the Kurevs, but not her husband. She made it back to the party without being missed, and she and Annika rode home, dropping off Ann Evalyn along the way.

Staying together in Sin's hotel room, they waited for Nick. Well, Sin waited, after fielding a late-hours call from Owen, Annika napped.

It was after four when the knock on the connecting door startled Sin and jolted her heavy heart. But she wasn't surprised by Nick coming through or that Owen walked in right behind him. His voice woke Annika, who hadn't been as asleep as she seemed.

"Anni." The single word conveyed happiness, relief, and a touch of irritation.

It was Nick who delved into the spoils of the night. Or lack thereof.

"I didn't get anything." He put both hands at his waist, clearly frustrated with the situation. He'd been casually prodding every Kurev contact he had for information on Lee and no one had produced anything useful. "I have near blueprint intel on most of their holdings, but until we have any idea where to start, it's useless."

His sigh reverberated around the room.

"I may have something." Annika spoke softly from the circle of her husband's arms. For a moment, Sin felt a stab of jealousy, but as with most feelings these days, she pushed it aside.

"What?" Every little bit helped. What seemed silly initially was sometimes later the most important thing. Sin retained all of it.

"So I was speaking to Sergei . . ."

Owen's arms visibly stiffened, though if it was the idea of his wife flirting with other men or the thought of her associating with such dangerous people was hard to tell.

Annika ignored the gesture and continued. "We spoke in Russian, so I'm sure several people there heard me, but it wasn't blatant. I was joking about how big and strong he was, and did he run a pirate ship?"

Owen frowned, but Sin understood Annika's workaround. She couldn't just ask the guy if he had a blond enemy locked up somewhere. "I asked him, 'Ah, ee gdyeh vih skrivayeetee plyenekov?' Which roughly translates to 'Where do you keep

your prisoners?' and he said, 'Mih pitayem eeh v temneetseh' . . .
'We torture them in the dungeon'."

Sin took in a quick breath. "The 'dungeon' was empty." Her
brain and heart struggled wanting to put pieces together. But how
would they even know if they held all the pieces.

Annika shrugged, as it seemed to be the appropriate gesture
for the whole operation. "I don't know if it means anything, but
he did claim to be Kaspar's right hand man."

"Oh, shit." Nick paced a tight circle. "Books."

"Books!" Owen popped up from his spot on the bed, leaving
Sin ready to scream, wondering what these amazing books were.

Annika seemed to be the only one who caught Sin's
confusion and explained while Nick and Owen scrambled to
boot up tablets and laptops, dug through bags producing USBs.
"Mug shots. Picture books. We have to remember faces."

That wasn't a problem. Sin always remembered faces. She'd
started memorizing anyone she had any level of interaction with
the night her home had been invaded. Even though those two
had long since been brought to account for what they'd done, she
could still have picked them from a line-up of a hundred similar
men. She would have no problems finding the party goers.

It was another hour and light was creeping around the edges
of the always-drawn curtains, when they checked their spoils.

Sergei was indeed Sergei. Sergei Orlov, well known Kurev
employee. They had also met and spoken with Jason Hulla, a
Pakistani associate believed to be trafficking Kurev goods
overseas.

The two women agreed on three more ID's, two known Kurev
associates and a third, a woman who was apparently very well
known in the wrong circles, Galina Casazza.

The last name alone was enough to make three of them upset,
but it was Owen who seemed to simply stop where he was,
frozen.

"Dr. Dunham?" Sin asked the simple question at the same

time Annika put her hand on her husband's arm and said, "Owen?"

Suddenly coming back to reality, he shook off his wife's hand and dug through his bag again, pulling up a file of paper copies. Too neat to be the actual file, this had been created for Owen, thus denoting its importance to Sin and making her more concerned.

"This." He stabbed his finger at page after page, opening the folder on the bed between her and Annika and flipping through almost too fast.

Printed picture after printed picture showed nothing of use. The man, always the same regardless of clothing, was clearly aware he was being photographed . . . Every single time. There was no picture of his face. A partial profile was the best Owen— and apparently the FBI—had to offer.

"Slow down." Gently pushing his hand away, Sin took control, turning back to the first picture. Watching Annika, she turned the pages, one by one, ignoring the stack of print behind the photos, she just concentrated on the match. But got none.

Neither did Annika.

Each time they said no, Owen let out another little piece of his breath. They went through the whole stack, Dunham's shoulders sagging with obvious relief.

Right as Sin said, "Nothing." Annika pulled the page from her hand, not noticing that her husband tensed right back up. She flipped to a blown-up, pixilated picture of a man, smoking on a dock, "This. When was it taken? And are you sure it's the same man?"

"It was taken a week ago in New York, and yes we're sure."

"How?" Sin had to ask, the picture was for crap. It looked like the same build, but . . . In a big city the chances of mistaken identity had to rise by too high a percent to make it worthwhile.

Owen crushed her question. "The photographer was following him with a team. Though the shot was terrible, they had a plainclothes pick up the cigarette after he dropped it three blocks later. DNA was a match."

Well, that cleared that up.

Annika nodded. "Look at his finger on his right hand."

Though the bandage wasn't overtly obvious, it was there. A black wrist brace slid along the palm of the hand and under the edge of his jacket. Nude colored bandages slimly wrapped his last two fingers together and with the other bandages it looked like he had several broken fingers.

The man was holding the cigarette with the broken hand, though whether that was a 'fuck you' to the damage or if the hand he kept in his pocket was simply worse off, she couldn't tell. Annika could though.

"He was there."

"SHIT!" Owen bellowed it loudly enough to blow Sin's hair back if it wasn't still plastered to her head from where she'd put the wig over it.

Ready to jump up and shut him up before he drew a noise complaint to their little illegal, four a.m. powwow, she stepped back as Annika did the job for her.

"You cannot yell like that!" She hissed the words in an accent strong enough to sound like she was maybe speaking her native tongue. "If you bring trouble on us, you bring it on Lee."

Sin was both shocked and touched by Annika's rage. For a moment, she simply glanced around. Both Nick and Annika were looking at Owen, Nick in surprise, Annika in anger, and they were all here for her. For Lee.

But she didn't get to bask in friendship for long. Owen nearly whirled on his wife. Though his voice was lower, his fear and fury were clear.

"That's the Mechanic. He's a known hitman of the worst kind—"

"Why is he called 'Mechanic'?" Annika asked as though she were asking about what to serve for dinner.

Owen was nearly sheet-white from holding back what boiled inside him. "Because he dismantles his victims by pieces. Sometimes he puts them back together."

Annika seemed almost impressed. "Well, he was there. And that picture is recent. I cannot tell you by his face, obviously, I can't match what you don't have. But I can tell you that the man I saw had that build and that hair and that damage to his right hand. . . I can give you a good drawing to go by if you want to bring in a police artist. But that's him; his hand is still healing. The other one is hurt, too. Someone did a number on him, but seemingly only on his hands."

*Lee.*

It rang through Sin's head with the clarity of a bell. Lee was chained to a chair, maybe because he'd done that. Though it was more likely he'd done that after he was chained. Had Lee not been tied down, he would have done a lot more damage than that . . .

Hope. It sprang up in her like weeds. And like weeds she would pull it out by the roots, not letting it interfere with the job she had to do.

Owen was silent for a minute, and Annika filled the void. "Get a sketch artist in. I can give you his face now. That would be a huge—"

"No." He cut her off, the sound low and deadly, pulling Sin from her planning. "I will not have either of you, any of us—" he threw a piercing glare at Nick, "—getting our names associated with that man in any way. It's bad enough he's seen your face . . ." He stopped.

"I am nothing to him. The sketch would help you catch him." Annika tried again.

"You ID him and you're not nothing anymore." Owen radiated frustration.

"How would they know? I can do it."

"No." He brooked no arguments. "There are leaks everywhere

—leaks back to the Kurevs, back to Vani Casazza. I can't put you at that kind of risk. I wouldn't do it myself. It's a ticket to hell."

Sin had never heard Owen speak like that. Apparently, Annika didn't hear that kind of vehemence that much, either.

Dunham was right, she decided. A link to The Mechanic was a link back to them. A sketch artist could easily render Annika's face from memory and put her on the books with disturbing ease. Sin changed the subject, "So Casazza has her daughter at this party, thus in close contact with either the Kurev boys or Ann Evalyn. Also, her henchman is here, . . . And a higher up says they keep their prisoners in the dungeon." She stood, walking her own tight circle for lack of room to move. "It may all be useless party talk, but it's the only thing we have to act on."

She looked up to see that they all agreed with her. "I'm going back to Ann Evalyn when she'll be awake."

Sin hated that she was catering to that she-demon, but a friendly Ann Evalyn was much more useful than an angry, hungover bitch. Sin was beginning to wonder if the woman really had sent her sons to an aunt's home or if it was cover because she'd literally eaten her own young.

The small hunting party broke up, with Nick deciding to crash next door and Owen and Annika heading back to their own hotel. Before they left, Owen looked at the group. "Everyone should be armed at all times."

"Always am." Nick replied quickly.

Sin just raised her eyebrows.

"That was stupid, Owen." Annika patted his arm, and he looked back at her.

And then they turned the knob, Annika shuffling her too-stiff hair into place, burying her face in Owen's shoulder, and they went off avoiding all cameras, while Sin tried to find a speck of sleep in the void they left behind.

For a while, sleep was hard fought, but eventually it hit her full force dragging her down. In the constant pull between Lee and her old life and the baby and a new life, Sin had no input. Her tired body overtook her brain and she crashed.

Even so, she woke, alert and on the prowl long before Ann Evalyn would be awake. But she had to figure out what the woman might know about the Kurev dungeons. Probably not much, but anything could help.

She rang the doorbell and pulled her scarf closer. Leggings kept her warm under a trendy pair of cargo pants. The deep cargo pockets hid weapons galore, including a flexible, short whip made of flat plastic that would extend her reach in a fight, slice a hand that tried to grab it, and evade detection in any kind of pat down.

So she stood on the stoop, a scarf for warmth when her jacket had to remain open to get to her weapons. And she rang the bell again.

Sure enough, Sin got a buzz on her phone, letting her know that Nick had intercepted some movement inside the house. He was running more back-up on Ann Evalyn, using time the night before to place tracking devices in the other phones she'd carried with her. Once they'd been in Nick's hands, she never should have trusted them, but Ann Evalyn was turning out to have a tendency for career ending mistakes.

The door jerked open, revealing an Ann Evalyn who was awake and in some kind of yoga outfit. Clearly she'd heard Sin at the door. She'd simply been ignoring her caller. *Bad idea.*

Not waiting for an invite, Sin pushed her way inside. "Did you get any intel last night?"

Not that she expected Ann Evalyn to be the best source, but it was worth a check.

"Kaspar is a horny man. Roman was stoned on Kurev meth, which he wants to move into the Czech Republic, and your man, Nick, is an unbelievable asshole." The woman could have been filing her nails while she spoke for all the disdain she put into the words.

As expected, it was nothing Sin didn't already know, and nothing she needed. But fuck Ann Evalyn. "How about this: tell me about the Kurev holdings in town. What buildings might have a dungeon? And where?"

A grunt came in response as Ann Evalyn turned her back on Sin and headed to her kitchen. Taking enough time to be a bitch and moving just fast enough to keep Sin from simply stabbing her, she gathered a single long-stemmed wine glass and a bottle of merlot and arranged them on the kitchen island. As Sin stood watching, the woman produced a corkscrew from the drawer, knowing she was burning time, she sniffed at the aroma of the wine before pouring herself a very old, very expensive merlot. Sin just offered a special smile at the pettiness. "Go on."

"I don't know anything." She offered a put-upon sigh, which Sin returned.

"If you don't know anything, then you're of no use to me." A shrug. "That's a problem."

A teenage eye-roll followed. Man, the woman was a ball of physical gestures, as though she needed to stay in motion today. Sin didn't take anything for granted. But she pushed. "Give me something. Now."

Sigh. "There's an old building they own, down by the docks."

It was so trite that Sin couldn't believe it was even true. Did every gangster own an old factory down by the docks? She waited.

A headshake. "It's still used as storage, but there are back rooms that Kaspar likes to use. Bear took me there once."

"What color is it? What street is it on?" Sin had flipped her phone to record earlier, with the mic turned up, she should be able to play this back later. Not that she would forget a single detail that might lead to Lee's whereabouts.

"Beige, with dirt. It's concrete, with square, high windows, not broken. It's on the street that crosses 102, off that Access road. 'G', I think." She took another sip of her wine as Sin eyed the glass.

It was too much information, too fast, on a topic Sin had brought up. It was probably mostly true. "Give me another."

Looking put out, again, she continued, rattling off three locations, a little description and what she knew of the street address for each. Leaving Sin with four places to check.

In exchange, Sin offered only a nod. Then she turned to go and Ann Evalyn made her mistake.

The sound was light, almost melodious—the sound of fine crystal breaking. Sin had expected nothing less, and sharp crystal was more deadly than glass.

Turning, Sin pulled a police baton from the old clip she had placed at her hip, the movement of her right hand fluid and unconscious. Her left hand pulled a second baton even as the first snapped open. It was the right-hand that led her turn, fake hair flying, as she countered the thrust of Ann Evalyn and her crystal knife.

More tinkling noises heralded the meeting of Sin's metal rod against the remainder of the goblet.

But Ann Evalyn now had a skewer made out of some of the sharpest edges known to man.

Sin's second baton crossed her first, the small ball at the end giving it weight and control as it came at the other woman at high speed. She didn't hit Ann Evalyn with the full force of it, still hoping to walk out of here with the other woman as her informant. Informants had to be alive.

Using the cross of the weapons in front of her, Sin stopped the other woman's forward momentum, keeping her crystal spear from coming closer. But Ann Evalyn was no untrained rube and though the force of Sin's push sent her stumbling backward, it wasn't from being off balance.

It took Sin a moment too long to see that the woman had purposefully fallen against the counter. The sound of a kitchen knife being drawn from a block was a siren call to kill.

Before the knife could come out, Sin made a short circle,

bringing her baton around and coming at Ann Evalyn from her less-defended side, the hand that still held what was left of the wine glass.

A look of fear passed the other woman's face as she saw the baton coming, but her movement—a sharp feint toward the counter—showed she was ready and Sin's hit missed the intended target.

She didn't have time to think, just to try to move out of the way as Ann Evalyn's knife, blade out, held in the grip of a trained fighter, came down on Sin's right arm.

# CHAPTER 17

This time Nick had a more direct line of sight to Dana. At this shop, his coffee was larger, with more caffeine, sugar, and other things he shouldn't have.

Nick never really thought about his health other than as a general way to feel good and stay in shape. For the first time he looked at the cocoa powder he'd added to the swirl of probably very heavy cream on something called a "Black Cat." It was wonderful, but it made him consider living to enjoy something as he got older.

He had no heir to kill him for the business. Nick's grandfather had killed Nick's great grandfather—his namesake—and while Nick hadn't killed his way in, he had certainly started the dominoes falling. His grandfather had been a bad businessman, an awful person in general, and terrible to Nick and his mother in particular. Nick had no regrets.

But he did need to change.

"I want to get out."

"We've talked about the money."

He sighed. "Can I keep some of it? Maybe a retirement fund? Give the rest to the dogs, IGF?" *In good faith.* He couldn't say that in a coffee shop, the feds followed the Kurevs around, the local police followed the Kurevs around, probably had undercover narcs in the Kurev establishment.

"You have to bail before the tide turns." He could see her head tip and her brown hair brush her shoulder.

"Yes. Sooner rather than later. Before the dogs do anything." If the police pulled a sting on the Kurevs and he was there . . . That would not be good. If they knew who he was, and he didn't doubt they did, he would be caught in the sweep.

He was Teflon on his home turf, but here? He wasn't so sure it would all roll off him. "I have to finish this. It may be another week. Maybe two."

Her shoulders heaved. "That may be too long."

There was a pause. He couldn't get out of what he was doing. Turning himself in, negotiating immunity, that would take time. He needed to finish finding Lee, then extricate himself from Sin. He'd hate himself forever if his change of sides brought her in as collateral. He wouldn't be able to protect her.

"I have to get this project finished before I start on the next thing. That's all there is to it. If it costs me the job . . . Then that's how it has to be." He stated it as though the project and the job were something that were expendable. Neither really was, but right now, he had to see Sin through finding Lee.

"Maybe there's another way." He could see her scratching notes on her notepad. He trusted her not to write anything incriminating. Their conversations were vaguely coded, surely her notes were, too.

Waiting for whatever she might say, Nick took a sip of his coffee and nodded mutely at the empty phone line. It took a few moments before she responded. "Do you have any friends in law enforcement?"

He laughed. He *owned* people in law enforcement, in several cities. And he had no idea what she was getting at.

"I mean federal level. Not someone you've *worked* with before, but someone entirely unassociated."

"So, bring in someone they trust."

"Yeah." She sighed. "You need to reach out soon. Get on the record now. Get the paperwork started, then sign on the dotted line in a few weeks."

He understood what she meant. "I think I'm catching a cold. My immune system isn't what it used to be."

"Do you want me to take care of that?" She understood. Nick wanted full immunity. He had a file thick enough to kill someone if dropped on their head. He knew it.

"It's a necessity." He'd leave the country before he'd rot in jail. But life in non-extraditing countries wasn't all it was cracked up to be. "Can you?"

"I need a few days."

She said goodbye. Nick didn't return the words, but lingered on the phone as though finishing a conversation. He said goodbye to a voice that told him his party had already hung up and would he like to call back?

Tucking the phone away, he took another sip of the coffee before reaching back into his pocket as though the phone had buzzed. Only the most alert coffee-goer would realize the phone he pulled out was not the same as the first one.

Nick texted Dana, making sure their methods of communication were scrambled, and never from the same number twice in a row.

I know someone. Higher up, like you wanted. Maybe could be a link?

What would Dunham think? Would he be willing to broker the deal? Did he even have an 'in' with the Feds anymore?

Nick didn't know any answers, only that Dunham was loyal to Sin.

Pocketing the second phone as smoothly as the first, he picked up his bag and left half of his Black Cat sitting on the table untouched.

Her arm stung and Sin pushed back against the knife. A red spot formed on her jacket letting her know that Ann Evalyn's blade had struck true and even pierced the leather of her coat. The fact that her hand still worked perfectly well told her that it was a nick, nothing more.

She'd underestimated her opponent. Hadn't counted that Ann Evalyn knew exactly where every weapon-at-hand could be found.

The Island and countertops were granite. The beveled edge would lessen a blow to the head, but it would still be pretty effective if she could get the woman's skull there.

Her left arm stayed across her body from where she'd struck and missed Ann Evalyn and the woman was still leaning in from her move. So Sin acted in the moment, twisting her wrist quickly up, snapping the ball end of the baton against the side of the other woman's skull, then followed through with the back of her hand, bashing it into the high cheekbone and hearing a small crunch.

Sin pushed forward, driving Ann back. They both had only a moment to recover from the crack to Ann's face and Sin took advantage, pressing her attack.

She simultaneously pushed the buttons and threw the batons, knowing they would retract as they flew away from her. It would cost her the weapons, but keep them away from Ann Evalyn, too, and Sin needed her grip.

Following the same arc she threw the batons with, she braced her hands against the counters on either side of her, the granite cold and thick beneath her hands. Bracing her arms added force to her kick, which she planted square against Ann Evalyn's collar bone.

It didn't yield the satisfying crack she was hoping for, and Sin wondered if the soles of her boots were simply not hard enough to cause the damage she wanted. Ann Evalyn kept her feet better than expected. By helping to throw herself backward, she stole some of Sin's momentum.

Even so, she cracked her back against the counter.

Not her head, as Sin had wanted, planned, but her spine wasn't a bad target either.

Still, Ann Evalyn stayed on her feet. Sin clearly surprised her by launching herself backward. Let Ann Evalyn scramble to keep up, Sin was moving the fight to somewhere better. Somewhere she wasn't pinned between the counters.

As she landed on her feet in the open spaces of the eat-in area of the kitchen, she let her jacket fall open. With a practiced move, she slipped her sais from their long pockets, knowing they appeared seemingly from nowhere.

It was the look on Ann Evalyn's face as the sais simply materialized that let Sin know the woman hadn't quite believed her before. Hadn't been positive that the same person who broke into her home, bugged her phone, and forced her to become an accomplice was the same one who left Kurev victims in a trail behind her. Sin almost smiled. "Wondering if I brought a big, red bow for you?"

There was no answer, but Sin enjoyed the expression.

It quickly changed from awe to rage.

Ann charged her with the knife slashing, her face contorting now, an odd look on a woman in yoga gear. But Sin didn't let the irony distract her.

The knife was heavy, sharp and definitely dangerous, so she side-stepped, knowing that not getting cut again was the best she could do. As she waited for an opening to get at Ann Evalyn, she noticed a drop of crimson on the near white carpet. Her own blood.

Without time to pay attention to the evidence she left behind, Sin sidestepped again, putting a chair between her and her attacker. The next time Ann Evalyn came at her, the woman veered slightly, making the mistake of expecting another evasive maneuver.

It cost her the knife as Sin wracked her arm with the side of one sai and used it to hold the arm in place while she punctured it with the point of her other sai.

Ann Evalyn dropped the knife, her other hand still lashed out with the crystal stem.

Though Sin was already moving out of the way, she couldn't completely escape the sharp object. Raising her left arm just a little higher, she ducked her head behind it, protecting what was important.

The edge of the crystal caught her jacket, tearing cleanly into the leather, but Sin was fast enough to keep this from getting to her skin—a feat neatly accomplished by sweeping Ann Evalyn's legs out from under her.

The floor was hard and the space was tight, but the other woman hit the ground already rolling. She was moving away from Sin even as she popped into a crouching position. Sin could have cornered her, but she didn't want a dog fight. Hoping for a neater end, she bided her time while Ann Evalyn regained her feet. Now too far away from the knife block, she was left with only the crystal stem and her own cunning as a weapon.

Sin now knew better and didn't put anything past this woman.

Ann Evalyn charged her, stem clutched downward now in her right hand, her thumb anchoring the base of the glass and giving her weapon an even more deadly force. Sin rolled her center of mass low and let Ann Evalyn come.

Though the kitchen was big, it took only two running steps for the woman to reach her. Ann Evalyn was ready for the immovable force that was Sin and she used her unarmed wrist to block the sais that were coming at her, making space to bring the stem down into Sin's shoulder—exposed where her jacket had fallen open during the fighting.

But Sin was fast. Faster than Ann Evalyn.

Dropping the sais, she ducked into the coming onslaught, letting them clatter to the expensive tile floor. Her movement into, rather than away from, the jab brought the sharp piece down behind her shoulder, not on it.

Standing suddenly, Sin used the target shoulder to force Ann Evalyn's arm up and her now free hands grabbed and controlled the one dangerous weapon the woman still had.

With one hand inside Ann Evalyn's elbow and the other at her wrist, Sin bent the offending arm backward. Though the other woman struggled, Sin remained in control. And the crystal, still firmly in Ann Evalyn's grip, was now aimed upward, just behind her own head.

Ann Evalyn fought to kick out a foot, forcing Sin around to the side. While that worked, Sin didn't let go of the arm she controlled, though her sudden movement did wrench it back just a little farther.

Seeing an opening, Sin took it. The stem and Ann Evalyn's arm were both pulled abnormally to the back of her head and Sin controlled Ann Evalyn's hand.

Aiming the sharp spear right at the back of the woman's head, Sin pushed.

A small sucking sound was the only noise as the sharp point slid neatly into the hole at the base of Ann Evalyn's skull.

She'd hit something good from the jerking motion that suddenly overtook Mrs. Kimmel's muscles. It wasn't done yet, but Sin didn't hesitate as she unfolded the clamped fingers from the wine stem and pushed the remainder of the shaft into the woman's brain.

With a gasp ending on a gurgled moan, Ann Evalyn Kimmel collapsed to the floor.

Owen looked over the map that Nick had spread out before him. It had been difficult to find a good paper map of Chicago. Since when had everyone gone digital? Thank god he had his own red pen.

He didn't consider himself behind the times, though maybe he should. He was definitely behind his wife, who easily worked her tablet, pulling up street views of many of the places he thought the Kurevs might be stashing Lee.

Nick told them what he remembered, while Owen circled things on the map, jotting down addresses and additional tidbits on sticky notes. Given the fact that he seemed so old school, he didn't mention his longing for a corkboard and a set of colored stick pins.

"Here." Nick pointed to another spot along the water. "It's a marina, there are lots of docks. I know Roman keeps a boat there."

"Hold on." Annika looked at Nick's finger, asked the exact address and while Owen made himself a sticky note, she tapped at her tablet. "I don't think so."

She had pulled up a photo of the building, a nice, clean looking marina center.

Owen looked at it a little more closely. "Maybe."

"Too nice." His wife countered, never afraid to tell him when she thought he was wrong. At least she wasn't mean about it.

"Actually, I think that's good. No one would expect it." He turned to Nick, who offered an agreeable shrug.

"I would—hypothetically, of course—keep a prisoner in an unexpected place. No one would look." The head of Vasilescu frowned at Owen's look of disbelief. *Hypothetically?* It was a reminder of who exactly he was working with.

Still, the man was Sin's brother. And while he might be the head of Vasilescu and own the Atlanta drug and gun trade, he was only frowning at Owen. He didn't look like a man who killed his own grandfather in the name of illegal business.

"Can you check out the nearby buildings?" Owen guessed the picture didn't show all of the marina holdings. And he was right. "Look there." He pointed as she pulled up a shot to the left, then the right of the first. "See? Those look like individual storage. They're numbered, key code locked?"

Annika moved her fingers, zooming in on the picture and nodded. "Individual number pads. High end, too. Possibly sound-proofed."

Owen put a green flag on the paper map, smiling in spite of feeling like a dinosaur. On his other side, Nick was pecking at his phone, his thumbs flying. Then he was on the line, talking to someone at the marina. Smart man. He was inquiring—as a buyer—what the storage was like, how much per year, and could he guarantee his privacy there?

Owen mouthed to him, "Ask who the owner is."

Nick complied then grabbed the pen, jotting the name down on a sticky note before clicking off. A spurt of satisfaction shot through Owen that someone else was using the paper. But it didn't last long. *Holden Enterprises.*

"Holden is owned by Jason Hulla. Known Kurev associate."

"He was at the party." Annika nodded. Owen should have known; she would never forget a name or a face that she had met that night. He shot up a small prayer that she'd escaped Belarus when she did. If her father had been KGB, it was even more likely that she would have been recruited as soon as they figured out how smart and adaptable she was. Owen still might have met her one day, but across the barrel of a gun. Instead, he smiled and planted an impromptu kiss on her mouth that Nick soundly ignored.

With Nick's new information, they were up to five possible locations where the Kurevs could hold a prisoner like Lee. Over the next hour, they found more. The Kurev brothers, through their shell corporations, held buildings all over town. Some were houses, which Owen thought should be crossed off the list out of hand, but Nick protested, pointing out that some had basements.

Owen had happily pulled out the photos Sin had been sent. Paper to the rescue.

These were the only copies of the photos, which Sin left behind when she went to see Ann Evalyn, as they might be some use to the "home team." No one had uploaded digital versions. It wasn't safe to have a picture like this anywhere digital. If a phone with that picture was searched by an officer, or even a Kurev associate, it could be the end of whoever was holding it.

Owen pointed. "It's dark, but it doesn't look like he's being held in the basement of a home." Square, concrete pillars rose behind the man in the chair. Owen pointed, though no one liked looking at the picture. He tried turning the image away from Anni, but she wasn't having it.

Her voice was soft. "These are support posts for a large building. Industrial."

"That takes out all homes." Nick added and Owen agreed.

"The floor is plain, poured concrete." Annika pointed to the lower part of the photograph, her finger avoiding blood in the picture as though it were on, rather than in, the photo.

Nodding, thinking, Nick spoke. "That rules out the boatyard, though I liked it."

"No." Annika countered, turning away from the bloody picture and back toward her tablet. "Given that Hulla owns the whole boatyard, it makes options. Lee isn't in a locked vessel storage unit, but he might be here . . ." She tapped, swiped and turned the tablet for the guys to see a warehouse on the site.

"Okay." Owen stuck the post-it note that he'd removed back onto the boathouse address. Two more locations fell away with added intel. While Owen scanned the map he noticed Annika fiddling with the manila envelope.

"Owen, Nick, where did this come from?" She didn't lift her eyes.

Nick ponied up the information. "It was a handoff. Someone at the restaurant, but I didn't see."

This time Annika looked at them. "Does that mean they know where Sin is? Someone found her. Several days ago, so why is she still here? They know that you know where she is?"

Adding those pieces together put Anni into an agitated state that Owen hated to see. But she held herself together admirably well. It was Nick who said the right thing.

"No they don't know. If this is them, they're stuck relying on bait. And I have one of my guys feeding them information with some errors."

"But why wouldn't they know where she is? What she looks like?" She was fast, Owen always gave her that. She and Sin were a force to be reckoned with. He only hoped they didn't stay that way much longer.

Nick shook his head calmly. "My guy says Kurev lost her after the cabin. Knows I knew her in Atlanta, and knows I'm here now. This is their only communication. They don't have good intel, or they would have recognized her, blond wig, green eyes and all, at the party. But they didn't."

"Roman was too stoned to recognize his own dog. I think he could barely tell guests from staff." Disgusted, but who knew with exactly what, Annika looked nearly ready to spit at the thought of the younger Kurev brother. "If it was Kaspar, then he's better than the rest of us put together."

"Exactly." Nick responded, opening the valve that let the tension out of Anni and thus out of Owen, too. "I don't think he is. Which means it's something else. I have guys deep enough in that they get me what they can, but I can't always get to them."

"How do you get that? I mean, how do you get guys like that?"

Owen almost jumped to cover her mouth the second the words fell out. His other option was covering his own ears and yelling, "Lalalallaaalaaalaaa" to drown out Nick's answer.

Fortunately, he didn't have to do either, Annika jumped in and saved them both.

"Never mind. I really don't want to know."

For his part, the Atlanta kingpin smiled, understanding.

At that moment, they were all interrupted by Sin coming through the door. Her dark sunglasses and blonde hair were in place as always, but while she looked cool coming through the door, the moment she crossed the threshold, her demeanor changed. Frustration, finally uncaged came off her in waves.

Annika saw something different. "Oh, Sin, you're injured!"

Did his wife even stop to think about *how* exactly this girl must have come by the injury? Probably not, for she jumped up and helped her new best friend remove her jacket with the holes and the single bloodstain on the arm.

Annika's eyebrows lifted as the removal of layers revealed a stack of paper towels held in place by clothing, the bottom one wet against the cut that was somewhere between superficial and serious. Blood began flowing as Annika peeled the paper away.

She sighed. "I had to get out and I couldn't touch anything that would leave behind any DNA evidence. I already left a few drops of blood on the carpet."

As Owen watched, Annika dragged Sin and the conversation into the bathroom. His wife patted at the wound much the way she would had one of their daughters been scraped up from riding her bike. "Any cuts or bruises anywhere else?"

"No, mom."

Sin had caught the gesture, too, but Anni didn't take it as an insult, even though Owen was pretty sure that Sin had never worried over a bruise. If it didn't bleed, she probably didn't pay it the slightest attention.

Nick came into the space, too. While it was plenty big for a bathroom, it had never been intended to hold four people, and this time it was Nick shoving people out of the way, his hands full of real bandages, butterfly strips, and some kind of glue. He held up a pack "Do you want stitches?"

Sin poked at the exposed spot on her arm, peered down into the hole that clearly didn't hurt her.

But before she answered, Annika asked, "What made the cut?"

Owen wanted to throttle her. They probably should have left Chicago a good two days before, but Annika wasn't having any of that. All his plausible deniability was jumping, piece by piece, from the tenth floor window. He shook his head and vacated the space even though Annika didn't. Instead, he tried to concentrate on the view of the city.

He could hear her, "Kitchen knife? Are you confident that it was clean?"

Sin's rich laugh wafted through the compact room. "I don't think that kitchen was used for anything but show."

"Still, we should wash it, but probably stitches aren't necessary."

Nick emerged, leaving the women to it. When he saw Owen looking out the window he was shaking his head, but changed his tack and spoke. "You probably shouldn't stand in front of the window like that."

It was a rude reminder. Nick had commented on his tendency to get as close to the view as possible. Though he didn't expect bullets through the window, he was mapping the likely locations of a hostage hold; not for law enforcement either. For people seeking their own brand of justice.

For a moment he scanned the room and realized there was no getting out. Covering his ears and screaming "Lalalaalaaa" at the top of his lungs wouldn't keep him out of jail. This had to go well. And Annika had to get out, too.

He was thinking their life savings might buy them a good lawyer, and was planning to hit Nick up for the money if this crazy adventure got him and his wife into legal trouble, when the sound came.

A heavy thump came behind him from the sky. In front of him, Nick startled, sending Owen swiftly around to look.

A small round pock marred the thick sheet of the window, cracks radiating out despite the fact that what had made the mark was gone.

Annika's voice called as he scanned the skies, fighting his urge to run closer to the glass and look for the source. "What was that?!"

Thank god she didn't come out of the bathroom. Nick was already in motion as Owen spoke as calmly as he could. "Bullet."

Two more quickly followed.

# CHAPTER 18

S in was not panicked. She'd expected this.

They had been found, and it wasn't shocking, despite the terror that had bloomed on Annika's face.

There had been no time to tell them about Ann Evalyn's demise, about nicking the woman's carotid artery for the point of making a mess. About using her old trick of mixing blood, so that no one spot on the carpet was purely her own blood. Once there existed a hair of hers from a crime scene. Somewhere there would be a fingerprint.

With Owen Dunham out of the FBI, there was no one there to kindly steal or replace her evidence. So Sin had to keep it from being found in the first place. That meant putting Ann Evalyn Kimmel's blood onto the carpet, diluting her own. That meant using a kitchen towel to wipe down anything that might have left a trace, including Ann Evalyn, whom she'd fought bare handed.

DNA could be lifted from so many places. It took Sin an hour to clean her evidence, locate the woman's phone—dropped in the scuffle—and remove the chip Nick had planted. Then she remembered to find the second phone.

Still, it was a lot of work getting out of there and not bleeding more while she did it. Luckily Annika had now done a nice job of pulling together the edges of the hole, though she'd been reluctant to just glue the skin together as Sin insisted.

The bullets changed everything.

It was an attempt on at least one of them, if not all of them.

It meant they'd been found.

But there was no way anyone could get up here and get them all. Thus, the end of the bullets was the end of the issue—at least until they got out of the building.

It was more important to leave no trace, than to leave quickly.

It meant her go-bag came out. Guns, spare weapons and cleaning supplies. She handed one compressed stack of antiseptic wipes to Nick, hair sprayed his hair and sent him into the next room. Without being asked, Dunham held his hand out for the spray and followed suit, though lacking the ease and adding a heavy dose of fatalism.

Silently, even Annika took a disposable wipe and cleaned every surface in the main room while Sin stole her own trash. She wasn't worried about her own hair, she hadn't even pulled the wig.

It took twenty minutes to leave. Maybe that was too long, but it was necessary. The bullet was just a message, she had every confidence of that. But from whom?

Owen was ready to pull Annika right out the door when she pointed out—not in so many words—that they were safer with the assassin and the mafia don. Owen disagreed, pulling his own gun from an ankle holster, another from the bag he carried. He handed the smaller one to Annika. With no goodbye other than a nod, he pulled her out into the hallway and through a nearby door.

Sin and Nick weren't too far behind, taking a different set of stairs which were a tomb of echoing concrete. The ability to sneak down them without alerting anyone coming up was almost a near impossibility. Sin and Nick both kept guns in their hands but held down and away, ready for any random guest or hotel employee to pop into the stairwell. She had a ready story that wouldn't arouse suspicion . . . Just in case.

Though she was alert for a battle, for Kaspar Kurev or the Mechanic or even a new face to pop out and try to kill her at a moment's notice, none of it happened. And she wasn't surprised by that. She wondered if the bullets had just been a message.

The "glass" in the hotel room windows wasn't glass. It was a thick polymer. Virtually bulletproof as a side effect of being high-wind pressure proof and idiot-trying-to-kill-himself-from-our-hotel-window proof. It was possible the bullets had never been intended to hit them, it had only been a way of saying "I know where you are."

So she would change that. They would move again.

She and Nick left the hotel going separate directions, Nick on foot, Sin in her car. He had less to carry, and she circled the city for a while, until she was certain she hadn't been followed. Then she headed to a motel on the outskirts of the city.

She'd been here before, with Lee.

They didn't check ID, didn't give a shit if she rented two rooms or ten. The place was a shithole, which meant it didn't require upkeep from her. So she'd gotten the room here about three days after she'd gotten to town, and for exactly this purpose.

Sin didn't contact any of the others. They would have to trust that she was okay, just like she would trust them. Opening phone lines now could ping where they were, what the new locations were. That could bring more trouble if the intent had simply been to divide and conquer.

Never one for praying before, she opened the space blanket and laid down on it, sandwiching herself inside, and found herself talking to any deity that would listen. She prayed for Owen and Annika, relative newbies at this game, probably the most likely to trip up. They should not get hurt for helping her. For Nick, who had something going on that he hadn't told her about. Sin was used to his secret meetings, but not to the heavy weight that settled around him. It had been there after Reese's death, but this was different. And lastly, always, for Lee.

*Hold on*, she thought, *I'm coming.*

She drifted into an uneasy rest.

---

Owen's heart had been close to beating out of his chest for about four hours. Annika was the calm one. And thank God, because if he was the one carrying their child it would have fled screaming for all the stress he was under.

Despite his raging heartbeat and labored breathing, all controlled by stark fear, he had nothing to feed his churning brain. Since they were holed up in a new hotel room after buying new, empty luggage to check in with, he didn't have any strategy to plan.

Annika laid back on the bed, nodding off with a paperback she'd picked up at the store where they'd gotten the luggage. She was so placid!

In a flash of insight, he saw her, nine-years-old and terrified, running through woods and clinging to a tiny boat on dark seas in a storm. She'd told him all of this. He'd always thought of her as brave, strong, smart, but he realized now that at a young age she had conquered a bone-chilling fear that most people never even came in contact with.

This was nothing to her.

This was helping a friend. Maybe this was payback. In the past she'd mentioned three different people, only one of whose names she knew, who had selflessly helped her and her mother escape Belarus. This was a woman who, as a mere child, had thrown herself on the mercy of an American consulate with legitimate cause to seek asylum.

He wouldn't have thought it possible, but his admiration for her went up.

A second flash came on the heels of the first, only this one was seven years too late. He suddenly understood why none of his good criminals seemed to care when he arrested them, why no one was afraid of him or the FBI.

He realized now, that anyone who was afraid of *him* was either a good, prison-fearing citizen or else knew that the FBI would expose them and they were afraid of their other enemies finding them. That was it. No one was afraid of Owen Dunham.

He was trained *not* to shoot. Not to kill. In fact, he was obligated to try to save anyone in his custody. While clearly, the other side was fucking, batshit crazy and had no compunctions about killing.

Just look at Sin. She said she'd taken care of the Ann Evalyn problem. Owen was pretty certain that meant Mrs. Kimmel was dead.

Just as he was thinking, once again, that no one was afraid of him, and with good cause, his phone rang. Nick.

"Yes?" No names, no ID. Vocal recognition was bad enough.

"I need to talk to you. I need your help." Nick's voice shook, just a little as he offered up the last word. "Please."

*Holy shit.* Maybe Nicolae Stelian was afraid of Owen Dunham. That was indeed a very scary thought.

It took an hour—an hour of watching Annika sleep with a peace he could not find for himself—before Nick managed to rent the room across the hall from Owen and Anni, and Owen headed over for this mysterious talk.

He left the door to his room ajar, and left the door to Nick's room open behind him. When Stelian raised his eyebrows, questioning the move, Owen didn't change his expression at all. Those were his terms. He had to be able to see Annika's foot on the bed, know when she woke up, if anyone came into the room or even checked it out. Paranoia was settling deep into his gut.

Nick invited him to sit, then proceeded to leave Owen with his jaw hanging open.

First, Nick pulled out a hundred dollar bill from his wallet and handed it to Owen with the words, "I'm hiring you as my attorney."

"I'm not an attorney." He shoved the money away, only to have it jabbed at him.

"You went to law school."

"I passed the bar but never worked as a lawyer." It took him far too long to realize what Nick wanted. "Attorney-client confidentiality."

Only a nod in response and another attempt to hand over that one-hundred dollar bill. "I'm not a lawyer, you need a real lawyer."

The words were necessary, though Owen admitted to wanting to take the money and the information. He was curious as hell, and the relationship would protect him, too.

Nick agreed. "Anyone can represent themselves. I don't have to have a licensed, practicing attorney. Find a loophole."

"It won't stand up in court."

"It doesn't need to. It just needs to get us to a place where we can talk."

This time, Owen took the money and thought for a while. Twice while he was thumbing through his mental inventory, he checked through the open doorways, looking for Annika. He took another twenty minutes to write out a document regarding the loopholes and that all agreed. He wrote Nick a receipt, and Nick signed everything, before telling him. "You have to close the door."

Big. It was going to be big. *Shit.*

With a nod, he went across the hall and woke Annika, though he hated to do it. She couldn't be there with him—no attorney client privilege. But she needed to be protected.

He left her there on the bed, book in one hand, gun in the other, looking as content as she might at home. His heart turned over and he wondered for the hundredth time today alone just what he'd gotten her into.

Owen had no sooner closed the door than Nick began speaking. "I'm getting out. I need immunity."

Everything in him froze. Stelian was done? Owen asked exactly that.

A nod, a few words. Nick was smart. He wasn't handing over anything of value until he had agreement. "You're FBI—"

"Former FBI." The distinction was important to Owen and should be to Nick.

"Former, but still with connections into the Bureau. Still with the trust of the current Agency. If I come in on my own, I'm not safe. I come in with you, you get the accolades and I get a deal. I *need* a deal. Or I stay where I am."

"What are you willing to trade?" Owen knew how this worked. He was shockingly ready despite the fact that this came at him entirely out of left field.

"Names, dates. Anything and everything I have on the Kurevs. And old intel about crimes committed under my grandfather. I can close a lot of cases."

"You're a detective in the Atlanta area, you can close them yourself."

A smirk and a nod. "Only by exposing what I do."

Oh, Owen was so curious. He could know what was happening and not become liable for it himself. The temptation was overwhelming. But the truth was the truth. "I can't guarantee you immunity."

"I know. But you can keep yourself from becoming involved because of your own knowledge and you can also negotiate the deal for me, even though you can't write the paperwork yourself anymore. You know who to go to. You can speak for me."

All true.

Though the papers were already signed, Owen held out his hand in a gesture of good faith, for the first time thinking that maybe his initial trust of this man had not been misplaced. The handshake felt like something solidified and Owen opened his mouth only to have his phone ring.

Sin.

---

She'd gone to them, to Owen and Annika, and Nick had been there, too. Something was going down with Nick and Owen. Sin had interrupted an important conversation, but she didn't have time to stay and find out what it was.

Ann Evalyn was no longer a source of information. It was only so long before she'd be found anyway. Maybe even already. She'd considered more than once that Ann Evalyn's demise triggered the bullet hole. There had been enough time that she could have been found and the order to say "hello" via gunfire could have been enacted. But Sin didn't think that was it.

She wasn't a big believer in coincidence, but shit was going down. Owen was scared. Annika wasn't but should be. And Nick was in up to his neck in something she didn't know about. So she interrupted and asked what they had.

Owen showed her the map, Annika chiming in about likelihoods and probabilities. Nick put in his two cents and she compiled a stack of post-it notes with addresses and names and scribbled notes on them. She would destroy them as she used them, rather than leave a manual for anyone to trace her steps. But there wasn't time to memorize them here. Her memory of the pictures Annika had pulled up for her might be enough.

She was headed out the door when Owen pulled her aside.

"We got DNA from the second person at the cabin."

Just the thought punched her in the gut and she fought not to let it show. "Who was it?"

She liked the past tense even as it came out of her mouth.

Didn't make it seem as if the problem was still ongoing, even though it was.

"We don't know."

She was turning away at the pitiful response when Owen grabbed her arm. Sin reached for his fingers, prepared to peel them back and bend them so that he would literally jump away from her to avoid the pain before she remembered whose hand was on her. And before he remembered it was a bad idea to grab her. Neither of them mentioned it.

"But we did get a lot of information. It was a female."

That matched the fuzzy memory she had of the night. For a moment it hit her that so much time had passed. She wondered if Lee could still be holding on. How would he have lasted? But she pushed the thought aside so that she didn't give up. Not yet anyway. She couldn't.

In the end, she took a note from Owen, it was just a list, and while she wanted to tuck it in her pocket for later, the sticky part clung to her fingers. And when the silence of everyone wondering what everyone else was up to began to permeate her thoughts, she pulled up the note and looked. Slavic—recent ancestry. Curly, dark hair. Neg. BRCA. Neg Genghis relative.

What the hell good was that? Was she supposed to go around asking people if they were related to one of the most evil and successful conquerors in history? She raised her eyebrows at Owen and he only shrugged in response.

Oh well, if she had to deal in terms like "lactose intolerant," "sprinter," and "likely cilantro adverse" then that's what she would deal in. "Brown eyes" would be a winner, but no one in her business used their real eye color. Not anyone of consequence. But she nodded and thanked him.

She was wondering how to get out of this impromptu gathering with any grace. How to let Owen and Nick get back to their conversation without making a scene. Though she wore black sweatpants and a baggy red turtleneck under her thick jacket, she was armed to the hilt. The jacket had changed, this one had no holes, though the same couldn't really be said for the arm under the sleeve.

She'd seen the picture of Lee. Alive or dead, he'd suffered much more than the puncture of a previously unused kitchen knife. The cut didn't bother her; thoughts of her husband did.

She turned to go when Annika asked the question that would start a shitstorm she didn't want.

"Where are you going?"

Shrugging it off, Sin simply looked at the other woman like, *What do you mean?*

It didn't work. "You're armed to the hilt. You're off to do something of importance. What?"

"I'm after the Mechanic."

# CHAPTER 19

Nick's night had been rough, and it had started early in the evening.

Dunham didn't want to leave Annika alone, and he also didn't want Sin out following the Mechanic. Though the former agent was trained in shadowing people, chances were next to nothing that he matched Sin's skills.

Thank god his sister had left before Dunham suggested that they tail Sin. Nick immediately pointed out that would mean leaving Annika alone, which effectively shut down that bad idea.

Also, Dunham wanted to hear what Nick knew. He started with some old murders. "My uncles—"

He didn't get a third word out before Owen interrupted him, "Italian uncles, or real blood relatives."

"We're not Italian." Nick deadpanned, and was met with a dead-on *you know what I mean* look from the former agent. "Actual relatives, but not my grandfather's sons. Not in direct line. They are Bun's cousin's sons." Jesus. Clarifying relation in a Romanian family was like restoring a tangled spider web. But he tried. It was another almost ten minutes of family tree organization before Nick could tell Dunham that he knew where Uncle Stefan had hid the body.

"Bun?"

"Romanian for grandfather." Nick clarified. "Emilian Doru Vasilescu."

"So this Stefan was accused of the murder of his girlfriend, in what year?"

Nick hadn't realized the process would be so tedious. He thought he'd sit down, tell Owen some secrets, throw some of his group under the bus, where they needed to be, and head out. Instead, Dunham wanted a full accounting. He wanted to know exactly where to find the body.

"Are you going to dig it up?" Surely he just needed to be able to say where it was.

"Yes, not personally, but I'm going to hire someone and have it genetically tested."

"Holy shit. Isn't the information good enough?" He and Dana had discussed that he would go through a lengthy process of being detained and relaying info, before he would walk out a free man.

Owen put down the pen and stared at Nick long and hard. Nick could feel the look in his bones and suddenly he was glad that the agent wasn't after him. Though surely some were literally on his case.

"You ran an organized ring of drugs and guns in Atlanta. That's huge Nick."

But he was offering good intel.

Owen had other thoughts. "You want to walk free. Do you have any idea what it will take for you to walk away from this without the sum total of the FBI's resources following you for the rest of your life?"

Apparently, he really hadn't. Dana had suggested this, but maybe he had misunderstood the grandeur of his need. Maybe she hadn't known. Maybe Dunham was wrong.

Dunham wasn't wrong. He was too methodical, knew exactly what he was doing.

When Nick glanced at the other man's notes, he saw that coordinates had been written down, along with a few other jottings that weren't English. "What's that?"

"My own personal shorthand so that these notes can't be used against you in a court of law." His eyes were dead serious and Nick thought about what else he had to offer. But Dunham asked the next question. "Where can we pick up this Stefan?"

"You can't. He's dead."

"That's not much help."

"But Uncle Dorin is alive. Barely. He killed Stefan."

Clearly, it was a great effort for the FBI man to keep from smacking his hand flat to his face. Nick was pretty sure he mumbled, "Of course he did" before continuing with the questioning.

Nick handed over three meth houses that he knew of in the Atlanta area.

"These are your meth houses?" Owen was strained by the information.

"No. I don't run meth. It's horrible for communities."

The *what the hell are you talking about?* stare that Dunham gave him told Nick what he was up against.

He tried again. "I run—"

"Shut up!" Owen held his hand out even as he jerked his head back, as though he could move far enough to stop the sound from traveling to his ears. He didn't have to worry, Nick shut up.

"Only answer the questions. I don't want to know about the rest." He muttered something Nick couldn't understand, again. Then said, "Not now, maybe not ever."

So Nick picked up the first thread. "I don't run meth. The Kurevs tried to filter it into my town without my permission."

"Didn't hear that last part."

*Jesus.* Nick sighed like a teenager. He felt like one too. "Can I tell you that I shut down meth houses left and right? Did you know that Atlanta has one of the lowest meth addiction rates of any major city in the US?"

"So you're just a mafia don with a heart of gold?" The words were harsh, damning.

Nick wanted to retort, sharply, but there was something to it.

He'd always considered Atlanta his town. Well, it had been Bun's town, and it had been pretty bad then. But Nick had been running White Oak. He put guns in hands; the gangs were his gangs. They kept Kurev meth out of his town and ran cocaine, the most innocuous of big money drugs. But Owen had a point.

Nick now ran Atlanta his way.

He'd never been brought up on charges. In fact, most of the word was that his people ran the show. He'd kept it so no one could get anything on him. Working a full time job with the White Oak PD was about the best cover he could get. The only thing that connected him to Vasilescu were rumors.

And large off-shore bank accounts.

"Fine." He sat back and waited for the next question.

"So where is your grandfather's body—" Owen held up a hand before. "Don't say anything that tells me *how* you know where it is, just *where* it is."

"I don't know."

Owen blinked. "That's seriously the most useful piece of information. How do you not know?"

"You just told me not to—"

But again, Dunham interrupted him. "You didn't—" He waved his hand, apparently not wanting to say the word,— "him?"

"No! I didn't—" he gestured wildly "—him."

Owen frowned. "But you ousted him."

"Yes." Nick waited for the next cue.

"He left quietly?"

"No." He sighed, Dunham was never going to get to what he needed with this binary questioning. Not tonight anyway. "Look. I never killed anyone. I set things into motion. The table turned on

Bun, plenty of people wanted me in and him out by the time it happened. It wasn't me. I don't know what happened to the body."

"You never killed anyone?"

"No. Well . . ." *Shit.* "Five times weapon drawn, three shots, one wounded, two killed as an officer. That's it. All three shots found 'righteous' by Internal Affairs."

"Which you had in your back pocket." It was just a statement, but Nick exploded.

"No!" He jumped up, nearly yelling. This was not going the way he planned. "Do you not trust anything I'm telling you?"

Dunham stayed seated, cool in the face of an outburst Nick was already not proud of. The man was steel in an interrogation. Nick wondered if he would have broken Sin had things gone another way back then.

Owen's voice was calm when he spoke, but he waited for Nick to sit down. The barely leashed frustration came through in his voice. "I'm trying to get you out. You said you wanted to get out. This is what it will take."

He took a deep breath through clenched teeth. "I do trust you. My pregnant wife is in the room across the hall. I'm here in Chicago on a dangerous mission to help a friend and I'm still here—" his voice started rising "—despite the fact that someone fired a long range rifle at me earlier today! So don't question my dedication to this shit-show!"

Nick nodded. Dunham was right on all counts. But before he could apologize, the man spoke again.

"Now do you want to get out or spend your life in prison?"

Nick thought there was a third option, which was just go on as he had been. No one had caught him yet. But he didn't think he'd last much longer that way. "I want out."

"How far out do you want to get?"

Nick didn't know there were variations on the theme. So he

asked. And Owen Dunham shocked the crap out of him with his next offer.

***

Sin sat back in her car, not tired at all. The subtle red-brown of her wig startled her each time she caught a glimpse of it in the rearview mirror. Occasionally she cranked the engine and drove around the block, stopping in a new but equally shaded parking spot each time. The Mechanic surely was keen on people tailing him. She would have to stay smart if she wanted to stay alive.

The awful car served its purpose, staying unobtrusive and running well. The time it took to find it was well spent. Lee had given her the tools she needed to find him. The knowledge of cars —how to find out which ones were common, how to walk into a dealership and buy a car with cash and not be remembered. She was using all of it now as she watched Kelly Gilligan in his hotel room.

If The Mechanic realized he'd been followed he didn't show it. When he arrived at the small house, he looked around then pushed the lock on the silver-colored sedan that he drove. He, too, seemed to have a good grasp of being unobtrusive. Probably why the FBI could never quite find him.

The man had let himself into the Kurev-owned property at 5436 South Ridgewood Court with no pretense of subterfuge, before disappearing behind the deep green door that looked like any other door in the neighborhood. The curtains didn't even twitch. For all that she could tell, he had no idea she was here, watching. And, while Sin knew the time would be uninteresting, she was interested.

Around nine in the evening, she circled the block again. She traded cars for a second, simple sedan at a nearby parking lot. This time she parked just a few spots away from his car, as she expected the Mechanic to leave the house soon. Surely he hadn't turned in for the day at 5p.m.

Getting out of the car as though she were headed somewhere, she walked down the block and grabbed a soda from a nearby gas station. Though the weather was chilly, she wasn't the only one out on foot and she blended in nicely. Even if Gilligan was watching specifically for her, he should have a hard time recognizing her. On her return walk to the car, she positioned herself away from his windows, so he couldn't see her even if he looked, then—for the benefit of anyone else—she let her purse slide off her shoulder just beside his car. When she stooped to pick it up she stuck a cheap tracking device under the bumper.

She'd had good luck using one in the past, as long as they weren't found. She wondered if Gilligan would look. Though this one was cheap, it operated on cell signals, not radio, which he might not check for, even though he should be sweeping his car every time he got in.

She climbed back into her car and drove around the block again. This time parking on the side street, where she could only see the car through a slit between the massive trunks of several trees. Had the season been different she wouldn't have been able to see, but the trees were bare and left her with a view of the Mechanic's car. If he was smart enough to look for a bug, then he'd also be smart enough to pop it off and leave it in the street. That way, anyone who was just watching the bug would sit quietly, thinking the car hadn't moved, and only when they got suspicious would they discover they'd been tracking an empty parking space.

Sin wasn't going to be that person.

By sitting and watching the car, she didn't have to turn on the tracker until he was already in motion. That would make it even harder to find, forcing a physical examination of the car to locate the actual signaling device.

It was three hours later that Gilligan came out the front door.

And he looked a hell of a lot more like The Mechanic this time. His hair was slicked back, his clothing dark. In the deep shadows surrounding him, only the streetlight caught him. If she hadn't been looking just then, she would have missed him. Probably the neighbors, if interviewed later, would never know that this man had left his home at 10p.m. dressed for a kill. He carried a duffel bag that Sin would have loved to get her hands on. Instead, she hoped he would lead her to Lee.

Dumping his bag into the passenger seat, he disappeared from view for a moment. Then reappeared on the other side of the car.

*Now or never*, Sin thought. He did sweep the car and she held her breath until he climbed in behind the wheel. As he started the car, her mood turned just a little lighter.

Still, when he pulled out and down the street, Sin didn't even start her car. She simply turned on the cell phone she'd linked the device to and waited for it to pick up the car.

A genuine smile bloomed on her face as the dot appeared on a map program and she pulled from her own spot, staying a good distance behind Gilligan. There were enough side streets and enough traffic crossing that she needed to keep reasonably close. That same problem luckily also afforded her cover. So she carefully balanced between too close and too far with the cars. There was always a danger of the Mechanic spotting her.

Turning on the audio switch on the tracking device, Sin listened as the car was filled with an obnoxious *beep beep beep*. The speed of the synthetic chirp was correspondent to the receiver's distance from the bug. Old school style, it got a little longer when the Mechanic made it through a stop light and Sin didn't, but the sounds came closer together as she got closer behind him. Using the map, she confidently pulled ahead of several other cars and caught up in time to see Gilligan take a turn and aim for the freeway on-ramp.

Sin simply followed.

In the past, she'd often followed people, often stayed awake and alert for days on end. But none of those times had the work been this important. She was alert, on task, and focused like never before. Lee's life depended on it.

Gilligan hit the gas and Sin hung back a little further, allowing the beeping of the bug to space out as he gained some distance. The freeway system here was rapidly changing and she didn't want to miss an interchange or an exit that Gilligan might take advantage of, so occasionally she got close enough to get a visual. She didn't want to have to turn around at the next exit and backtrack and play a bad game of 'hotter/colder' in busy city traffic.

Cars in between shielded her from his view, and then there was the forgettableness that she had worked so hard for that worked to his advantage as well. Just like Lee had taught her, she had on a non-descript baseball cap, and sat in the car in such a way that it was difficult to discern her gender. The Mechanic probably wouldn't recognize her even if she pulled up even with his car. But she didn't take that chance.

Twenty minutes and two interchanges later, she exited onto a cross road that was smaller and seemed to lead to better places, but it wasn't a stop, only a turn. A single gas station sat at the exit, and the building didn't look as though anyone of any class had graced it in a long while. This was exactly what she was hoping for. Something out of the way; someplace a person could stash a dangerous prisoner.

He took two corners onto smaller and smaller roads, forcing Sin to hang back to not be noticed.

Then the car stopped.

Sin hit the brakes, not wanting to pull up beside him, and she waited a beat or two. Let another car pass her and take the turn taking it past the point where the Mechanic had stopped. Then she drove past herself, looking straight ahead, not as though she were lost, but as though she were curious about the area.

The Mechanic's car was empty.

He'd simply parked it and walked away.

But to where?

Though there were buildings on all sides of her, these looked like small shops. He'd parked in a lot with a four-hour parking sign. Given the looks of the place, none of that seemed well-enforced.

Had she lost him?

She fought a bitter laugh as she tracked down the road. She'd been shaken off. And good.

Sure none of the shoppers had looked like the Mechanic, but she didn't expect them too. About to rail at the universe for its cruelty, she turned the car around and headed for home, wondering when she'd find him again and how.

As she pulled up to the light, several cars pulled up behind her.

*Holy shit.*

The Mechanic was in the car behind her.

What the hell. It wasn't like she could follow him from in front, especially without her tracker. The worst part was that she knew she was onto something. She believed she was being led to Lee. So she acted lost, carefully turned to the right, hoping that was the direction he was headed. She kept him stuck behind her, letting the Mechanic get antsy and pull around. Then she tailed him down the street. The car stopped less than two miles later, purging itself of a lone rider.

The Mechanic headed into a closed bar.

While she was thrilled that she'd made a good guess, Sin was also pretty certain that this little operation was over. He walked into the bar midday, blending right in with the local scenery. The kind of service was noted only by the faded sign hanging from the narrow porch. The windows were boarded up, the door bolted heavily. No one would notice him. But they would notice her.

Though she was dressed to blend in, she was dressed for the area where his house was, not here by the warehouses. And how would she get into the building without him seeing or hearing her?

Disgust filled her, to be so close, and yet be so thwarted. The Mechanic had disappeared, bag and all, into a locked building. If she went in, she had to be prepared for a fight. And she wasn't prepared. She had no clue what or who awaited her. What if Lee wasn't even in there but others on the Kurev payroll were? What if she got herself caught? No offense to her friends, but between Nick, Annika and Owen, it was a crapshoot between Annika and Nick who could take this guy, and Sin wouldn't honestly bet on either of them given what she'd read in Owen's files.

Unable to stay sitting in the car here at the curb, she had to go find a parking spot, then scope out what she could. Big mess.

She normally wouldn't have done it. But the decision was made simply because she didn't have anything better to do. She didn't have any other real leads on where Lee might be held. And Gilligan hadn't quite sloughed her off yet, though he sure was giving her a good rub.

Parking close to the building but around back from the entrance, she managed to get the scope of the place. Three stories, covered windows except for the top floor. The staircase leading up to the porch and the cinderblock that made up the base of the building suggested a partially sunk basement.

She had done her recon, and made it back into her car to sit and wait.

For fifteen minutes she tortured herself with the thought that Lee was in that building. That she was so close, but couldn't risk it.

As far as she could see, the only person in there was the Mechanic—no one else had gone in. She was watching from her driver's seat, map ready at hand in case she needed to look lost.

From a safe distance she watched as Kelly Gilligan headed back to his car. His bag was noticeably lighter.

He didn't seem to notice her car, though her job was now considerably more difficult without the tracer. She had to keep visual tabs on him and though she kept him in sight, she wasn't certain she'd done it without alerting him. There was every possibility by this point that he'd figured out the dark blue car was everywhere he was. Still, she had to stay on his tail.

He hit three more spots that night, each time taking the bag in with him. Each time he entered a door that was heavily locked. Each time he emerged the bag was lighter. The third place was the last. At least Sin thought that because the bag was wadded and tucked under his arm as he exited the building behind a nicer boat dock.

While she managed to walk the perimeter of the large building set a ways back from the dock, she wanted to case the place more thoroughly. As it was, she was out of the car when Kelly Gilligan returned to his own ride.

For a moment, she fought indecision. Should she stay? Go inside? It had all the same problems as the bar. And now there was a one-in-four chance that Lee was inside. Lower odds than were safe for a breach of that risk.

Barely making it back to the car, she managed to follow him back to the first sedan. At that point, she quit tailing him.

Better to not get caught. Better to get out while she might still be ahead. The tracker meant she could sit where she was and watch as he drove home, parking in front of the small house again.

She wanted to go back to each of the four places, but it was going on four a.m. Figuring Nick was in bed asleep by now, she called him anyway.

# CHAPTER 20

"Shit."

Sin felt as much as heard the word pass her.

It wasn't like being out with Lee. Nick was lighter, willing to swear because he stepped in an icy puddle of mud just under the window to the bar. Lee wouldn't have noticed.

But Nick was who she had and though he was normally good, he seemed distracted tonight.

"Get your head in this." She hissed at him under her voice. Ironically, whispers carried farther than normal vocal tones, and Sin knew not to give away anything she didn't have to.

A nod, and Nick literally straightened up.

There were no windows into the lower level of the closed bar. Multiple bolts on each door made picking their way in time consuming. A window was the fastest method, if the most obvious.

They brought a lightweight foldable ladder, and positioned it under the window. Sin kept watch as Nick stood atop the ladder and pried the wood before holding an old baby blanket over the glass. He then smashed it with his elbow, the blanket both protecting him and muffling the noise.

Sin was on lookout and, given the neighborhood, it seemed lonely work. A good place to store a prisoner.

She'd brought Nick back here, thinking this was the best of the four places Gilligan had gone to. His car remained at the rental house, which was a good indicator that he was home, though not proof. With Lee on her mind, she'd bumped the timescale.

They had no idea what was on the other side. Unable to see in, they were unable to predict. What Sin could tell was that something of value was inside.

Though all the windows were boarded, some of the boards were new. Someone had fought down the telltale signs of recent activity, and the fact that someone had gone to the trouble to replace the broken boards without looking like they had done it, told an important story. One that had drawn her here tonight.

She heard Nick's breath escape him as the window came loose of its moorings, pushing inward and revealing nothing of value. He nodded down to her and with minimal noise climbed inside, using the blanket to cover the jagged edges of broken glass.

Sin followed him up and into a darkened back room. Old, scuffed wood floors creaked softly under their feet, a ceiling fan hung unmoving over their heads, and in the faint light she could see a doorway ahead of her.

With a nod, she pulled a Springfield from her holster and slipped a lone kama from its moorings along her leg. Long range and close range, she was ready as she led Nick through the door.

The darkness closed around them and, as much as she wanted to run through the place, checking behind every door and around every corner, Sin's discipline held her rigidly in check. She was no good to Lee if she was caught. It was the only thought that was keeping her sane at this point.

Standing still, she let her eyes adjust for a moment, then pulled out night vision goggles, motioning Nick to do the same.

They couldn't wear them on the way into the building. In this neighborhood, robbery didn't seem like that big a deal. But robbers with NVGs? That would earn a call to someone . . . and Sin didn't know who.

The world around her narrowed to a strip of information ringed in green. The edge of a table in the next room popped into relief and a set of doors leading off the front room to various locations gave her information. She walked through the kitchen, then leaned over and blew across the stove top. A puff of dust revealed that the area had not been touched in some time. Had she touched it, she would have left information that she had been there, that she had been checking things out.

The floor told another story. A path had been worn from the front door through the room out the second door to their left. Sin motioned to Nick, who pointed to the table.

Though most of it bore the same dust as the stove, the corner nearest them showed evidence that something had been set there recently. It also said that whoever had made the marks didn't have any real concern about people finding it.

She loosely followed the path along the floor, but she checked through every doorway before continuing on. Nick stayed at her back, giving them a three-sixty fighting radius should it turn out they weren't alone.

But all measures seemed to indicate that they were. There were no stray noises, and Sin listened deep into the corners. There were no movements at the corner of her vision. While trying to dart behind her would be monumentally stupid, some people were just that dumb. However, she didn't think the Mechanic was, and she doubted anyone who worked for or with him would be either.

It took so long to make it to the doorway they needed, and she almost laughed when they got there. She and Nick both had been trained by the blue to take down doors, make safe entry. Before that, she had been only relatively safe. When she was an officer she'd learned what it took to make the safest breach possible.

Anyone who looked would see the classic pair of cops bracketing the closed door using the hand signals learned at the academy. The only thing out of place was clothing—dark and with no identifying marks at all it screamed of illegal activities. Her kama, low and ready at her right, also told the story that they weren't quite what they looked like. If anyone around here knew enough to report them, well, the local PD would have a field day.

With a nod, she signaled Nick to turn the knob and push open the door. She swung inward with it, her gun leading the way. She didn't use the classic flashlight hold, though she knew it. While it would blind anyone it hit, it also gave away your location. Sin wasn't giving anything. Tonight she was only taking.

The floor fell away and her brain took a moment to process that they'd found the steps to the basement and that this was the path the person had worn in the dust on the floor. Not *a* person, the Mechanic. The man who most likely had Lee.

So she turned the narrow scope of her vision down the steps.

There were corners and shadows that even the NVGs couldn't penetrate, she aimed her gun there and hoped one wasn't aimed back at her. Taking an old piece of advice from Lee, she and Nick wore body armor. But it wouldn't stop her from bleeding out or protect against a head wound.

She stepped softly down at first, but the squeak of the wooden step broadcast her position and Sin changed tactics.

If someone was down there, they expected a soft, slow entry.

She ran.

Down the steps. Two at a time, her feet no longer worried about silence.

Nick came down behind her, taking her lead, and aiming his gun to the left where she'd aimed to the right. Another ingrained cop move; don't swing a loaded weapon in the direction of your partner.

She was tensed, ready for the Mechanic to pop up and fight for his life.

But nothing came.

Just as quickly, she spoke to Nick. One word. "Daylight."

An uncommon code, it wouldn't alert anyone waiting, but both of them simultaneously flipped up their goggles and turned their flashlights to "flood."

For a half second she held her breath, until all the corners were illuminated, until she was certain there wasn't anything down here.

Yes, she knew that there could be someone in the upper floors. That person could try to trap them down here, shoot down the staircase, any variety of options, but the breath eased out of her as she scanned the area.

A dirt floor stretched to the cinderblock walls. In the corners the dirt seemed to drift as though some wind had piled it there. Recent scuffings showed shoeprints and the dirt changed colors, darker in some areas, lighter in others.

She pulled out her phone and snapped two pictures of clear footprints she'd located. She was about to get a third when Nick touched her on the shoulder and pointed down where she was standing in the multi-colored dirt.

His voice was not a whisper, but even the carefully modulated tone didn't hide his concern. "Sin, that's blood."

---

Owen thought Nick looked bone tired, but Sin appeared to almost bounce in her shoes. Though she didn't move a muscle, there was a disturbing energy about her. He didn't know how she held up. Weren't pregnant women supposed to be tired? Even now, with all their awareness heightened, Annika would still be sleeping had Owen not woken her.

It was all tangled together. He wouldn't have woken her if he hadn't been afraid of her being alone, asleep, and maybe someone finding her. But then, once she was alert, she refused to be left behind. He was a trained agent, but she'd seen more war than he had. There was something about her like Sin—if the shit hit the fan, Annika might very well be the only one left standing. He had to trust in that even if he didn't feel comfortable with it.

He was even more uncomfortable with the comparison to Sin. Sin hadn't been normal since she was eleven, and given the way she'd come up fighting then, Owen would bet good money that she hadn't been normal even before that. She'd probably always been bright, steady, single-minded, and stubborn as fuck. It shouldn't surprise him now. But somehow it always did.

As he stood in yet another hotel room Sin had procured and watched dawn crack open, he reminded himself of his purpose. He'd thought his issues would untangle with time. Instead Nick Stelian had only tied the knots tighter.

"Here's the sample." Nick had carried it, and Owen was glad Sin didn't have to reach into a pocket and wonder if she carried her husband's blood. They'd scraped some of the soil into a plastic sample tube, functioning like cops though everything they did was patently illegal.

Owen pushed the thought aside and pocketed the sample, thinking to get it out of sight. "I'll overnight it ASAP. We might have results tomorrow."

"Do you need a sample from Lee to match?" Sin asked. She knew how this worked.

Owen fought the mild nausea that threatened. "We have the sheets from the cabin."

Only a nod as she compartmentalized that and shelved it for later, if at all. He was opening his mouth to say more when Nick beat him to the punch.

"Did you need to talk to me more . . . About our agreement?"

Sin chased the conversation, obviously behind and obviously perturbed by that fact. She didn't ask.

As Owen shook his head, he felt Annika's hand slide into his. She didn't know this either, but Nick's deep breath told them they were about to all come up to speed on yesterday's game of cops and robbers.

Nick's voice was steady. "I've been thinking for a while, Sin. Running Atlanta isn't what I need it to be."

When he paused, she nodded back at him, though Owen had no idea what passed between them. But Nick continued. "I want to live to spend the money I made—" a quick, fierce glance at Owen spoke volumes about his desire to retain some of what he had. Owen had other thoughts about that and kept his expression bland. "—at least some of it. And I need a challenge that doesn't make me sick to my stomach some days."

"This?" She asked him softly.

"Among other things, but yes. This was a tipping point."

"Reese." Her word was soft, Owen almost missed it and it took a moment of brain searching to recall that was the female officer lost when the Kurevs found Lee and Sin living and working as Will and Diana Kincaid just outside Atlanta.

Nick nodded in return and was opening his mouth when Annika's voice unexpectedly filled the gap. "You two made a deal."

She pointed back and forth between Nick and Owen, her brain chugging as the pieces fell together.

It was Sin who leapt into the fray. "You can't go to prison Nick!" She grabbed at her brother's arm, protective and fierce. Owen had to admire it though part of him thought that was exactly where Nick belonged.

Unfortunately, prison didn't bring exchanges. If Nick went inside, he would do so quietly. If Nick stayed out, he could topple his own empire in his wake. Owen also thought there were greater and lesser evils in the world. The lesser evil here was definitely Nick.

Sin had other ideas. "Nick, what about the head of the dragon?"

He shrugged back at her. "I can't be it anymore."

"Did you not believe it?" She let his hand drop, stepped back, and eyed him warily all during a cryptic conversation that Owen wasn't following.

Never one to be unaware of her surroundings, Sin crossed her arms. "Tell them, Nick. If you believe it, tell them."

Owen wanted to hear this.

"If you cut off the head of the dragon, another grows back in its place." Nick sighed, reciting the words like a child forced into an insincere apology.

Turning to Owen, Sin stared him down. "Nick is the head, Owen. You take him out and Atlanta goes to hell in a handbasket. You can't do this."

It hit him like a shotgun blast, nearly throwing him backward. She might as well have simply hit him, he thought.

Her words came before he could respond. "Do you not see what's going on in Chicago? Atlanta doesn't have the hits that Chicago does. No families are being taken out, like mine! Like Lee's! No one crosses Nick because they don't have to."

"There are deaths in Atlanta, Sin. Drug related, gang shootings." He wasn't taking this mafia-boss-with-a-heart-of-gold shit any longer. "Is Nick in charge of that, too?"

She shook her head, breathing heavily, her fists and power on tight rein. "That shit is Kurev shit. They've been trying to push into Atlanta for years. Heroin, meth, you name it. Nick keeps that shit out."

"Sin—Sin!" Nick's words seemed to reach her, stalling her tirade if not her anger. Owen still felt the white anger of her glare while Nick spoke.

"Stop talking, Sin, you're giving away my bargaining chips."

It wasn't true. But it worked. A little.

Sin stepped back. Her anger still evident.

Owen didn't buy it all, but he knew where the better decision was. It was with Nick Stelian.

"Tell him, Nick." Sin didn't turn away.

"No. I'm pleading the damn fifth." He tugged at her hand again, then spoke more softly. "I went to him. I asked for a deal."

That knocked her off her high demon-horse. Shaking her head, suddenly confused, she turned to Nick. "What?"

"He thinks he can get me a job . . . with the FBI."

It was Annika who suddenly burst into laughter.

Sin whipped back around to face Owen and if he didn't know better he would think she'd hurt her neck doing it. He just shrugged.

"Crimi—" She cut herself off. "People with Nick's history can't become agents."

Owen just shrugged. "You can say 'criminals'—it doesn't indict Nick. And there are a lot of former criminals working for the FBI. Who can think like a mafia don better than a mafia don?"

Lesser of the evils, he reminded himself. While his brain was okay with that outcome, his gut still hadn't quite come to terms with it.

"No!" Her outburst surprised him out of his thoughts. Before he could ask about it, she clarified. "You can't have any ties to Nick or to me!"

"It's a little late for that, don't you think?" After all, a bullet hadn't hit the window he'd been standing at the day before because of anything Owen had done.

Frustrated with his lack of comprehension, she blurted out, "No traceable connections."

"It's still too late, Sin."

She looked heartbroken. Maybe overly so for someone who had come to him to ask for help. The lack of logic in her thoughts concerned him, for if anyone was purely logical, it was her. She nodded slowly, "Don't connect too closely to Nick. I'll get out of your life as soon as this is over, and we'll make sure there's no trail."

She thought for a moment, "None of the Kurevs should have any way to trace the woman at the party back to Annika."

Unless they were vetting their visitors more than it appeared. Owen didn't put it past them.

For a moment, they were all lost in thought, then Annika spoke up.

"Owen and I took a drive through the Kimmel neighborhood this morning. We went twice in two different cars." She smiled at the thought and continued, this time talking directly to Sin. "I thought Ann Evalyn was gone, the way you spoke yesterday, but she was out jogging this morning."

There was a pause, and Owen saw the incredulous look on Sin's face.

"What?"

Annika shrugged. "You had a cut and some bruises, but she didn't look any the worse for wear."

# CHAPTER 21

Nick sat quietly in the passenger seat, fiddling with the radio as Sin pulled up to a block near the house the Mechanic was staying in. As soon as she pulled up to the curb, he climbed out, keys in hand.

There was every possibility this was a fool's errand. Every chance it would get them killed. But so was every day and Nick was becoming a believer in doing what he could. He'd always had his heart in Atlanta, in Vasilescu, but he'd done that.

Nick had rebelled against his grandfather's traditional strong-arming ways, realizing early that everyone could have a lot if no one got too greedy.

Something he'd learned though was that people just got too greedy. The species wasn't very evolved and it was starting to depress him. A lot. "Are you ready?"

She nodded with a small smile, though if it was for anything but cover, he couldn't tell.

They wore long coats with thick padding at the necks. Sin had on a ball cap and a wig of short pale brown hair. They both wore sunglasses against a thankfully bright sun. Even their leather gloves looked perfectly in keeping with the day. Unless they were physically detained, no one would ever know this was them.

Having waited until fifteen minutes after the man left, they casually walked down the street, and went up to the Mechanic's door. Sin knocked, waited, knocked again.

When the door remained unanswered, they headed back down the walkway and directly to Gilligan's car as though it were their own. Even as they walked he began repeatedly pushing the button on the small device in his pocket.

Bracketing the car on either side, Nick immediately pulled his "key fob" and began openly trying the options. At the passenger side door, Sin was doing the same with her half of a carefully divided set of codes.

After a moment, he made a point to appear frustrated—the way anyone would if they went to their car and the fob wasn't working. He was about to hold it up, motion to Sin some inane act for any old biddies watching through their curtains, when the car beeped and blinked the running lights at them.

The door popped open and they both climbed in. There was no telling whose code had opened the door, and Nick couldn't care less. They'd gotten in.

Getting out was going to be harder. Because who would climb into a car, program the GPS and get out? So they had to go for a drive and get back before the Mechanic noticed his car was missing.

They didn't know how long he'd be out, but Sin voted that it was worth the chance and Nick had agreed.

"Two birds?" He asked and his sister nodded back.

He headed for Ann Evalyn's neighborhood.

As soon as Annika had made her comment, Sin had pressed the Dunhams for details. How was Kimmel out running around?

They'd grilled Annika and Owen.

The woman had looked like Ann Evalyn, but they hadn't gotten too close. Annika would have recognized her face, but it was hard to see without stalking her. The woman had picked up some piece of mail and grabbed a small towel by the door, clearly left there for returning from her run, waved to a neighbor, and headed inside.

Sin and Nick both agreed that was all wrong. Ann Evalyn was a bitch through and through. She didn't run and she sure as hell didn't wave to her neighbors.

The Dunhams had interrogated Sin in return, leading her to start telling about Ann Evalyn's death. Which in turn left Owen nearly yelling, "No, no! No Sin! No Anni, everyone shut up!"

Owen Dunham was in enough shit with his open deal with Nick. Right now, the former agent knew everything and couldn't move anything. Nick stipulated they had to find Lee before anything could be negotiated with the FBI. Having Dunham on his side protected the ex-agent but also bought Nick a get-out-of-jail card should shit go sideways on them. Sin had no such deal, only the goodwill of the others.

She had sighed at them. "I am confident that Ann Evalyn Kimmel was deceased. And that's something I actually know a bit about."

Dunham had coughed into his hand, choking on air, as she said that. But in the end it only meant that Nick and Sin were driving around the neighborhood, trying to figure out what the hell was going on. The dead didn't rise again, and this one sure as hell wouldn't have gone jogging.

Sin was messing with Gilligan's GPS and a moment later she exclaimed, "They've been trading the GPSes out!"

That got Nick's attention. "Who would do that?"

"Paranoid people!" She laughed but it came out more as a cynical bark. "I turned on the tracer in the unit and it doesn't even have last night when I followed him out to the other car."

"He could erase it." A good tech guy could dig out the info, but the standard tools allowed you to erase your tracks.

"No. It has tons of back information, just not for this car."

Nick nodded, and about five minutes later, he was turning into Ann Evalyn's neighborhood, and trying to get his sister's attention from where it was focused on the panel that housed the built-in system. She sighed. Loudly.

"Nothing. . . . If the system was ever turned on, it's been erased since then. No matter what I try, it gives me an error code." At last she gave up on it and looked up at her surroundings.

"Wow." It wasn't surprised, but definitely not what she expected. "No police crime scene tape, no gawking neighbors. Her car is right there. I'm impressed."

Nick was, too. Impressed and concerned. The complete lack of any detail about the owner dying meant the Kurevs had come in, and fast. They had managed to remove the body without anyone really noticing, or else it was still in there. Nick told this theory to Sin.

"It's not still in there. Someone is living there as Ann Evalyn. The smell alone would be unbearable. The body's gone."

"Which means they figured out that she was missing very, very fast."

Sin nodded absently and Nick wondered, too, if Ann Evalyn had tipped the brothers off to her entrapment.

None of it boded well.

---

Owen had no idea what he was doing here. Except that he had every idea.

He followed Sin out of the car and into the brush separating them from the large boathouse building. Dressed in his casual clothes—did he own anything else anymore?—in colors and fabrics she picked from his suitcase to blend in.

What was he blending into, he wondered. Urban decay? Old boathouse?

Nick should be here. Except he couldn't be and that was

Owen's own damn fault. Well, it was indirectly for not stating in no uncertain terms exactly what Nick could and couldn't tell him.

"You can't strike a deal with me then tell me you're headed off to perform *yet another* illegal activity!" He shouldn't be yelling. He rarely yelled. Except lately, when it was hard to keep his voice below alerting-everyone-in-a-mile level. "I'm not your get out of jail card! If you keep doing this shit, it gets harder to cut the deal and impossible to keep you out of prison."

He remembered grinding his teeth. Owen only hoped he wouldn't need massive dental work when he got home. They had to find Lee, quick.

"Someone needs to go with her!" Nick seemed to have plenty of practice at being angry without yelling. Just another thing that grated on Owen's nerves lately. He wanted to help. He just didn't want to be . . . *Here.*

"If you tell me and I don't stop you, then I'm not a very good representative of the law, am I?" It felt like yelling at a teenager. Nick looked like he didn't care or didn't understand. Owen had set him straight. "I'm your broker, you idiot. If you compromise me, you compromise your deal!"

"Are they really going to ask you about this?" Nick hadn't even flinched at being called an idiot and Owen wasn't sure if he was glad that it rolled off his back or mad that it didn't stick into him and hurt the way it was supposed to.

And the question just pissed him off. "No, probably not. Not this, specifically. But they WILL ask something that would require evasion if you tell me these things."

"You can't evade?" Nick asked, straight-faced.

*Why was this conversation still going on?* Owen wanted to bury his face in his hands, buy a plane ticket, and get the hell out. He didn't want to broker a deal for Nicolae Stelian.

But he did.

"No, Nick. I can't evade. I'm the worst liar on the face of the earth."

Nick's gaze suddenly flew beyond Owen's shoulder and he turned to find Annika nodding in agreement with his statement. She shrugged one shoulder and said simply, "Well, you are."

The conversation had somehow still gone on with Owen nearly yelling again, "No, I can't forget I heard this. You can't go do this. You can't or your deal is over."

So Owen wound up coming along with Sin. He consoled himself that he hadn't committed any crimes . . . Yet. He was merely skulking around, carrying tools used in the commission of crimes, and following a known and wanted criminal with the intent of committing a crime. He hoped he got to meet his youngest child face-to-face and not through bullet-proof prison glass.

Sin motioned him to tuck in tight against the wall, as though he wasn't trained in search and seizure procedures. He did what she told him.

They were on point two of the four point list—Nick and Sin having apparently 'scoped out' the bar the night before. They didn't give Owen and Annika any details and Owen didn't ask.

The sun was out, typical of a Chicago cold snap apparently. Sin had insisted that his clothes be matte colors and his shoes have common treads. He wasn't used to this.

They slunk through the bushes, Sin nearly disappearing into the sparse foliage even though she was barely a few feet ahead of him. Dressed in greys, like she'd managed to get him partially into, she was just another smudge on the unkempt boathouse wall. Owen tried to do the same.

They slid around to the front, the small parking area deserted, and headed straight for the door. Owen tucked in behind Sin, his Glock already in hand because he didn't like the feel of the place. Still, he kept it out of sight, prepared to act casual and wave to anyone who came by.

"Don't look." Sin spoke after trying the knob on the door.

Turning his head away, he waited through the clicks that

indicated she was picking the lock. He told himself he didn't know that.

As they came through the door, a noise came from the back, instantly changing the rigor of Sin's stance. Even he thought, *Lee!* But he didn't move forward. Not yet.

The bright daylight outside bounced off everything and slightly illuminated an open space in front of them. But once Sin closed the door behind them, the dark inside was more than their eyes could take.

That part, he wasn't used to. He'd been part of assault teams that kicked their way in or used battering rams. They didn't go in and close the door behind them so no one would know that they were there.

His heart rate ticked up a notch. The corners were blanketed in darkness; he couldn't tell what might pop out at him, but Sin never faltered. A new revelation hit him: he'd always been taught to protect his own life. Every agent knew there were things they might die for, but agent safety was always made a priority.

Sin did no such thing.

She stood there inside the doorway, Owen at her back, ready to face bullets while her eyes still adjusted.

She must be made for the dark, because Owen's eyes hadn't yet adjusted and he'd always been one of the first in the crowd to dark adapt. He trusted her. He had to, she was already moving.

The sound came again from the back room.

A moan, a query buried beneath it.

Owen thought it could be a trap, but that didn't matter, as Sin was leading. And she was smart enough to head to the quiet room. It only took seconds to get to the peeling, teal blue door that stood sentry to the second room. As Owen adapted to the dim interior, he saw the large warehouse was shortened by the two rooms cut into it for some kind of locked space.

He was turned, checking behind him, when the sound came

again. But it was the sight his adjusted eyes saw that stopped him. "Hey."

He spoke softly, didn't use her name, made sure the sound carried no farther than the five feet separating them. It took her a moment to check in front of her before she turned around to look.

His hand still on the gun, he used the other to gesture into the room.

She nodded.

The square, dirty pillars went all the way to the roof.

The general debris along the floor showed someone had been coming and going recently. As Owen scanned farther into the room, no longer convinced someone was going to jump out before he and Sin opened one of the doors, he saw the damage in the far corner.

Something had been there. The floor showed signs of a struggle, maybe several of them. The position of the pillar matched the photo of Lee.

He didn't get Sin's attention, her focus had returned to the door in front of her and he saw that while he now gripped his gun in two hands, Sin used only one. Her other hand held a kama, a weapon he'd never heard of before encountering her work.

They progressed within kicking distance of the first door and placed themselves on either side of it. At her nod he bashed the door, barely getting his foot out of the way as she blazed in, a wraith streaming by.

She was shaking her head before he even entered.

The room was empty and the barely human noise came from next door.

Owen didn't trust the sound. It could be Lee, trying to call out through a gag or a hood. It could be a looped sound recording, enticing them to a door that would explode when kicked open. Owen had seen stranger shit.

Only he didn't think the darker possibilities mattered, and he and Sin did their choreographed dance at the second door, though with more trepidation. If a door was going to combust or hide men with machine guns it would be the one with the bait-sound behind it.

But as he pulled his foot back, Owen found he was still alive and Sin was rushing into the gap, unconcerned with what lay beyond. Through the opening all Owen could see was that she'd lowered her weapons as she dashed inside.

---

Sin figured she might as well be chewing gum as she stepped up the long, fancy driveway on Nick's arm. Her wig was in place, as was the overabundance of make-up and the leathers combined with cheap, buy-anywhere clothing. She'd leave her skin cells behind, but she couldn't change that.

Sin knew what she was doing. She had a clear goal here: get into the Kurev house again, scout more info about the holdings, and get a glimpse of the new Ann Evalyn. What Sin wasn't sure of was if she was doing the right thing.

There were still two more locations that made Owen Dunham's list. New info might narrow it down, though Sin would bet hard their list was actually incomplete. The boathouse earlier had been proof that the Kurevs were up to far more than she had expected. But she tried to shake off the memory and focus on moving forward.

Ann Evalyn might not even be here. Sin might have gotten dressed up for nothing.

The concern that she'd made the wrong decision was new to her. While lives had sometimes hung in the balance, she always trusted her decision. This time the life was Lee's and the weight seemed more than she could bear, swaying her decisions one way then another.

Nick subtly reached out and touched one of the cars parked along the side of the drive, leaving fingerprints on it. They'd both rubbed their three middle fingers in a black light gel before walking up the drive. Sin had a spare tiny pot of it in her purse, Nick had one in his pocket, and they were marking the cars as they went by.

She reached out and touched the next one—three fingers against the paint, low on the support that bracketed the back window. It might be useful later to see who had been here.

They could mark household objects, too. While Sin didn't know how that might be useful, she was a regular boy scout of the underworld—always prepared. Nick almost smiled about something, but Sin was already speaking when she realized it.

"Three."

"Yes, Hayley." The conversation was a simple code, a reminder of their breakaway signal to each other. This wasn't the cleanest entry, but it didn't make sense to be obvious about it either.

Sin didn't like going in this way; she hadn't vetted the people here. At all. Well, some of them were Nick's people, but they wouldn't act out tonight. They had strict instructions to fly under the radar until he gave the signal. He hadn't given it yet.

And she was walking into a situation almost completely out of her control.

Probably Ann Evalyn wouldn't be here tonight. How could she be? Wouldn't people recognize if someone tried to pass herself off as another person? Then again, Nick and Sin hadn't made the list, they'd simply invited themselves. So maybe she *would* be here.

Sin wondered again if the gamble was worth it.

Then she forced the thought aside as she reached the front entrance and the doors pulled wide, the servant stood guard against the cold but not the intruders on the doorstep. Instead, he ushered them right inside.

They found their way back to the same party room, only this

time Sin arrived well into the party. She listened with half an ear as Nick mentioned running into Hayley out on the street where she'd been forced to park so far back.

It took only a moment for a few hellos as a party girl looking for a good time. She fought the urge to make conversation.

Casually, she and Nick went their separate ways, friends for a walk up a long driveway, nothing more. She scanned the people around her, looking for this new Ann Evalyn, checking for faces from the last party, wondering if any of them saw through the alterations to her appearance and recognized Sin beneath.

The crowd was as dense as it had been the last time she'd been here. Only this time she knew what the Kurevs could do. Not just the picture that had been mailed. She understood now the broken jaws, shin bones protruding through the skin, untreated. She understood ragged fingernails, bloodied from being broken beneath the quick.

Previously she'd lumped the Kurev boys in with Nick to a certain extent; they ran drugs, guns, made money illegally. But she was off that bandwagon. The stories she'd heard in the last twenty four hours were as depraved as any she'd heard before.

Kaspar and Roman had no morals. None at all.

They trafficked in human lives, some of them kids.

She was thinking about the possibility that her trajectory might change. If Owen got enough information, there would be no stemming the tide. The feds would crash down on this place and Sin would have to slip away. Find the Mechanic, make sure he didn't tie up loose ends like Lee.

If the Feds came in, the Teflon brothers would lock up everything they could. She might never find Lee. But she'd gone hunting with Owen today and Owen Dunham operated only one way.

He was right. There had been only one choice, get the man to a hospital or let him die.

That was it. *How* they got him to a hospital was another story.

A story Owen was writing while she and Nick were here, scouting, scouring, for anything. Just in case.

Her anger was laser sharp. Where before it had simmered just below the surface, now it pierced and she had a harder time playing the fool amongst the monsters.

For a moment, Sin thought of what she'd seen today, then thought back to what she'd done. Even recently. But she'd never moved without proof. While her methods were similar, her morals were very different. Her level of vetting a potential victim much clearer. Even Owen said he'd hesitated to bring her in more than once.

Had Dr. Dunham wanted to take her and Lee down, he could have. Where she'd always thought herself invincible, she understood now that she was a mere mortal like everyone else, and that she'd always had and always would have weak points.

It took a moment to remind herself to keep a happy face on. She was at a party and supposedly too stupid to worry about anything. That was why she almost walked into the line of sight of the woman in the red dress.

She casually ate a handful of chips, brushing back her dark hair. Her brown eyes smiled at her companion, and she might have spotted Sin had someone not called to her as he walked up.

"Ann Evalyn!"

She turned to him, giving a clear view of her face, halting Sin's breath and freezing time.

She pushed the button on her phone, signaling the abort to Nick and turned to walk out of the party.

It wasn't Ann Evalyn.

It was worse.

# CHAPTER 22

Owen sat waiting in the hospital room for thirty minutes before they found him a more secure position.

He flashed his ID. But it wasn't worth much. He did have credentials; he was an honorary badge holder for his state Bureau of Investigation. At least it was a real badge even if it wasn't FBI. It really meant he consulted on cases and that they could cut him a check out of the standard payroll budget.

It did not mean that he could bring severely wounded patients into the ER and claim that the staff should not call the local police. But that's exactly what he did. He was trying it anyway and sitting next to the wounded man, reading a magazine that was about fifteen months out of date, and hoping like hell he didn't get arrested for impersonating someone more important than himself.

He called Nguyen.

Nguyen might come with his real FBI badge and help bail Owen out as a pure favor. He'd bitch the whole time. So Owen dangled the bait.

He hit send on his phone, putting in a picture of the victim and telling exactly where he'd had the hospital staff take DNA swabs.

The text came back immediately.

I'm in. Who do I call?

Owen smiled. He'd told the staff that the out-of-state badge was because of dirty local cops. He insinuated that members of the police force had been involved in the beating of this man. Told them he was going to get them an FBI agent on the phone and they wouldn't want to interfere with an open investigation into corruption. Then he had prayed that it held.

Prayed they believed him.

Prayed nothing happened to Annika while he was out here playing the dirty hero again.

The man had been tied to a chair, his wounds grotesque and obviously human inflicted. It was the kind of image that would stick. The smell of the infected wounds lingered, molecules lodged in Owen's olfactory senses. He told himself that it was just scent memory. But he couldn't help the belief that he carried some part of that violence inside him now. That by seeing it and being there, he had somehow inhaled it into his own system.

He focused on his phone, on the sounds from the room next door where they worked on repairing the broken man even as they washed away the evidence. He texted Nguyen back, giving a name and a number.

Owen would have really brought the FBI in, but that would have compromised his deal with Nick. So Nguyen would have to do.

As he and Sin had hauled the man away—stopping to put the boathouse back in order, so no one would know until they entered the small room that their guy was gone—Sin had pointed out that they still didn't have Lee.

Bringing in the full weight of the Feds could and most likely would get Lee killed.

His thoughts festered a while longer but were then interrupted by a nurse. He looked no-nonsense in his blue scrubs, but the blood smears down the sides told a different story. He'd come from right next door.

"Agent Dunham?"

Owen didn't correct him.

"We received a call as you said from an Agent, verifying your work here. Also the patient has asked for you."

Snapping upright, Owen tossed the magazine to the tabletop. He pocketed his phone and followed the nurse into the hall and the short distance to the next room.

The man must not be completely passed out, as Owen had feared. The nurse pulled a paper towel from his pocket and wrapped it around the knob before pushing the door open. "Don't touch anything." He tossed the towel onto a trash can piled high with them.

When Owen only began to look like he was going to ask, the nurse pertly stated, "Outbreaks. And no idea what came in with him. Also, he's worried about his car?"

A frown was forming on his own face, Owen could feel it. But the next words smoothed it out, even though they shouldn't.

"He keeps asking for a mechanic."

"Can I talk to him?"

A shrug was the simple response. "Sure, don't make him talk too much. He's not communicating all that well to us." Then he leaned over the patient, ignoring the other staff running portable x-rays and doing blood draws. "Your jaw is broken. Try to speak without moving it. You're going into surgery shortly."

Looking around the room, Owen searched the faces. "Why wasn't he taken directly in?"

Another physician finally looked up from his chart. "He's not good, but he's stable. We assess before we cut."

"Do you have his name?" Owen pulled out a small notepad to take notes. Most used their phones, but phones could be hacked. While Owen could lose the notepad just as easily, someone would have to decipher his shorthand.

"He says he's Officer Doug Hellico. Chicago PD."

Owen's head jerked toward the man, and he leaned in close, "Don't move your head, just answer quietly: did you follow the girl?"

"Yes."

Owen's heart sank. Their inside guy had been compromised.

"How many days have you been in there?"

The croak was barely discernable. "Five."

He didn't like to think that the leg must have been broken on the first day and left to cause pain. Why hadn't he died?

"The other man?" Owen didn't want the answer, but he needed it.

"Gone."

*Shit.*

*Shitshitshit.*

There was no telling what "gone" meant. Dead? Moved?

He wanted to ask, but it wasn't a binary question and it wasn't healthy to get the man talking. Owen did scribble in his notebook, and was writing a few questions for later when the doctor pulled him aside.

He kept his voice low but clearly the officer on the bed could hear him. "You should see this."

Slowly, he lifted the old shirt the man was still wearing and exposed a set of crude stitches.

The officer didn't move, but he gathered himself and muttered what sounded like, "Keep me alive."

The doctor pulled Owen into the hallway. "We're taking him into surgery in about fifteen minutes. As soon as the first specialist arrives, we'll prep him."

Owen only managed a nod before the doctor spoke again.

"Clearly this man was tortured. It sounds and looks like the . . . Monster that did this enjoyed the work a little too much."

Leverage.

Owen played it, used it, twisted the doctor.

"We know. We're looking for another of his victims currently. We have reason to believe the man is still alive." A lie. But the Mechanic apparently did go to lengths to keep them from bleeding out. Owen didn't comment with his opinion of whether it was a blessing or not. "This man was an undercover cop. We also know there are other officers involved in this. We think a dirty officer recognized him and that's why this happened."

He paused, letting the drama seep into the moment. He needed this doctor to believe.

"If you report this to the local authorities, you'll sign this man's death warrant. We don't know how far the corruption goes. And you may even bring the man who did this to your doorstep. He works for hire."

As Owen watched the doctor slowly tilted away, his feet planted but his torso tipping back, an unconscious sign that what Owen said bothered him deeply. "My FBI Agency contact will be in touch. You need to make certain no one on your staff talks about this. No matter how much they trust their spouses. They aren't even to say that they treated someone they can't talk about."

He waited.

"Do you understand?"

The doctor offered a slow nod.

Owen changed tacks. "Can I talk to the staff who worked with this man? As soon as he's in surgery, you gather them in the room and I'll make sure they understand what needs to be done."

A faster nod this time.

An expected response to an old trick. Take authority, assign a detested task, then take it over yourself. Owen had just earned not only control of the staff—as much as anyone could control what they said at home—but he got the doctor on board with a good level of gravity.

His phone rang then, his actual phone. Nguyen.

"What do you have?"

His friend started rattling off what he'd told the hospital. That he'd verified Owen Dunham was no longer an Agent but had been with the Bureau and during what years. He stated consultant status and mentioned a very difficult current case in Chicago right now.

That was all well and good, but . . . "We need protection here for him. Now."

"Like what?"

"Like I'm all there is here and I'm not currently an agent. I'm not ready to open a case. But we need this guy protected. How do we get agents here?"

Nguyen shook his head. Owen could almost hear it through the phone, the breath sucked in, the push of air accompanied by a sound meaning he had nothing to contribute. "If you want agents, you need Agency. And you can't get that without explaining why."

*Shit.* Again, *Shit.*

"Okay, let me try someone here."

Standing in the bleak hospital hall, he hugged the wall, trying to keep his voice from carrying, either to the staff passing by or to the crowd in the small room. Officer Hellico had probably heard all he needed to.

Nick's voice came through, concern lacing his words. "Is he alive?"

Sin had dropped Owen and the man at the hospital after they had traded the three of them to his car. The hospital had cameras and Owen couldn't be seen getting out of a car registered to a strange woman in Chicago, not with the crap that was flying about, ready to hit the fan. He and Sin had made the same decision that the hospital staff had made: Hellico was in pretty bad shape, but he'd held steady, staying alive despite conditions. It was better to do it right than fast.

Owen was glad now.

"Yes, he's headed into surgery. In spite of multiple wounds and a bad infection, he should make it."

"That's good."

"Yes and no." Owen took a breath. "He's a CPD officer. Do you know him? Doug Hellico?"

Nick's swift, vehement response was all Owen needed. This was one of his guys. Owen found himself a bit startled at how much it bothered Nick that one of his guys was caught. He was startled more when Nick didn't ask if he'd been compromised. Maybe he was simply washing his hands of it.

But he didn't. "He's a good guy. What's his condition like?"

"He should make it, but he's got a broken jaw . . ." Owen rattled off a few more bits of information about the surgery, things Nick wouldn't know from Sin already. "Thing is, the doctors said he was asking about his car."

"What?"

"Yeah, he clearly said 'Mechanic.'"

There was nothing Nick could say. It was the obvious conclusion.

"I only got to ask a few questions, but he said he followed her." Owen didn't dare say her name. "Which means he's compromised."

"Jesus."

"It gets worse." Owen waited while Nick took in a breath, probably bracing himself. "I don't know what got him caught, but he said they moved the other guy."

"What?"

"I'm convinced the picture you saw was from the same building. But . . . The man you saw isn't there anymore. He was moved."

There was a long pause, then Nick asked softly, "Is there any information on him?"

"Only what I can extrapolate." Owen rubbed the bridge of his nose. His head hurt as though a spontaneous sinus infection had popped up. "This guy has been tortured and stitched. The monster likes to keep them alive. So the bad news is he's in the worst possible hands. The good news is that he'll be kept as long as possible."

"I don't even know what to tell her." Sadness, deep enough to be true despair, washed across the line.

No names. But it was Sin and Lee they were all concerned about.

"We keep going." Owen wondered if he was reading into the tone. If Nick was as selfish and greedy as he'd first thought, or if Owen consistently painted the man with different brushes depending on his expectations. He couldn't untangle any of it. So he went for logistics. "Listen, we need guards. If I can't find guards I can trust, I have to call in the FBI."

"I can get you men."

Owen had thought so. Nick had his fingers deep into the Chicago PD, deeper maybe than the Kurevs. "They have to be trusted. Not compromised."

"I know." He didn't even sound irritated at a reminder of the basics.

"I'm here until you can get your people here. We'll make arrangements as soon as possible. He's headed into surgery now."

Owen looked up and saw the gurney being wheeled out of the room, a semi-lucid Doug Hellico reaching for Owen's hand as he was wheeled by.

"I owe you, man." But then his eyes rolled back as he'd clearly already been given some drugs.

Owen hung up with Nick and prepared to face the staff.

He delivered as harsh a message as he could. The staff were white-faced at his pronouncement that the man who tortured

Officer Hellico was a mercenary who had no issues with families and kids.

In the end, he was as assured as he could be that they would stay quiet. It would be up to them to uphold any lies they managed to tell. He would have tried to drill the necessity of compliance into their heads a little deeper, but his phone buzzed, the alternate phone, the one that made him feel like a criminal.

"What you got for me?" He hoped Nick had news. He was ready to go home, even though home wasn't an option. He needed, at least, to see Annika.

"Nothing."

*Shit.*

He should just recite the word in his head over and over, as though it were a talisman to ward off bad things. "What? Why? I thought you had cops."

That was a bad thing to say in the corner of the hallway of the hospital. Owen was getting tired. He'd been out for nearly eleven hours now. And he desperately needed a damn nap.

"I do. But given Hellico, I have to assume that the brothers know that I do. And they may have already tried to find and turn others." There was a shrug, a well of disappointment in his voice. "If I burn bridges, my guys will want to be on my side of the river when the flames start, but I haven't had a chance to talk to them yet."

Owen felt his breath rush out of his body, escaping the bad juju that was taking residence.

Nick spoke again before Owen could gather his thoughts. At the news, they'd taken flight and scattered like birds.

"Honestly, I may not have the crowd I had before." Another pause, another telling break that sank in his chest. "There's nothing I can do to counter the Mechanic. If they choose by fear, I lose. I don't have that in me."

That statement, the disappointment was strangely the most

comforting thing he'd heard all day. Owen spoke briefly, "I understand," and extricated himself from the call.

Standing in the hallway in the same clothes he'd gone scouting a boathouse in earlier today, still sporting a few smears of Hellico's blood from where he and Sin had dragged the man out of the boathouse, Owen did the only thing he knew would work: he called his wife.

Ten minutes later he wanted to kiss her. He hung up praying to God that she never realized how much better than him she could have done.

Then he called the FBI.

---

Sin staggered out of the party. The heels she wore were normally perfectly serviceable, but the shock and the driveway cobblestones tripped her up every fourth or fifth step. She fought to stay upright and consoled herself that an obviously drunk woman leaving a Kurev party was not an unusual sight.

Her mind reeled.

Had the new Ann Evalyn seen her?

Sin had been at the party for a while. She'd separated from Nick as per the plan and wandered around. It had taken a while for her to find the woman posing as the dead woman.

She'd heard Kaspar's voice. "This is Ann Evalyn Kimmel, I believe you met her once long ago."

An introduction taking place beyond a stand of drinkers chatting about nothing useful to Sin. So she'd rounded the corner and lost her instincts for self-preservation. Images flashed at her and she'd fled the party.

Finally making it to the car, she let herself in, sitting in the driver's seat ready to take off. But she wasn't ready. She was nearly shaking. And it was a sensation so foreign to her that she didn't know what to do with it.

As she tried to settle back into her skin, waiting until she could drive without getting pulled over, she rewound the events in her head. It was Kaspar's voice that introduced the woman as Ann Evalyn. But it was Sergei Orlov who had been speaking to her.

Sin gripped the steering wheel tighter and started the car.

Ann Evalyn had introduced Annika and Sin to Orlov at the first party. So Sergei Orlov *knew* the illustrious Mrs. Kimmel been replaced and he was part of the cohort feeding out the lie that Ann Evalyn was still alive.

Sin smacked her hand against the steering wheel and hit the gas, almost running into Nick as he crossed in front of her car on the way to his own.

Paranoid now, she waved him around and drove on. She couldn't be seen talking to him out here. She needed to get back to the motel.

The drive was congested with Saturday night traffic and crowds like this made it hard to tell if you were being tailed. She wasn't, but it took a long time to be certain. She took surface roads instead of freeways, spiraled in on the motel rather than going straight toward it.

Halfway there she realized that her paranoia had not extended far enough tonight. So she pulled into the parking lot of a drive-through restaurant and checked under the car.

She was ass in the air when a friendly employee came out and asked if she needed help. Thinking as fast as she could, Sin pulled out an old favorite.

"I drove over a plastic bag back there, and I didn't see it come out from under my car." She offered a stupid what-are-you-gonna-do shrug. "I'm just paranoid."

He nodded and she tacked on, "I mean, my car can't catch on fire if that bag got stuck under there, could it?"

When he scratched his head and shrugged back at her, Sin went back to her work, a legitimate excuse for stacking her radio scanner behind her phone and pretending she was using the light of the display to check for stray plastic bags.

She didn't find anything and by the time she pulled up to the motel Nick was waiting in her room as were Annika and Owen Dunham.

He didn't answer the door for her, but stuck three toothpicks through the space above the lock so she would know before she opened the door that her tag was gone—someone had been in the room—and there were three of them inside waiting for her. She walked in as though she were alone. Still paranoid, not bothering to acknowledge them until the door was closed and locked.

She stayed on her feet even as Nick spoke.

"I told them that Ann Evalyn wasn't Ann Evalyn. And that several of the Kurev group are saying she is." He tipped his head a little, scanned her for flaws, then kept talking. "I only saw her from the back. But I get the feeling I've met her before."

Sin stared him dead in the eyes, "You have."

Then she turned to Owen. "I thought I saw her standing over my bed the night Lee was taken, but I was certain I must be wrong." She sucked in a breath, the telling harder than she thought it would be. "Ironically, the woman playing the role of Ann Evalyn really is resurrected from the grave."

She turned back to Nick, giving him a name that would make his blood boil like hers did.

"That was Yulia Churkin."

# CHAPTER 23

"What!" Roaring the word, Nick jumped straight off the bed, nearly pushing his head into a low hanging ceiling fan. Churkin? That bitch was Yulia Churkin?

He and Sin had only been at the party a short time. He'd bailed soon after arriving, bidding the brothers good-bye, saying he'd been called away on business. It was a perfectly reasonable excuse in their line of business. Even in his police work, a call could come at any time.

No one questioned his leaving. And in trying to stay with his story, he'd walked briskly out the door, not realizing the woman he wanted to kill more than anything had stood merely inches away.

It was Annika who broke through the cloud of rage that extended from Nick to Sin and back again. "I thought she was dead."

"We all did." Sin muttered through clenched teeth.

Owen joined in. "But . . ." It lingered there on his lips, falling carelessly like thoughts onto the ground. He looked up again. "Nick shot her in the head."

"And the bullet bounced off that god-damned skull of hers." Sin put her hands up as though she didn't need a recitation of events. Nick sure didn't. "You were the one who texted me and told me she was finally dead."

Nick should have pulled her back from turning on the ex-Agent, but instead he joined her. Churkin should be dead. Rotting in her grave. Better yet in an unmarked grave or eaten by animals.

It was Annika who stood, putting herself between her new friends and her husband. Her back was to Owen and the daggers she glared at Nick and Sin were no match for sais or bullets but were pure malice from the normally genteel woman. She was the one who curbed anger in favor of pertinent questions. "Owen wasn't there. We left before she died. Owen, who told you she was dead?"

"Um. The Agent there with her." His eyes looked up.

As Nick watched, Dunham's gaze connected with Sin's then found Nick's. The man was baffled.

"They said her body was taken to be cremated." He turned away, shoving his hands through his hair in a gesture of pure frustration. "I wanted Nguyen to check the body, but it was gone before I could intervene."

Dunham walked a tight circle, his breath laboring like his thoughts. As Nick watched he fought to direct the roiling boil in his blood. He didn't really think Dunham was to blame for the fiasco, but he had nowhere else to point his rage right now.

They stood that way for a moment. Annika guarding her husband. Dunham pacing and thinking. Sin looking shell-shocked and Nick clenching his fists and thinking that if he didn't hit someone soon he might burst.

That bitch had killed Reese.

Churkin and her sidekick Shvernik had come to clean up Sin and Lee and had shot his newly minted girlfriend mid-skull, killing her instantly.

There had never been a question that they were taking out Reese. The bullet wasn't meant for anyone else, Churkin and

Shvernik didn't miss. Reese had become part of the party, so they'd killed her.

Nick had put a bullet in Churkin's skull from closer range.

The thought that his revenge shot didn't take—didn't put a hole on the other side of her head and left her bleeding out the way Reese had—always made him angry. Until now, he consoled himself that she was dead anyway. That while the shot hadn't spilled her brains on the grass, she had died from it.

Now . . .

Now he was wrong.

Now the one consolation he had was stolen back from him.

She should be dead.

And Nick aimed to correct that error in universal logic.

As he was thinking that, Dunham stopped his pacing and faced the others. "Shit."

It was whispered, barely tapping the bars of the personal prisons each of them floundered in.

"Shit." He whispered the same word again.

But no one had to prod him. "It means there's a mole in the Bureau."

He looked sad. Defeated.

"It was the Bureau watching her in the hospital. They had men on rotation. I don't know who was there when she 'died.' I don't have any idea who pushed her body to the morgue or where she disappeared between there and the crematorium. But someone in the Bureau does. Someone at the very least lost her. And that would be very hard to have happen."

Nick heard him suck in a breath. "Someone let her go."

For a moment Nick felt bad for the man.

But the feeling was overpowered by his anger. The same anger he could feel radiating off his sister. They were vibrating at the same frequency—to the tuning fork that was Yulia Churkin, alive and walking around as Ann Evalyn Kimmel.

At one point Nick thought Mrs. Kimmel to be the worst of his problems. How easily that fallacy had fallen away.

As though he had run into a wall, Owen Dunham began repeating himself. "There's a mole in Bureau. There's a mole in the Bureau."

He grabbed his gun, his coat, his wallet and started off while the others looked at him, utterly confused.

At the door he turned back, looking at Nick as though why didn't he follow.

Dunham looked spooked, saying the same words again. "There's a mole in the Bureau."

Nick didn't know why that meant he had to run out the door right now, and he must have shaken his head, shrugged, something, because Owen Dunham looked scared.

"I called the Bureau to arrange for protection for Officer Hellico!"

---

Owen bolted from the motel room, flying down the second floor walkway and cursing Sin and her inability to get a ground floor room. She said it was safer, but she was talking in terms he had not yet come to terms with.

She spoke of forcing anyone coming to climb stairs, come at her from two directions. She spoke of vaulting over the railing, onto a car that she had waiting in the spot below for just that purpose.

They trailed him out of the room, not quite as fast as him.

He'd been ready to run, only stopping to throw Anni the keys to their car and tell her—ask her—to please return to their hotel room. Even as he scuttled his feet down the steps as fast as he could without tripping, he thought how he didn't fit in here. Sin shouldn't have let him come. He and Annika stuck out like sore thumbs.

A lone idiot, smoking in a chair outside his ground floor room, looked at Owen like he was the idiot, running around in his nice jacket and khakis, fleeing like his ass was on fire. Maybe he was.

His heart raced and he got to the car only a moment before Sin and Nick who were in much better shape than him. The only thing he was certain of was that Sin had not vaulted the railing and landed on the roof of her car. Though she had parked nose out for a fast getaway, a fact Owen was grateful for even as she refused to peel the mid-sized SUV out of the lot.

"That room is shot now."

Breaking his concentration on all the things that could go wrong while they drove to the hospital, Owen looked at her from the passenger seat. Sin kept her eyes on the road.

"Why is the room shot?" he asked.

"Because we bolted out of there like wild monkeys. We made a scene. We'll be remembered." She turned, hand over hand, refusing to go too fast. Refusing to make another 'scene'.

Owen understood.

But he wanted her to speed, dammit! "Can you not go any faster?"

"And get pulled over? At least you would look believably shocked at what's in the tire well in my trunk."

From the back seat, Nick Stelian snorted. Owen wanted to tell him that he could rescind the deal they had. No one else knew about it at this point. Owen hadn't sold Nick out to get the agents to the hospital. He'd used bait for a specific young agent. And it had worked.

Maybe too well.

His toes tapped the floor of the foot well, his knee jostled with the movement, his hand gripped and released the door handle as though his energy might make the car go faster. As if he could clear the road in front of them. He couldn't.

Owen tried to think about Annika, hoped she was resting, but had no idea how she might find sleep in this surreal and dangerous landscape he'd dropped her into. As always, he had to consciously remind himself that she handled it better than he did. So he sat there, continuing to wish he could bend time.

He'd called Agent Tex Pillow, knowing the kid had been given the thankless task of tracking the Mechanic. Told him he had one of the Mechanic's victims, alive and ready to talk when he came out of surgery.

Checking his watch, he saw that it was a crapshoot who would get to the hospital first—him or Agent Pillow.

Forcibly he turned his attention to the mole. Churkin had been 'lost' in Atlanta. Under local agency jurisdiction. So he knew there was a mole in the Atlanta area at that time. But that didn't tell him a lot. Turning in his seat, he tried to be useful and started questioning Nick.

"Did you have Agents in your pocket?"

Eyebrows raised at the bluntness of the question. "I wish."

"That's not an answer." Too used to the casual evasions practiced criminals gave, he had immediately shot back. It wasn't the way he should handle Stelian.

Owen had never brought in the Grudge Ninja. She would have made his career, but he'd made different choices. So he now sat in the car beside her with the opportunity to bring in possibly the most well-hidden and enigmatic crime lord in the US.

Keeping his job as a detective with the White Oak Police Department just outside of Atlanta was brilliant. The district was small enough that Nick could control his image, and close enough to the city he ran to allow him legal jurisdiction into crimes. Add in the cops in his own pocket and Stelian was well covered. Enough to earn Owen a huge boost when he worked the deal. A deal that had fallen into his lap from the very man he'd just insulted.

"No." Nick deadpanned. "I don't have federal agents in my pocket. If I had them, Churkin wouldn't be popping back up alive." The way his jaw clenched harder and harder as he spoke told Owen the truth of it.

"Do the Kurevs?"

"Probably. They're bigger than me and meaner. And it's their guy—woman—who's turning back up after dying in Bureau hands. So my guess is: yes, they do."

"But you don't know anything about it?"

Nick shook his head at Owen where he was cranked around, looking over the seat.

Owen had to agree with him. Too much evidence. Not enough information. Story of his life.

The question was, *is there a mole in Chicago now?* And the answer had to be, *Probably.* If the Kurevs had agents in Nick's city they either owned Atlanta guys—which was a possibility, or they sent them—also a possibility. Either way, there was no reasoning whatsoever that led Owen to believe they had gotten Bureau agents into an Atlanta hospital but couldn't do the same here.

It had been less than twenty-four hours since he and Sin had hauled the man out of the boathouse hell he was in. Unfortunately, that was more than plenty for the Kurevs to know he was missing and to react.

His toe tapped harder as the hospital came into view.

Sin swung near the sidewalk and stopped, missing the turnaround and the higher likelihood of a camera grabbing her license plate clearly. Owen blessed her for letting them out and practically ran inside, Nick Stelian hot on his heels.

Hellico was in Intensive Care, which meant he was down the long hall past the information desk. Getting to the ICU involved a disturbingly long wait at the elevator that was in fact only about fifty seconds. Owen knew because he checked his watch every three and contemplated taking the stairs. Even Nick looked nervous.

They rode up with someone in scrubs carrying a shower caddy full of needles, drugs, and plastic tubing, so Owen couldn't talk. He wasn't sure if Nick should go with him and as soon as they stepped out of the elevator, he said so.

"I know him."

"I know." Owen responded. "But what reason is there for you and me to be here together? If the FBI has eyes on us—which they will—there's nothing I can give them now."

Nick was nodding. "And if Kurev's people see me with you . . . I'm calling Sin." He muttered an expletive and took a side hallway as though he had always intended to go that way. Owen didn't point out that the sign he was heading toward said "Maternity" just kept his pace clean as he made his way through the tangle of hospital wards. It wouldn't do to rush.

It seemed ages before he turned the corner into the section housing ICU. A reverent silence was overlaid with irreverent beeping, breaking his thoughts as Owen scanned the area. Only a mild amount of natural light came in to the central area, mostly it was illuminated by fluorescents lending more power to the eerie feel of the place.

Owen wondered if anyone else knew that Nick knew Hellico. It might be a good thing he hadn't shown up.

Forcing his heart rate to slow, so that he didn't look like a crazed maniac, he leaned on the central counter and was roundly ignored by the man typing away on one of the computer systems. It was probably only ten or so seconds, but Owen didn't have it. Instead of being a complete ass, he went for half-ass and reached into his jacket and pulled out his state Bureau of Investigation badge, then held it over the counter where it was sure to catch the man's eye.

"Can I help you?"

He didn't seem bored, per se, but he didn't look like he'd completely come to attention either. The stress was eating Owen alive. This was exactly why he'd left the job.

"I'm here to see about Officer Doug Hellico?"

There was a shuffling of paper charts, and the man picked up a tablet, tapped in some info and looked up. "ID?"

Owen pulled his driver's license and the small ID that went with his badge. He waited impatiently while the Nurse scanned it, then checked it against something on his screen, then looked up at Owen's face, before handing it back. "Right behind you."

Of course.

The room full of staff, running a code while this guy sat at the desk and tapped away. He knew that's how the job worked. You couldn't have a personal emergency every time something emergent happened, but Owen resented the nurse's easy demeanor anyway. It was easier than fearing for Hellico.

Needing to act, he walked to the door where a federal type was standing awkwardly just outside the door.

"Owen Dunham. Former Field Agent."

The other man held out his hand at Owen's offer and they briefly connected as he asked, "Bureau?"

Owen nodded. "I brought this guy in. How's it look?"

"Not good." The man chanced a glance over his shoulder and Owen had to wonder if he wanted the man in the bed to live or if he was waiting for him to die.

Not knowing what to say to the other Agent, he decided to update Nick and Sin and sent each of them a separate text, letting them know that Hellico was coding as he wrote.

It seemed to go on forever as Owen watched. Long enough for Nick to text back a string of expletives.

Owen was about to find someone to ask what was happening when a different answer walked up to him and shook his hand.

"Agent Pillow." Owen had been expecting him. He was even expecting the new-agent-in-a-big-world nervousness and the attempted cover ups. Pillow had them all.

He ran his hand down his tie several times and muttered under his breath even as he tried to be polite to the man who'd handed him this break in his case. He kept tilting his head to peer into the room where the staff worked as though that would allow him to see through the doctors and nurses to the patient behind them.

Owen figured they were still working, which meant there was still hope.

Looking back at Agent Pillow he saw the frustration on the younger man's face and Owen tapped him on the arm. "A word of advice?"

"Sure." But Pillow didn't look at him.

"That's a person in there. With a wife and kids." Owen made that part up. He didn't know, but it made his case. "To you and me, he's valuable information that might jeopardize a case or future lives. To the people who work here, he's a patient. They don't care what he knows. And those nurses don't do this job for the pay."

Pillow was looking at him now, understanding on his face. But Owen kept talking.

"And you can't turn it on and off. Not only when you're talking to them. They're smarter than that. So no matter what you really think, you have to understand how to get what you want."

From the look on his face, Agent Pillow wasn't the cold prick he'd appeared when frowning over Hellico's horribly inopportune choice of death time. He nodded and his face took on a look that let through he'd simply forgotten it was a person under the needles and wires.

Owen let it drop. He'd been there—the eager agent, catching a break. Only no one had told him his zeal showed through when he was interviewing the wife of the dead man they'd found. He'd been off base. He'd alienated his best witness and been generally offensive. Maybe Pillow would turn out better for it. Who knew?

They watched the progress with Hellico, standing together just outside the door close enough to help if needed, far enough back to be out of the way. And a few moments later the doctors started stepping back, wiping brows, stripping gloves.

Only the steady beeping of the monitor told them the outcome was a positive one. Or at least as positive as it could be.

Owen was taking his first steady breath, wanting to reach for his phone, wanting to update Nick and Sin who were waiting anxiously out of the way. Or not so much as Owen caught Sin walking by down a far hall.

He tried not to look at her as she scoped out the scene without looking like it. She was that good.

"May I speak to you?"

The voice turned him back to the situation at hand. A nurse stood before him, a wadded up yellow gown in her hand, hair in a pony-tail, harried look from the recent battle to hold death at bay.

Before he could say anything, Agent Pillow answered, "Yes, of course."

But she only looked at the agent askance before saying, almost politely, "I need him." And pointing to Owen.

Shocked, Owen offered a slight shrug to the younger agent and followed her down the hallway. She dunked the wadded paper casually into a biohazard bin, stating "One in the room was full," as though he cared. Something in her voice triggered a reaction in him, fear? Maybe a thin layer under it? She'd just come out of a code, but . . .?

Owen didn't know. Not until she ducked into an empty room, closed the door and turned on him, eyes wide, acute terror showing on her features.

Reaching out to touch her shoulders and calm her didn't work. She broke on her own.

"I drugged Officer Hellico. Potassium Chloride to send him into heart failure!"

His mind reeled. A confession? A death attempt from this scared nurse?

She kept talking and Owen let her, his brain scrambling to keep up.

"A man came and told me I had to do it. He told me he'd kill me and my family. But it was about . . ." She checked her watch, her hand shaking too badly to read the time. Still she offered one. "About fifteen minutes ago. He stayed until the patient started seizing."

Her breathing came more raggedly now, her own fear about to claw out of her chest and reach for Owen. "I tried to turn it around. Save him with calcium chloride, dextrose, and insulin. But the man is gone now and I'm afraid he'll go after my family."

She sucked in air. "You said there were dirty cops involved. You're the only one I trust." Now she grabbed his shirt, her fists tight on the fabric as she shook him and demanded, "I saved your guy, now you save my family!"

# CHAPTER 24

Nick stood in the hospital hallway, his phone ringing. Not good news. "Yes?"

"One sec." Then Owen's voice turned away speaking to someone else. "Wait outside. I'll take care of this."

"Fast! I live about thirty minutes from here. They're all at home! You have to get there before he does." The woman's voice was frantic, sobs interlacing the words.

There was some kind of response from Owen before he spoke to Nick again. "The Mechanic was here."

"Hellico?" Nick asked. The man was a goldmine, no wonder the Mechanic had showed up.

"He's pulled through. A nurse was coerced to induce the problem and she didn't do the whole job. Needless to say she saved him." The words poured out of Owen almost too fast to keep up as Nick paced the hallway, nodding to doctors and patients who passed by.

Harsh, wooden chairs were parked in a row under a large window framing a gray sky outside, but Nick couldn't sit. In the next moment he was running.

Out of the hospital, telling Owen to call Sin, Nick fled the thoughts in his head as he fled the hospital. He spared a brief hope that it wasn't too odd to run in the hospital halls. It didn't matter. He needed the speed, the Mechanic was ahead of him.

Owen couldn't trust the FBI, certainly not Agent Pillow. Young as he was he had no proven record. And clearly Gilligan wasn't above threatening families, creating leverage.

Owen also couldn't trust the Chicago Police Department. There were too many in the Kurev pockets. Some in Nick's but it was a slow cultivation. He had numbers here, Nick wracked his brain for his best. The problem was both Nick and the Kurevs held something on his men. Nick's promise was to remove the Kurev threat, that's when the PD Officers would truly become his. Not yet.

The fact that Hellico was in the hospital after the Mechanic had worked him over was solid proof that the Kurevs knew Nick had at least one of their people. They would be activating higher alerts, watching more closely, monitoring, testing faith.

There were two officers Nick *knew* he could call. That was it.

He skidded out the door into the thick, cold air, dialing the first number. Unable to go farther, not knowing where Sin had parked, he was stuck there.

It was two minutes later that he found the man and promptly hung up. The officer was on active duty. There was no way Nick could take him away without arousing further suspicion from the Kurev camp. His goal had been to steal Kurev associates. Thus all his own men were also Kurev men.

Only now did he see his error . . . He needed others, other officers, those who didn't report to the Kurevs at all. But it was too late. Cultivation took time. Necessity had to lend a hand. Because, unlike Kaspar and Kolya before him, Nick wasn't willing to trap an innocent man to turn him. It was bad business in his mind— no help at all if they were always struggling to get out from under him.

So now he had one last call.

Sin blasted past him, a bolt of dull colors, pulling her hood up as she raced for the car; Nick took off after her. Sin was like the wind. She practiced for speed and distance, rough terrain, and apparently bolting from hospitals. She had the car started and was pulling out of the spot before Nick caught up with her, dialing as he ran.

The cell in his hand was ringing his second call as he slid into the passenger seat.

"Hello?"

The number would be unrecognizable, but the lone word Nick spoke told the man he needed to be alone to take the call.

"I'm good. What do you need?"

Nick rattled off the address he'd written on his hand, started the officer in that direction, and told him to arm himself with anything he could. Thank God Duffy wasn't on duty. He wasn't far from the nurse's home either.

Grasping the phone as Sin took a turn as fast as she could, Nick tried to stay on task. There was no picture, only Annika Dunham knew what the man looked like. Sin hadn't even seen him at the party. He'd only been there for a minute or two, while Mrs. Dunham had been talking to Sergei. So Nick did his best to repeat the description of the man's face. They had height, build, hair color from the pictures. "And his right hand has some kind of damage. Probably broken fingers, maybe a week or so ago."

Nick took a breath in while Sin sat at a traffic light that might cost the nurse's family their lives. But blazing through it and getting stopped would get them all killed. Nick and Sin in lockup wouldn't stop the Mechanic from torturing the family. At the green light, Sin jogged several lanes and exited at the next option.

"You have the right to shoot this man on sight. Do you understand?"

Duffy should have been a squeaky clean cop. When he pulled people over, he didn't even want to ticket them, he just wanted to stop speeding. He was calm in a crisis and cried over domestic abuse cases he couldn't fix. The Kurevs had spattered the man's white hat and he'd never been quite the same. Shooting someone on sight was not in his wheelhouse.

Nick did his best to persuade him. "He's a known assassin. Worse, he tortures his victims. Seems to enjoy it."

"Hence the name?"

"Yeah. And if you see him and don't stop him, he'll come after you. He told the nurse he'd come after her family if she didn't kill a patient." They took another turn and Sin took her chances, speeding up through the neighborhood.

With one hand she rifled in the backseat and under her own seat, pulling out weapons as they went. Sounds of Duffy driving through noisy streets broke into Nick's wandering thoughts.

"She believed him?" Duffy's car stopped and Nick heard the door opening.

"You there?" Nick shouldn't have asked. "Stay clear. She believed him because she was treating his latest prisoner. She'd seen what he was capable of. Don't engage him. Just get the family. We're . . ." Nick looked to Sin who flashed him three fingers "three minutes out."

"On it."

He was about to get hung up on, Nick knew it, so he yelled out, "Leave the line open." And hit the record button on his phone.

Sin raised her eyebrows at him.

Nick shrugged. "We can playback if we need to. I'll erase it. But . . ."

Only a nod accompanied the words as she scanned her way through a four-way stop, not stopping at all. No one followed. No blue lights came to life and followed them. A former cop herself, she knew all the hiding places and the chances. She'd taken them.

"Two blocks." She said. "We're going in the back. Not the alley."

As they parked, Nick heard knocking through the phone and

thought about how much of the day he'd spent listening in on the happenings rather than acting. But as Sin pulled the car to a stop under a tree in a disturbingly idyllic neighborhood, Nick was about to get in on the action.

He only hoped it didn't leave him in the same shape as Hellico.

Through the phone he heard Duffy identify himself as an officer and wondered what the woman had told her husband, if anything. He didn't wonder for long. He was stuffing spare magazines into his pocket as the phone chirped another call coming in. He didn't have time for it, but he also couldn't afford to miss something important.

Nick checked the number and didn't recognize it, so he answered it. "Hello?" Probably a wrong number. But the thought had no more flashed through his brain than he recognized the jilted cadence of a man under severe stress.

"This is Randall Holder, my wife gave me this number, she's a nurse—"

Nick interrupted him. Owen shouldn't have given out the number to one of Nick's burners but he still didn't have time to listen to a full explanation. "What do you need?"

"Nikki told me not to trust the police but the man at my door just identified himself as an officer with Chicago PD."

"Duffy?" Nick nearly barked it over the sound of the door slamming.

"Yes."

Walking briskly down the street, trying to both look casual and keep up with his smaller sister, Nick kept talking, giving Holder assurances that the man at his door was safe. Within moments he heard the door opening and Duffy's voice coming through the line. "Give the phone to the officer."

He didn't wait for the man to speak, Nick just started barking orders. "I can see the back door of the house, and I don't see anyone there."

"Husband says the inside is clear." Duffy reported back from a much calmer sounding Randall Holder.

"Don't trust it." Nick almost yelled back. There was no telling if the Mechanic had slipped inside while they made dinner or watched tv. Sin could do it. "Check for yourself or just wait for us."

He heard some back and forth where Duffy made sure that the family understood they couldn't pack anything, even though Holder made a case for his daughter's stuffed rabbit up in her bed.

Nick interrupted through the phone as they hit the back alley. "Don't you dare let them upstairs. They do not split up! Looks like—"

A little voice cut in, faint, but Nick could just make out the words. "There's another man coming up the front walk, Daddy. Should I get the door for him, too?"

"No!" He broke into a run. He was farther from the house than the Mechanic was. Gripping the phone in front of him as though he could make them understand, he yelled. "Get them out the back, NOW."

Sin heard all of this and broke her steady stride. There was no longer time to not draw attention to themselves. Gunshots would bring more attention. And they would have to shoot the mechanic. Nick couldn't go as fast and still bark instructions. He had to trust Sin. They had to be a team.

She was not the team he was used to, but they'd done okay the other night. Now he had to depend on her even more. Lee's life still hung in question and only the Mechanic seemed to know where he was. While Nick didn't want the man dead, he didn't know of any way to get the information out of him alive. He shouted to Duffy. "Get out, if he gets in range you have to kill him."

Hearing Nick's loud words, Sin threw open the back screen and kicked at the door, throwing a look over her shoulder that said she didn't agree with Nick. Though about what, he couldn't understand.

As he watched, she vanished into the house, gun in one hand, kama in the other.

Running across the back lawn and jumping over toys, Nick bolted toward where he'd last seen Sin. The back stoop was narrow, barely big enough for one person to stand and pull the door open.

Just as Nick was about to leap up the stairs, Sin appeared, nearly crashing into him as she sprinted out the back door. A small child clung to her like a monkey, Sin with a single arm around the bundle of pink clothes.

Nick held the door where it flapped behind her.

Sin was only the front of the brigade.

Holder, a middle-aged man not made for running, practically pushed a teenaged boy out the door. The kid leaped to the dead grass and followed Sin like a heat seeking missile. Somehow he had gotten the message better than the father. The father held the hand of an elementary aged boy and behind them Duffy was pushing them both out the door.

Nick immediately identified the pair as the weakest link.

Holder turned to him, apparently trusting Nick because Duffy did. "He knocked on the door."

Good to know, but . . . "Shut up and run."

The man looked offended but Nick pushed his shoulder and let Duffy pass, taking up rear guard.

Sin would stuff them all in her car, luckily an SUV today. But it was a block away.

She was almost there, Nick was still walking sideways, his gun out while trying not to look like it. He still harbored some hope that a neighbor wasn't reporting the Holder family being kidnapped. That would bring a shitstorm down. So he kept his back to the street, and his hope high.

Putting himself between the father-son duo and the space at

the side of the house, Nick tried to block for them. The afternoon wasn't quiet, with cars going by on neighborhood streets and birds calling from trees, but Nick thought he heard something from the space between the houses.

In a moment he was rewarded with the sight of a man matching their description coming around the corner and stepping over a bush that supposedly guarded the edge of the house. As he came around, he lifted his gun.

# CHAPTER 25

O wen met them at yet another motel. Since he didn't have the time to set it up, he asked Annika.

That was heart stopping—both in sending her out to do it and wondering if she would be okay. Then it hit him again when he arrived at the incredibly cheap looking motel with a new duffel bag full of medical supplies and didn't see Annika anywhere.

He didn't see Sin or Nick either. There was no real information coming in, only one message that they were en route and needed care for a bullet wound. It didn't tell him whether someone had been grazed or was bleeding out of their aorta. His return question had not been answered.

Annika had told him their room was the middle door of the back row. Though he parked—nose out, as Sin had drilled into him—a check of his mirror revealed only two old men sitting outside sipping forties. They appeared too drunk to realize they were going to freeze their balls off. One decrepit looking woman who had to be a cheap prostitute stood sentry.

Owen figured he had a moment and took stock. His clothing was too nice for this neighborhood. Zipping the jacket would help as he'd bought a cheaper one just for blending in. He didn't even want to think about the money he was hemorrhaging during this little 'trip'. Hotel rooms, extra clothing, phones, even duffle bags and medical supplies.

The bag itself was clearly new. Shit, he hadn't even pulled the tag. Though he did that immediately, it still looked shiny, like he was a courier for a drug lord or something. By his own measure he now wasn't that much above what he'd thought of those guys. Somehow his motives made the difference.

Or did they?

Was he where he'd always felt others deserved to be when they found themselves on the wrong side of the law or a gun or a powerful criminal like Kurev? Was he simply the victim of a series of poor decisions? Not bad decisions, and certainly decisions made for the right reasons—helping a friend, ending the Kurevs, upholding the moral right if not the legal one . . .

For a moment Owen considered starting the car and driving away. But Anni would be here any moment. She'd gotten a room for them, and Sin and Nick would show up with a family, an officer, and a gunshot wound and . . . *Shit*. He *was* on the wrong side of it. But he got out of the car anyway and went under the tree as the wind picked up making the air colder than a subarctic witch hunt. He kicked at the grass a little, hidden from the view of the old men and the hooker as he battered the duffel, destroying its eye-grabbing shininess and hopefully not the supplies inside.

After scuffing his shoes a bit, too—they also clearly identified him as not belonging—he headed toward the middle of the old, faded paint doors. The hooker looked up at him and asked if he wanted anything. But he waved her off only to find she'd stood and followed him, flashing a room key dangling from the end of a sawed-off hunk of broom.

He needed a better life. He needed to get back to his daughters and school-drop-off lines and soccer practice and over-privileged college kids who thought they deserved an A.

He was ready to brush the woman off again when she shoved

her way close to him and put her mouth on his ear, nearly making him retch. He was turning away, but she put a hand on his arm, stopping him.

It was only then that he noticed she didn't smell as bad as he expected. Only then did he let the familiarity of her seep through with the words.

"Baby, it's me." She laughed then stepped back, still waggling the key. "Come in the room with me."

This time he did, trying to look as though he had chosen to go rather than that he'd discovered the hooker was his pregnant wife. No sooner had he closed the door than he turned on her, "Please tell me you didn't get propositioned while you waited."

She smirked at him and shook her head. "I said I had a fancy date coming to get me."

He was willing to bet the slight Russian lilt to her words only made her more believable. Plenty of women had come over the way she did, but didn't have mothers who educated them the way hers had. Again he found himself wondering about the people he'd arrested in the past and whether they might have been victims of circumstance more than actual criminals.

Owen pulled his phone and gave Nikki Holder his information while his wife stripped out of her bright, cheery puffy coat and ragged-cut, carrot red wig. As he talked, Annika quickly swapped out the skirt and knee high boots for jeans and sneakers.

Gratitude filled Mrs. Holder's words, "I'll tell them I don't feel well. I'll be there in about . . . Thirty minutes. Oh, thank you!"

Yeah, he thought as he hung up, he hadn't told her about the gunshot wound yet.

Annika was laughing and Owen was still upset about the fact that he hadn't recognized her when Sin pulled up in an SUV less than a minute later. It didn't look like it fit here any better than he did.

Briefly he considered going out to greet them, but that wasn't normal in a place like this. Annika was already through the door that adjoined the two rooms, the flimsy chain swinging as she left the door open. He heard her as she ushered the family inside as though she were the wife.

"Honey!"

From the small portion he could see, the Holders looked confused. But they were pushed along by Sin and Nick, the teenaged son seeming to get into the play for a moment.

Tipping his head to the other side, Owen looked to see what kind of impression the family made on the two men drinking and smoking in the frigid weather. But he couldn't see them and he couldn't go outside and check while he was supposed to be in here boinking his cheap-hooker wife. He was perhaps most disturbed by the way Annika entered this world so easily, how much she seemed to enjoy it.

Whatever happened out on the walkway, no one seemed to be making a fuss about the SUV that pulled up and dumped a family out into the parking lot. No one cared as they all headed into one room.

Owen went back to his task, opening the duffel bag and lining up what supplies might be needed for a gunshot wound.

Inside of a few seconds, Nick and Sin came into this room, another man trailing them. In Nick's brief introductions, it didn't escape Owen's notice than no one's full name was used.

"Owen, Duffy. Duffy," He pointed between them. "Owen."

Duffy wrapped his left hand around the meat of his right bicep and only raised his fingers a little in greeting, telling Owen all he needed to know.

"Is that the only wound?"

Sin nodded. "Gunshot. Mechanic. Duffy, the dad, the youngest son, and Nick have now all seen his face."

She seemed frustrated not to be able to count herself among that number. But Owen didn't have time to linger on that thought. Duffy was peeling his damaged jacket and revealing a t-shirt tied around the wound.

As they watched, the adrenaline drained out of the officer and he started to tilt. Mercifully he passed out fully while Owen cleaned the wound and Sin went to work stitching him, her sewing disturbingly neat.

Owen would never want motel room stitches himself, but he didn't start that argument. There wasn't time.

Nikki Holder showed up then, still in scrubs, another person too nice-looking for this backwater motel. Annika in her hooker get-up had been the only one to really fit in.

Owen left them where they were and went into the other room to see his wife serving crackers and sodas. *What the hell?* She must have hit the door the moment he hung up with her and ran roughshod through a box store getting all this stuff. He'd be amazed if he wasn't so distressed by it.

Nikki was touching her family, stroking hair, holding the little one, her relief at their safety pouring from her. Owen interrupted —she could start talking and they could figure this out or it might be the last time she touched them.

"Why you?" He asked bluntly.

Nikki Holder looked at him blankly, then shrugged. "I guess because I had access to the patient and only a few of us did."

Owen nodded, trying to remember his own advice to Agent Pillow, *that's a person in there. And she'll give you more if you're nice.* "Tell me how it happened."

"He had a chart, scrubs, looked like one of the staff. Pulled me aside to talk about one of the other patients, but when he had me there, he slipped the potassium chloride into my pocket and told what he would do to my family." Tears shimmered in her eyes but didn't fall. Only then did she seem to consider maybe she shouldn't be telling this story in front of the kids, but she didn't stop.

Owen couldn't make the pieces fit; it nagged at him. Turning back to her, he picked at threads. "He knew about your family?"

She nodded. "He knew the address, the kid's ages, where they went to school."

That. Right there. That was the problem. "The kids go to public school?"

"No. Private." She hugged the smaller one to her. He'd go to a daycare.

Owen asked.

Nikki gave him the name of a place, and shrugged again. "It's closer to Rand's work than home."

Sin stepped through the doorway, clearly having been paying attention to the conversation. "That's a lot of info. Really specific for . . . What? Ten hours Hellico was in the hospital? Sounds like he had a file on her beforehand."

Both the Holders stifled gasps as Sin spoke. Owen understood. It was hard to think about. A madman like the Mechanic coming after you. And it wasn't anything they could brush off as paranoid either. The man had shown up and even shot Officer Duffy, who was now sleeping off motel-room surgery next door.

Owen was thinking: Public schools were an easy guess, private wasn't. Knowing the daycare was even odder, because it wasn't near their home. Owen picked another thread. This time he turned to the husband. "Where do you work?"

"Blackwell." There was a pause. "I'm a CPA."

The words came out of Sin's mouth and Owen turned just in time to catch her dark look.

"Sonofabitch."

---

Sin closed the door between the two rooms. "She *was* targeted."

Annika looked at her oddly, but Nick understood.

Sin didn't let them get a word in edgewise. "Blackwell is a

Kurev firm. It owns a bunch of other companies. Some of which pretty clearly launder money."

Owen sighed. "I thought we shut them down?"

Years ago, Sin and Lee had delivered an accountant, tied to a tree, wearing a necklace of computer information. They'd also "convinced" several other employees to talk. And the firm had shut down with Owen's help.

"No. We shut down Black and Associates." Pure frustration boiled in her. Another firm had sprung up to replace what was lost. Just like the one before. Just like Nick had always told her.

Just like Kaspar had come up worse than Kolya before him.

Just like Churkin and Shvernik had come, and now Kelly Gilligan . . . Each one worse than the ones before.

Her heart clenched.

This was her life's work.

Sadly, it seemed Nick's cynical predictions were cold truth. Severing the head of the dragon should have been a success. But she was not the victor, she was merely stuck back where she started.

Tromping to the other side of the room, unable to stop the anger in her footfalls, she opened the door and stared at Randall Holder.

Hand still resting on the knob, she looked him in the eye and asked, "Do you know what you do for a job?"

His gaze dropped to the floor, while his wife looked back and forth between Sin and her husband. All the answers were right there. Sin wanted to tell him he disgusted her, but stopped herself. His children didn't need to hear that. She wouldn't have heard it when she was a kid, no matter how loudly or clearly it had been stated. Instead she closed the door and turned to the rest of the group.

"Nick, Owen, are you ready to launch the deal you have? Get Nick out as soon as this is cleaned up?"

Nick shrugged, seeming like it really wasn't up to him, but

Owen nodded. Then he frowned suddenly and reached for his jacket, rumbling around for a pocket. As Sin watched he pulled out one phone then another, checking each screen. "I forgot. . . Here . . ."

He looked up at her.

"Sin. The bloodwork came back."

She just stared at him.

"It's Lee's."

That made her brain feel funny. "How do they know it's Lee's? I thought no one had our DNA on file! You said—" Her trust faltered. Owen promised them the old evidence against them was gone. "Is there a new case on us?"

Her heart rate sped up. This would kill Nick's deal, make it harder to get Lee into a hospital. After seeing Hellico, it was clear there was no way Lee would get through alive without surgery, and that meant using the fake IDs she always carried for them. He had a new one, from the go-bag she'd dug up that first night outside the cabin. But his DNA on file? That meant anything could pull him up into the FBI's crosshairs. Especially with Hellico already in.

Sin couldn't imagine that the Mechanic's work wouldn't be matched between the two. There would be no way . . .

Suddenly, Owen was in front of her, grabbing her shoulders and shaking her. "No, it's not on file. Listen to me."

Sin looked up. He seemed serious. Finally, she listened.

"I sent it to a private lab. To my friend. He's the only one who touched it. He hand matched it to a piece of the sheets from your cabin. That's it. That's how I know it was Lee's."

For a moment her head spun with images of the blood soaked sheets. But she forcibly pushed them out of the way.

Owen was still talking. "—fresher than a week ago. So Lee was in that basement more than two days ago but fewer than seven."

Sin nodded. Lee was still out there. She had to believe.

With one deep breath, she stopped herself. Staying still was the only way to hear what might be coming up behind you. "I have to find him soon. We're running out of time."

They all nodded.

*Good.*

"Churkin is out and about with the Kurevs. She'll recognize me."

Annika shook her head. "I barely recognize you. You'll be fine. We'll be fine."

"She's good. And she hates me. She'll be looking for me in every face she sees." Sin shook her head. "The way Ann Evalyn died . . . She'll know that was me. Just like I would know it was her."

Sin took another deep breath. "Annika, Owen, you should take the people next door somewhere safe. You know the drill."

Owen would understand about taking their phones, tossing the pieces and destroying any GPS. He understood about disguising the family. Annika would think of anything else they needed, like clothes or food for the toddler.

Just as Owen was about to protest, Sin held up her hand.

"Nick and I are going a separate way. You can't hear any of this."

Seeming to catch on, and obviously ready to be out of here, Owen pointed to the unconscious man on the bed. "Duffy?"

"Take Duffy with you." The officer was starting to come around, the conversation taking place over his head clearly getting into his psyche.

But Owen didn't wait. He tugged at the man's hand, pulling him up to sitting and then braced himself under Duffy's good arm to walk him out the other door.

It was Nick who stopped Annika, "Trade me cars."

Sin only caught this out of the corner of her eye. She was looking at Owen as he turned around in the doorway. Her heart was heavy, but she was starting to form a plan.

"I'm going to hand you the Kurevs on a platter."

# CHAPTER 26

Nick Stelian was nervous. That was not normal for him.
He'd talked to his lawyer, Dana, and for the first time, he'd given her Owen's information. That way she could decide how to contact the man, what to reveal and what not to reveal.

Owen wasn't really his lawyer. That relationship had a lot of legal loopholes in it, but Dana really was. She was the one Nick met up with while Sin planned. She was the one he spoke to about taking down the Kurevs. Her questions had been to the point.

"Will people die?"

"Most likely." He knew better than to fully admit what they were up to. He'd learned a long time ago—at his grandfather's feet—to only express concern for the outcome, to only offer projections rather than plans.

"Will you be involved in that happening?" Dana knew the lingo, too. She was morally and legally obligated to report any suggestion a client was about to go commit a crime. Particularly one of the nature Nick described.

Nick knew her morals lay along the same lines as his own. They made a good team that way. And he answered accordingly. "It would be the likely outcome."

She'd left him with one piece of legal advice, "Don't get caught."

It would jeopardize his standing with Dunham, his chances at getting a sweet deal with the feds, any money he might retain. It would jeopardize his chances to walk around as a free man.

If he didn't do this though, it would jeopardize Lee's chances to walk around as a live man. He didn't mention it to Sin.

The Kurevs were first on the list. Churkin would be there with him tonight. That's what they hoped.

Sin stood in the doorway of yet another motel. They'd abandoned the first room, but aside from the fact that it wasn't the same place, it was the same place.

She was in her wig, though tonight her eyes were her own brown. She couldn't risk the contact lenses she often wore. Her purse hung over her shoulder, and she had on leather pants and boots that laced tightly to her feet. While she did look party ready, she also looked fight ready.

Nick did not.

He was in his slacks and button down shirt.

"You don't have a vest on." She meant the Kevlar she wanted him to wear.

"Neither do you."

She shook her head. "Too obvious."

"Same here." He shrugged at her. He'd tried it. At best it looked like a sudden weight gain in only his chest. The Kurevs would notice. And the two of them needed access—they needed to get into the back rooms. They needed to walk in, not fight their way in.

Fighting their way in would get them killed. The vest would not protect from that. So he only had on his usual slacks and button down shirt.

He stuck a gun in the back of his waistband, but it was a flag for the men at the door. An offering for them to take upon his entry.

"Are you ready?"

He nodded, but said, "I want Churkin."

Sin knew it. He still needed the closure for Reese.

He wanted Churkin because he thought he'd already won that game and that small consolation had been yanked out from under him.

Then he shook the thoughts and started the engine. It wasn't long before he passed the spare car parked just beyond the Kurev's north entry. There was another spare waiting out back. Each of them had keys for each car. Getting "in" was the issue, "out" was already in place as much as it could be.

Two cars, separate arrivals. And Nick wondered how the Kurevs got anything done when they kept inviting random people inside their home, especially when they kept letting Sin in.

He checked his weapons, and took his shinier car in one direction, Sin split off down the road. With phone contact, they timed it perfectly, Nick pulling in before her.

At the door, he was checked and his gun taken from him, just as he suspected. But he walked slowly down the hallway, heading toward the sounds of yet another gathering, stalling for time.

Nick tugged at the tie, pulling it from his neck, they hadn't taken it, and he wasn't going to wear it into this little impromptu get together. They hadn't taken all of his other weapons either.

He ambled along, waiting to hear Sin behind him, so he headed further down the hall. He didn't doubt Churkin would recognize him, so he and Sin had to enter together. As he swung past the open double doors, he heard Sin's voice in the entry behind him.

"Really, you're going to check my purse?"

They'd find cigarettes, a lighter, hairspray, another small hairspray . . . It couldn't be helped. Nick kept his hand down by his side, showing her an open five fingers. He estimated almost fifty people in the room. He ducked into the restroom and burned a minute while he listened to them check out his sister.

"Thank you." He heard her finally heading down the hallway just as Nick was finishing washing his hands.

His nerves kicked up.

Though it didn't change his ability to function, he felt it.

He came through the door from one side, Sin from another, still fumbling in her purse as though the check had messed things up.

Nick saw Yulia Churkin look up as they entered.

For just a moment, he watched her eyes recognize him then flit to the woman next to him. They were narrowing as she looked.

Sin produced the small hairspray bottle then yanked it apart, throwing it at Churkin and Kaspar's feet. Though both jumped, too slow to avoid the world going white and wild for a moment.

It was all he and Sin needed and they worked while the others fought off the disorienting effects of the flash bang.

He heard screaming and suspected that Churkin and Kaspar would come around the fastest. It didn't matter though. Sin was reaching for the other little can of hairspray.

Still blinded, their ears would be ringing. They wouldn't hear it hit or see the smoke sizzling out in a stream that was quickly dissipating into the air.

Nick reached into his jacket and ripped out the lining he'd pulled then tacked down earlier that day. Sin was already yanking at the fabric on the side of her purse. Each pulled out a thin, clear mask with a rubber, sealing rim around the edges and under the eyes to prevent fogging. A small filter on the front let them breathe, both of them getting it onto their faces just as the CS gas hit their side of the room.

The air was cloudy with the stuff, but through the faint haze they could see people coughing and rubbing their faces. Many dropped down on all fours as though that would help. Nick felt it too as it started to seep into his pores.

But that had been expected. This was a police issued canister he'd brought with him. The same stuff he and Sin had trained on in White Oak. They already knew how it would feel, though Nick could admit that the memory never quite added up to reality. The shit burned. His armpits were the worst as the stuff attacked glands, but he pushed aside the pain, taking his advantage. He went after the people around Yulia Churkin.

The room was brightly lit. So with his clear shield on his face —which wasn't as good as a real gas mask—he was able to make out Sin signal him as she tossed him some cosmetic canister from her purse.

Nick knew what it was.

Yanking the lid, he pulled the trigger, streaming OC spray into the faces of the nearby partiers. Oleoresin Capsaicin was a purse standard, but this was military grade. Nick wasn't surprised that people went from crying and rubbing at their faces to curled on their hands and knees, clearly feeling a burn akin to razor blades in their throats. A few were even trying to scream, though they couldn't really make sounds. Pepper spray was bad when you saw it coming. And though the effects were only temporary, having it hit you when you were already blind had to be scary.

Nick didn't care. They shouldn't have been here. Everyone knew what Kurev really was, and those who didn't deserved it for being stupid.

The OC was starting to hint at Nick's skin, but again he'd been ready.

As he headed forward he searched the people who were down. Which one was Churkin?

Nick scanned the space, looking for the woman who didn't quite pass as Ann Evalyn. Nothing popped out at him. He was scanning the people coughing and yelling on the floor a second time when one of them stood up.

She stood tall, staring at him. Her brown eyes watered at the gas, but that was the only thing masking the hatred radiating from her. Of course she hated him, he'd shot her in the head. And he intended to do it again, only with better results this time.

Reaching into his pocket to finger the tie he'd stashed there, Nick took stock.

The way she blinked, the OC gas was having little effect on her. Police training warned him that a few people were nearly immune to the stuff. It would just figure Churkin was one of them. The other possibility was that she'd trained with it, just as he and Sin had. Maybe she knew how to handle the pain, understood that it would fade and she should breathe shallowly. But the subtle shifts in her stance looked like the CS gas was getting into her skin.

Good.

It was easy to see why she'd been mistaken for Sin once upon a time. Her hair and eye color were the same; she stood like a fighter, just like Sin, and she was dressed to literally kill if necessary. In the short skirt and tightly laced boots, she could have been Sin through the haze in his eyes. But he knew better.

They looked alike because the two were cousins. In fact, Churkin was his cousin, too.

That was all it took.

The convoluted web of relationships that Kolya Kurev had spun during his life lived on long after his death. Nick didn't care that she was his cousin. He *hated* her. She'd killed the one good thing he'd found, the one person who made him think he could be more than just the head of the Vasilescu crime family, more than just a backward cop living two lives.

He pulled the tie out, the silk slipping through his fingers. He didn't have Sin's moves; he relied on guns, Tasers, pepper spray, and cuffs. None of which he had now. And Churkin did have Sin's moves.

Not turning his head, Nick listened for sounds of his sister behind him. From what he could see from the corner of his eye, she was grabbing shoulders and turning people over looking for

Kurevs. But movement in front of him brought him back to his own fight.

Yulia Churkin stepped over the writhing body on the ground in front of her, her eyes wet but clear. Through his mask he could see the anger on her face and for the first time he wondered if Stanislav Shvernik had meant anything to her personally. He could only hope that Shvernik getting his face blown off in Nick's front yard had hurt her as much as Reese's death had hurt him.

Nick decided he didn't care. He only knew that his fighting skills were at a disadvantage here, but his anger, his hatred, would carry him through.

The punch would have connected with his jaw had he not seen it coming. As it was, she was so fast he almost didn't get out of the way in time.

Even in heels, even with her fist not connecting, even given the writhing, crying bodies at her feet, Yulia Churkin didn't stumble. She was that good.

Nick took a deep breath of tainted air and reminded himself that her air was worse. She didn't have the mask.

With a quick step to his left, he used his right leg to sweep out hers. But—like her—he missed.

She simply wasn't there when his foot went by.

Her own leg connected to the back of his standing leg, taking it out, neatly reversing his move onto him. While he wasn't her caliber, Nick was good. He'd lived his whole life knowing there was a punch flying, a hit coming, a gun aimed at him, and though she made contact, she didn't take him down either.

Her elbow came at him in an arc that looked nearly graceful through the time gap of adrenaline.

This time she hit. He'd moved, taking the blow in a glance on the shoulder and using it to his advantage, Nick went down of his own accord. Two steps into clearer space, away from the crying, sniveling party guests. His left hand coming up to grip his upper arm as though in pain. He would have a bruise, but it was nothing to worry over, he just made it look like it was.

From over his own shoulder he could see her taking the bait, following him to where he was crouched, his back to her.

It was dangerous, baiting her with his spine. He didn't doubt she'd cripple, crush, or even kill him in a heartbeat.

The boot came down next to his left foot, his hand still clutching his arm as he hunched over. He knew she was coming in, but he couldn't see how so he just exploded.

Levering his right hand against his left fist, he led with his elbow, shooting upward into whatever she was bringing.

Nick felt it contact before he even knew what he'd hit.

She kept coming forward, the long bone of his arm bearing the brunt of her weight. For once, she hadn't seen it coming. But Nick kept going.

Letting go with his right hand, he curled his fingers. He'd been taught this, but in the moment it was instinctual, and he jammed the knuckles up under her jaw.

Only, it wasn't her jaw.

Behind him, some part of her—elbow, fist, knee?—connected into what was surely his kidney. He was going to piss blood for a few days, but Nick didn't care. The thought flitted away as he realized what he was hitting. Not her chin, but some part of her shoulder.

Clenching his fist, he went for a different approach, hammering down onto the top of her clavicle. Two hits, three, four, he kept going, knowing that sooner or later he would hit the nerve cluster there. He aimed into the meat of her trapezius, hoping he hit it before she stopped him.

A muffled grunt, followed by her stumbling backward, was his answer.

*Bitch.* She deserved it.

He was facing her now, though his feet were twisted under

him from when he'd come up so abruptly, and he first straightened them out.

For a moment, they circled each other, Nick knowing the time he spent getting his breath back was also time Churkin used to regain her own footing. Everything else in the room had fallen away, except it hadn't.

Too well trained to look away, Nick still took in the partier on the floor, her dress hiked up in a decidedly un-lady-like manner. Not that she'd been a lady before he'd thrown CS and OC gas on them all. One of her sparkly, spiked, fuck-me heels was missing and her face oozed tears and mucus. Nick didn't care. He only cared that she was crying and feeling her way around behind Churkin. And Churkin didn't see her.

With a rush of speed from adrenaline and sheer anger, Nick charged her. His hands didn't come up until the last moment, deliberately deceiving her from knowing where he would strike.

And he didn't strike. He pushed.

A quick shove to her hips, a shoulder into her chest, hitting all her major points of gravity. The woman on the ground behind her became no more than a tool for him, but she ensured that Churkin could not keep her feet.

Nick landed on top of her, hearing the breath whoosh out of her. But she wasn't in a street fight. She was in a gas fight and Nick had the mask. Flimsy as it might be, it was a benefit.

Churkin was coughing as she reached for his face. Her eyes were squeezed shut and he could only hope the gas was getting to them, finally. Her hands clawed at him, a nail peeling a good strip from his cheek, the burn worse in the toxic air. Nick didn't care.

He shoved the heel of his hand into her chin, slamming her head back against the floor. It was a good hit, but the thick, garish carpet made a mockery of his anger, padding her against the blow.

She twisted, using her hips and shoulders to create momentum and shove him off.

More startled than he should have been, Nick jolted backward but was stopped by someone on the floor behind him. The grunt—a guttural break from the whining—signaled that the other person hadn't been expecting the hit either. Nick paid no attention and spent his energy faking confusion.

He didn't have to do it long; Churkin gained her feet almost faster than humanly possible. Just another reminder that he was fighting an expert. But he shot his hands out, grasping her ankles just as she got upright, and with a quick jerk using all his weight, he took her stability right back out from under her.

This time when her head hit, he heard it.

Though her breath whooshed out again in an attempt to control the fall, it wasn't enough.

Crawling forward, even as she thrashed a bit in surprise, he could see her eyes and the stunned confusion there. Though the carpet was still thick and still ugly, this time the force had been hard enough. Churkin blinked, stunned by the blow to her head. Even though her limbs were already in motion from years of training, it wasn't enough. She wasn't aware of what exactly she was fighting against, which Nick used to his advantage.

He wished he had a gun, he wanted bullet holes in her; he wanted actual blood. But he couldn't get a gun past the front door. Instead he had his tie. Reaching into his pocket he easily grabbed at the only thing in there.

Kneeling over her, Nick watched as her eyes began to focus. It all happened so quickly that he couldn't have counted it off had he tried. What mattered was that the tie was in his hands.

Long and silk, it was sturdy enough for the job he had in mind. Without thinking of anything other than killing this woman—again—he wound the ends around his hands, the grip reassuring him.

Before she could react to bring her hands up, Nick straddled her and brought the fabric down across her neck, the muffled thunk of her head hitting the floor again satisfying deep in his gut.

Churkin struggled, but Nick didn't let up. He thought only of Sin and how Churkin had ambushed her in Atlanta. Of Lee, asleep in his bed as Churkin and her friend poisoned them and opened fire. He remembered Reese, and how he had tried to hold her skull together after Churkin and Shvernik had shot her in the middle of Nick's living room.

At that last thought, he unconsciously gave the tie an extra yank and watched as her face started to change color.

And she was starting to fight back despite that fact.

He expected her hips to come up, her feet bracing under her to throw him.

Though she did lift him off her, he didn't let it stop him. Coming up off the floor, pushing into the necktie, she sacrificed a little of her own pain to get out of what he held her in. Nick wasn't having it.

As she lifted her head, he took advantage and jerked his right hand quickly around her head, keeping the pressure on her windpipe as best he could. He now had the tie wrapped entirely around her neck. Wherever she went, he need only pull on the ends to cut off her air.

So when she gained a position of advantage and pressed her own bare hands to his neck, Nick held tight. He yanked the ends of his neck tie, satisfied with the changing shades of her skin. It wasn't fast, he had to hold on a long time, but it was effective.

When her fingers pressed into the flesh at his neck and he felt the floor pressing up behind him, he yanked harder on the silk.

And when his own vision started to sparkle and dim, he reminded himself that it was a game of time and he'd started first.

# CHAPTER 27

S in watched through the shiny film of her mask as Nick went
after Churkin. The gas made the air a little cloudy. The
party-goers crawling, crying and wheezing toward the door made
the going rough. Sin didn't care.

She was more worried that Nick was outmatched. When he
had a gun in his hand, her brother was fine. He had plenty of
training and no compunction about pulling the trigger. But he
didn't have his gun and Sin was confident that he was wholly
outclassed at hand-to-hand with Churkin.

But she had other fish to fry.

The mask interfered with her peripheral vision and she
needed to turn her head from side to side to sweep the room.
There was no disguising that she was looking for someone, and
had anyone been paying attention, it wouldn't be a surprise that
she was looking for the Kurev brothers and Kelly Gilligan.

Gilligan was nowhere to be seen, but Roman was easy to find.

The noise alone led her right to him.

Though he usually spoke clean, American English, he fought
for air with a hint of an accent.

"Kahs-par?" The letters were muffled by the effects of the gas,
but he was calling for his brother. He was leaking water from

both eyes and making odd, jerky movements as though he could escape the gas that had already seeped into his pores.

Sin was used to it. The younger Kurev clearly was not.

"Roman?" She walked over to him and stood, tilting her head to stare down at his position on the floor.

Though he wasn't rolling around wailing as some had, he had only managed to gain his hands and knees. Sin corrected that.

With a quick, head-turning scan of the room, she spotted Kaspar making his way for the door. She wanted him dead, but that would have to wait, Roman was her better bet.

The black boots proved useful as she ground one heel into the base of his spine and forced him flat.

Though he rolled partway to face her, he didn't fight back.

She scanned the area, checking for anyone who was focused on her, then reached into the side of her trendy polyester pants. The stripes each hid a plastic whip; grabbing the tops, she pulled them free. They easily survived a good pat-down, but the small weights on the ends packed a punch.

Rheumy eyes widened as Roman watched her pull them loose.

*Good.*

"Roman," She leaned down, "Where's Lee?"

"I don't know who you're—"

She didn't let him finish. The whip cracked across the side of his head, leaving a short gash.

He hadn't yet finished corralling the pain that had fled his lips when she asked again. "Where's Lee?"

His hand came up, as though he could hold her off. As though she would show him mercy for his weakness.

Wishing she could shoot him again, Sin went back to the work she'd resigned herself to. Torturing Roman was almost like hurting the dumb kid who didn't know any better. But Roman was no stupid kid, he was just a bastard who valued his meth and his big house and his coke and his shiny car more than he valued other lives. Namely Lee's.

The whip cracked again, this time across his face, letting him know he'd better get his shit together and speak quickly.

"I—" He held the hand up again, palm out, though it hadn't protected him the last time. "You're my sister."

It almost had a question mark, as though a few genes from their asshole of a father made him a victim here. He almost seemed surprised that she would do this to him. "Oh, no. I'm no sister of yours."

He frowned as though his genetics had somehow betrayed him.

This time the whip caught him across the open palm of his hand even as she scanned the room.

She was getting impatient.

Kaspar had managed to get near the door and was folding himself into the writhing mass trying to shove its way, unseeing, through the narrow space. Sin would have laughed, but Roman was finally talking.

"Basement. Old bar. South town." His words were punctuated by gasps. Though if the sounds were from the gas or the gashes she'd laid open, Sin couldn't tell.

He rolled over, face down, cradling his split hand. He was high as a damn kite, so she was shocked he even had that much self-preservation in him. And she didn't let it work.

Her heel, despite the fact that she was still bent over him, again jammed into his lumbar vertebrae. "No. He was there last week."

Angry now, she pushed against his spine until it forced a sound out of his lungs. This asshole knew where Lee was. He was soaking in a mix of two gases, had cuts from her whips, was clearly being dominated and was *still* trying to bullshit her.

The whips were designed to hurt.

Plastic and definitely not mainstream, they had taken her a

while to master. So she didn't worry about tossing them away in favor of something more useful; she didn't think anyone could really pick them up and use them. But he still hadn't told her what she needed.

His now almost completely face-down position presented her with his clothing, and too many layers to do maximal damage. "Roll over."

"No." He yelled it like a kid who didn't want to go to bed.

"Roman. You will tell me where my husband is or I'll kill you."

He didn't budge.

"Then I'll kill your brother."

He still didn't budge.

He couldn't see clearly enough to block her. Only able to tell that she was coming at him, he held his hands up in defense, unaware that was exactly what she wanted him to do.

There was no telling what might be crawling in his blood, but it was a chance she needed to take. Grabbing at his hand, she forced her thumb into the open wound.

The sound of Roman screaming would have been music to her ears, but it didn't contain any words.

It wasn't enough. She switched her grip, pressing against his wrist and the back of his hand, forcing the bones in his wrist to start separating. In another minute she would snap it. "Lee?"

"I don't kn—"

The sound of bone cracking was buried under the scream he let loose. He tried to stop it but failed. Being high didn't help his self-control. Sin had hoped to use that in her favor, instead it just seemed to make Roman cry.

And it turned out his screaming had attracted attention.

As she swept her head to the side, always scanning the room, she saw a figure break away from the pack.

Kaspar.

He was coming to help his brother.

Luckily the people in between were hindering his progress.

They only knew they were in danger, so they panicked like gazelles and trampled like hippos.

Where Roman was an idiot, Kaspar was a machine. He was not high. He was angry. And he was trained.

Pushing harder, she felt another of Roman's bones snap and watched the full-body jerk from the fresh spurt of pain layering on everything else she'd delivered.

For a moment she thought about feeling bad about what she was doing, about what she'd become. Then she thought about Roman and half a second later she snapped a third small bone.

"Last chance."

"I . . . don't . . . know." Snot came out of his nose, tears poured out of his eyes, and he blubbered at her like a playground bully finally learning what it meant to be down.

She let go of his hand and watched his body relax at the release.

With one finger, she pulled the flat knife from the inside of her boot. Unadorned and sharpened just enough to do damage, it too had passed the pat-down at the door. Like the knives she had used when she started, but ceramic, this one passed the metal wand, too.

Kaspar was headed toward her and Sin turned her head to watch him as he approached. She didn't need to see; she could operate the knife by feel.

So she placed the tip into the fabric of Roman's shirt and began rotating it. She felt the give as it slipped into the groove between his ribs.

Kaspar's eyes darted to her hand. Rage, already present, sharpened as he watched her push the blade smoothly into his brother's torso.

Roman jerked more harshly this time, his whole body stiffening. The reaction out of his control as she hit nerves and pushed him beyond pain. Kaspar's eyes narrowed, but he was watching from over the shoulders of a pair of women, screaming and shoving blindly against him in their push toward the door.

*Good*, Sin thought, *let him watch his brother die.*

She pulled the corner of her mouth up in a twitch as she swept the blade through Roman's torso, ending the struggle.

At that moment, an inhuman growl burst forth from the elder Kurev's snarled mouth, startling the women into scattering, setting him free to rush at Sin, drawing his gun as he came.

---

Owen watched Annika as she bustled around the motel rooms. Once again, he'd managed to get two with an adjoining door. There were just so many people. Him, his wife, five in the Holder family and Officer Duffy, who was refusing a hospital.

Sin had suspected as much and already texted him a name and address and the word "dermatologist."

Anyone else might have needed more information. But Owen knew he could take Officer Duffy to this man. Todd Maxwell would want information in exchange for the work though.

With a sigh, he put his hand out to stop his wife's perpetual motion. He wanted her to be still, be pregnant, and not have to worry about anything except the baby. But it was finally sinking in what she'd said—well, yelled actually—when she carried Virginia. Something to the effect of, "I'm not just a damn Tupperware for this baby!"

He saw it now, in a way he didn't the last time. Last time, someone else could have driven the kids to gymnastics, school clubs, etc. But he didn't realize how much that had devalued Annika herself. He hadn't understood that being a vessel for a child, then losing that child for whatever reason, was a loss of nearly your entire life for the months invested.

Annika was braver than he was. Smarter than he was. And the only one who could walk into the Kurev house with Sin, speak Russian to find Lee, then play hooker, only to turn around and mother an abused and shot-up family. Asking her to not participate was to ask her not to be.

So he would ask her to participate again, in a game he shouldn't be playing. He was making decisions in hopes they were the safe ones—not the necessary ones, not even the right ones. Everything had gone out the window.

"Anni, can you stay here and hold down the fort? I need to get Duffy to a doctor."

"That's not safe, is it?" She looked worried and he could almost see the gears turning.

Owen had learned long ago to let her think, as she often came up with things he didn't see. How was he fifteen years into his marriage and only now really gripping why her view was so different from his?

"Sin recommends this guy." He showed her the message and watched as comprehension dawned. "Of course. You know what you'll tell him?"

"What can I?" Owen shrugged. It was the worst kind of news he would be bringing. "I'll be about three hours or more."

He hated leaving her for that long, but she'd lived with him being called out in the middle of the night more times than he could count. And now it was her turn. She was the best one for the situation and he was just the designated driver.

That trust that he would make the best decision in a given situation, that he would do his best, and get himself safely home had to be given to her now. It was much easier to expect and even demand it than it was to give, he was finding out.

With a quick kiss, lest he change his mind, he let her go and headed out the door with Officer Duffy, who was bleeding a bit and in need of more help than Sin's home sewing kit could offer.

The man slid into the passenger seat as though he hadn't been shot just a few hours before, but once the door was closed the tension fell away leaving wariness in its place. "I don't trust doctors right now."

"I know. I trust this one." Owen took the turn onto the freeway, trying to blend with traffic in every way possible.

"You've used him before."

"No." That didn't help matters, but Owen opted for honesty. "I've never met him before, but he's our missing man's brother."

An understanding nod from Duffy was all he got before the man fell asleep, leaving Owen on the road in a sea of taillights. His thoughts swam as the night got darker around him and he wasn't surprised that the voice answering the unknown number was cautious.

"I have a friend of your brother's wife—"

"Oh." That was all Todd Maxwell offered, letting Owen know he knew the score. He didn't mention Lee in any way, and was probably unaware of the trouble his brother was in. Owen would have to deliver that news along with the patient. "Do you know where to meet me?"

"Headed there now."

That was it. Todd Maxwell hung up. He'd helped Lee once before, according to Sin.

His office was embedded in the end of a strip mall that was actually in good shape. Pulling into the back lot, Owen tried to wake Duffy and for the first time became concerned when the man was hard to rouse.

Dr. Maxwell appeared in street clothes, knocking on Owen's window before Duffy even began to come around. Duffy's unexpected lethargy created urgency in the two fully functional men as they hauled the officer out of the passenger's seat and through the back door.

It was over an hour later that Owen waited on a colorful chair in a room obviously intended for children and watched as Maxwell put the final touches on Duffy. He offered to load them up with enough samples to make a prescription, rather than have

Duffy's name appear on pharmacy records. It was safer for all of them not to be linked.

The officer lay still for a moment after the last stitch was in, then tried to sit up. Still too woozy to manage it, he triggered both Owen and Dr. Maxwell to jump up, urging him to lie back down for a moment.

While Duffy had his hand on his eyes, shielding the light, Todd Maxwell finally turned to Owen and asked the million dollar question, "Do you have news of my brother?"

# CHAPTER 28

The sparkles came in at the edge of his vision with greater force, and Nick began wondering why Churkin wasn't passing out and rolling over.

With a show of force he didn't have enough oxygen for, he yanked at the ends of his tie, tightening the silk around her throat. Though it obviously affected her, it seemed to affect him more and the dancing lights at the edge of his vision were pushed inward by black. His world slowly narrowed as he and Churkin held onto each other, each trying to outlast the other. He could only see her face above him, her anger and determination, as he concluding that he was losing the game he started.

Then she jerked suddenly.

The movement loosened her grip on his throat, and through bruised chords and the constriction of the mask he gulped air as best he could before her fingers clamped again.

The clarity of his brain and her slight movement backwards allowed him to twist his arms, effectively garroting the tie. Her eyes started to redden even as she managed to close his oxygen off again.

Abruptly, Churkin jerked backward again, this time farther. Though her hold loosened from around his throat, so did his hold on the tie. As he gulped in precious air, he wondered who had hit her.

Not shockingly, it was his sister.

Sin stood over Churkin and not only managed to do something that made her release him, but she added her own plastic whip to the pressure on the woman's neck. He barely managed to let go of the tie as clarity flooded his brain along with oxygen.

As he watched, Churkin lifted off of him, though it was unclear from his position if Sin was pulling her up by her throat, or if Churkin was trying to throw his sister. Maybe both.

Finally free of the woman, Nick managed to gain his feet just as the other two did. He barely resisted the urge to rub his throat, the raw skin was suffering enough from being exposed to the gas they'd let loose in the room. At least Churkin was breathing the stuff straight.

Still, she managed to shake Sin loose and turn on her.

Trying to figure out how he could help rather than hinder his sister, Nick tried to analyze the fight in front of him and the room in general.

Neither gave him good news.

Sin, still managing to stay behind Churkin, put a couple punches into the other woman's kidneys. But Churkin was a nearly unstoppable force.

So was Sin.

Watching the two of them hit, miss, and swing again, was almost like watching giants fight.

Sin's arm struck out lightning fast, only clipping Churkin on the chin because the other woman carefully moved two inches in exactly the right direction. Used on anyone else, that punch would have made a head roll.

Yulia Churkin returned the favor by sweeping a foot out. But it affected Sin no more than a spider web, not even making contact as she'd seen it coming and feinted right. Churkin still managed to connect, but Sin claimed the other woman's hand and pulled her along. She used her plastic whip, but on Churkin's leather top, it had less effect than she clearly hoped.

Nick kept trying to insert himself in the fight, but there was no way to do it in a way that would actually help Sin.

Seeing him, she managed to hang onto Churkin's wrist, while planting a foot in the other woman's belly and pushing her body away. She was effectively holding the other woman out so Nick could do something.

Finally.

But no.

He couldn't really end Churkin, because behind Sin, Kaspar Kurev was finally breaking through the mass of crying people. His face was twisted into a mask of hatred that let Nick know he'd seen too much.

As Nick looked back to warn Sin, Churkin reached her arm back in a confusing move.

*Shit.*

*Gun.* He knew it the moment Yulia Churkin's hand began to emerge from behind her. Nick recognized the pieces now: Sin had been trying to get behind Churkin, trying to turn the woman around so Sin could get the gun. But it hadn't happened.

Luckily Sin saw the movement, too. Because the women were still too tangled for Nick to try to get a hit in edgewise. He felt useless standing there, waiting, no real weapon, even his tie gone.

Frustrated, he circled.

As Churkin pulled the gun forward, Sin grabbed for the woman's hand. Though she most needed to keep the gun aimed away from herself, Sin was clearly trying to get it twisted back to point at Yulia.

The other woman jumped out of the way, feinting right and dodging the bullet the struggle released.

The sound brought a sharp staccato to the screaming, which

quickly turned from crying and worry to abject fear at the retort of the bullet.

The stakes had just gotten higher. If one or the other got the right move, it would all be over. With a rapid movement, Sin got her left hand pushing Churkin's gun hand away as her right hand came up with the knife.

But the other woman was just as good. She dodged, though Sin grabbed at Churkin and didn't let her completely escape. Though the knife made contact, it appeared she only managed to get through the jacket. No blood bloomed or ran on Churkin. Her arm swung back, making strong contact with Sin's shoulder, sending her body swinging away from Nick's in the effort to regain control.

*Now.* Churkin was sufficiently apart from Sin, the gun was pointed away from Nick; he could be helpful. But just as he reached out to hold Churkin and help Sin, he saw Kaspar, appearing through the people, still scattering like ants.

Kaspar had a gun, too. The rest of them couldn't get one into the mansion, but his people had them. Kaspar probably had one on him at all times, necessary if one ran a business the way the Kurevs did.

As he tried to move forward, a few people screamed in the background, probably just barely managing to get their eyes open through the gas.

Though Kaspar's own eyes teared from the poison in the air, his gaze was steady and so was his aim. It was clear he intended to fire a bullet into the fighting women and didn't care who he hit.

Nick did the only thing he could do.

---

Sin stared at Yulia Churkin. Finally the woman was right where she wanted her to be.

Raising her left foot this time, Sin went for her second knife. It slid cleanly from her boot, the result of rounds of practice. Even with that, Sin knew Churkin saw it coming.

It was impossible to hide a move from a seasoned fighter, but it was easier to get her own knife than to disarm the other woman, so Sin pulled it. But Nick was interfering.

Standing on the fringes, Nick had tried to break into the fight for a while. It was his fight; he wanted to take Churkin, but there was no good way to hand her back over. Besides, Sin had broken in only because she had to. Clearly Churkin had been outlasting Nick in the air battle, something she'd probably specifically trained. Sin had.

But now?

She didn't want to look at Nick. Couldn't afford to communicate, as anything she said would be heard by Churkin and easily counteracted. It wasn't like fighting with Lee.

That thought flitted through her head and was punctuated by the butt of Churkin's gun thumping against her head.

*Shit.*

No time for melancholy thoughts. Churkin would and did take any advantage.

Ducking, Sin punched with her right hand, the hand not holding the knife.

This knife had been in the left boot, thus it was now in her left hand. And while the other hold—right hand weapon, left hand defense—might be more advantageous in a normal fight, nothing normal was helpful with Churkin.

Crossing her left hand to the right, Sin brought the back of the knife hard against the woman's right temple in a hope of re-damaging the scar from the bullet Nick had put there last time they'd fought.

Though she hit the spot and heard a grunt, Churkin didn't fall the way she should.

To Sin's surprise, she lifted, her feet flying upward, her body slamming into Sin's rather than falling away from the hit.

Sin lived and died by physics.

Hit Churkin from her left, she falls to her right, feints backward, smacks her head forward. Though there was no guarantee, lifting and slamming the opposite direction wasn't something Sin was ready to counter and she lost her air as the two bodies smacked together with a sound much louder than they should have made.

The only consolation was that Churkin looked even more surprised than Sin was and they hit the floor in a tangle of limbs exceeding the number they had.

Two hands pushed on her back—*Nick!*—Sin realized. He was shoving himself out from under her. While she tried to help him, Churkin flailed above her, oddly out of character.

To Sin's left, Churkin's hand hit the floor and the gun clattered out of her grip.

In a flash of adrenaline-fueled thought, Sin considered grabbing it, but it was enough that her opponent didn't have it, while Sin retained control of her knife.

In another shocking move, Churkin rolled away, barely leaving Sin time to catalog what she saw.

Her opponent lay beside her, mouth open, sucking in the bad air like a fish.

Sin could taste the gas now, not having realized while she fought that her mask had been knocked askew. She was reaching to straighten it, to filter her air again, when another hand smashed her to the ground.

From her odd angle, laying on her back, she saw Nick rise up to a knee in the same smooth motion with which he'd shoved her down. As she watched, his hands wrapped the butt of the gun and his shoulders relaxed. With Churkin's gun firmly in hand, he laid out three perfect shots.

Only then could Sin raise her head and look.

Kaspar Kurev, the last of the live Kurev boys, stood stock still, a shocked expression forever frozen on his face while blood seeped from a perfect hole in the left side of his forehead.

---

Owen was returning to Chicago with Duffy by his side. The man was much more alert this time, though Owen wasn't exactly sure why.

Once again, he was finding himself on the wrong side of things. Unfortunately he was also on the right side of them. Getting this man medical help without alerting the Kurevs was definitely the right thing to do.

The fact that he had to deliver news to Todd Maxwell about his brother—a fugitive, from the law that Owen so desperately wanted to uphold—was the price of the treatment. It didn't seem to matter that the news was not good. Dr. Todd Maxwell wanted anything he could hear. That it hurt Owen to tell it didn't factor in.

In a fit of not-thinking-things-through, Owen opened his mouth before contemplating what he might hear back. "What made you throw in with Vasilescu?"

"Nick?"

Owen nodded quickly. That response, as much as anything, told volumes. This man questioned the family name but clearly called Nick by his first. The tone told Owen Nick was respected and anything he heard here would be in the positive. He should have stopped, he didn't really want to know.

But he did.

"Yeah. Why are you on his short list of people to call?"

"Because he trusts me not to notify Kurev." Duffy tried a tentative roll of his injured shoulder. It was an alpha male thing —the need to test limits even when those limits were stitched onto your skin at the moment.

"You aren't in Kurev's pocket?" Owen understood that Nick had a handful of people he'd already swayed from the Kurev camp. Owen understood that Nick had faith those officers and officials would stand up against Kurev and be the tide when Nick decided to part the seas. It was ambitious and depended on loyalty. Something these people were torn between.

But Duffy wasn't on that list.

And Duffy was eying him from the other side of the car. "What's your standing with the Feebs?"

"I'm not FBI anymore. I'm just a college professor with a badge for my state bureau of investigation." Owen took a turn onto the freeway heading back to Annika and trying to alleviate the itch that was building at the back of his neck.

Taking that in for a moment and turning it over, Duffy slowly nodded his head. The he followed up, showing Owen exactly why Nick had chosen him. Though he looked a bit like the donut-loving kind of cop people either loved or hated, he was smart. Calculating. And made sure he was solid before he spoke. Not only would he not betray Nick, he also wouldn't accidentally let things slip.

Still, Duffy waited another moment. Clearly feeling out the situation, trying to consider not only his own loyalties, but the loyalties of those he was loyal to.

Again, Owen had what he needed.

Though it was disturbing to think of Nick as honorable in any way, Owen had long ago faced the fact that his world was neither black nor white. He'd accepted Sin in her single-mindedness. He'd begun to understand that, though he wanted the law to work, it sometimes didn't. He'd also accepted that Sin was often the better alternative than waiting for legal remedies to catch up. Good people suffered and died while Owen's hands were tied by laws. But Sin's weren't.

It had been harder to put Nick into that category.

Owen had wanted Nick in the negatives column. But the

ledger didn't want to accept him there. Though the edges of the law had never been certain—what was illegal one day was legal the next—the core had been pretty stable. Though now that was shifting too.

Nick was up to his neck in more than just drugs, but even so, even in shades of gray, he had his own code. Owen was just trying to figure it out.

Duffy spoke again. "He's not perfect, but he's consistent. . . Nick wants cleaner streets, stronger communities, and more opportunities for the kids who grow up in the wrong neighborhoods." There was a longer pause this time. "I don't always agree with where his line is, but the fact is: Nick's line is far more reasonable than the blue one and if you check Atlanta, he's holding it."

*Well, Holy shit.* Owen blinked, thinking he could be knocked over with a feather. He had not expected a well-rounded commentary on the state of society from friend-of-the-godfather Officer Duffy.

His estimation of both Duffy and Nick went up several notches.

At least he felt better about getting Nick immunity. But he was starting to wonder if the better deal wasn't to leave Nick in place. It wouldn't happen. Whatever Duffy and Owen might think, there was no way the legal line would move to Nick's line, whether he could hold it or not.

But Duffy was talking again, still not incriminating anyone, but giving out more details, more of what he seemed to sense Owen wanted. "I've done some things for him. Helped him find a few people, take down a few harmful groups. He's stepped up and always gave me full credit on stings or arrests."

"So you're indebted to him?"

"No. It goes both ways." He looked out the window and rolled that injured shoulder again, but he spoke before Owen could activate his parental vibes and slap him. "I've never seen him take advantage of anything for personal gain. I know he lost someone, but I've never seen him go off the rails over it. He's had opportunity. He could be wealthier than he is. His moral compass doesn't point due north, but it stays damn steady. Which is more than I can say for a lot of my true-blue brothers."

Owen was absorbing that when Duffy said something that made his blood run cold.

"I mean, if you put a tracer on that guy, you'd never find a step out of order with what he says." Duffy looked at Owen then. "Fuck. A tracer."

He'd put it together, too.

The mechanic had a bead on a straight line to Annika and the Holders.

# CHAPTER 29

S in pulled the face mask and crushed it back inside her purse as she wound her way through the trees behind the house.

Blue lights were fast approaching the house, but the people wandering back here would serve as camouflage if she didn't stand out. Most of them would never be able to identify her given all the crying and eye-rubbing.

Being a former cop was an advantage here. She knew how they were trained, what pattern they would use to clear the house, and how quickly they would pull out their gas masks and get to work. Only one look at all the partiers drooling tears and snot down their faces and it would become clear that gas canisters had been deployed.

Sin had lost track of Nick as they left the room. Churkin had taken advantage of the melee—the gunshots an added impulse to not just cry out but to trample their friends.

For some reason that bitch still wasn't dead.

She was even on her feet.

And she'd eluded Sin.

Sin only hoped Nick had a bead on her. He'd put Churkin down if he had the opportunity.

She, on the other hand, was weaving through the crying

people, reaching out as though she couldn't see, marking a crooked path with a very clear destination. As soon as she reached the tree cover, she quit pretending and beelined for the high wall.

The high wall was topped with embedded glass shards, ensuring that anyone who made it to the top sliced themselves to ribbons.

Picking her way through the shards, Sin balanced on her sturdy heels for about ten feet, heading from the tree she climbed on the yard side of the fence to the tree on the outside. The trees were carefully spaced and pruned so that an intruder could not climb from one to the other; the wall with its irregular glass spikes separated them. But the odd steps did their trick and she came abreast of the second tree and reached out just as she heard voices behind her.

The police had made their way into the back yard.

That likely meant that some had masks on and were already inside the house. They would have found two Kurev sons dead on the floor.

She couldn't find it in herself to be upset about it.

What she was upset about was that Churkin, despite being shot by Kaspar, was still up and around. And that Kelly Gilligan had been nowhere near the party.

Then again, he wasn't the party type.

Her inquisition with Roman had not gone as hoped either. He had either taken the secret of Lee's location to his grave or he really hadn't known. She now suspected the latter.

Likely Kaspar had known, but that gate was closed now too.

She swung down from the tree on the other side of the wall before any of the officers could see her. They would be finding the gas canisters and putting the pieces together about ...

*Now.* The yells and radios squawking said the canisters had been found. But she and Nick wouldn't leave the masks behind. For a moment, she double-checked her steps, taking stock. There would be nothing to pull minute traces of DNA that could tie the job back to them. The gun was Churkin's and likely untraceable. Nick had taken it. Churkin had been shot by Kaspar's gun, still in his hand, and his hand would test positive for residue. If anyone located her, Churkin's own hand would test positive, too. The Chicago PD would find the gas canisters were from their own store.

She should be clear.

Sin climbed into the car she'd stashed back here and waited for word from Nick.

For two minutes she just sat. It wasn't really long enough for him to get to his car and contact her. But she couldn't stay there any longer. Not without getting found out.

So she pulled away just as her own phone buzzed quietly by her leg. The number said it was Nick, but her voice never did. Always no names, dates, addresses, just in case someone was listening in. "Yes?"

"You out okay?"

"Yes. You?"

"Clean." He answered calmly. "Where to?"

Though she was fresh off a fight, and sporting new bruises she wished she didn't have, Sin wasn't wearing a bullet wound like Churkin, or a death stare like the Kurevs. Still, if they didn't get to Churkin fast, she would come back like the damn plague. Lord knows they thought they'd killed her once before.

Sin sighed. "I think we have to go to the house."

"Really?" Nick's disbelief was clear.

Sin understood. Churkin wouldn't go where expected, but she was bleeding. Badly. She'd need supplies.

Sin also was banking on Churkin assuming that Sin and Nick would never think she'd go back home. Thus the most obvious place was the least obvious. It was a mind game of the worst order. "I think so..."

Letting the words hang in the air for a moment, Sin allowed

Nick to think. But when he responded all he said was, "Meet you there."

Which meant either he agreed or he couldn't come up with anything better. She had no clue which. But if they were going to take Churkin out it would likely take both of them to be sure the job was finished. The bitch just kept getting away.

Without the Kurevs as anchor, there was no telling what kind of personal vendetta Churkin would run. And Sin's mind drifted to the possibility the Kurev legacy might be over. None of the sons had any known heirs. She had no idea if anyone was ready for the eventuality of all three of them passing. But it had happened.

She thought about the house, the land, the money . . . while Nick and Sin were half siblings of the Kurevs, neither was legitimate. Unless Nick came forward as a blood heir, he couldn't inherit. Sin couldn't be found, so she wouldn't. But Churkin was a legitimate cousin.

*Holy shit.* Churkin might be running the Kurev Family now. Getting Sin and Lee and then Nick would be her full time focus. Sin hoped Nick understood.

There was a window of maybe an hour to find her or she'd be in the wind again. And the last time she'd been in the wind, she'd turned up standing over Sin's bed in the middle of the night.

Just then her phone buzzed again.

Sin frowned for a moment before realizing it was Owen. "Yes?"

"Are you okay?" He didn't wait for an answer. "I need you. I think the Mechanic has a tracer on Mrs. Holder. I think he probably followed her to Annika and the family."

*Oh shit.*

Churkin.

Or Annika and the Holders?

---

Owen was the present. Sin and Nick were the future.

Owen was to go after the Mechanic and make sure that Annika and the Holders were okay.

In his brain, a litany of swear words buzzed. Words he didn't even realize he knew.

Sin's argument was that if they didn't take out Churkin now, she would come back later. Owen didn't give any fucks about later. Not if Annika wasn't there. What if the Mechanic got her? He'd seen the man's handiwork.

Churkin could wait.

Sin disagreed.

Churkin would be in the wind within the hour.

That, at least, was true. What they disagreed about was the importance of keeping her out of the wind.

Trying to pull back, Owen thought about looking at the problem like a cop. Where were his best odds going to be?

He smacked his hand against the steering wheel, earning him a sideways glance from Duffy, but nothing more as he steered the car off the nearest exit and pulled into a gas station. Winding amid the semis fueling up, Owen found a spot out of the way and simply pushed the gear into park.

Neither man spoke, but in unison they got out of the car and began checking common spots. Owen didn't find anything, but Duffy did. Silently, he held up the small black box and nodded at Owen. As the officer casually attached the device to the underside of a truck whose driver wasn't paying attention, Owen kept checking.

The simple tandem work was as soothing as anything could be right now. Owen was vibrating with nervous energy, but seeing that Duffy understood the problem and responded the same way was helpful.

They silently climbed back into the car and Owen started the engine, figuring they had done their best. If there was a second tracker on the car—which was the smart move—they hadn't found it. Ultimately, Owen counted the possibility of a second device as relatively low, since the Mechanic had already tracked Mrs. Holder and Annika. Which led Owen right back to his earlier train of thought.

When he looked at things rationally, the problem was that no one was looking at things rationally.

Owen wanted to save Annika—logic be damned. Sin wanted to go after Churkin, because she wanted to save Lee. Nick was after Sin to find Lee and get himself out of the pyramid he'd spent his whole life building.

It was basically a shitstorm of emotions with no one really thinking straight.

He would never change Sin's mind. Just like she would never change his.

Though he'd come here just to help, he was in it up to his neck now. No, he was over his head.

And he was on his own.

His eyeballs hurt. The kind of pale burn that came with the pain of severe loss.

Two deep, tight breaths later, Owen took stock.

The only good news was he wasn't on his own.

Turning to the man beside him, he asked, "Are you in?"

"Damn straight." Just a small lift of the chin defined his dedication. "I'm going to take this asshole down. I saw what he did to Hellico."

*Shit.*

"I have men on Hellico." No, that was wrong. "Nick has men on Hellico."

For a moment, Owen bathed in the irony. He didn't trust the FBI. Not at all. Not even that young upstart, Pillow. He was entrusting a human life to dirty cops in the mafia's back pocket. He almost snorted because he was making distinctions based on *which* mafia.

How had he gotten so twisted around?

Owen didn't answer himself. Instead he took a sharp turn at a speed that would get him there as fast as he could arrive without getting pulled over. In this town, these days, he wasn't sure he wouldn't be recognized as Nick's ally and take a bullet right on the side of the road.

That was a sobering thought.

So though his foot itched as it stayed gentle on the gas, he didn't press it harder.

He had himself, he had Duffy . . . And he had Annika.

He'd been undervaluing her for years, apparently. She knew how to shoot. She was good at it, too. And Owen was willing to bet in the end she'd have fewer qualms about killing someone than he did. If she laid out the Mechanic, she'd probably throw herself a party. He almost smiled.

Then he didn't.

He'd called her; he'd warned her. She'd checked back in a moment later and said she'd found it.

Owen had sworn out loud.

Annika had reasoned. "Owen, if the tracker is on this car . . ." She didn't have to finish the sentence for him, but she did anyway, "He was at the other motel. Saw that we switched cars and put a tracker on this car, too."

He consoled himself that she still hadn't seen the guy. The Mechanic might be right there and may have watched her find the tracker on the car.

"Dunham."

The word came from the other side of the car, breaking into his worried thoughts. It was a welcome relief, as Owen had asked the man how they might get Annika and the Holder family out of the room without the Mechanic knowing.

While Owen was confident that Annika's phone wasn't bugged, he was not as confident that Gilligan didn't have some other way to listen in on the conversation. So even if there was a plan, getting it to her was a problem.

He turned to Duffy, "Give me something good."

"Sorry man." He shrugged, the movement truncated by the fresh stitches in his shoulder, reminding Owen that even though he had Duffy, Duffy wasn't a hundred percent. "I got more bad. If the Mechanic got a tracker on Mrs. Dunham and the family, he probably also got one on your friend and Nick."

Duffy didn't seem to know the relationship between Sin and Nick. Owen noted that but opted for the bigger picture. "Shit."

"Yeah. I'm calling Nick." He already had his phone out, but seemed to hesitate until Owen gave him a nod.

Another interesting fact. But Owen shuffled it away as he took the last turn toward the motel. Duffy was on the phone but reached out to Owen's arm, stopping him.

For a moment, his nerves flashed in anger. Then he stopped himself and decided to be grateful for the fact that the other man knew what he was doing. They would not drive blindly into an ambush.

They were three blocks away when Owen stopped the car. Though Duffy had been checking his weapon and patting himself down, familiarizing himself with his options and the limitations of his arm, Owen had been driving. He grabbed the spare he'd stuffed under the seat, an unregistered gun from Nick. And while he walked, he tried to casually load and rack this second gun. If he was caught with it, he would be brought up on felony charges at the least.

Owen didn't care.

The walk in was slow. There was no telling where the Mechanic was camped out. He might not even be here. He might be in a tree—something the FBI figured out Sin and Lee had done, using parabolic listening devices the agents later found at one of their scenes. He might be sitting in a car, listening to the radio, right outside the room. He could be anywhere.

It took forever for the two men to make it to the side of the motel. Street lights were random, providing strange puddles of light and swirls of dark beyond them. To the side, several men sat on the hood of an old car, drinking something and down the street a woman walked alone, her gait solid and far more confident than the environment should have allowed.

There was no sign of the Mechanic as they reached the room.

They stood in front of the door the Holder family had entered with Sin and Duffy. As he checked the surroundings he noticed dents in the metal but they didn't look fresh. There was no evidence of a break-in.

The knob turned easily in his grip, his heart near to bursting from his chest as he trusted his exposed back to Duffy's protection. As the door swung wide, he noticed two things simultaneously.

The room was empty.

There was disturbing three-foot-wide hole busted in the back wall.

# CHAPTER 30

S in didn't bother with climbing the tree or going in through
an upper level window.

Though she and Nick did park a block away and come over
the back fence—Sin more gracefully than Nick—it was the only
concession to stealth.

This whole thing was crap. Owen was trying to keep the
Mechanic away from Annika and the Holders and he was doing it
with the help of Duffy. Officer Duffy seemed like good backup,
but what did she know? One adrenaline-fueled face-off with a
madman did not a partner make. Also, he was likely an arm shy
of a full set.

But she *knew*, if they didn't get Churkin now, she would turn
up over someone's bed. Since she'd been hanging out with the
Mechanic, she likely knew all the tricks. Lee was likely only still
alive because they kept him that way, probably to tell them where
she was. Sin was only still alive because of Lee.

Torn over her decisions, Sin was simply backed into a corner.

She would love to make Yulia Churkin suffer. And she did
need to get Lee's whereabouts from the woman. But it needed to
be fast. They needed to get back to Owen, help with Annika and
the Holders.

Sin's jury was still out on the parents in that family, too. Randall Holder *knew* he worked for the Kurevs.

But she could see almost a complete circle there. Her own father had known what he did, too. Her mother had slept with her husband's boss. In the end, they had gone quickly. Painlessly, compared to what their girls had endured. Sin and her sister Wendy had been innocent, even if they were a genetic blueprint of their family's transgressions.

When Sin thought of the Holder family, she thought of getting back there to save the kids from following in her footsteps. That meant saving the parents. And turning the father over to Owen . . . If everyone lived long enough.

So she lifted her gun, counted on the fact that Churkin was already shot, and nodded at Nick. The drops of blood, already seeping into the cement at the back door, told them that Churkin had parked in the detached garage and headed in this way.

He kicked the door in.

It gave way surprisingly easily. These houses were lavish but not as solid as they looked. If they were lucky, Yulia Churkin was only just now jerking her head up in response to the noise.

Sin went through the open door first. She could almost feel the blue uniform she'd worn for so long, the belt riding heavy just below her waist. They acted like cops again, clearing the first room silently, nearly floating in tandem.

There was no way Yulia Churkin didn't know they were coming.

The lower floor was empty, but there was blood heading up the stairs . . . More than on the back steps. If it were anyone else, Sin would count them as easy prey. She would never count Churkin that way.

She and Nick looked at each other for a moment.

There was no movement upstairs, but the staircase was a plush tunnel of death favoring whoever held the top. Reminding herself that she was going to get some kind of information about

Lee out of Churkin, she motioned to Nick to cover her and stuck her head into the open space of the staircase.

Though she held her gun in front of her, ready to shoot if she saw the woman—or God forbid, someone else!—it was scant protection against bullets. But a heartbeat later nothing had come her way and she started up the steps.

She hugged the lower right hand side, shimmying along the corner. It was a game of speed versus safety. Lower profile meant she was harder to hit; leading with her head meant she was dead if she was hit.

Though time spun out as she crawled, it was only a few seconds until she reached the top. Unfortunately, the top was even less protected than the stairs themselves. The low railing wall on her left opened to the landing and doors to all the rooms were flung open.

Quietly, she sucked in a slow, deep breath and steadied herself as she motioned Nick to come up behind her.

He let only a little noise into the eerie stillness of the house, but just beyond the landing, more noise came. Breathing—soft and shallow—came from the other room. Low shuffling noises indicated that Churkin was slowly moving from one spot to another.

Unable to wait for Nick, and relying on the guess that Churkin was alone in the house, Sin bolted forward.

Though the door to the room was ajar, she couldn't see inside and so she slammed through it, sending it swinging wide. It hit the wall hard enough to bounce back and click shut behind her.

Sin pulled up short.

Training—motor memory—left her positioned in the correct stance. Though she had no recollection of getting there, she crouched in the middle of the room, gun out.

The Sai in her left hand meant the gun was held only in her right, not standard police grasp. But thousands of push-ups, hundreds of rounds, recoil after recoil, left her arm steady and her aim true with just one hand. Her last fingers wrapped around the butt of the gun that she'd retrofitted to her hand. The smaller grasp meant she could get a tight grip and still have her middle finger on the trigger and her first finger aimed down the barrel.

It was Lee who taught her that technique. It seemed fitting that Lee's own methods were going to save him.

In her left hand the sai waited, ready to do damage. For a moment, she flashed outside herself, recognizing the hybrid she'd become. For a moment she was forced to consider that if Lee was gone, he was already in her. She alone may be his legacy.

Forcing her attention to the present, she took in the scene before her.

Yulia Churkin lay on the ground in front of her, blood pooled behind her from a clearly nasty gunshot wound to her lower torso. Not fatal. Not yet.

Because, despite the gauze, tape, and supplies strewn on the floor around her, and despite the fact that she was very injured, Yulia Churkin held her own nine millimeter in two steady hands. She was too far away for Sin to make a move, and her hands were steady as she aimed for Sin, center mass.

---

Owen's chest constricted and he couldn't breathe.

Anni was gone.

*Gone.*

So were the Holders . . . The whole family.

Glancing around the room he tried to take stock and make an assessment, but his brain flitted from object to object, not grasping the meaning of any.

An open duffel bag sagged at the edge of one bed. A pale blue purse, not Anni's, was left on the dresser as though it had just been set down as the person came in. The table held crackers, crumbs, and a sippy cup of juice.

"They left in a hurry." Duffy's voice came through the fog of his brain.

The Mechanic had them. He had Annika.

But it was Duffy who quelled that thought. "No sign of struggle."

Owen had fought that conclusion as it was the one he wanted. But Duffy was right—there was zero sign of conflict in here. It was almost as though they'd been abducted by aliens. The only earthly sign was the hole in the wall. "No, he doesn't have them."

Which meant he could call his wife.

The ringing phone wouldn't put her in jeopardy, wouldn't turn Owen into a player in a sick game where he jumped through hoops to set his family free. There was no telling what depraved chores the Mechanic might come up with for an ex-FBI agent and an active duty police officer.

His fingers were pressing the numbers on his phone, shaking even though it was from a flood of relief and no longer from terror.

"Hel—"

"Anni!" He breathed the word out even though he shouldn't have said her name.

Saner than him, she adopted a southern twang, replying, "I'm sorry, you have the wrong number." And promptly hung up.

Throwing his head back, Owen laughed loud and deep, until Duffy tapped him on the shoulder and frowned.

*Shit.*

The Mechanic could still be here. Even so, he turned to his new partner and smiled. "She's fine."

She'd followed the exact protocol she'd been given should someone screw up and use a name. Right down to the accent. Anni was good.

He called her right back. "Hey, Baby. How'd you get out?"

There was a smile in her voice. "I didn't. The hooker did. Used the other door."

His smile was as wide as the sun. "Very smart. Are you safe?"

"All of us."

"Were you followed?" If she had been, it would give him an idea where to start.

"I don't think he even knew we were gone."

Yep. He and Duffy had fucked that up. If the Mechanic had been outside, waiting to get them all together, he now knew that a good portion of the party was AWOL. Though one of the worst humans Owen had ever heard of might burst through the door and kill him at any moment, Owen found a measure of peace.

Annika was safe.

"I have to go."

"I know. I'll wait for you." She paused. "Call me if you need anything."

He didn't want to need anything. But he did. "I need you safe."

In the end, that was everything.

But the Mechanic had just been bested by his very own wife, and that was probably not going to stand. He hung up and turned to Duffy. "Figure it out yet?"

The man was still frowning.

"She put her hooker clothes back on—it's how she got the room, unnoticed in the first place—and went out the adjoining door." He pointed to the other room, where Duffy had been subjected to Sin's handiwork. "She went to the front desk and rented that room." This time he pointed to the hole in the wall. "She busted through, pulled them out and walked out the door on the front side of the motel."

"Holy shit."

"She's something else." Owen smiled again.

"She busted through a fucking wall is what she did." Duffy stared at a hole just big enough for each of the Holders to climb through and escape to somewhere the Mechanic wasn't watching. Then he shook his head and turned back to Owen, "Where now?"

Owen had no clue and he shrugged. "We scour this place.

And if he's not here, I have a list of addresses, any one of which might be the right one."

Guns drawn but low to their sides to not draw attention, the two men slowly rolled out the motel door. Owen's eyes darted left then right, scanning for any sketchy looking characters in a land of sketchy looking characters.

---

Nick stared at the closed door from his low position at the top of the stairs.

He'd been further down when he heard Sin make her move, so he couldn't see anything. But now there was only silence.

His brain churned. He needed to check the other rooms, but he needed to not make any noise. Which was like not breathing in a tomb. Every sound echoed off the plush walls and decadent design that contradicted the strict reality of Yulia Churkin but fit the self-indulgent Ann Evalyn Kimmel. Carpet that thick should absorb his sounds, even if it didn't feel like it.

Slowly he crept forward, watching for enemies that might rush him from any angle and keeping an ear toward the closed door that held Sin and Churkin. But he didn't hear anything.

At each door he held his breath, stood flat against the outside wall and popped into the doorway. If anything went down he would be the one doing the surprising, not getting surprised.

Unless, of course, he heard a gunshot from behind the closed door, or someone popped up behind him. Someone he'd missed as he cleared each door.

But he found no one—else—and he was getting more worried.

As fast as he was, Sin and Churkin should not have been at a standstill the whole time. Sin had not yelled out that she was the victor and the bitch was dead.

So he stood, his body trying to barely breathe yet take in

enough oxygen, and his brain at war trying to figure out if he helped or hurt by busting in.

The snail pace of time in his adrenaline washed-brain told him that it hadn't been as long as he thought, but it had been too long.

In his head, he counted.

Jabbing his heel just above the knob, he kicked the door wide in one loud crack. For a split moment, he imagined Sin standing behind the door not ready.

But it was her back that he saw, her arm raised slightly, the gun aimed down at Yulia Churkin.

Churkin lay on the floor, her hips turned, her arms raised, her own gun pointed at Sin's open chest while the odd curl of her body protected her own.

It looked like neither had moved.

But his brash entry put everything in motion.

Physics could not be denied and the door slapped back at him, but Nick was there to catch it. The swinging panel was lighter than the mahogany the paint job made it look like, and as he deflected it he watched Sin take advantage of the momentary flicker of Churkin's eyes to him.

Aside from Churkin's bullet wound, the two were well matched. But that and Nick acting as Sin's backup were enough to sway the odds.

With grace and an economy of motion that still amazed him, Sin covered the several steps separating the two women. The distance had been too great to cross until his momentary distraction gave her the opening she needed.

The sai, which he only now saw in her left hand, was swinging even before she reached her destination. Acting as an extension of her arm, it reached Churkin's hands, before Sin's hand ever would have. Solid metal, it didn't give the other woman any room to argue, and her hands and thus the gun were forced to sway, just a little off their aim.

The retort of the gun cracked inside his skull, always louder than he was prepared for. But even with the shot ringing in the air, almost as though he could see the bullet fly by, he understood that Churkin had fired and that Sin had moved the gun far enough that the shot didn't get her.

Though he was still cataloging what had happened, Sin was onto the next move.

As he stood sentry, she dropped to her right knee next to Churkin. With small circular motions of her hands, she swept her gun hand around, catching Churkin's wrists and replacing the sai that held her hands away with her own arm.

As quick as it happened, Churkin had only a few choices. She could drop the gun, which she didn't do, or she could allow Sin to hold her aim at bay until she was able to do something else to get herself out of the disadvantage. Not surprisingly, she chose the second option, obviously thinking she had time to make a counter move.

It was a mistake.

As Nick watched, his sister's sai hand swept out from under her own hold, the blade waving its threat across the other woman's field of vision.

Lightning fast, the grip switched almost as though the blade itself performed the action. No longer gripped upward but now aimed down, it stopped for less than half a heartbeat while Sin used her other hand to push Churkin's two-handed grip on her own gun down toward her own knees.

The blade plunged into the small space framed by Churkin's upper arms.

The metal hit something vital.

Churkin straightening and dropping the gun was out of her control. For a woman used to being a master of both her surroundings and herself, the blow was clearly a surprise. She'd seen it coming, but Nick had seen her eyes.

She'd seemed to think she'd find a moment to roll, deflect, escape.

She'd not found it.

Her chest expanded with a slight sucking sound that might have only been his imagination.

"Sin." He growled her name, maybe loud, his head buzzing with the echo of the bullet and the ring of revenge he thought he'd completed once before.

Sin did not look up, but she did sway away, so slightly from Churkin. Nick waited.

With a shove against the hands that had not quite gone limp, Sin created a counter force and pulled her blade free from Churkin's torso.

The exit of the blade was nearly as painful as the entry.

That much was obvious from the woman's face. Nick had expected her to die as she had lived—cold, merciless, inhuman.

Though he was shocked, he didn't care. It was him—thinking of holding Reese's head in his hands while her blood pooled on the floor behind her—that was cold, merciless, inhuman.

Something shifted in his sister's stance. Though he could only see her from the back, he could tell she was pissed. Probably angry that Churkin could not speak and they had no leads on where Lee might be.

Sin's shoulders dropped, but not in defeat, and as he watched she wiped Churkin's blood from the blade by running it across the woman's shirt.

Once, twice.

One side, then the other, until the blade was clean, and Churkin's shirt had been used as a rag to clean her own mess.

It was the ultimate insult she could deliver.

But she stepped back to let Nick level his own.

Churkin could no longer lift her arms. Her legs were eerily still, as though no longer attached at all. Sin must have hit a nerve, and Nick didn't doubt it. She'd trained herself not just on fighting but on anatomy.

Churkin's eyes darted to him as he stepped up beside her.

There.

That was the moment, where she gave up. No longer surprised, she accepted what happened, and in the end she would not give him the satisfaction of her fear. Nick didn't want it.

He wanted her dead.

His gun was still in his hand and he didn't have to think about it as he shot a bullet into her torso.

Her eyes didn't move, but the twitch of her muscles acknowledged the hit.

He aimed a little higher, her wounds now bleeding freely into the carpet fibers as he leveled another bullet into her.

He fired a third time, and as the determination in her eyes started to fade, he emptied his gun into her.

Bullet after bullet flew, the noise no longer registering. He put the last several into her brain, making sure this time they didn't bounce off her skull.

This time she would not be saved by a bad agent swapping a body at the morgue and declaring her dead.

This time she was done.

"Nick!"

The urgency in her voice, the tension in her grip told him it was not the first time Sin called his name.

"Nick! Someone's downstairs."

# CHAPTER 31

O wen was as relaxed as he could be when he made it to the plush hotel where Annika had taken the Holders. Maybe it wasn't exactly 'plush' but it was a hell of a lot better than the ratty motels they'd been staying at.

The sun was still about an hour away, but he'd passed most of the night content in Annika's safety. Though he hadn't found the Mechanic, he hadn't found anything else either. That alone was a victory.

While he'd always wanted Lee brought home, Owen now found himself wanting Nick to succeed, too. Originally, for Owen it had just been about Sin, about finding Lee, about not crossing his own moral boundaries.

Instead, he found he had not crossed them, they'd simply dissolved away in the face of the choices he had to make. There was no going back, because there were no lines remaining to cross back over.

For a man who'd lived his life clearly inside the lines being without boundaries was like tilting the world off its axis. And he was glad to be back where he knew how things stood.

He looked around the lobby, one he was more familiar with

than the places Sin and Nick had been taking him. Annika the illegal Russian hooker would not have made it past the desk here.

He almost smiled at the thought.

Had he known that Sin and Nick had found Lee, or even just taken care of the Mechanic, he would have been able to relax even more.

As it was, Owen was able to roll his shoulders, stand at the front desk and pick up his room key. Plastic this time. Not metal. Not with a chunk of some broken tool hanging off it to make it too big to put in your pocket and carry it off.

He and Duffy stood quietly waiting at the front desk while the nice man tapped on his keyboard and told them about the Wi-Fi. Despite it being the dark of night, and despite Annika leaving the key for them, it took almost as long to check in as normal. Still, Owen almost smiled to himself.

Trust Annika to get them out of that motel and out of the Mechanic's line of sight. Trust her to leave a three-foot hole in the wall when she left. He wondered if he should call later and pay for the damage. As his mind wandered through iterations of how to do that without confessing to a crime, the man behind the desk looked up at him. Taking the key, Owen suddenly felt free.

Annika waited at the other end of the elevator ride.

The Mechanic didn't know where they were. Duffy was stitched up and alive. He was out—

*Shit.*

The tracker.

With a motion to Duffy to wait a moment, Owen pulled out his phone and dialed once more the number Sin had given him.

This time, Todd Maxwell answered perfectly alert.

Smart like his brother, he said no names, gave no identifying information. "Yes? Is everything okay?"

Owen sighed. "I don't know." Owen felt his hand grasping at his own face is frustration. The move purely involuntary. "We found a tracker on our car. On the way back."

"Oh."

Yes. Good. "This means there's a trace to your place. I'll leave it up to you how you deal with that."

Owen waited for the blow-up. Waited for Dr. Todd Maxwell, dermatologist, to light into a string of swear words that Owen had brought this to his office.

But he didn't do it. There was only a small comment. "I understand."

"I'm so sorry."

"Will it clear up?"

It was a good question. Luckily, Owen felt there was a good answer. "Yes, hopefully within twenty-four hours. I'll call with news when I have it. Is that okay?"

"I would appreciate it."

Of course he would. Maxwell now knew that his brother was being held by one of the worst human beings on the planet. He must have been desperate to help. Desperate for information. He obviously needed that more than he needed his own safety.

But there was nothing more to say, so Owen quietly hung up the phone.

Todd Maxwell had been good to them in the face of overwhelming trouble to himself. Given that Sin said Lee had gone to him before, this wasn't the first time he'd been generous. He'd refused any kind of payment. And now wasn't upset that Owen had laid a tracer path to the door of his business.

He could easily see what little he knew of Lee in Todd.

The thoughts pinged around his head as they rode the elevator up. Now that he was no longer concerned with Anni's survival, other thoughts broke free of their moorings and Owen felt them careening around his brain, crashing into each other, and lying about like wreckage. His head hurt.

He slipped the plastic key into the slot and grasped the room handle, his only thoughts of holding Anni and falling deep, deep asleep.

Though Anni had gotten two rooms, one for them and one for the Holders, he opened his own door not to a waiting Annika, but to a gun aimed but wavering.

Behind him he heard Duffy pull his weapon as Owen tried to process, why Annika was so still on the bed and Nikki Holder was holding the gun on her and crying.

He must have made a noise, because the woman gulped and the weapon jerked. "Don't move."

"Owen." The word was soft, simple and meant nothing other than his name. There was not a wealth of meaning behind it. But it made him look. Take stock. And that was more disturbing than he could have imagined.

Annika's hands were tied behind her back with ripped fabric. She sat on the bed, up against the headboard, obviously stressed. From her position, there was nowhere she could go, no fast move she could make, hindered by fluffy white pillows and the awkward alignment of her seating.

Owen looked back and forth between the women. His brain registered sounds but felt as though he was trying to understand a surrealist painting rather than seeing something real in front of his eyes.

Behind him, he heard Duffy click the door shut.

Probably a good idea. Anyone walking by—at one a.m.?—could interfere. With two guns drawn now, that was a recipe for problems. And Duffy already had one bullet wound.

For a moment, Owen's tired and scattered brain shot off on a tangent he could grasp: Duffy had suffered one fucking bad day. And it had all occurred because of Owen.

"Owen."

His attention zeroed in on his wife again, his brain careening back to the present. But she didn't say anything else. No, the sound of ocean waves crashing was really the sound of Nikki Holder, crying as she spoke.

"I have to."

"No you don't."

Owen frowned. The words didn't come from him. Nor from Duffy.

Only then did he spot Randall Holder behind his wife, his hands gently lifting to settle on her shoulders.

"I do!" Tears ran down a face already blotchy and Owen's brain sharpened.

Professionally, he knew he should never work a case with his own family involved. He also understood there was no choice here. No back-up.

Everyone who could solve the problem was in the room.

*Assets*: Annika—smarter than she looked. Duffy—gun already drawn. Pretty good shot and police trained. He and Owen could work in tandem without speaking. Himself—trained FBI agent with some hostage negotiation training he would have to pull out of the back of his brain.

*Detriments*: Duffy was shot. No one was coming. Nikki Holder was clearly insane with worry or grief. Annika was tied up and put in an untenable position. Himself—his brain was fucking shot because that was Anni tied up on the bed.

He opened his mouth. *First names. Gentle voice.* "Nikki."

Though her hands continued to shake ever so slightly, she didn't take her eyes off Annika. But her chin lifted and he knew she was listening. "Nikki, what's going on here?"

"I have to kill her."

*That was a terrible opening statement. Was she mentally ill?* He prayed not.

"Why?"

Hoping she wouldn't say the voices told her to, because that was hard to combat, he waited.

They all waited. Nikki Holder just kept her gun aimed and sniffed. Unable to wipe the tears from her face, they ran unchecked onto her shirt. The size of the wet spot told him she and Annika had been at this for a while before he and Duffy burst in like idiots. Maybe the fact that Annika was still alive was a good sign. A sign that Mrs. Holder wouldn't pull the trigger.

But Owen couldn't bank on that. "Tell me why . . ."

Another sniff. Another moment passing with nothing.

Owen let his question sit and get heavy.

Annika must be about to die of heart failure. He knew what it was like to look into a loaded gun. But he didn't think he'd ever held his cool as long as she had. His wife managed to express a perfect combination of sympathy and boredom.

He couldn't look at her.

Had to pretend it wasn't Anni on the bed.

He waited.

"He called. He'll kill my family."

Owen wanted to collapse. It wasn't schizophrenia. Just the Mechanic. He tried to talk, but found his voice didn't work. He tried again.

"Nikki." *Use names.* "Annika saved you. If you pull the trigger —" He didn't say 'kill her'. He couldn't live with the thought. "—you'll live with that forever. . . And it won't protect your family."

Another sniff.

The only acknowledgement he was getting.

"Nikki, baby." Her husband pleaded. Owen wanted to stop the man but the words were coming out too fast. "I know you'd do anything for me and the kids. But not this. Please don't kill her."

*Sonofabitch.*

Owen didn't remember his whole hostage negotiation training class, but he did remember that you didn't speak what you didn't want to happen. You repeated what you did want.

He was opening his mouth, when Nikki Holder opened hers.

She was the hostage taker. When she was speaking, her likelihood of shooting was way down. "He'll kill you. I saw what he did to that officer."

Owen stepped back in, attempting to take control of the

situation. "This will not keep him from hurting your family. Who saved your family a little while ago?"

Another sniff.

Another pause.

Then, finally, words. "She did."

"That's right. If he finds you, he will kill you and your family. Nothing here will change that."

*If he finds you . . .*

The words echoed in Owen's brain. When they connected to thought, it was all he could do not to roar. He began to wish that Duffy would just shoot the woman, so they could get out of here.

But he had to know. He already knew. But he had to be certain.

"Did he call you, Nikki?"

"Yes."

He bit his tongue. Tasted blood. Wished again for Duffy to shoot.

She'd kept a phone from them. A phone with access to the Mechanic.

Which meant she was more in the assassin's pocket than Owen had even guessed.

And it meant that the man who had already found them twice, could trace her cell phone signal and find them all here.

Or maybe he already had.

―――――

Sin's heart beat loudly in her chest and the adrenaline spiked through her system.

It had been beating like this almost consistently since she and Nick fled Ann Evalyn's place, escaping but never seeing who had come in downstairs.

She now stood in the overgrown back yard of an abandoned house among abandoned houses in a crap neighborhood. To say it was run-down would be like saying the Titanic had a fender bender. Most importantly, it was the last place. She was betting everything that Lee was behind the closed door.

It took everything she had to calm her nerves. Though she was very good at staying focused, she hadn't had to fight for it like this in so long that she had almost forgotten how.

She had forgotten her hands would shake, her heart would try to escape her chest, her legs would turn to stone. She was almost fourteen again, picking her fights, taking the hits and creating the bruises that would hide any damage sustained in her first kill.

Since then, she'd taken bullets. Not today, but other days, other fights, Churkin had laid some damage on her.

Now she stood on one side of a door that closed off the biggest part of her life.

Nick's eyes darted toward hers. A slight lift of his chin signaled. Was it time?

She shook her head and leaned forward.

Pressing her ear to the door, Sin listened for what she could get. Though she didn't hear anything, that didn't mean anything either. The Mechanic was a professional: more cunning than Sin, colder than Kaspar Kurev, and meaner than Churkin. Sin wasn't surprised that sound was nonexistent on the other side of the door.

She offered a small shrug to Nick, who didn't respond.

Without moving her head, she darted her glance around, wondering if there was no noise because the Mechanic wasn't inside. If she were holding someone here—not her style, but if she were doing it—she'd be smart to be outside, to be watching.

But she couldn't find anyone.

No one had opened fire on them. Then again, they'd chosen the back because it would be hard to get a steady line on them and stay hidden. The yard had grown up so long ago that many of the weeds had become slim trees. She and Nick had slowly pushed their own path to the door. Anyone coming after them would have to do the same. Would have to rustle the weeds and bushes and give themselves away.

Nick pointed at his own chest, asking "Me first?"

And she wanted to say "yes." Wanted him to bust in the door, scream their way in with bullets and declarations. But she shook her head.

It was a house. Full of doors. Though she didn't hear anything inside, there was plenty outside. Rustling in the undergrowth, the occasional car on a street she couldn't see, the click and whine of a failing streetlamp trying to quit the world.

Reaching out, she grabbed the knob and turned it as slowly as she could.

It gave way with such shocking ease that she almost slammed it open. It creaked with wild abandon, happy to finally be used or shouting a warning to whomever waited inside. Sin had no idea which, so she opted for the safer route and assumed someone in the house was armed and dangerous.

Though the place was clearly abandoned, it was a Kurev holding. Sin was disturbed to come full circle and still be using the same methods from her first encounter taking down the Kurevs.

She stepped slowly into a room that was too much like the bar in Southtown to be coincidental. Though it was clearly a home, the abandoned furniture and the layer of dust, the recent disturbances to the dust were all the same. Someone had been using this place. Probably within the past two weeks.

The question was, were they here now?

Sin's answer: they had to be.

She and Nick had picked, busted, and shot their way into every other address on the list. This was the last one. Left because it was in a neighborhood and thus an unlikely place for the Mechanic to hold a live hostage. But when they'd arrived, Sin had seen the usefulness of the place. The weeds would muffle the sound, obscure the view. There wasn't anyone around to hear anything. And no one here called the police when they had a problem.

It was actually the perfect place.

Sin took a deep breath and smelled ... A tinge of blood.

At least she thought it was that. Could be her imagination. Her desire to find Lee. Standing in the darkened kitchen, her eyes adjusting, her nose forcibly holding back the sneeze the stirred dust wanted to force on her, she understood how sad it was that the smell of blood was something good in her life.

With a low signal from her, she and Nick started pacing the area.

Her heart still beat erratically, fueled by wishes and real fear.

They clung to the edges of the room when they could do it without running into furniture. Still the wood creaked.

Knowing there was no way around it, that their arrival had already been announced, she made a series of short motions to Nick, sending him down the hall. Watching as he moved, she placed her feet only when he did, hung back so that any door he opened would reveal only one person to whomever waited.

It was a dangerous position she put her brother in. As she watched him position himself to the side of the door, grasp and turn the knob, she realized she might be sacrificing the only family she had left in an attempt to find the only family she had made.

Nick held his gun in one hand, and as she watched and held back, ready to spring in surprise, he counted down on the fingers on the knob.

He turned the knob, swinging the door in, leading with his gun.

And was greeted with nothing.

He entered purposefully, swinging the gun with his gaze, taking in every corner.

Though Nick stepped back out into the hallway and shook his

head at her, she'd known from the way his shoulders fell as he'd swept the room.

Lee was not in there.

Though Sin had monitored her brother, she'd also kept her eyes on the hallway. It was dangerous for Nick to burst into the rooms, but it was also dangerous to take their eyes off the other doors. Anyone worth anything in this business would take the offensive at first opportunity.

There were no running feet. No clicks behind the other doors. And nothing burst open. Including her heart.

Quickly, without giving anyone time to prepare, Nick backed across the hallway, using Sin for cover. He grasped the next doorknob, and didn't even wait through a countdown. Sin's gun was in her right hand, her sai in her left; she was as ready as she could be, as he swung the next door open.

Again, he stepped in, meaning he didn't see anyone in there. Again, Sin felt the pop of relief mixed with disappointment. And Nick stepped backward into the hall. This time he didn't shake his head at her, just turned to the next door.

He turned the knob, swinging the door open.

And this time his shoulders popped up. The gun stopped mid-sweep and aimed, and without thinking Sin stepped into action.

She felt his spine against her own as she moved into place with a single step. Her own weapons pointed out, she rolled along Nick's back, listening to his voice but missing the words as her own adrenaline screamed through her system.

The hallway empty, no one jumping out, she could no longer stay behind. She had to see. So she continued to turn, swinging around to face Lee.

Only it wasn't Lee.

Wasn't the Mechanic.

A teenager, blankets strewn as recklessly around him as the needles on the floor, tried to press himself into the wall. Too high or too scared to make a noise, he stared silently as he pushed empty air out of his mouth.

Nick motioned the kid to be quiet and stepped back, lowering the gun enough to not be a threat. It was too cold at night to be here. The house wasn't 'on'. The kid was not a player in this game. Sin fought the despair that was working cold fingers into her heart.

Two more doors.

But much less hope.

Her breathing shallowed out, a bad thing in her world. Her weapons stayed up, but her arms lost the tension of a player ready to enter the fray. She now believed there was no fray to enter.

Nick opened the fourth door, saving the one at the dead end of the hall for last.

He looked at her, his eyes sharp, square, but clearly now believing as she did: Lee was not here.

They opened the last door without the tight readiness that they'd had for all the others. Convinced the space held nothing, Nick swung the door wide, gun leading, but trigger finger not quite ready for the shape that jumped out at him.

# CHAPTER 32

Owen hated the woman in front of him. Nikki Holder suddenly represented everything wrong in the world.

Like every fighter, Owen quickly assessed his options. Could he pull his gun and shoot her before she squeezed the trigger and killed Annika? Could he talk her down? Would her own sniveling lead her to accidentally pull the trigger?

Like every lawman, Owen's thoughts went further. If he shot her, would it be justified? What would he do if Nikki did manage to shoot Annika? What if it killed his wife?

He tried to keep the contempt out of his voice, but wasn't sure he fully succeeded. "Nikki. You had the opportunity to cut ties with the Mechanic. But you chose to keep them. You kept that phone. And the woman you are aiming at is pregnant. And even if you do this—" He still couldn't say 'kill her,' not without vomiting—"can you live with it?"

Nikki's face squeezed with frustration and Owen thought he saw regret.

*Regret?*

Had she already decided to pull the trigger?

Slowly he moved his hand behind him and motioned Duffy.

Duffy didn't move.

Did he see the signal? Owen couldn't be sure.

He waited.

Tried to stay calm.

"Nikki. Look at me."

But she just stared at Annika.

Annika stared back.

From the edge of his vision, Owen could see she spat daggers at Nikki Holder.

She should. She'd committed a crime and put herself in the path of a madman to get this family out of harm's way . . . And this was what she got for it.

Owen wouldn't have been surprised if Nikki Holder suddenly began to freeze solid from Annika's dark gaze. Or maybe she'd just spontaneously combust.

Stopping his mind from wandering, he surveyed the scene and prayed Duffy had seen him and was on board. The problem was, the correct thing for another officer to do—if he was already in the right place—was nothing. The situation sucked.

"Look at me, Nikki."

She still didn't. The woman shook her head, her hands still twitching, her nose running. "He'll kill my kids. Torture them."

Randall Holder stood behind his wife only occasionally speaking, and each time he did he got in the way. He always managed to say something that should never be said to an unstable hostage taker.

So when he opened his mouth, Owen didn't wait any longer.

He yelled. Let the hotel patrons call the front desk. Hell, let them call the police. He was going to end this. *Now*.

"That bastard is going to kill your kids because *you* led him here, you fucking bitch!" He leaned in, probably spitting with the hatred he felt. The release would have been cathartic, but it wasn't over. There was no time for catharsis yet.

He moved just a little forward as though his yelling was the major point. "If you kill my pregnant wife I swear *I'll* kill you and your *whole damn family!*" He only paused long enough to breathe in, to suck in a tiny prayer before he spewed all the venom he felt again, and leaned just a little closer. "*You* did this. *You.* Touch one more fucking hair on her and I will torture you until you beg me to kill you. The Mechanic has nothing on me because I will dismember you while you are *still fucking alive!*"

With each phrase of his rant, Nikki reacted.

She sucked in air, sniffed, pressed her lips together.

So while it wasn't standard hostage negotiation, he was getting to her, he was getting at least part of the job done. What he was also doing, unfortunately, was destabilizing her. Her hands, already twitchy, were outright shaking now.

The good news was: her aim was for shit.

The bad news was: her aim was for shit.

And she might just twitch and pull the trigger at any time. He'd never hated anyone the way he hated Nikki Holder right now.

There was every possibility that he was going to disarm her just in time for the Mechanic to get here and deliver them all a long, slow death. Owen was trained to talk down hostages slowly; he'd not gone far enough in the coursework to handle a situation that might explode from the outside as easily as from the inside.

But while his anger had been real, his tactics had been planned. He was now much closer to Nikki Holder, and she was much less stable, much less alert to him, than she'd been a few moments ago.

He had only a moment to make a move, but making it in the right split second meant everything.

He stood, maintaining his heavy breathing, keeping her off balance, looking for a way in . . . He was still too far away, it would take a step to reach her, and if she saw it coming, she could pull the trigger.

His rescue came in the form of Randall Holder doing something stupid.

The man leaned in and put his hands on his wife's shoulders even as he leaned closer to say something into her ear. Not surprisingly, it startled her.

The good news was that, while Randall Holder clearly had no clue what to do in this situation, neither really did his wife. She sniffed and jerked her shoulders. She thrust the gun forward, a dangerous move for everyone involved and yet another indicator that she should never had been allowed to pick up a gun in the first place. And she turned, just a little, toward her right shoulder. Away from Owen.

It was the best he was going to get and he took it.

"Anni!" He used the sharp yell as a notice to his wife to make a dive for it at the same time he rushed Nikki Holder.

His right shoulder down, he went for her locked arms, striking the elbow closest to him. The move gave her two options: get her joint forced backward or move her arms up.

The blow jerked her arms skyward, her foot stepped back and her fingers twitched, pulling the trigger and sending the gun bucking.

Owen couldn't see her face, he had aimed his shoulders so that he was looking down her arms at the gun. In his field of vision he could see her hands grasping for the weapon as it tried to escape her. And beyond his immediate area, he could see Annika's legs as she disappeared down behind the bed, her tied hands flailing behind her. She'd probably caught herself with a shoulder or a knee, nothing good. He clenched his teeth at the thought of the abuse his wife was taking at the hands of this woman.

While he thought of Annika, behind the bed, out of sight but not out of danger, he reached for the gun. A bullet would go through the mattress without changing trajectory or slowing enough to make any difference. It was a fact Lee himself had inadvertently taught Owen and his FBI team years ago.

Palms out, he overlapped his hands, making a V almost as if

he were about to choke someone. The reinforced position along with the shape meant that he need only push upward to corner Nikki Holder's hands in his own.

As he felt his own grasp cover hers, he fought for control of the gun. Her fingers fumbled. She still didn't have control of the weapon, having lost it when she shot and the slide came back on her hands.

Slippery with blood—hers? Had the slide sliced her?—Owen had a hard time getting a hold of her.

Ever the one to do the opposite of what she should, Nikki let go of the gun.

As Owen watched, Randall Holder dove for the weapon. Normally, it would have been okay. Normally, Owen would have trusted this man to hold the weapon. But his wife had just pulled a gun on Annika, and Owen had had beyond enough of the Holders and 'normally.'

"Don't. Fucking. Move."

The words weren't Owen's. He almost sighed in relief.

Duffy had known to stay out of the way for the second and a half that everything had gone down. Owen's move had put him in between Duffy's drawn weapon and Mrs. Holder. But now that Owen was grasping her wrists as best he could and twisting her into a position of submission, Duffy was back in play.

But Owen was still in between them. He still partially provided a shield for the Holders from the one person who was on his side.

Sparing a quick glance to the other side of the room, he realized that Annika had not popped up yet. He had to attribute that to the fact that she was smart and would stay down and quiet until she was called out to. The alternative was unthinkable.

"Ah!" Nikki holder cried out and pulled against his grasp as he applied sharp pressure to her wrist bones.

This was a trick he'd practiced after reading about it in a paper written by a college student in one of his classes. That student had been Diana Kincaid—Sin, really. He almost swore at the crap she'd gotten him into, and that it was her moves getting him out.

As he watched, Randall Holder managed to pick up the gun because Duffy wasn't quite willing yet to shoot the man until he'd assessed him as an actual threat rather than just a dumb-ass. He was a good cop.

To counter Holder, Owen pressed against Nikki's wrists even harder, and when she yelped again, he growled out, "Shut up, bitch."

"Don't you speak to my wife that way!" Randall Holder's reaction would have been reasonable in any other situation but this one.

Owen snapped.

He twisted Nikki's wrists, hoping for, but not hearing, a crunch of bone, squeezing until she dropped to the ground.

Duffy might not be willing to shoot these assholes, but Owen now was. With Nikki whimpering on the ground at his feet, Owen reached out and grasped Randall's wrist this time.

With a wrench of his hand, he changed the man's hold on the gun from casual to simply releasing the weapon into the air. Having known that would happen, Owen shot out his left hand and caught it before it hit the ground, before it got near that simpering bitch at his feet.

She was playing it up, ready to jump up and come at him. Owen had seen it all before. It was part of why he'd left the FBI—the deceit and the skills to suss it out had bothered him. But apparently they were still there and plenty sharp.

Transferring the bloody gun to his right hand—he wasn't Lee after all—Owen pointed it at Randall. "Don't you dare defend her."

One breath in and he found he couldn't stop.

"My wife is pregnant. The Mechanic knows where you are now, despite Annika's efforts to stop that. You would have been safe except your stupid wife kept a phone and tracking line open. So don't you dare suggest that I cut her any slack. I've had enough of her shit . . . and yours."

Randall stepped back, hands up, palms out. He moved his hands back and forth as though to say, "I don't have any problem with you." But he did.

Nikki, simpering at his feet, shot upward, reaching for the gun.

Duffy had her in his sights in a split second, excellent back-up. But Owen had known the amateur move was coming, and he brought the gun down as she brought her own head up.

The two connected with a thud that should have been sickening, but to Owen it was only satisfying. His heart felt better as he watched her crumple back to the ground, unmoving.

"Nikki!" Randall dove for her, but managed to stop himself when he realized that both Owen and Duffy had their guns now trained on him. Nikki was no longer a threat, only Randall's stupidity was in play.

Owen's hand stayed steady despite the shaking in his heart and he did the first thing necessary. "Annika?"

"I'm fine."

God bless her. Years ago, she'd trained him and Charlotte to not cry out or yell "What!?" after a crashing noise or an accident. The whole family, first words out of their mouths, were, "I'm fine." "I'm hurt." Or "I will be fine in a minute. I need a hand." He'd never been so grateful as right now.

He couldn't wait to see her pop up over the edge of the bed. He couldn't hop over and untie her like he wanted. There was still crap to take care of. Crap that Nikki Holder had dished up.

"Right now, you can help me save your wife and kids from the Mechanic. Or I'll take your kids and you and your wife can stay here and wait for him." It was the only deal he was offering.

Only then did he hear the pounding at the connecting door,

as one of the Holder kids fought to get into a room where a gun had just fired. Was the whole family idiots?

Still, no one deserved face-to-face time with the Mechanic. Though Owen had never heard of him working on kids, he didn't doubt the sadistic bastard would do it.

"Duffy." He handed the gun into the waiting hand of the officer, never more grateful for backup than he was right now.

Not lifting his feet from the floor, not giving anyone the chance to take him off balance, Duffy kept his gun trained on Randall and one eye on the crumpled Nikki. At last, Owen took his own gaze from the two who had made his most recent moments a living hell and headed to the other side of the bed.

Only as he passed around the corner could he see Annika. She'd pressed herself against the board sealing the underside of the bed to stay out of sight and to be as close to what little protection the bed offered as possible. She was rolling over to smile at him as he knelt down.

"Oh, baby." He reached out, only to pull his hand back at the last moment. Touching the abrasion on her cheek wouldn't make anything any better. "Here, let me get you."

She seemed in remarkably good spirits for someone who pitched head first off a bed with her hands tied. But as she looked at him, she frowned. "You're a mess."

Of course he was. He sighed wondering how he looked. Then he caught sight of his own hands, leaving bloody prints on her as he untied her.

"You're bloody." She commented calmly, as though seeing blood on her husband was a regular occurrence. The woman was a fucking godsend. Calm in a crisis and vicious as a grizzly when the situation warranted. Once again he was struck that this was not the most serious situation she'd ever been in.

"It's not mine." The blood was already on her; he'd already messed her up. Nothing for it but to clean it up later, so he continued working the knot until it gave way and she could sit up.

Rubbing at her wrists and the transferred red, she smiled at him. "Good."

That was it. No questions about what she'd seen. She was on her feet before he could offer her a hand.

By the time he caught up to her she was standing over the still crumpled Nikki Holder gazing down. He'd seen the look on her face when she was pissed before, so he could only imagine what Randall Holder saw, why he pulled back and didn't speak. Annika turned to him after staring at his wife for a moment and simply said, "Good."

She was reaching for Owen's hand when Duffy started giving crisp orders to Randall. "Get the kids in here. Tell them to bring only necessary items."

"Food for the baby." Annika said, but didn't look at any of them as she dragged Owen to the bathroom.

Had he looked anywhere other than at Annika, he might have gotten a glimpse of himself and not been so shocked when he looked into the mirror over the sink.

His face was haggard; clearly he was drained. Worse still, there was blood all up his sleeves and in his hair. He must have run his fingers through it out of habit. He cringed.

He couldn't pass through the lobby like this, but they needed to get out of here. There was no telling where the mechanic was or how close. Also, anyone with half a brain would have called in the gunshot, though no one at the hotel should deal with them. The police were likely on their way, too, and he was no longer actually with the FBI. No doubt young Agent Pillow would have a few things to say about that. Might even lock his ass up.

He hadn't figured out how to scrub up, when Annika finished washing the blood off her own hands. Leaving the water running, she pushed his head toward the basin even though he didn't understand.

"We have to leave fast. In the sink."

Another push and his hair was washed with the hotel bar soap. She used a washcloth on his face and was rubbing his hair as dry as possible with a fluffy white towel. Streaks of pink tinged the bleached cloth as she pulled it away.

There wasn't time to wash it all.

It was just enough to get out of the hotel without looking bloody. He smiled at her wondering how his old life had collided so spectacularly with his new one. How it had smacked into hers and how amazingly she'd adapted. "Thank you."

Just the briefest smile returned the moment, but she was still all business. "Change your shirt."

As he unbuttoned, he headed out into the main room where he found Duffy with the Holders lined up like they were ready for a firing squad. Owen wanted to console them, tell them it wasn't as bad as it seemed.

When the oldest turned an appealing gaze to him, Owen felt his heart harden. He didn't stop rifling through his suitcase, but he did explain.

"This was brought on by your mother who not only turned a gun on my pregnant wife . . ." He stared the boy in the eyes as he slipped one shirt off and the other on, stuffing the wet and bloody shirt into a side pocket. "But she also stayed in contact with the man who showed up at your house and tried to kidnap and/or kill you."

The kid's adam's apple chugged once as the seriousness of the new—worse—situation set in. Owen kept talking.

"I stopped your mother. I'm trying to help your family, but I won't let any member of your family hurt any member of mine anymore. Do you understand?"

The kid only nodded, his eyes glued to Owen's.

"Can you make your brother and sister understand?"

"I think so." It came out as a guttural whisper, forced through a blanket of fear. Owen remembered those days. He nodded to the kid and turned to Randall as he pushed the last buttons into place and slicked back wet hair in a farce of normalcy. Grabbing his and Annika's bags he spoke to the man. "If you want your wife to come with us, you carry her. I'm being generous by not leaving her here. If she breaks protocol again I will either shoot her or throw her to the Mechanic to save your kids. Do. You. Understand?"

Randall nodded and scooped up his wife, who lolled backwards in his arms, dead weight.

Owen nodded to the kids to line up at the door, but turned to the man. "Make her look asleep or passed out. You can't come with us if she looks like that. She'll attract attention."

With a quick nod and a rapid side glance at the gun Duffy now held on him more surreptitiously, Holder shifted his wife in his arms until her head rested against his shoulder and her arms curled inward, innocent looking. Owen hated her.

He was nodding to the family—he'd be first into the hallway.

Standing at the door, he motioned everyone to be quiet as he listened.

Footsteps made their way down the corridor, but didn't seem rushed or heavy. He would wait until whoever it was went into their room.

But the steps stopped in front of their door.

And a key slid into the lock.

# CHAPTER 33

S in did not expect the scene that awaited her.

Owen and Officer Duffy stood on either side of the door with guns braced, ready to take out whoever came through.

She looked from side to side as they slowly lowered their weapons. "What the hell is going on?"

Even before either man could answer, she shook her head. "There's something going down in the lobby, too."

"Shit." Duffy was the one who muttered it, but it was Owen who moved.

"We have to leave. Now."

Seeing the necessity in his eyes, Sin adopted an *act now, ask questions later* attitude. "Which way?"

"I don't know." Owen appeared both in control and at a loss. "I know the lobby is probably a bad idea. We had a shot fired."

The look in his eyes and her own knowledge of procedure told them the hotel staff would hang back, knowing they were untrained in diffusing these situations. But the police would be here any second. If they were smart, they'd come in quietly through a back entrance.

"Just one shot?" It was a pertinent question.

One shot followed by silence meant the situation might be

over, but likely wasn't still an issue. Paramedics might be in order, but the likelihood of bystanders getting shot went down—at least somewhat. Multiple shots meant an active shooter; it meant they would run a raid, going in fast and hard.

"Just one."

Sin turned inward. This night was a clusterfuck. Though the sun was coming up, the night was continuing. She wanted to sigh, but there was too much adrenaline for that. "Split up."

She turned to Duffy. "Can you take the Holders?"

"Not all of them." He tipped his head, never setting down the gun he now casually aimed on Randall Holder.

Before Sin could process that Owen jumped in, "Nikki led the Mechanic to us."

Automatically, she leaned forward, her mouth wanting to fall open. Only years of training her face not to react kept her from screaming at the heavens. "Then leave her for him."

"No!—" Randall holder yelled

Sin turned to respond, but it was Duffy who beat her to it. "Keep your fat mouth shut or I will drop you where you stand. Do you read me?"

A stiff nod followed from the older man who looked like he was about to crumble.

As Sin followed the rapid-fire conversation, she saw that it was Owen who both damned the couple and saved them. He pointed at Holder, still stiffly cradling his wife. "Duffy, just them?"

This time the officer nodded. And Sin got on board. "We'll text with an address. You take them out the side. If you need to, drop them both—shoot them, leave them, I don't care."

It was Owen's look of agreement that led her to understand she wasn't being too harsh. Apparently Nikki had led the Mechanic here on purpose. Sin took in the blood on the woman's forehead as Randall passed by holding her. Maybe she wasn't asleep . . .

With a quick click, Owen opened the door to the hallway

after listening for a second. He didn't pop his head out or check. Duffy went out first, heading across the hall to the small room for ice, the bucket he'd grabbed concealing the gun ready in his grip.

After a moment he came back and joined Randall Holder as they headed with Nikki, the bin of ice, and the hidden gun down the hallway toward the exit sign. Randall Holder would have to carry his wife down the stairs. But according to the he-didn't-give-one-fuck look on Owen's face, one or the other of them had earned it.

It was up to Duffy and Mr. Holder to make people think it was normal for them to walk down the hall carrying a completely passed out woman.

While they waited only as long as they had to for some semblance of normalcy, Sin traded her jacket for one from Annika.

Still in her clothing from kicking in doors, she and Nick had come in a side entrance. If the police were here already from the gunshot . . . "When was the shot fired Owen?"

"Ten minutes ago?" He looked to Annika, who nodded her best agreement in response.

It was hairy, if you weren't used to guns going off. It could have been anything as long as twenty minutes or as short as two. Sin only knew it wasn't less time or she would have heard as she and Nick climbed the steps.

While she watched, her brother traded his shirt for one of Owen's and they all tried to look different and normal. The three kids didn't help. She pulled out her phone and an address that she'd banked a while ago. "Let's try this one."

Transferring the data to Owen might leave a trail, so she waited while he copied it into a note for himself. "You tell Duffy— and only Duffy—once you're on the road."

It was Annika who nodded as she zipped up her bag.

Sin was about ready to shove the five of them out the door

when the Holder boy spoke up. "Are my dad and mom going to be okay?"

"That's entirely up to them." Owen's face looked grim. But there wasn't time for more. "Right now, we are your family. We need to get out of here."

Sin held her breath, because it got sticky from here on out. Dirty cops, no one to trust, kids in the mix. But Annika handled it fine.

Her hand creeped to her lower abdomen as she spoke to the kids. She looked at all of them with a mother's understanding, and for a moment Sin felt so much at a loss. She didn't understand anything about these kids. Not even their fear. She'd never been afraid for her own parents; her change had been massive and momentary. One minute everything was fine. The next they were gone and everything was wrong. She'd never had a chance to help, to contribute, to save them, not like the Holder kids.

Annika's words were true but guarded. She didn't lie, but neither did she tell the whole truth. "Duffy doesn't want to hurt them. He's trying to save us and you. Owen chose him because he's on our side. The rest of the officers we don't know about. So we're going to get out of here as a team." She nodded at each of the kids, and it worked so well even the toddler nodded back in understanding. "Then we'll find your parents and we'll figure out who to trust and how to get you guys back home."

That involved killing the Mechanic, Sin knew. Annika knew that, too, but didn't say they might be on the run forever if the rest of them couldn't take him out of commission. But Annika's words were all that was necessary to send them through the adjoining door and out into the hallway.

At least if anyone was watching the hotel cameras—a reasonable likelihood given the gunshot—they would look like a happy family leaving early for something. The oldest boy's backpack and the diaper bag would help with the illusion. They should make it through the lobby without being stopped.

For a moment Sin wondered if they should have kept one of the kids behind, to help her and Nick get out. People just didn't suspect parents or kids of much as long as they were clean and seemed happy.

She turned to Nick. They had no kids, no bags, nothing—only different jackets than they came in with. If they were seen coming in, they might be recognized going out. If not, then they were at risk for coming out of the same room as Duffy and the Holders just moments ago.

If someone were watching this hallway, simply their pattern of entering and leaving the rooms would be suspicious. "Do we wait?"

Waiting would allow Owen, Annika and the kids to maybe get out before the real red flags were raised about these two rooms. Someone downstairs could be punching keys right now to see that both rooms were rented by the same person and that the connecting door had been opened.

"I don't think we can."

It's what Sin hated about nice hotels. When it was just her, nice was easy. She came and went on her own. A lone woman with odd hours in a big city hotel raised zero flags. But this? This was a mess. Waiting meant a head start for the others. It also meant the Mechanic might be one step closer to them.

For a moment Sin contemplated that.

"Will he come if we wait him out?"

It would be an almost-too-easy way to find the elusive man.

But even as Nick shook his head, she understood. The risk was too great. Someone would pinpoint the gunshot to this room. Or at least come knocking on doors and ask about it. With a grim nod, she turned the knob, smiled over her shoulder at him, expecting Nick to watch her back in the face of her attempted normalcy as she stepped blindly into the hallway.

Just then the elevator doors opened with a ding, spilling several officers into the space. Their dark blue uniforms spoke in deep contrast to the plush cream decor. The hands that rested casually on their weapons stated that all was not casual.

"Ma'am?"

Though she'd seen them in her peripheral vision, Sin turned, acting surprised and slightly confused. "Officer."

She knew how innocent people acted, and how guilty people acted, so she spun her own response. A small smile, a bit of a dismissal as she turned back to Nick portrayed someone who knew they hadn't done anything wrong. Still she wasn't surprised as several of them fanned out and knocked on doors while two approached her and Nick.

As the officers stopped them, Sin and Nick looked to each other, and Nick frowned slightly, "Is there a problem?"

There would only be one if one of these guys recognized Nick. If one of these guys was in a Kurev pocket and wasn't happy to be suddenly liberated from it. "There were gunshots. Did you hear them?"

Sin pulled back, a planned reaction. "Here? . . . No."

Then she looked at the floor in the distance and stopped her facial muscles before looking back up at the officer. "Is that what that was?"

"What did you hear?"

She shrugged as though struggling for words. She wasn't struggling, she was stealing. Borrowing from a woman she'd interviewed a small handful of years ago, she gave a plausible lie. "It sounded like someone cracked something wooden. I thought maybe someone was having a fight, but then there was no more noise, so I thought I was mistaken. Maybe someone dropped something?" She shook her head a little. "You think it was a gunshot?"

It was a great deflection.

"We're not sure ma'am. But we are checking everything. Can

you tell us where it came from?" His hand still rested on his gun and the snap was still flipped up for an easy draw.

She was just grateful she hadn't fired her weapon tonight. If they were hauled to the station and checked for residue on their hands at least they would come up negative. She needed to get out. She needed to find Lee and that was seeming harder and harder to accomplish. But though pressure pushed at the back of her eyes, she didn't let it show. Breaking down here would get her hauled in for sure.

Pointing back at the door, she spoke again. "That's our room, so it was maybe ... that side?" She put a question on the end of it. "But it might have been above us or below us."

It took three more minutes, as the officer took their names and info. Nick gave his family name, and Sin wondered if maybe word had gotten around. Whether "Vasilescu" would help them or hurt them, she didn't know. She gave them the name on the ID she carried. They were asked to approximate the time of the shot, which they both did poorly, even arguing a little about it, before they were told they might not be able to get back into their room later.

"We'll be out most of the day. Do you think it will be okay when we return then? No one will go in our room, go through our things, right?" She played the concern well.

"No ma'am, and you should be fine coming back then. We should have this all cleared up soon we hope."

"Oh good." Only then were she and Nick allowed on the elevator and she fought a smile.

The officers wouldn't wrap it up. Unless the shot went through the ceiling into another room, they would have to get into that very room to discover the source of the bullet. And they'd just promised her they wouldn't.

In the lobby, they passed several other officers stopping people as they left or entered. But they were allowed to go by after mentioning the officers questioning them on their floor.

Sin stepped out the sliding doors into the cold Chicago sunshine and wondered when in the hell she was going to get to see Lee again.

---

Nick drove the car to the next stop, wondering if there was a motel or hotel in the entire city they hadn't yet stayed at. He wasn't used to all this running. He usually hid in the open—did deals behind Kaspar's back, stole his officers out from under him, tried to get them to reveal tidbits that Nick could later use against him.

He'd played the meek brother, not as strong, not as capable, for so long that being free and yet still under the gun was bizarre to him. Nick fought the sigh that wanted to escape. He'd been up all night and they had jack shit to show for it. "Is this the right place?"

"Yeah." She nodded and checked her phone.

A lone number had been sent from Annika's phone indicating the room number. Owen had sent a message. "Just come in when you get here."

Room 141 had a blue door—different from each of the others down the hallway. It would have been cute had the colors had any relationship to each other. Instead it looked as though the owners had bought out the incorrectly mixed paints at a store. Glosses and eggshells made random patterns. Some of the uglier colors must have come in bigger cans, because two or three doors would be painted in the worst options. There were colors that Sin didn't even have names for . . . and she'd worked clothing retail in another life.

Annika smiled at them as the door opened. Owen did not— he held a gun on them until the backlighting of the sun cleared their faces and allowed him to see who they were.

"Put that away Owen." Annika shoved at his shoulder just as the man was holstering the weapon anyway.

For a brief moment, Nick saw himself and Reese the same way.

He wouldn't be here if she were alive.

He didn't know where he would be. If he were honest, he knew their relationship had been new enough that it wasn't necessarily the real deal. But their friendship had been old enough that he'd been willing to bet on it.

And he had to let it go.

If he was going to have any semblance of a life, he had to let Reese go. Turning to his sister, he watched her become engulfed in a hug from Annika, partially against Sin's will. But it was good for her. He hoped she didn't have to get over Lee.

The spurt of hope—the punch of knowing it wasn't over yet —woke him back up. He turned to Owen, "We didn't find Lee."

But the former agent nodded. "So what didn't you check?"

He couldn't ask what they did or if they'd shot anyone. Dunham didn't want to know and would be in legal trouble if he did. But he could ask where they'd been in vague terms.

"Nowhere. We checked them all."

All of them. He and Sin had kicked in every door. Nearly shot a homeless teenager. Waited for the Mechanic around every door.

"All of them?" Owen looked shocked. Nick understood.

They'd been so certain. They thought they knew how the Kurevs were operating. But there'd been nothing.

"Maybe he moved him earlier in the evening."

Nick shook his head. Impossible. "There was blood, evidence that someone had been there, but nothing recent enough to be from tonight."

Owen put his hands on his hips and stared blindly into space, thinking. Nick recognized the look, he'd been doing it too.

While Owen tried to sort it out, Sin extracted herself from

Annika's grip and frowned briefly at the other woman. Annika gave a tight nod back, making Sin change the topic. Nick wondered if it was one of those "between women" things.

Sin floored them all. "It was Churkin in the cabin that night."

They all thought it was a possibility.

But Nick had never heard her say that as a definitive before. "What makes you certain?"

# CHAPTER 34

O wen had never been so frustrated.

His older kids were safe, but he wasn't certain about the newest one. Annika kept touching her belly in that way pregnant women did. Except she'd only started doing it two days ago. Owen was always afraid something was wrong. With all the previous pregnancies they'd shared and only two actual children to show for it, he didn't like the odds on this one.

Randall Holder was with Duffy and Duffy had cuffed the wife. She'd stayed that way all day with just her husband to help her. Mr. Holder was pissed. Apparently Duffy threatened to leave them chained to the radiator and let them fend for themselves. The fact that there was a radiator to chain them to told Owen they were in an even shittier place than this vomit-colored-door no-tell motel.

"Why do you think it was Churkin?" They'd known since the woman had taken over as Ann Evalyn that it was a distinct possibility. But now Sin was convinced.

"The genetic testing." Her gaze was solid. The idea never wavered for her.

"We didn't test the blood against anyone." Owen shook his head. Annika and Nick looked at her and the kids sat quietly in the corner hopefully not listening to discussions of which assassin had committed which crime.

"You can now." She held out a baggie with a piece of blood-smeared gauze inside.

Owen took it from her and nodded. His lip curled involuntarily as he saw that some little something clung to the threads, too pink to be blood. He didn't want to think about it. Though he'd been to more gory crime scenes than he could count, unlike his lab friend Nguyen—and now apparently Sin—he didn't go around collecting parts.

"I'm sure it's her though."

Owen waited while she explained.

"All that weird genetic testing your friend did on the blood so we could find the perp? I think it made a difference." She shoved her hands in her pockets, an uncharacteristic gesture that worried Owen. "We know she's female, probably with dark curly hair. That's Churkin—"

Sin held up a hand to stop his protest. "I know. There are a ton of curly-haired brunettes in the world. But there are only a very small, small handful who could get into my cabin."

Owen wondered at her use of "my" for the cabin. Had she already discounted Lee?

"You said she's cilantro averse." Her mouth quirked up. "While it's ridiculous, I noticed her eating a handful of chips at the party. No salsa." Her head shook softly. "It doesn't mean anything. But it adds up."

She turned to Nick. "She outlasted you in a battle for air." Then she turned back to Owen. "You said the woman in the cabin was a sprinter."

He was putting the pieces together now.

Sin and Lee had always thoroughly vetted their targets, never taking out anyone they were unsure of. The only exception had been self-defense. She wanted enough to know she'd gotten the woman at the cabin—that she was done with that search.

"What do you mean she 'outlasted Nick'?" He asked.

"They had their hands around each other's necks—"

"I even started first!" Nick's anger showed through as he pushed his fists to his hips and walked a tight circle.

"But if she's built for sprinting that would explain it. . . ." She turned to look at Nick, "You're more of a distance guy. You'll depend on a steady flow of oxygen. Sprinters are made for working without it." Somehow the physiology lesson calmed Nick and she turned back to Owen, as he asked a tongue-in-cheek question, trying to lighten the mood.

"Did you see her drink milk? The woman in the cabin should be lactose intolerant."

"I didn't get a chance to check her fridge. There was someone in the house when we left."

"What?" Owen started. He hadn't heard that before.

Nick jumped into the conversation more then. "I'm pretty sure it was the Mechanic. Whoever it was was skilled. There weren't many footsteps, we didn't hear them come in the door or anything."

*Shit.* It was the first Owen heard of them meeting up with the man. "Can you confirm it was him?"

"Mostly." Sin answered. "I saw him from the top of the stairs as he checked out the lower floor. He went by the staircase."

"Me too." Nick added. "It wasn't well lit, but I think given his body type and the way he moved that it was him." He paused a moment. "It makes sense that Churkin would have called him. We went out the roof vent and down a tree."

The glare he sent his sister suggested that was a much easier route for her than him.

But Sin only nodded and gestured to the bag Owen had already tucked out of sight. She had an agenda there, he understood. "You have enough information to test it against the blood in the cabin. I know those tests get expensive."

"I would have tested it anyway."

A slow nod was the only thanks he expected. What he didn't see coming was the slight, grim smile. "I want to be able to tell Lee that she's gone. That the people who breeched the cabin don't exist anymore. It has taken so long to find him, . . . I need to have something to show for it."

That was something Owen understood. He'd never needed to chase Annika's demons—she'd done that on her own. But he had more than once needed to close a case, to finish it, before he would be able to walk through the door of his nice home as his complete self. Somehow he understood this woman better than he'd ever thought he would. Somehow his life had become entwined with hers, with a killer's, with a cop's, with Nick's . . . For the first time he saw the other side and wondered how he'd steeped in it all those years and never really examined it.

It was Nick who stepped up next. "We need to find Lee."

"You checked everywhere?" It was a stupid question, but no one seemed offended. Stupid questions often garnered the best results.

Nick started listing all the locations as Owen rifled through his bag and searched for the paper map he'd marked before. While Nick stated what they found at each place, Sin helped mark the spots.

Owen sighed. They had hit everything.

"There's a trail." Sin pointed and Nick leaned over the map as did Annika, her hand once again quietly covering her lower belly.

Trying to be discrete, Owen glanced her way, but she only shook her head slightly and moved her hand away. He had no idea what that even meant, but as his heart started racing at the possibilities he reminded himself that Lee was very much alive—at least they thought so—and needed to be found.

"See?" Sin pointed. "Here's the oldest evidence." She moved her finger to two more locations, then a third. "This is the most recent."

"We hit them in fast enough succession that he couldn't have moved around too much." Nick put his hands flat on the table to think.

As Owen watched, he and Nick came to the same conclusion at the same time. It was Owen who spoke first. "If he was at Churkin's at the beginning of the night then he found her after you guys left."

"And he contacted Nikki Holder . . . When?" Nick looked to Owen.

"Probably about five a.m.? Anni?" He looked to his wife.

Annika shrugged. "I checked the clock at four-forty-seven. That's the last time I remember seeing. She came in with the gun sometime after that."

"It was at four-fifty-one." The voice was quiet but firm. The older boy spoke from the corner. Apparently he'd been listening to everything. "That was the time on the hotel clock when her phone buzzed. I don't think she knew I was awake."

Owen's heart broke. The kid was somewhere between fourteen and seventeen—hard to tell sometimes—and he'd seen his home raided, his family shot at, and his mother go dark. He still stepped up and did the right thing. Somehow the boy had assessed the situation on his own and decided to help, even though his parents were basically Duffy's hostages somewhere across town.

Sin put the pieces together now, too. "So he didn't have time to move anyone tonight. He probably didn't even have time to go visit while we were out hunting him."

"Which means we missed one." Owen sighed. There were so many sites, so many possibilities. *How did the bastard have another one?*

"Money." Sin responded before Owen even realized he'd said it out loud. "He has his own money and the Kurev money. And the Kurev holdings."

"We checked the Kurev houses." Nick blew out a frustrated breath.

"Then we *missed* one!" Sin growled it out, as close to losing her cool as Owen had ever seen. From the way Nick jerked back at the words, it was probably more than he expected, too.

"So how do we find him?" Nick asked the room at large.

Owen did not want to be a part of this. Legally, it was a web that could tangle him and bring him and Annika down.

But he needed to be a part of this. He'd been loyal to the law out of belief that it was the thing that maintained what order existed. Now he knew that Sin and Lee would always have his back. "Anni? Take the kids and—"

"No."

That was it. Just 'no.' Annika wasn't going anywhere. His shoulders dropped as the weight of trying to convince her lifted. Her stubbornness at least made her participation easier to bear.

"So how do we find him?" Nick asked again. "Can we bait him?"

Sin looked at the far corner, irritation and defeat starting to color her features. "I don't know how to find him except to watch the places we already know. And I don't know how long that will take. He knows we're after him. He doesn't have to ransom Lee . . . And now that the Kurevs are gone . . ." Her voice caught.

*Shit.* Owen hadn't thought of that possibility. The local police scanner and Agent Pillow had kept him somewhat up to speed on the happenings of the night. Both the remaining Kurev boys were dead in a raid on the Kurev mansion. No one else was hurt . . . At least not beyond the burning eyes and lungs and one spot of blood on the carpet that the crime scene guys couldn't match to anyone.

With Kaspar and even Roman out of the picture—and finally with Churkin gone, too—there was no one left to pay the Mechanic.

The clock had been ticking before, but they were in countdown now. Unless the Mechanic reached out to them for money . . . But ransom wasn't his style. He was pay for kill, and play for fun. *Shit.*

Owen leaned over the now useless map. "If he reaches out to us, great, but we have to assume we need to find him. We don't know where to go. So how do we get him out?"

"My mom has his number." The voice from the corner again.

Still Owen didn't call the kid over to join in the conversation. This wasn't a place for a kid. Especially when Owen started considering using Nikki Holder as bait. "We took her phone."

Actually, they destroyed it.

Owen loved the thought that there were no bad ideas in a brainstorm. Though the truth was some ideas were pure shit. Just sometimes those shitty ideas were the spark that led to great ones. So he threw it out there. "If Mrs. Holder knows his phone number, I could get the FBI to triangulate his phone."

It was a bad idea and one that Nick rejected right away.

"I don't trust the FBI. Plus, if they know where the Mechanic is, we can't go in and get him. Best case, they save Lee and bust him for being Lee. Worst case, the Mechanic . . ." He just stopped talking. No one wanted to say the worst case out loud or discuss the possibility that it was already done.

It was Sin who spoke up next. Whether her voice was steady because she was remarkably resilient or because talking kept her from imagining the possibilities, Owen couldn't tell. "Can we get Nikki to call him from a pay phone and bait him?"

Oh lord. She'd gone there . . . And in front of the Holder kids. Sin obviously didn't have children. But not being an idiot, she picked up on it and added on quickly. "We get her out of there and somewhere new, ASAP. Then we wait for him ourselves."

Nick shook his head again. "We don't actually want him. I mean we do, but the Mechanic isn't our priority. He's job two. And he won't crack. I don't doubt for a minute that we can hold him forever and he'll never lead us to Lee."

Owen took a deep breath and he could hear the same from

Sin. He added his two cents. "I don't want Nikki Holder in on it if we can help it. I don't trust her. She seems to think the Mechanic is her best bet."

A short nod confirmed Sin's thoughts. "She doesn't know she's dealing with the devil."

But then the room went quiet. And quiet was bad in a brainstorm. There were no ideas to throw onto the table. There was only breathing. Nick walked another tight circle while Sin stood stock still. Owen searched the map for clues but none came.

He breathed in. Breathed in again.

Nothing.

"Who else can search the phone records? Triangulate a particular cell without permission?" Annika's voice was soft, simple, and finally offering up something worthwhile.

Owen didn't know anyone who could do that . . . Not off the grid. Everything he did would involve an agency. But he looked to Sin first—she had all those IDs—then Nick. It was Nick who was nodding.

"I can find someone. But it's a crapshoot."

"Why?" He either knew someone he could trust or he didn't.

"With the Kurevs down, the people I know are going to be scrambling. Some of my guys are my guys so that they aren't truly Kurev guys. They may not need me now." He shrugged.

But Sin's face said to go with it and Owen generally agreed. They didn't have time for a better idea or a safer route. The whole city was in flux with the "Kurev Massacre" that he'd seen in the news feed on his phone. Never mind that only two people had died. Journalism had gone to hell and the definition of the word "massacre" had been greatly exaggerated. Needless to say, it was going to be a bitch.

It was also the perfect time for Nick to insert himself as head of state. He could easily gain control of Chicago, link it to Atlanta and . . . Owen didn't even know what the 'and' might entail. He looked to Nick. "Are you still in for a deal?"

It had to be asked.

"Yes." Nick didn't hesitate, didn't falter, and Owen's respect for him went up. Nick wanted out. Even when everything he'd seemingly worked for had fallen into place, he was still willing to get out. Though he added sharply, "Don't know how excited I am to go work for the organization you don't trust."

Owen took that with a grain of salt. "Every branch of law enforcement has its dirty members."

Nick changed the topic. "What if we get Nikki's phone and turn it on enough to find the number? Then we trace it."

Duffy was supposed to throw the pieces out the window near the hotel, so it wouldn't look much like she'd moved. "It's gone."

The voice came from the corner again. "She'll know it."

Owen looked over at this kid, wondering where he'd found the very thing his parents lacked. Must be innate. "You sure?"

It didn't matter if he was sure. Owen was calling Duffy and Duffy was getting the number out of Mrs. Holder. It was their best chance.

The kid nodded, and Owen turned to Nick. "Find us someone."

He called Duffy, and quickly got a return call with the number. He didn't know what Duffy had said to make that happen so fast but whatever it was, Owen was glad. He would have left Nikki Holder to rot had she not had three kids depending on her.

Before he could hang up, Nick asked for his phone.

Surprised by his reluctance, Owen handed it to the other man. It felt odd enough to be working with Nick, to be on the same side of things. But handing over his phone or anything of his own felt foreign and wrong.

Nick nodded his thanks and ran his choice by Duffy.

A good call. If Duffy was clean—or as clean as anyone

working with Nick could be—then he would know who else was.

"Thanks man. I'll check with him." Nick already tucked his first phone away and had a second phone out. The fingers of his left hand were turning on the other phone as he wiped Owen's phone clean and returned it. The movement was so natural that Owen felt he was getting a glimpse into the life of a man who ran everything underground. He wouldn't talk on the same phone twice, didn't leave his prints behind.

It was a smart move, Owen thought. Having Nick on the home team would be a boon. The FBI would be able to put his techniques to use against others. Owen told himself that's why he was doing this. He almost believed it as he tucked the phone away and Nick made his next call, handing over the number they'd gotten from Nikki Holder.

Nicolae Stelian was a smooth operator, staying on the line while the number ran.

Owen waited with him. They all did: Annika sitting on the bed, her hand once again straying to her lower stomach. Sin watched the movement through tired eyes but didn't react. Her own hand never moved. She never touched her belly or really acknowledged the life inside her. Owen almost wondered about the outcome, but the live children in the corner distracted him.

The toddler had fallen asleep in her big brother's arms. The middle kid fiddled with a small toy in his hands and the older one watched the adults, far more wary than he should have to be.

"Thanks man."

The repeated words brought everyone's attention around to Nick again as he hung up the phone. But it was Owen Nick looked to.

"You aren't going to believe the address."

Owen shook his head, the look on Nick's face was bad, worried, and too obscure to be understood.

But Nick didn't hold out. "He—or at least his phone—is at the Kurev Mansion."

# CHAPTER 35

Nick didn't like this one bit.

The police scanner was correct: the mansion was still crawling.

Crime Scene people combed the yard and the house, though the only thing he and Sin could see clearly was the front door from this vantage point. The steady stream of people in and out —most of them in paper suits and carrying evidence in some form—told them local agencies were stripping the house.

The place was ablaze, both from the inside and from Klieg lights placed strategically. Occasionally a shadow passed in front of a window, letting them know that the place was full. It was going to be a bitch getting in.

"We need another entry. This sure as shit isn't the way in." She sounded about as excited as if she was in a dental office waiting room. Maybe less so.

Nick understood. He felt the fear, too, his nerves screaming that their timeline had a short downward spiral. They would crash soon and probably not really know when the end came— only that they had been too late.

She was already walking away and Nick followed, climbing into the car and driving the long way around. It was ten minutes later that they managed to park and enter the yard of a quiet home behind the Kurev mansion.

They hadn't been all that stealthy, but Nick was counting on Sin being able to fight their way out if necessary or him being able to talk them out. He had friends in there. But those friends might not be able to openly acknowledge him.

Sin popped up onto the fence, placing her hands carefully between shards of glass protruding from the top. There weren't trees here that would get them over. Only a ladder would do it.

After bracing herself up for a few moments on rigid arms, she cursed and dropped back down.

"What?"

"The back is lit up like the front. They've covered the whole grounds." She shook her head. "They almost spotted me. That would not be good."

Nick wasn't surprised the techs were all over the place. "Hey, who owns it now?"

Churkin was kin. He knew that.

While he'd found Kolya's bastards all over the US, most of them didn't know it. Even if they did know, they would only have a claim if Kaspar and Roman didn't have anything in writing. Nick didn't think that would be an issue. The Kurevs were a family—with a capital F—first and foremost.

"I don't know. I should have looked into it before we killed them."

Nick's eyeballs almost popped out of his head. It was probably the first time he'd ever heard Sin speak of something she'd done, something that would incriminate her. Either she was losing it or she'd simply ceased to care. Neither option was good. He changed the subject. "Did you see anything useful?"

"There are FBI agents hauling out everything—even some of the art."

"The art?" Nick thought about it. He'd seen huge canvases

featuring both realistic and abstract works. The frames alone had been gilded and ornate, probably worth a fortune.

"I thought I saw a Vermeer in there. And a Godlevsky. Maybe they were stolen?"

"Doubt it." Nick shook his head. "Too much attention to have stolen work. But it is a sound investment. Few people know exactly what a painting is worth."

Sin nodded at him, her attention clearly not on the art. She was looking at the wall as though she could see through it. As though, if she could see the back of the house, she could figure out how to get into it.

Nick was wondering the same thing when one of his own phones buzzed. He reached into his pocket and plucked out the one that vibrated. Flipping it open, he looked at the incoming number.

He'd only given this number on Duffy's recommendation. There wasn't much else Duffy could do to prove his loyalty to Nick, and Duffy trusted this guy completely. So Nick had given his number to a man he'd never met—hindering the ability of anyone keeping tabs on him to track him, but making it much easier for this one man to do it.

"Yes?" He answered the call.

"It's moving." The voice was clear. Even though the words all came through cleanly, Nick didn't process them well.

He tried to sort it out. "Same number? Where is it?"

"Yes, same number. Same place. I'm on a precise map now. Ready for coordinates?" The voice stayed calm, clearly used to tracking people with GPS.

"Okay, give me a minute."

He fumbled the phone, turned to Sin and had her open a map she could plug coordinates into. Her fingers moved, but her eyes stayed on the house in the middle of the yard they'd trespassed.

They waited until the dot popped up, then she turned to Nick. "Give them to me again."

He would have put her on the phone. But he didn't want anything else incriminating. It was enough that this man—whoever he was—had several of Nick's numbers. Nick wouldn't hand over his sister, too, nor even implicate her in being here. So he played middleman, rattling off the numbers again, waiting for Sin to input them to the system again.

It took a minute, but she asked, "How accurate are these?"

Nick asked, and the answer came back almost immediately.

"Very. Very very. I'm pinging him off four towers, and the signal is faint, which is odd. But even though it drops out some, the readings are consistent."

Nick was holding the phone out so Sin could hear, but put his hand over the mic when she started to ask a question.

"Get him to give us the first place he located the phone . . ." She was still looking at the red dot on her map and frowning.

Five minutes later, Nick thanked the guy and hung up. Despite all their questions, the man had never faltered, never gotten frustrated with them. Which meant he was either used to this, or he was pinging Nick's phone and someone was going to show up for them any minute.

Nick pulled Sin aside. They'd been standing in the middle of the backyard, the tall fences obscuring this house from the others around it. No one seemed to be home despite the single light left on. Still, they were safer in the shadows.

She didn't pay attention to his movements, but as soon as they were more safely tucked away, she held up the phone to him. A series of dots showed on the map, some directly on top of the overhead picture of the Kurev mansion, some out in the backyard.

She was shaking her head, and Nick felt his own frown begin to form. His mouth started working through the problem that was worming around in his head. "If these are accurate, then he was inside the Kurev house and is now in the back yard."

"I know." She simply handed him the phone and headed for the wall again.

Hands feeling around for a spot with no glass shards, she muscled herself up and peered over the top again. Nick didn't speak. He didn't think this was her smartest move, but he wasn't going to make noise and draw attention to her. It was well known there was a criminal tendency to visit the scene of the crime. Not that it was common, but it was common enough that anyone popping their face over a wall at a recent gas release and double murder would get their asses questioned.

Finally, she let go and dropped to the ground. "He's not there. How recent was the data?"

"He couldn't be in the backyard anyway. You would have seen the Feds questioning him." Nick shook his head.

"Or he could have gotten himself a jacket and hat and no one looked twice. The place is crawling. I've seen three different agencies; they can't all recognize each other."

While that was certainly true, Nick added another piece. "That last set of numbers was supposedly getting recorded while we talked."

Sin sighed. "So according to this, he was in the backyard less than two minutes ago."

"Or his phone was."

"The Mechanic is not a man to lose his phone." She shook her head, then countered her own statement. "But he would plant it on someone else to keep us guessing."

"Or," Nick added, "to keep it on and let it ping so we'll come to him. He knows Nikki Holder didn't get Annika. And he knows she knows his number."

"True." She looked at the wall again, still thinking. "And this place is so big that your guy's numbers would have to be way, way off to have the mechanic not be on the property."

There was no good answer. Nothing to really act on. And it wasn't like they could get into the house anyway.

Just then a noise came from the house behind them. Something subtle, but not the wind, not the night around them.

They stilled and as they did, they heard the front door open. With his hand flat and pushing toward the ground, Nick signaled his sister to stay low and quiet as they quickly paced the side yard to see the front.

A lone officer walked down the front walk, jacket on, flashlight swinging at his side. As they watched, he turned right at the sidewalk and headed down the street to a cruiser parked just around the corner.

Nick's own breathing became faster as Sin looked at him with wide eyes. Her voice was steady, but clearly surprised. "What's the street address here?"

"You're the one with the map!" He motioned to her as they stayed tucked in the shrubbery that helped baffle the sound from one house to another.

She pulled out the phone and checked what she could, her words rambling from one statement to another. "This is one of the properties, I think. There were so many, even in just Chicago. I didn't memorize them all, but . . . I think this is one of them."

Nick wasn't even watching his surroundings, his brain was working so fast. It explained so much. The times the feds had watched the house . . . And gotten nothing. The times Nick had looked for Kaspar and wondered why he stayed inside so long, or why he'd missed the man.

When he looked up, he saw Sin watching the house with wide eyes. "We have to go in."

"Wait." He put his hand to her arm, as though he could truly hold her back. "That was an officer. If they know about it, the place will be swamped."

She shook her head, but didn't shake him off. "They'd be

watching this house to see who tried to enter this way. If they knew, we would've already been pulled aside and questioned."

"Unless they're waiting for us to go in." Nick didn't like it.

"That's a risk I have to take." He could see the clock running down in her eyes.

His hand still rested on her arm. "We."

She nodded and smiled. Really smiled.

He'd seen that before. But it wasn't common.

An image flashed through his head of all the time he'd spent hunting down Kolya's bastards. They were far and wide, varied and many in number. But only one had turned into the family he'd been looking for. Nick smiled back.

Without speaking, they agreed to enter through the back door, a lock pick making short work of a place that wasn't sealed all that tightly. Once inside, they stood in the kitchen as Sin absorbed her surroundings. It became apparent to Nick pretty quickly that a family lived here. There were kid cups and baby bottles in cabinets when he took a quick glance. Luckily the low stock in the pantry and sparse fridge led him to believe this was a planned absence.

When he looked up, Sin was checking other rooms. He found her in a closet, pushing on the back wall.

"Narnia?"

She snorted. "The exact opposite of Narnia." But the wall didn't budge.

Believing the house to be empty, and needing to make short work of time, they split up. Nick checked walls, looked for seams, anything. The door would have to be able to open from either side, or it wasn't useful as a real method of entering and leaving the Kurev house. It would have to be difficult to find—in both places. Police raids, Feds, even DEA visits had to be common occurrences for Kolya's sons.

But he was back in the main room, trying not to make shadows from the single light in the living room, when it popped off.

His heart stopped, his gun was out, safety off, in a two-hand grip before he heard his sister's voice. "Timer."

*Shit.* His heart slowed and he didn't even react as another light popped on in the other room with a click. He was glad he wasn't standing there. He would have been outlined perfectly in the window. But Sin no longer cared about the lights.

"We have to go down, not up. But I'm not finding it."

"Me either." He'd checked the floors in the closets, looked for signs, but found nothing.

Sin stood still. "We have to look again, but smarter. If you were going to design a way between the houses, where would you put the entry?"

"Back of the house." He answered without thinking. "In the house, so as not to be seen, but the back rooms are easier to get to. . . . Not the kids' bedrooms, or mine."

Nodding, Sin agreed with him. "I think all the bedrooms are upstairs. But back of the house means the kitchen, the office, or the guest room."

They split up again, not speaking. The best case scenario was that another person would come out and they'd see exactly where the door was. Nick didn't want to alert that person that someone was here.

It took ten minutes before he made it to the office and realized the rug wasn't tacked in the far corner. No furniture covered the space. Sure enough, under the padding was a wood flooring, and near the wall, one short board had a gouge missing, just big enough to get a man's fingers under.

He lifted the flooring and saw the soft low light emanating. When nothing changed, he had to believe it was always on. It impressed him how the door was square, but the flooring lifted in the pattern it had been laid, leaving one edge step-and-finger shaped, so that the boards didn't have a seam that gave it away. Only the gouge in the wood, under the padding, under the carpet, in a fully furnished room told of the door.

Letting it softly down he headed out to grab his sister from where she was once again in a closet. "I've got it."

She smiled and followed him into the other room, watching as he went through all the steps.

"Clever." She commented. "Actually pretty easy—fast maybe —once you know what you're doing, but certainly not obvious."

Nick smiled. She would know.

But now they lifted the door together, watched the light, and Sin nodded, heading down the neat staircase into the tunnel that had to lead under the Kurev mansion.

Nick followed in the glow from small overhead fixtures, the ceilings a good eight feet tall as they hit the bottom. The cinderblock hallway was cool but not cold, the blue color probably a sealant rather than a paint choice. His fingers drifted out and trailed along the plasticky coating that didn't completely conceal the rough block beneath.

Though comfortably wide—enough for several people to pass each other, it was otherwise eerily quiet. The flooring was a soft polymer, ironically printed to look like tile. As he walked, Nick noted that it absorbed their steps. Or at least his—he had no doubt his sister could walk quietly in a pit of bells.

The hallway looked as though it came to an abrupt end in front of them, but as they approached it became clear that it was just a jog. Ninety degrees to the left, probably followed by another ninety to the right that would aim them directly under the Kurev mansion. The shift kept anyone from seeing directly down the long hall, from firing bullets over long distances, and probably more.

Nick wondered if there were cameras down here, but he hadn't seen any. There probably weren't. These days the worst thing you could do was link something to a digital feed, then anyone could hack it, see where you were. Now, the oldest ways were the most secretive and Nick didn't worry that someone would see them coming. He also didn't care.

After they made the turns, slowly, the hallway changed. Though still empty, there were now doors on either side. Nick's heart stilled—Rooms. A whole cavern of them. Who knew what the Kurevs were keeping?

Sin was shaking her head as she took in everything around them.

Windows were set into the walls next to the doors. Blinds or various coverings kept the people in the hall from looking in. Numbers delineated each doorway. Nick's heart rate kicked into high gear.

If the Mechanic was here, then Lee might be too.

Sin's hand was on a doorknob even before his was.

His gun in his hand, ready for anything that jumped out or hit or shot at him, Nick calmed his breathing and opened the door too quickly for anyone on the other side to react.

But no one met him.

It took a moment for the contents of the room to sink in.

Paintings, covered in fabric, hid in the shadows, stacked against the walls. A few corners peeked out where drapes had slid away and Nick's breath caught. He wasn't knowledgeable about art, but it looked like the real deal. He was trying to imagine the worth of the room when Sin called to him, her voice low and carrying only over the short distance.

He closed the door, berating himself for getting sidetracked. Sin shouldn't have had to call out.

As he turned, she pointed to two rooms that she must have checked. She mouthed the word "Empty" and pointed to the door she had open.

This time when he looked in, he faced an armory.

His chest felt like it was caving in.

He had guns. His grandfather's home in Atlanta was armed to the hilt. Nick had inherited it. As the head of Vasilescu and as an officer, he'd fired most everything. But this made his stomach turn.

The thought of taking over the Kurev holding curdled in his gut. He was not on their level. They were armed for Armageddon. They could turn Chicago into a militarized zone with what they had. By his calculations, they weren't under the home. They should still be under the long property behind the house. This was not their armory—this was just the spare.

Sin's expression told him her thoughts were the same. Slowly, she closed the door and they resumed checking rooms.

Nick moved a little faster this time, finding most of the rooms empty and waiting. His hand was on the knob to open yet another, ready to find the Mechanic, or Lee, or something of value, when he heard the man's voice.

"Stop."

It was slow, controlled and in charge.

Nick didn't open the door in front of him. He just turned in time to see Sin, held in front of the man.

He didn't put her in a choke hold, which she could have easily escaped. No, he had his arm snaked around her right arm, applying pressure at the back of her hand. Though she didn't drop the sai she held there, she could no longer control it. Her other arm was trapped in his as well.

But the most damning part was the .45 that he had jammed into her ribs.

# CHAPTER 36

S in faced Nick in the hallway. The hand that gripped hers was expertly placed, proving once again that the Kurevs had stepped up their game since Sin and Lee had begun picking them off so long ago.

The problem that Sin had now—aside from the obvious gun in her ribs—was that she didn't know who this man worked for. Though she desperately wanted to ask, she wasn't in any position for an interrogation. She didn't have time. The easiest thing was to let him grab her, let him think he had the upper hand. He was better trained than she'd expected.

As she watched, Nick lowered his gun.

She mouthed to him, "Don't drop it."

Whether he understood or not, he still held onto the weapon, though it was no longer pointed at the man who held her.

For a moment, she began to relax and sniffle a little bit. Whether this was believable or not depended on the gullibility of a man holding a woman holding a sai. The very fact that she was here in the tunnel meant she was probably someone who knew what she was doing.

Though that said the same thing about the man who held her.

But did he know enough?

She sniffled again, this time taking a deep, choking breath, as though she were crying. The sound hopefully distracted him from the fact that she raised her ribcage as she sucked in air. He jammed the gun into her side again, though this time it was tucked just under her last rib, where she wanted it.

It hurt like a bitch, but she did it anyway. It certainly hurt less than a bullet would and less than getting in a fight.

Despite the bite of the muzzle, she sniffled and mewed and worked her ribcage as though she was afraid. Though he pressed his thumb against the bones of her hand, he didn't force her grip to open. It could be done, and there wasn't much a person could do about it. It was just physiology. The fact that he didn't led her to believe he wasn't as trained as he could be. Churkin would have had the sai clattering to the floor long before this.

Another mew from her, another dirty look from Nick at the man whose face she couldn't see, and she pushed her flesh into the front of the gun. Making another noise, she took another breath, and as he pulled her position tighter, she worked the muzzle further under her ribcage.

She only knew two things about this man. One—he wasn't aware of what she was doing or he wouldn't have let her do it. And two—he wasn't the mechanic.

Without moving her head she blinked rapidly at Nick. If her captor was any good, he would detect if she nodded or moved her hand. Nick's long breath out told her he was ready, even if he didn't know her play.

She mewled again, rocking herself into the gun to the point that the slide pushed back and only the actual barrel gouged at her. She blinked once. Twice.

And she moved.

Leaning into gun, Sin rolled around to face the man. Even as she did it, he pulled the trigger.

The bastard actually shot her.

Her breath held against the possible pain. She didn't pause, couldn't afford to.

But the pain never came.

By leaning into the gun and pushing the slide back, she'd made it impossible for the weapon to fire. Score one for her.

Sin was smiling when she came face to face with him. His trigger clicked only once, and after that she had her left hand wrapped across the front of her body, holding onto the slide, forcing it back, making firing it impossible. His surprise was all she needed.

He couldn't control her sai hand as she rolled out of his grip. And his concern turned to his suddenly useless gun. He didn't even try to hold the weapon at bay.

*Amateur*, she thought.

Holding the gun by the muzzle, she pulled it outward as her sai came up across his throat.

The fist holding the sai pushed into his collar bone, forcing him back into the wall as she plucked the gun from his hand, his arm stretching all the way out before he finally relinquished the weapon.

Even so, she brought it quickly back to him in the form of a blunt object under his jaw line.

Hitting the nerve box there with the added weight of the gun knocked him out cold.

She stepped back as he slid down the wall, his eyes rolling upward in a grotesque parody of a perturbed teenager.

Sin turned to Nick. "Let's get him in one of these rooms."

She was greeted with reluctant help and a sigh. Nick was already grabbing the man under his arms, even as he complained. "We could have questioned him. He would have cracked like a nut."

While she agreed, she had a different take on it. "He pulled the trigger! He tried to actually shoot me."

Folding the man unceremoniously onto the cold floor, Nick

pulled the door closed behind him. "I'm not convinced he didn't just jerk in surprise. But it's done now. Keep going."

Handing Nick the purloined gun, she watched as he tucked it into the back of his pants. While the thought made her cringe, it wasn't as though she could carry it. Armed to the hilt, she was out of room.

Stepping foot over foot, they moved at a slower pace now. This time she and Nick shared the task, slowing them down immeasurably.

Normally her heart didn't thump in situations like this. She had trained enough, and fought enough, that she had her adrenaline under control. Once she'd read that parachuting was at its most dangerous when the skydiver no longer got the heart-pounding rush from the jump. Before this month, she would have said she was at the same place.

She didn't fear for herself. She had believed there was nothing that could be done to her that was worse than what had already been done. And she never worried about Lee; she knew he could hold his own.

This, . . . This was new.

Now it was her fear for Lee, her fear that she was too late, that made her heart thump loudly. The sound of her own blood pumping made an oceanic roar in her ears and fogged her brain. It was a fog she couldn't afford.

She held the gun down at her side, concerned the Mechanic might throw a bound Lee at them, hoping they would shoot their own man. And why not? He wasn't getting paid for the kill anymore. He needed only to escape to the next job.

Three of the windows they passed were bare. The rooms beyond them dark. Still she and Nick opened the doors with caution, sweeping their weapons into the corners, ready to kill what popped out at them. But nothing came.

Nodding to Nick, she put her hand on the fourth knob and made a motion.

The light was on behind the shade. The thick walls would have made anything short of machine gun fire or screaming all but impossible to hear. With no idea what waited on the other side—and hoping it was Lee—Sin turned the knob.

Nick swung into the doorway, legs braced wide, gun sweeping the area as four officers stood up abruptly. Chairs scraped back, unnoticed as hands went for guns or into the air.

"Nick!" One of the officers with his hands in air offered an oily smile. "Didn't expect to see you here."

As soon as the door opened, she positioned herself at Nick's knee level, weapons in hand and ready. Most people still didn't expect an attacker not fully on their feet and that played out here as well when one of the men spotted her.

He almost laughed, his hand reaching for his gun. "The girl has a knife."

He was sliding the gun from the holster while Nick kept his gun trained on the oily one. The woman and the third man were keeping their hands still if not high. Sin took Nick's lack of relaxation as a sign that all was not as copacetic as the greasy cop wanted to portray.

And the other one was being a dick.

She didn't know if she was more offended by his calling her a 'girl' or his belief that her knife was somehow lesser. Or maybe she was just enjoying the surprise.

Letting him draw his weapon, knowing he intended to use it before she acted, Sin waited until he had his grip and the gun was rising.

So many hours of training. So many moving targets Lee had rigged for her. All paying off.

Keeping her wrist straight and throwing from the elbow, she let the unadorned knife fly.

He was reaching for his chest and feeling the blade embedded there before he realized she'd thrown it. His hands involuntarily spasmed, dropping the gun with a heavy clatter to the cement floor.

The noise must have jarred the other officers from their stupor, because they now reached for their weapons and turned to her. They no longer thought Nick was the primary threat.

But Sin was already holding the next knife, having plucked it from the pockets she'd sewn into the jacket lining so long ago.

This time they saw the knife and lowered their weapons.

"Nick." The only officer talking acted as though Nick should be friendly with him. Sin had doubts about any officer that left a brother gurgling in his own pool of blood.

For a moment she felt a pang about taking down a man in uniform. She had a deep love/hate relationship with that particular shade of blue, but there was still something about a crooked cop that bothered her more than anything. She didn't regret the hit.

Nick didn't speak. Only looked at the man he must have known. Something in his eyes said Nick was disappointed.

"Nick, I'm your guy here."

"No. You knew about this place and you didn't tell me. You were Kaspar's guy all along."

Sin understood then. Nick would not take his aim off of Oily.

Slowly standing, she kept one eye on the two remaining officers who were now looking around as though seeking escape. Their buddy was dying at their feet and while they didn't move to help him, they also no longer reached for their weapons.

"I only just found out about this place!" The officer lifted his hands higher.

As convincing performances went, it ranked pretty low. Sin was just about to remind Nick that they had an agenda, when he beat her to it.

"I don't believe you. But I'm looking for a man held prisoner, probably down here." Nick watched the other man's eyes.

"No prisoners down here." He shook his head, his smile and

his confidence betraying his earlier lie. "Just some guns, some art, some safes."

"You know a lot for a man who just learned about this." Nick smiled as he stepped further into the room and kicked the door shut behind him.

Her knife was quiet, gunfire not so much.

The door clicked only half a moment before Nick's gun went off and the oily officer dropped to the floor with a look of surprise on his face.

Two remained standing, their eyes wide, hands now flying into the air.

"Guns." Sin held out her hand.

The man handed his over to Nick who promptly knocked him out with it as Sin had done earlier. The woman tried to be a hero.

"Seriously?" Sin grabbed the woman's wrist and twisted until it broke, the Taser in her hand falling to the floor. "That was dumb as shit. If you survive, you'll need surgery now." And she leaned over and picked up the weapon knowing Nick had her back.

The trigger felt familiar under her finger even if the anger in her system did not. Sin actually enjoyed tasing the bitch, watching her muscles lock and her stone statue body fall to the concrete with a thud. Normally, shocks were administered over grass to avoid head injuries. Sin didn't give a shit.

Using the officers' cuffs from the backs of their belts, Nick and Sin made short work of leaving them hog tied. Two dead meant extra cuffs for the living. When the woman moaned, coming around from the shock just as Sin finished, she was rewarded with another conk on the head. Then Sin pulled off shoes and stuffed the woman's socks into the mouths of the two remaining live officers. "Now they can't scream if they come around while we're still down here."

Nick turned away in disgust.

"Really?" She looked at him. He'd committed far worse himself.

"Dirty socks?" His mouth curled.

Shaking her head, she turned and headed to the next room.

Jogs in the hallways both slowed them down and provided cover.

As they stood at the third one they encountered, Nick pointed upward. Though there was nothing to hear, they were under the backyard now.

Standing side by side, pressed against the cold wall, Sin felt her heart give a sick turn. Lee had not been in any of the rooms they had opened. The tunnel itself was an unexpected revelation. The rooms offered finds that would have been fascinating on any other day. But today each open door was another room Lee wasn't in. Another drastic drop in the likelihood that they would find him around the corner.

And if he wasn't here, then where would he be?

There was nowhere else she knew to look.

Breathing in through her nose, Sin looked at Nick and forced her concerns back. They would find Lee or they wouldn't. If they didn't, she would get through it. She'd gotten through the worst before. Only this time she was older. She understood the loss she faced.

But this time she had Nick.

Looking up at her older brother and realizing he had become her family in a way that even her sister Wendy had never been, she did something she rarely did. She told him, "Thank you."

He only offered a small smile and a nod asking if she was ready.

Knife in one hand, sai at the ready in the other, they softly turned to face what was in the corridor ahead.

As she looked down the long hallway, a door slid slowly closed.

# CHAPTER 37

Owen hung up the phone.

He missed the old rotary phones, missed slamming the handset back into the cradle when he was finished. He missed that they were sturdy enough to handle his fury. This phone would shatter if he did the slightest thing to it.

Though the thought was tempting, he needed the line open.

"What was it?" Annika put her hand on his arm, the motion alone infusing some calm into him.

He'd never wanted to go home as badly as he did right now. Not in all his long years with the FBI, and never in his time as a teacher. He missed his kids and he hated this shit.

"It was Duffy." He sighed. He didn't want to tell her what had happened. But he had to. "An officer showed up at their hotel. Handed him a piece of paper."

She frowned at him, her face modeling the exact emotions he'd felt himself when he heard from the officer. "The Mechanic sent the message that he has our guy and is willing to sell him to us."

Only Annika didn't get frustrated or angry about it. She lit up like the fourth of July. "He's alive!"

Yes. It meant Lee was alive.

But the cynic in him hated the rest of what it meant.

"For how long?"

Annika shook her head at him. "For at least as long as it takes to get his money."

"We don't have it." That was the least of their worries, but it was what rolled out of his mouth.

"Sin might." She frowned at him again. "Nick will. What's the problem?"

"I don't believe for one second that he's going to just hand Lee over for cash." His neck hurt from tension he'd been carrying there. Now he wasn't nearly in the kind of physical shape he needed for this kind of stress. "He lives on business. He needs repeat business and personal referrals. We can't offer that." Owen held up his hand to stop her before she spoke. "They'll go after him. Even if there's a successful exchange of money for Lee."

Annika nodded. "And he can't have that."

There was a beat of silence before she spoke again. "Okay, so it's only a temporary fix, but isn't that better than none?"

"I'd say yes, but I don't think it's even temporary. My guess is that at best, it's a trap. If they leave alive, he's left highly skilled operatives who will hunt him down and stop at nothing." Owen hated the churning in his gut and thought for a fleeting moment of his superior at the Bureau, Agent in Charge Bean, and all his ulcer medications. What Owen wouldn't give for his own bottle of Pepto right now.

"So he's hoping for money and then he'll kill them. Can they trap him?"

Owen shook his head. Every fucking way he turned was a brick wall. "Not if I can't get in touch with them. Sin and Nick have been radio silent for well over an hour."

"I saw you getting frustrated. Didn't realize that's what it was." She reached up to rub his shoulders, but he shrugged her off. He fed off the low, pervasive pain that radiated from his shoulders down his back. It kept him sharp.

Sharp enough to see that her hand fluttered down to her belly again. "Are you all right?"

She shrugged but changed the subject. "They'll either come back with Lee and it will be done, or they'll come back without him."

He loved that about Annika—she counterbalanced him. She never even considered the third option: that they didn't come back.

Continuing, she stayed in her positive light. "If they come back without him, we give them the message. It's the first real link we've had."

He didn't speak the words. There was every chance Lee was already dead. Sin was in no position to demand proof of life. She might show without the money, laying a trap of her own, but that likely wouldn't get her Lee. Worst case the Mechanic took the money then killed them all.

"What?" The single gentle word broke through his thoughts.

But he shook his head.

"You're still upset."

This time he nodded and lowered his voice. Regardless of the money, regardless of any traps, plans, or outcomes, there was something else inherently wrong from the start.

"Duffy chose his own location."

Annika's eyes opened wide as she put two and two together. Even they didn't know exactly where Duffy was.

But somehow the Mechanic did.

---

Sin nodded to Nick as the door swung closed with a click. Given what they'd already found, there was every possibility it was just another group of who-knew-what gathering in the Kurev hold.

But it could be Lee.

It could always be Lee.

At least here they knew there was at least one person in the room. Previously they'd run full breach protocol on what turned out to be empty rooms. It was one of the true and boring aspects of police work that she'd actually always liked. But not tonight. Tonight she wanted the rooms full. She wanted Lee or at least someone who could tell her where he was.

Positioning herself on the hinge side of the door, she grabbed the knob and waited for Nick's signal. On his count, she threw the door wide and let him gain his stance, gun aimed, into the room.

She had this down, she'd opened so many damn doors in this hallway, that she spun easily into place staying low near Nick's knees, her knife and sai ready.

What wasn't ready was her heart.

Lee was slumped into a chair, alert but badly hurt.

A man stood in front of him, his back to Nick and the open doorway.

He was turning at the sound.

Even from the back she could tell it was the Mechanic and she had to get the hell out of view before he turned.

Faster than she may ever have moved in her life, she continued the rotation she'd started and nearly seamlessly darted low across the doorway, crossing from one side to the other. Hopefully she was out of sight before the Mechanic saw.

She'd just abandoned Nick with the man, but if he hadn't seen her it would give her the element of surprise.

Lee had seen her.

But he hadn't twitched, hadn't given either of them away, only the faint sound of well-oiled hinges had done that. Only Nick's feet planting softly, but firmly into the space had done that.

While she plastered herself to the wall, Sin fought to get all the pieces of her under control.

"Don't move." Nick barked.

Her heart soared, floating upward—they'd found Lee. Still, her gut sank. He was in bad shape. She'd had her share of sprains, broken bones, and even bullet wounds. But this was worse than she'd ever seen. Much like Officer Hellico, Lee had open wounds. In her mind's eye, when she revisited her brief glimpse of him, she saw broken bones. She saw that he was bound to a thick, heavy, wood chair with tie down straps. The webbing could be cut, but was nearly impossible to break out of. She could only conclude that Lee had gotten out of easier holds at some point, because this looked like overkill.

From the room she didn't hear anything and her brain played out possible scenarios. It didn't sound like the Mechanic had moved. He would be smart not to.

Nick would shoot him. Lee was there, Nick had no qualms.

But the Mechanic would want Nick to get in closer.

Why hadn't Nick shot already?

Just kill the bastard and be done with it.

Nick's right foot, the one closest to her, twitched, motioning her to look inside.

Her eyes strayed straight to Lee.

Though he looked at Nick and didn't change his gaze, she knew he saw her. Something changed in his eyes, his face. While she appreciated it, she hoped the Mechanic couldn't see it.

Though she wanted to look all day, it was action that would get things done, so she scanned the area. That was when she saw that the Mechanic had his gun pointed center mass at Lee.

No wonder Nick hadn't just laid the man out.

A good shot would make him twitch and send a bullet wild. But with his starting aim so clear, he'd likely hit something. And he knew they'd come this far, they wouldn't gamble like that with Lee.

If she was lucky, the man didn't know she was here, and wouldn't until it was too late. If she was unlucky, he already knew.

Action, she reminded herself, and slid slowly around the door frame not making a sound. She already had her sai and her knife drawn. Not lucky, just ready. Just in case.

And here she was staring at 'just in case'.

One foot over the other, she rolled her feet through each position, never breaking contact with the floor. For a moment she was grateful she'd spent so long practicing. . . . Today it might make all the difference in the world.

Sin wasn't used to being the recipient of her actions. But saving Lee? That was just for her.

And her heart rate proved it.

She was to Nick's right and almost directly behind the Mechanic, when Nick took a step to his left.

Coming a little more into the man's peripheral vision, he spoke. "If you shoot him I will kill you slowly and painfully. I'll use your own tools on you."

The action and the words drew the man's gaze around to his left. Leaving his right open for Sin.

*Thank you, Nick!*

She began moving just a little faster, any sounds she might have made covered by Nick's incessant threats. He spoke of pulling teeth, shoving bamboo under fingernails, plucking hair one by one by one. The mechanic laughed but didn't pull the trigger.

As she looked from her new vantage point, Sin fought the roiling of her stomach.

The bastard was using Vermont technique—his right forefinger was laid along the underside of the barrel, his middle finger on the trigger. It gave him excellent aim even if he wasn't looking directly at his target. Sin knew this because Lee had taught her this same method.

*Fuck.*

His ability to hit Lee was far more acute than they'd realized.

Still, the Mechanic hadn't seemed to notice Sin.

She wanted to believe it was because she was that good. But

putting all her stock in that was a mistake. Underestimating this man or his tolerance for his own pain was a mistake. Everything Nick threatened worked on normal people, but Sin was certain the Mechanic wasn't normal. He might enjoy his own pain as much as he enjoyed others. No, he was still standing because he wanted to stay alive.

She was banking on that.

If he turned to her, that would be ideal. She could take him or at least give him a run for his money. But if he heard her and just shot Lee . . . That would be the end.

She and Nick would be standing there over two bodies in less than a heartbeat. Almost able to smell the blood, she could envision the Mechanic dead at her feet, riddled with bullet holes from Nick and knives from her. But Lee would be still tied to the chair, a single well placed bullet putting shame to all he'd endured to get to this day.

She mentally shook the vision off.

She would not let Lee die this way. But the image of the Mechanic with blades in him made her think and she crept a little more slowly around to the man's right.

Only then did the words get to her.

"Where's my money?" The mechanic asked.

Nick had maneuvered around to be just inside his line of vision and as he did, Kelly Gilligan's shoulders bunched. Clearly Nick was obviously not carrying the money the man wanted.

Putting the pieces together, Sin realized that Gilligan believed Nick knew what he was talking about.

*Bluff!* She yelled it in her mind. Whether he heard her or not, she didn't know.

Nick didn't get the chance.

The Mechanic growled again, giving cover to her movements, keeping his focus toward Nick. "This isn't the meeting place or time."

"We set our own."

"Where's the money?"

"Just outside the door." Her heart almost sank in gratitude for her brother's stellar lying skills. It had rolled off his tongue easy and clear. She took another step. Any closer and he might sense her there.

Sin slowed her breathing, moved stealthily, and listened to the conversation.

"How much?" The Mechanic barked.

"One million." It was cool, sharp. A simple lie told in a simple way. Nick never faltered.

She could see Lee now, in the chair, unmoving. His left hand gripped the armrest it was tied to, but his right was too swollen to do much. He moaned a little, changing the game and suddenly pulling the Mechanic's attention back to him.

Sin froze. She was in position to surprise him if he was focused on Nick. He'd more likely spot her coming up on his right side, if he were aiming his attention toward Lee.

But Lee rolled his shoulders, moaned again, and flexed the fingers of his left hand several times. His right foot tapped but his left didn't.

"Shut up and don't move." The Mechanic gave the gun a tiny jerk. Not enough to change his aim or give Sin the opening she wanted. Just enough to let Lee know he meant it.

Lee stilled.

But he'd done his job. Even as the Mechanic turned his attention back to Nick and growled yet again, Sin had inventory.

"That's not enough!"

"We're playing our own game, Gilligan." Nick used his real name, though the Mechanic didn't seem startled by that. From the back Sin could see the subtle changes that indicated the man was paying attention to her brother again.

And she now knew what Lee could do and what he couldn't.

Nick kept talking.

"You can have the rest after we get our man."

The Mechanic wanted a way out, and he wanted money. Why in hell he thought they knew about it, she had no clue. But she was grateful he'd asked. Knowing what he wanted helped.

Kelly Gilligan got nothing but wounds and death from them if he killed Lee. So killing Lee wasn't on his agenda though she had no doubt he'd kill her husband if he felt that was his only way to walk out of here. And none of this prevented him from further wounding Lee.

If the Mechanic walked away, he just might come back after them. And she would definitely go after Gilligan if he escaped.

She had to wonder if he knew he couldn't walk away.

He probably did. But her priority would be Lee, and that would be his ticket.

*Shit.* Nothing she could do about that.

The words came and they were her cue.

"I want all of it or you don't get him." Gilligan shifted the gun and Sin could see him aiming for a leg. He'd wound Lee at best and maim him at worst. But not killing him wouldn't void his transaction with Nick.

From just behind him on the right, Sin popped up. At the same time she threw her knife to Lee. His left hand lifted as she had, and the tip of the blade buried itself into the wood just below his fingertips. It wasn't in his hand yet, but it was now where he could get to it.

She didn't have time to see him grab it, or even watch it plant in the wood. Her speed was how she would win this.

She'd dropped her Sai, needing both her hands to control his gun—anything less and he could fire it.

Before the metal of her weapon even hit the ground she had her hand over Gilligan's gun. His hand was much bigger than hers, and while her left hand wrapped the barrel and her elbow came down, wrapping his forearm for control, she found her fingers weren't long enough to control his own grip on the trigger.

Even though she had his first finger trapped along the barrel, the third could still fire the gun.

And he fought her.

Surprised as he was, he reacted quicker. Pulling back, he used brute strength to try and wrest his arm out from under hers. Knowing that she wouldn't win muscle-to-muscle, Sin was ready. She only needed to control the weapon a little bit; just enough to make a bullet miss Lee.

Shifting her grip slightly, she rotated her left hand around where she could twist his hold. Letting go with her right hand, she spun backwards, her right elbow coming around behind her aiming for under his ear. A knockout shot if she made it. Her spin took her left hand and his gun hand with her and as she twisted his hand he was forced to drop the gun or let her break at least his finger and maybe his arm.

She felt rather than saw his grip open and the gun release.

Her elbow encountered the hard bone of skull, rather than the underside of his jaw, as he ducked away from her shot. Without control of his right arm to block her, he took the brunt of the blow, but so did she. Fingers of electric pain shot up her forearm as her elbow smashed into his head.

She had to let go of his arm, or they'd both fall to the floor in a heap, but his gun was gone. He could no longer shoot Lee. Still, he'd maneuvered better than she'd anticipated.

Sin followed the pain in her elbow, spinning around to face him, ready to deliver the next blow. Her left hand balled into a fist and she used her momentum and the moment she had to spot her target, to get him in the kidney.

Air and a grunt belched from his open mouth as he took that shot full force.

But he was ready.

Though the blow hit him square on, and he moved backward with it, it didn't seem to cause lingering pain in him. He popped back up almost immediately. The hits didn't seem to scramble his thoughts as happened to most in a fight.

And the game had changed while Sin moved.

Nick had lowered his gun, unable to fire at a man in a fight with his sister. He'd scrambled to Lee's side, attempting to pull another knife and help with the knots.

Which left him open.

The mechanic had a second gun in hand, pulled from somewhere unknown while Sin knocked him backward. So as he regained his feet, he regained control of the situation.

Not surprisingly, the barrel was now aimed at Nick.

His voice was like gravel rubbed in an open wound. "Don't move, sweetheart."

# CHAPTER 38

Nick stopped cutting the webbing at Lee's foot. It had been wrapped around his leg enough times that when Nick quit it slowly unwound just a little to where Lee could move his foot back and forth to shake the rest off. Before he looked up at Gilligan, Nick spotted the gash the tie strap had concealed. And he saw that it was starting to bleed again.

Looking down the barrel of a gun was something Nick had done before.

He'd felt his gut tie up in knots, his heart churn, and his brain calculate his last moments.

*Dammit.* He'd been looking forward to working for the FBI. Though he dreamed his whole life of running Vasilescu, it hadn't turned out as he wanted. The police work had been more satisfying to him and he hadn't understood until his later years. Until Reese had shown him something other than where he was.

His legacy—the new one he'd reached for—would have been her legacy. He was pissed that he was going to die a criminal, under the house of those stupid asshole brothers of his.

The mechanic held his gun on Nick, but he spoke to Sin. "Get over there next to the boys, baby."

She shook her head.

*Good girl*, Nick thought.

If the Mechanic managed to corral the three of them together, with himself between them and the door, he could spray bullets before they could do anything. Right now, Sin was on her feet and apart from the other two. She was their only hope.

"Move it, or I'll shoot your brother."

Nick's heart tumbled. *How the hell had he known that?*

But Sin still wasn't playing that game.

"Lee," she called out, "I'm pregnant."

For the first time, Lee jerked his head up. Whether he was playing along, or if he could read the truth on her like an open book, Nick couldn't tell. But his reaction seemed genuine.

The Mechanic looked at her. "Really?"

As though his reaction mattered.

"Yes." She stared at him but didn't move.

"Well, then both of you need to move over there. Last call."

Setting her jaw as Nick watched, she took the first step toward him.

*No!* The thought rang through his head. She couldn't come their way.

And she didn't.

Only one step toward them and she suddenly switched directions, dropping to the ground before Nick even comprehended.

Ready for what was coming, Nick ducked back, he wouldn't use Lee as a shield, but he would cover himself. Turning his head away, he tucked his right arm up along his side and brought his left around to cover his head as best he could.

The sound of the bullet leaving the chamber was an afterthought. Something he heard as he fell backward onto the cold cement floor.

His hands didn't move and he couldn't catch himself, so he took the brunt of the fall on his shoulder, his muscles unable to keep his skull from cracking against the hard ground.

Pain radiated up and through his skull, but it only served to light up all his nerves. He felt the heat in his right side as the bullet tore through his arm. It had been a crappy defense against a bullet and the wild sting let him know that.

Even as he fell, he knew the sequence was wrong. The bullet wasn't still moving through him. But in slow motion he felt it rip past his ribs and up through his organs, sucking everything inside him into a black hole of searing pain.

His eyes still worked, his brain still worked, though he questioned both.

He waited to hear the bullet exit the other side of his body and hit the flooring, but the sound never came. In front of him, he could see the thick, square back legs of the chair. Under each foot was a small, dried puddle. Most likely blood. Most likely Lee's.

The small movements in the wood told him Lee was still moving above him, but he couldn't redirect his eyes to learn more. The pain was all consuming now, having traveled his torso to his legs and feet. He could no longer pinpoint the bullet that was apparently still inside him.

Nick tried to take a deep breath, but it felt as though the air was being sucked out of him instead. At the edges of his vision, blackness pushed down on him. And underneath him, warm blood began to pool while he felt himself growing colder.

---

Sin heard the crack of the gun, but there was nothing she could do about it. She wasn't the praying sort—in a situation like this, prayer took time and focus. She didn't have either to spare.

While the gun had fired and that was not good, she did use it to her advantage.

Knowing from experience that any gunshot required the shooter to brace, she moved as fast as she could, accomplishing as much as possible in the short window while he fought the recoil.

She'd hit the ground and come back up with her sai gripped tightly. Her left hand dove into the front of her jacket and another throwing knife came out. By the time the Mechanic had swung his gun around to her, she was ready.

The knife flew from her hand as she'd pulled another and let it fly before the first even hit its mark.

A third knife appeared from inside her jacket. If she wasn't good enough to save Lee and Nick, then it was all a waste. She wouldn't let it be.

The first knife buried in his right bicep, causing twitches in his gun arm. Just out of range of controlling his arm, Sin kept throwing. He'd either hit her or he wouldn't. She figured she could keep going with a bullet or two in her.

She didn't look at Nick as the third knife flew as the handle of the second sagged, the tip buried in his abdomen near his right hip.

He staggered backward, the metal of her knives hitting nerves and causing him problems.

*Good.*

As he turned to face her, his eyes wide at what she'd done, the third knife buried itself in his chest. He gurgled, but stumbled backward, farther out of her reach.

Now she could move toward him. She could manipulate him.

Though his right hand still clutched the gun, it was useless, and Sin stepped into his sphere. With her sai in her right hand, she slashed it across his arm. When the sharp point hit bone, she pulled, severing muscle and tendon.

The twitching in his hand stopped and his hand lolled back as he watched.

Kelly Gilligan still seemed to not understand what was happening to him.

Sin did.

She couldn't look at her brother, didn't acknowledge the tang in the air from blood both fresh and old. As she pulled her right hand back she reached forward with her left, grabbing his shoulder. She braced his foot with her own, needing him upright. Behind her, the sai switched grips in her right hand. Lee had once said it looked like the weapons floated, turning one way and then another. He said it was scary as shit. It was just the result of years of practice. But the sai came back in a downward facing grip and she didn't hide the high arc of her swing because there was nothing the Mechanic could do about it.

The tip went through shirt and skin like it was butter. She must have hit his collarbone, but it didn't matter. Though the blade glanced slightly, her momentum carried it until the sai buried itself almost to the hilt.

This time, he sucked air in.

And failed.

When she pulled—not wanting the blade to stop any bleeding she'd caused, wanting to get more damage on the way out—the blade resisted. She'd buried it so deep it didn't want to come back.

But she kept her foot behind his and pushed with her left hand, relishing the feel of his flesh falling away from her. Holding the sai handle tighter than she maybe ever had before, she let the force of his falling body dislodge the blade. It was hers. He would not take this from her. She would not give him anything.

He hit the floor with a heavy thud, the concrete absorbing most of the blow. His head made a second sound, harder, less heavy, clunking a half moment after his back hit.

The Mechanic's eyes rolled back and stopped and Sin finally turned away to assess the situation.

Lee was just getting free from seemingly miles of ties, each of which had to be cut. She grabbed his head, held his face to hers and kissed him, something flowing through her at the touch of his lips to hers. He kissed her back, just for a moment, despite the bruising and swelling that marked so much of his face.

He uttered one word. "Nick."

Nodding, she turned to her brother. The concrete didn't absorb blood like carpet, didn't direct it like wood. She'd seen blood under a body in so many ways, but nothing spread like concrete. As though his life was trying to get as far as possible, it ran in all directions, the front slowly folding under itself as more came up behind.

She touched his arm, where the bullet had torn a hole in his jacket, where the material had soaked the blood from the hole in his skin.

Moving his arm aside, she then pushed away his jacket and found the corresponding hole near his ribs. Not too bad from the outside.

"Nick? Nick!" She shook him for lack of something better to do.

"Sthnnnn?" he mumbled, maybe her name, definitely incoherent. Still alive.

She smiled. "We have to get you out of here."

It took a few minutes. She tore shirts, bandaged Nick's gunshot first with Lee's help and the nylon straps for tension. There were plenty to wrap around Nick, then she bound Lee's leg, the wound now stuffed with a piece of shirt.

He looked at her as she tied one of the straps in a tight knot. "Are you really pregnant?"

"Yes."

The left side of his mouth didn't move, but the right side quirked up in some semblance of a grin.

There was no way to tell him it was stupid, they couldn't have a child, there was too much at stake. Let him grin for a moment. They could make decisions later. Right now they needed to get out, but weren't ready yet.

She insisted on wrapping his arm, too, where a long cut had

broken back open and was oozing fresh blood over the old. The webbing, once bright orange was already dark with Lee's blood, probably from days past. But neither of them mentioned it.

He stood, wobbly, breathing heavily, and she reached to help him. Lee pushed her away, saying only, "Nick."

Her brother still sucked air, looked a bit gray, but he made it to his feet, though a sound like wind cutting a desert storm came from him as she pulled him fully upright.

Bracing Nick's good arm across her shoulders, Sin lifted, watching as Lee attempted to get under his other side. But Nick's side wasn't up for it and neither was Lee.

She made it two steps with Nick bearing heavily on her, Lee hobbling and hopping at her side, when the Mechanic moved.

There was nothing she could do, burdened with an injured man on either side of her, Nick's weight making her too slow to react.

Gilligan hadn't died yet. And he didn't want to die alone.

His first shot went a bit wild, cutting the air beside her head.

But he kept firing. He needed only the one finger to keep pulling the trigger. And he did.

The next shot came before she could react at all. She was tossing Nick's arm up and away from her despite his sounds of pain. She shoved his torso as she felt the bullet graze her arm. But it didn't stop her.

Lee did.

Unencumbered, he was still slow, but not slow enough.

His body turned, and he was facing her, directly in front of her when the bullet hit him.

Small changes in his momentum told her he was hit, but it didn't stop his trajectory.

Lee fell to her side, leaving her the view of the Mechanic, still laying on the floor, gun aimed but wavering.

The scream tore out of her, the sound reverberating through the chamber as though it came from the walls themselves.

Unburdened now, she pulled the sai from where she'd sheathed it along her thigh. Her booted foot hit Gilligan's wrist where he held the gun and shoved it to the side. Her foot ground his hand into the unforgiving floor so he would never use it again.

Her right foot planting on his gun hand was just the first part of her arc. Falling to her knee in a controlled thrust, she brought the sai around, sailing point-first into his chest and through his heart so hard that it passed through his torso and hit the concrete behind him.

She felt the tip break off as the force reverberated up her arm and blood misted from his mouth.

# CHAPTER 39

As Sin turned back to look at Lee and Nick, her heart beat wildly.

She'd come all this way, fought so hard to save Lee. Here he was bleeding out—again. This time under the Kurev house. This time after weeks in the Mechanic's 'care'.

Her chest felt like it caved in, but she didn't have time to break.

She'd stabbed the Mechanic three more times, making certain he was dead. Her thoughts flooded with guilty questions and her own answers. Why hadn't she checked him better the first time? He'd seemed dead. Sin knew what 'dead' looked like, how 'dead' acted. They were out of time. He'd been dead. How he wasn't actually gone was something she'd have to face at another time.

Lee had only been shot once. But the shot was to his torso, into his back, because he'd been looking at her as the bullet hit.

Nick started to come around, using one elbow to come toward her as she rolled Lee, looking for an exit wound.

Footsteps broke her concentration. They rang through the concrete flooring and she wasn't sure if she heard them or felt them. But she'd grabbed Nick's gun and pulled a knife and stood, every muscle ready as she watched the open doorway.

Surely someone had heard something.

The steps slowed and Sin lifted the gun, waiting for the person to show themselves. Ready to kill again, she forced her breathing to a steady pace, and tried to reign in her senses.

She could hear Lee on the floor, tiny movements telling her he was still alive. Nick was trying to get to her husband, trying to help and stay quiet at the same time. The Mechanic made no more changes in the atmosphere, well and truly dispatched to his own hell this time. And the footsteps around the door had given way to breathing.

A head and a gun rotated slowly into view, the gun leading, cop style.

Blonde hair.

Sin aimed, her finger twitchy, ready to kill. Ready to make up for what she'd screwed up.

As she watched, the gun flipped upward, out of the way and Owen slowly stepped into view. He'd recognized her before she recognized him.

At the sight of him, she almost cracked.

She wanted to.

For a fraction of a second, an image slashed through her brain of running to her father for a hug after falling and scraping her elbow. Her own father was almost twenty years gone, but here was another. This man understood her, knew what she was, what she'd become. And he still showed up.

He was moving toward Lee and Nick even before she was.

On the floor, the two of them worked with rapid coordination. Owen peeling his jacket even before she saw that he was intending to use it on Lee. Wadding the material, Owen rapidly located the worst of the damage and shoved the jacket against the wound to stem the bleeding.

When he looked up at Sin, there was no mistaking the fact

that he'd already seen that Lee was in grave shape. But he didn't say so. Instead, he took over, giving instructions.

"Others are coming. I heard something from the Kurev house." He pushed harder on the wound, eliciting a small groan from Lee. Then he shoved his shoulder at her husband and Sin's hands moved to help, as he grunted to lift the grown man without making his injuries worse. "Get Nick. We're heading out the way we came in."

Sin only nodded and reached out for her brother, her eyes still on Owen as he turned and started walking, bearing the full weight of her husband.

They pushed themselves—Owen carrying Lee, Sin supporting Nick—as they made their way down the tunnel.

Noises behind them made Sin turn and look, but the jogs in the hallways bent sounds and made it impossible to tell how close anyone was. Someone was coming from the direction of the mansion, and if the bouncing tones of voices were believed, more than one person was coming.

Sin had no strength left, but she dug in. Somehow, she dragged Nick despite her exhaustion, somehow she kept up with Owen, and even heard Lee mutter "this time" more than once. Though she had no idea what he meant.

The noises were louder behind them, and it was difficult to turn and check with Nick draped over her the way he was, but she managed a glance. She still couldn't see them, but they had to be close. If they made the turn, whoever it was would see them, and there was no way they wouldn't be faster. There was no way a bullet wouldn't find them all. Only Owen was in any capacity to escape and Sin knew he would never drop Lee and run. Not while Lee was alive.

Owen must have heard it too, for his pace somehow managed to pick up. Hers did too, and the four of them threw themselves into the turn at what was probably the last second.

The stairs leading up into the back street house were a

welcome sight, and she could only hope no one had figured it out. That no one waited at the top to kill them or take them in.

At that moment, she decided she'd gladly trade her freedom for Lee's life.

It wasn't something she'd ever had to consider before. But here, now, it became a probability. Suddenly, she *hoped* someone was waiting.

But she set Nick on a step and pushed open the trap door for Owen to carry Lee up . . . and no one was there.

The house was empty and they didn't even hide their tracks as they gave one final push out to Owen's car.

He nearly dumped Lee in the backseat, the effort having bordered on superhuman to carry another man that far, that fast. Sin was grateful, but she only managed to push Nick into the passenger's side before climbing in the back and cradling Lee's head in her lap.

"Sin."

He smiled up at her. At least alert enough to do that. She took it as a good sign and almost didn't notice as the car lurched forward. Owen took turns at high speeds but Sin stayed focused on her husband.

"Lee, you're going to be fine." So much of what she'd held so tight loosened at what she took as a good sign.

"No." He didn't shake his head, but he was firm enough that her heart clenched.

"Yes." It was the only argument she could fathom. As she pushed one hand against the wadded jacket holding back the blood and ran her other hand over his hair, she wondered if this was the last time she might ever touch him alive.

She didn't cry.

She couldn't.

His eyes found hers, and he found enough voice to speak. "I did it this time. I'm ready to go."

She opened her mouth to protest, but he spoke instead.

"I'm so cold. I've lost too much blood. I'm at peace with my decisions."

He closed his eyes and for a moment she panicked until she saw him breathe, felt his hand twitch where it rested against her own.

"Owen, drive!" She nearly yelled it. But Owen was going as fast as he could.

# CHAPTER 40

Owen stood by Annika as the rain came down, the umbrellas of little use in the Chicago storm. Her eyes were wet, and her black dress had been bought for this somber occasion, styled to emphasize her pregnancy.

She wasn't pregnant, not anymore. But she'd been pregnant before and she carried the false bump convincingly.

He hated the lies, but understood their necessity.

There was no minister here. Just a small crowd, mostly keeping their distance from each other. He and Annika huddled under one umbrella; the rain had been a blessing, keeping any crowds or curiosities at bay.

Sin had asked him to bury Lee next to Samantha and Bethany —his first wife and their daughter. Though Lee had purchased the three plots together when he laid his family to rest, it had taken Owen months to convince the authorities that this man was in fact Lee Maxwell, missing these nearly ten years.

DNA tests had finally solved his problems, but running them quietly, making sure the cemetery kept it out of the press had taken coercion, money, and his badge. The rain made it better.

Several FBI agents stood quietly in attendance. Though their dark suits hid them among the raindrops and the funeral goers, their eyes were on alert, hoping Sin would show herself. They were ready to take her in.

Gavin Reil—formerly Nicolae Stelian of the Vasilescu family, but only witness protection and Owen knew that—stood to Owen's left, several yards away. He held an umbrella, but his expression was stoic as he stood in the downpour. He was here in an official capacity, but had considered Lee a friend, and had known him far better than Owen had. Somewhere inside, Nick was mourning. Or maybe he'd come to terms with Lee's death in the months it had taken to get here.

Todd Maxwell stood alone on the other side of the open grave as they lowered the shiny casket, devoid of flowers, into the earth. His suit was ruined and he cried openly. Owen knew he had daughters, but they weren't here. Probably had never met their uncle Lee. Todd was the only one left to mourn.

About ten other people stood in attendance. Several co-workers from Lee's days as an accountant with Black and Associates remembered him from before everything went south, before Sam and Bethy had been shot down, before Lee went crazy and fell off the grid. Maybe they felt guilty that they worked for the company that had been exposed as a key player in the Kurev mafia. Maybe they were just gawking.

Samantha's father had shown. He stood silently, alone, her mother having passed several years before. His stoicism matched the downpour and he didn't even speak to several friends of his daughter's who remembered happier times with the couple.

They had all been asked to show ID to attend. The FBI had insisted.

Cynthia May Beller, known associate of Lee Maxwell and wanted woman, did not show.

No one suspected the green-eyed, blond woman who stayed dry-eyed through the ceremony, her hand resting casually on her own round belly.

Her ID had passed and she spoke only to Samantha's father,

saying that she'd been a friend from school, had visited Sam and Lee and met Bethany when she was tiny. She was sorry she hadn't made it to Samantha's funeral, and she was here to rectify that. The man shook her hand and nodded, but didn't speak.

Owen watched the whole exchange, listening quietly from several feet away.

After the dirt was thrown with no fanfare, she turned and left, following several of the other attendees through the wet grass and out through the gates.

Putting his hand on Annika's back and holding the large umbrella with the other, he motioned for them to follow.

---

Nick didn't smile much when he got the mail, but today he did. Though the mail was addressed to his new self, Gavin Reil, it was meant for Nick.

Months of physical therapy had overlapped months of interrogation, but Owen Dunham and Dana Block had played the FBI like a fiddle for him and his deal had come through.

He would pass his ninety-day mark with the Bureau next week. He was only a consultant, no badge. He could never have one after what he'd confessed to.

He'd given them some of the people from Vasilescu, making it clear from the opening negotiations that he would pick who he leveled evidence against and they could take it or leave it. They had nothing on him.

In the tunnels under the Kurev mansion, he'd been afraid. After Sin had dropped him and Lee had been shot, he realized that he was going to live. His lung was collapsed, and he needed surgery, but he'd make it through.

The gunshots and her screams of rage and fear had brought in the cavalry. To this day Nick didn't know if she would have left Lee's body behind to save him or not.

As the footsteps had come down the hallway, Nick had scrambled for a gun, his hands and legs not working well enough.

Luckily, it was Owen who had come in.

He'd pulled them out, driven them to a hospital and managed to get both men admitted under false identities. Two weeks and three surgeries later, Nick began the process of turning states evidence.

The Mechanic had picked the house behind the Kurev mansion as the drop point for his demanded exchange. So when Owen arrived and found the carpet up and the door exposed, he'd come down. It was probably the thing that saved him. Sin, too.

There was no telling what would have happened had they still been there when the pounding footsteps of whoever had been coming from the Kurev house arrived.

He hadn't been with her when she'd had the baby. He'd seen her once a week later when she passed through, not telling him where she was headed. He knew he would see her again, he just didn't know when.

Sliding his finger under the flap of the thick envelope, he popped the seal and grinned. The note came from the Dunham family, announcing their newest daughter, Georgia Reese Dunham.

For a moment his heart stopped.

*Reese.*

Probably the closest nod they could give to the baby's origins. A nod to both him and Sin and the friend they'd both lost.

*Georgia.* Perfectly in keeping with their older daughters, Charlotte and Virginia. But again a note to where this baby had likely been conceived, where her birth parents were last together.

He looked at the picture, the round face so much like Sin's. Like his own infant picture, and he could see traces of Lee there, too. But she looked enough like Annika and Owen that he hoped no one would ever question it.

The page was thick, and he frowned as he turned it over.

A sealed envelope was stuck to the back of the high grade announcement paper. This one had no return address, but the front was set to be mailed to Todd Maxell.

Nick held it for a moment. The Dunhams couldn't send it themselves, but he could drop it in a distant post box when he got the chance. He'd never actually met Lee's brother—not as Nick and not even at the funeral as Gavin.

It was a week later that he dropped the envelope in the mail for Maxwell.

As the vellum left his fingertips it took a huge weight with it, setting him free of Nick's mistakes and Nick's past. He turned to the sunshine and walked into Gavin Reil's life.

---

She didn't know why she was here.

It was a seedy bar and she wasn't even drinking. Just a coke. She ate some peanuts from the bowl and thought that if she hadn't lived the life she had, the unclean bowl would kill her. But these days, probably nothing would.

She hadn't died giving birth, though she wouldn't have been horribly upset by that outcome.

She hadn't cracked in half when she'd made it to the cabin and cleared their stuff out from under layers of dust and bugs and leaves.

Sin had finally gone back to the last place she'd shared with Lee, bolstered by the picture in her heart of Owen and Annika leaving the home with their new baby. The midwife had been paid very handsomely to put their names on her certification and never acknowledge that Annika had not actually given birth to the child.

Sin had never thought of the baby as anything but theirs and held her only once before handing her over.

Holding the infant was something Annika insisted on. She wouldn't take the dark-haired girl unless Sin did it. So she'd held her, looked for Lee in her tiny face, and softly brushed her head.

But it hadn't been a problem to give her away. The Dunhams were her only chance. Being Sin was dangerous and so was being with Sin. If Lee couldn't survive their life, how could a child? And the Dunhams wanted her. The rightness of it sat well in her heart and she didn't live with regrets.

But thoughts plagued her.

She dreamed of her sister Wendy and the baby that died in her when Wendy died. So young. So long ago. Sin had now lived without Wendy for longer than she'd had her.

For months while she'd been pregnant, Sin lived above the surface. She had a fake ID, moved to an apartment in a mid-sized city. She saw a doctor for her check-ups, and worked part time in a shop—almost the way she had for cover when she was a teenager, before Lee had insisted they be dedicated. She'd gotten the proper care, then moved away as she approached her due date.

She'd followed the news and the police reports about the dismantling of the Kurev holdings. Much of the art in the tunnels had been stolen; not surprisingly, some of it dated back to World War Two and pilfered Nazi treasures. While the house had survived scrutiny, the tunnels were damning. The guns were militia level. The police force had been shaken down for Kurev sympathizers, leaving Chicago PD decimated in one of the most thorough Internal Affairs cases in history. Nick had helped put that in motion.

Vasilescu had been dismantled, too, the reigning theory that attorney Phil Megan had taken over after Emilian Vasilescu had died a handful of years ago. Megan—from prison—insisted police detective Nick Stelian had been the real head of the crime family, but no evidence supported it. Only Nick's subsequent disappearance gave any credence to Megan's story. But another rumor suggested Megan had him removed to make him seem guilty.

Sin had laughed when Gavin told her he thought Megan was full of shit.

He'd had some plastic surgery, courtesy of the US government, but she still saw Nick in him. Years of practice kept her from slipping up with the name.

She'd stopped by his place after the baby was born, showing up in his living room one night. Slightly out of shape from having birthed another human, she didn't make as quiet of an entry as she'd planned and he walked out to meet her.

But that had been several months ago.

The cabin was now dismantled, cleared of any evidence. Storage lockers in various states held her prized possessions; spare keys were buried on their property out west. She'd camped there and trained. She'd moved again. Trained more.

And wondered why she didn't have a short shelf life.

She was still here.

Lee insisted he'd lived much longer than he expected to, but Sin had never thought of herself as dying, just as going on. But all she was doing now was going on.

Her husband had lived four hours after leaving the tunnels. Broken physically and losing blood that couldn't be stemmed, he'd managed to grab her hand before he was wheeled into surgery.

Though his voice was raspy and shallow, she managed to hear him and soak in what he spent his last energy on.

He'd told her he was dead before she found him.

At first she'd taken that to mean 'before they met,' but after hearing Lee's medical report from Owen, she realized he meant this time. The Mechanic had killed him. He was dead before Sin and Nick came in. The damage was too extensive. The surgeons couldn't have saved him even if he hadn't been shot. His words rang even truer after she heard that.

"I was always waiting for you. I lived longer than I ever thought I would, and better than I ever imagined. I accomplished so much, because I was with you. But you were always the stronger one." He'd stopped and slowly sucked in more air before continuing. "You and our child are the true sum of my life's work. So you have to go on. When you stop, I stop."

He'd squeezed her hand and she'd seen what was in his eyes before he'd closed them for the last time. Though he technically died on the surgical table, he was gone before they'd wheeled his body down the hall.

Sin had disappeared before they could take her, knowing it was what Lee wanted. Though she'd waited for word from Owen, wishing the outcome would be a good one, that Lee would wake up from surgery, she'd not been surprised by the verdict.

She'd thanked Dr. Dunham and hung up the call, trusting him with Lee's remains. Then she'd picked up the already packed bag and left the hotel room where she'd awaited the news, walking out into her solo life.

She'd grown more pregnant, given birth, and given her child to a better world. Then she'd walked out into yet another phase of her life, this time wondering how many times she could do it.

Though she was alone again, she was lighter.

Sin had relived the night in the tunnels under the Kurev house more times than she cared to admit. She'd second-guessed her every decision—thinking the Mechanic was dead. But even looking back she couldn't figure out what signs she'd missed. She wished she'd done more, but she was trying to get them out of there. Fast.

In the end, Lee had saved her.

Twice.

He'd pushed her out of bed in the cabin when Churkin and the Mechanic had come to kill them. And he'd saved her again, by jumping in front of her. He'd made it clear later that he was at peace with his decisions and she had to be, too.

He'd lived longer than he'd thought. And he'd been given a rare second chance. Lee had not been able to save Sam and Bethy. But he'd saved Sin and their baby. He died having righted the one failure that had always driven him.

He'd died for her.

Lee had come full circle.

Truthfully, so had she. She'd begun so many years ago when her home was invaded and she'd lost everything. This time she hadn't lost herself. She'd saved her daughter. She'd found Lee.

And now she had to find a way to go on. To make it worthy of his sacrifice.

Though she lived with no burden, she had no major goal. She wandered, almost lost.

She wore her sais, her knives, carried a gun when possible. But there was nothing to do.

Picking up the Coke once more, she took a sip only to be confronted by the wet clunk of ice in an empty glass.

"Need another?" The bartender asked.

Sin shook her head. She could easily identify the man in a line-up though she'd never looked at him directly. She could ID everyone in here, knew who was carrying and who was trained. One of the guys in the corner was a cop.

Old habits died hard.

She was putting a bill on the bar when the woman at the end sputtered, "What a pig."

Several patrons looked over, then up at the old TV above the bar. Not a new model, it threatened to come crashing down at any moment. The color was too blue, too bright, the man on the news too orange.

But the story grabbed them all.

A college professor at a school in nearby Denver was wanted for trafficking some of his students in exchange for grades. He'd been caught when the third one failed to return home at break.

Sin turned to leave, the professor's name stuck in her head by default—an excellent memory and years of training still inherent in who she was. The need to find the missing student, or at least set the situation to justice, suddenly grabbed her.

The gravity and necessity of who she was settled once more into her bones and she pushed her way out the heavy front door into a dark night, at last having a direction.

Two steps down and she was in an alley between two buildings. The bar was old and tucked into a dead part of town. Only the faintest traces of neon lit dirty brick walls that corralled three sides of the rough asphalt. It glistened with old rain or old beer, reflecting rainbows and taking Sin back to a memory of another alley, of Lee, and a fight.

Only this time no one was around, just her and her memories of a decade ago. She hadn't known in that alley fight that she would love that man, have his child, spend what was left of her life striving to make him proud, but here she was.

Denver wasn't far.

The police couldn't do what she could do.

The old standards still applied—do the research, be certain, be swift.

There was no one around to see as she reached into what looked like the flap of a pocket on her cargo pants. The sai pulled free easily and for a moment it danced in her hand as she walked down the alley toward her own justice.

# ABOUT THE AUTHOR

At heart a biologist and avid student, AJ writes about the possibilities that keep us up late at night. Previous novels have won numerous awards including a Booky Top Ten Fiction Novel of 2011, several USA Book Awards for Best Fiction of the Year and Best Suspense of the Year, multiple Best Audio Fiction of the Year awards, as well as others. Audio formats have even garnered 2 Audie Nominations. AJ also writes the "Archives" Hybrid Novel Series for Game Nation.

*For more information*
www.ReadAJS.com
AJ@ReadAJS.com

www.ingramcontent.com/pod-product-compliance
Lightning Source LLC
Chambersburg PA
CBHW021957050726
47498CB00001BB/152